BLOOD LETTERS

A NOVEL

RANDY NERI

Crystal Mill Press

Copyright © 2018 by Randy Neri.

All rights reserved. No part of this publication may be reproduced, distributed or transmitted in any form or by any means, including photocopying, recording, or other electronic or mechanical methods, without the prior written permission of the publisher, except in the case of brief quotations embodied in critical reviews and certain other noncommercial uses permitted by copyright law.

Randy Neri/Crystal Mill Press
Printed in the United States of America

Publisher's Note: This is a work of fiction. Names, characters, places, and incidents are a product of the author's imagination. Locales and public names are sometimes used for atmospheric purposes. Any resemblance to actual people, living or dead, or to businesses, companies, events, institutions, or locales is completely coincidental.

Blood Letters/ Randy Neri. -- 1st ed.

ISBN 978-1-7321583-0-6 Print Edition

ISBN 978-1-7321583-1-3 Ebook Edition

This book is dedicated to my wife, Penny, who encouraged me, and when necessary, chastised me if I got cocky. Her patience with me, and understanding that writing is a solitary endeavor, gave me the time and space to focus on my writing.

And a very special thank you my friend and fellow author, Nat Jackson, for his listening skills and gentle nudges when I veered off course.

"It is a man's own mind,
not his enemy or foe,
that lures him to evil ways."
– Buddha –

Prologue

AS NYPD CRIME LAB SERGEANT Detective Specialist Hunter Stone turned the corner, a kaleidoscope of red, blue, and white flashing lights bounced off vehicles and houses, irradiating the night. The light show reflected off the wet snow falling from a winter storm. Stone parked his personal Chevy Tahoe in the middle of the street near the scene. Through the wet streaks on his windshield, he saw the yellow crime scene tape flapping in the stiff, cold wind.

Police officers milled about outside the tape, sipping from steaming cups of coffee, some huddling in small groups to fight the cold. Like the night, the scene frozen in time awaited Stone's arrival. His captain had called waking him from a deep sleep, because this was another murder scene staged by a serial killer with a personal beef against Stone.

He walked toward a sergeant he knew, the wet snow slapping his face. "Sergeant Matthews, you know where my crime scene people are?"

"Yeah. They're waiting for you inside the front door," the Sergeant said, poking a gloved finger toward the house. "Hell of a night. They drag you out?"

Stone nodded, ducked under the tape, and headed for the house. As he approached the front door, he stomped his feet, knocking off what little snow had accumulated. Before he could enter, an arm sheathed in a white biohazard suit, with a latex gloved hand on the end, popped out of the darkness with a pair of blue sterile booties. He donned the booties and stepped through the doorway into the inky interior. The only illumination, other than muted red, blue, and white light filtering in through drawn drapes, was three flashlight beams from the crime scene investigators waiting inside.

Skipping any salutations, Stone got down to business and ordered, “Tell me.”

One of Stone’s lead investigators, Larry Hanson, adjusted his flashlight beam and flipped open a notebook. “Dispatch received a suspicious person call at 0203 hours from a neighbor who lives on the next street over. The neighbor’s backyard abuts with the victims’ yard. They dispatched patrol at 0205, and two cars arrived at 0211. They searched the area but came up dry. They contacted the witness, who said she saw someone in the backyard of the victims’ house. Officers found the back door open and cleared the house. Found the victims, an elderly couple, deceased in bed upstairs and secured the scene.”

Stone asked, “Any suspect description?”

“The complainant is elderly too and couldn’t give them much,” Hanson said. “Told the officers she couldn’t sleep and was at the kitchen sink getting a glass of water when she saw a shadow exit the victims’ house through the back door and run south. Best description they could get was tall, average build, and black.”

“African-American?” Stone asked.

“Can’t say for sure. She said he was black from head to toe. Sounds like maybe what she saw was his clothing. She couldn’t give them anything else. Patrol’s canvassed the surrounding houses, but no one saw or heard anything.”

“Where’re we with our investigation? Stone asked.

Hanson said, “We photographed and videotaped the exterior.

No tracks in the snow, meaning the suspect and officers were back there prior to the snow sticking. Nothing of interest going south for a block. Back door has a cheap knob lock and the door looks pried. We conducted a preliminary check of the house interior but backed out to the foyer per Captain Baxter's order to wait for you."

"Okay. Give me some latex gloves," Stone ordered. He donned the gloves and said, "Everyone, quiet. Give me a minute."

As it always did, the eerie silence of a death scene caused Stone's senses to sharpen. His ears strained to hear any extraneous sounds. Other than the refrigerator humming and the oil heater kicking on, it was quiet as a tomb. His sharpened sense of smell detected everyday household odors: the faint smell of furniture polish, last night's fish dinner, and a pet—a cat.

"Watch out for a cat," Stone said to the group. "Okay. Hanson, you lead, I'll follow. You two stay here until we get back," Stone ordered.

As they approached the staircase, Hanson said, "Didn't find anything unusual until we—"

"Don't tell me," Stone interrupted. "I want my mind clear."

As they began to climb, Hanson pointed out suspected blood smears on the wooden handrail and on the carpeted stairs with his flashlight beam. At the top of the staircase, Hanson shined his flashlight to the left at an open bedroom door. "The victims are in there," he said.

Stone pulled out his own small flashlight, turned it on, and adjusted the beam. He ordered, "Go back downstairs with the others, and give me a few minutes." Without waiting for a reply, he walked to the bedroom door, careful to avoid other areas of blood on the carpet—and stopped. He could smell the familiar, coppery scent of blood.

Lots of blood.

From another pocket, he pulled a small digital recorder and turned it on. He shined his flashlight beam on the floor. As he moved into the room, he began recording his observations.

"Bloody footwear impressions indicate someone moved back and forth around the bed. The impressions appear to lead out of the bedroom and down the stairs. No discernable footwear pattern, but a size may be obtainable."

Mixed in with the footwear impressions, bloody cat prints led into a closet. The door was open about four inches.

Smart cat, Stone thought.

Stone shifted the flashlight beam onto the bed and victims. "Two victims. An elderly white male and female. Probably attacked in their sleep, based on the blood spatter. Each has had their throat cut—and—Jesus! They're missing their eyes."

Stone scanned the room with his flashlight, and the beam came to rest on a dresser against the wall. Four eyeballs sat, lined up like soldiers. Stone shifted his flashlight beam to a bloody message in familiar print on the dresser mirror. The inference of the message was unmistakable.

NYPD ARE YOU WACHING STONE!

PART I

BEGINNINGS AND ENDINGS

Chapter 1

STONES A LIER !

STONE SAT AT HIS DESK in the Crime Scene Unit of the NYPD Crime Lab, scrolling through digital photographs on his computer, well after his shift had ended. At thirteen brutal murder scenes, they had found messages left in the victims' blood—messages directed at him that assailed his honesty, integrity, and abilities. This particular photograph tied this case to the other unsolved murders committed over seven months.

Each murder as heinous as the last, the victim mutilations paralleled the messages. In the Stones a Lier Murder, the suspect used the victim's severed tongue as the writing instrument to pen his message. The media was aware of the messages—but unaware of their content. They were aware of the mutilations too, but unaware how they corresponded to the messages. As usual, what the media lacked in facts, they substituted with unsubstantiated speculation.

Stone found the lack of physical evidence puzzling. Other than a few black nylon fibers found at some of the scenes, and a few measurable footwear impressions, they had recovered no other physical evidence. The pathologist's report stated the direction and angle of the wounds at the various scenes indicated a right-handed suspect. The wound configuration and depth of the stab wounds indicated the use of a knife with a large, single-edged, serrated blade, similar to an old military-style knife. The pathologist further speculated the killer might have used the same weapon to commit all the murders.

No victim connections. No witnesses. No fingerprints. No hair. No DNA.

Unless you counted the misspellings in the messages, little evidence existed. The questioned document examiners, experts at tying an offender to particular nuances in the style of writing, might match the bloody messages to a specific person—assuming they ever caught him.

An FBI profile of the suspect failed to provide any useful information. A white male (because most serial killers were), between the ages of twenty-one and thirty-five, with limited education and low self-esteem. He might have been an abused child. Even with some additional information provided in the profile, little of it was useful when solving the cases.

Someone has a real hard-on for me, Stone thought.

With nineteen years on the job, the pool of reprobates numbered in the thousands. The NYPD brass, the people with stars on their collars, focused the investigative efforts on narrowing the number of suspects, a colossal waste of time in Stone's opinion. The offender could be anyone he'd contacted, someone he'd arrested, or a relative of someone he'd arrested. Hell, it could be a friend, or a friend of a friend, of someone he'd busted. The potential culprit cluster was too vast to make it an effective investigative strategy.

To waste additional time and resources, Inspector McFarland, Stone's boss's boss's boss, had ordered an internal affairs investigation to see if they could find some meat on the bones of the killer's bloody accusations. It was routine for the NYPD to look into citizen complaints to see if they merited further investigation. McFarland, the consummate ass, had stretched the bounds of the complaint process, using the messages to bring in Internal Affairs. Of course, the IAB found nothing.

Apparently, the list of people with a hard-on for him extended beyond the serial killer.

Stone glanced at his watch. Past ten. The nightshift was out, processing various scenes—no one to catch him rummaging through the investigations.

What a ridiculous way to conduct an investigation, he thought.

Over three months since the last Blood Letter Killer Homicide, as the media had dubbed the murders, and he was no damn closer to catching the killer. An expert in crime scene reconstruction, known for his ability to find innocuous clues that had resulted in numerous arrests, he refused to accept defeat. Determined to find something to break the cases, he had no intention of quitting, even though his captain had ordered him to drop his unauthorized investigation.

Stone's captain was right, of course. His assignment as the SDS in the NYPD's Crime Laboratory entailed supervision of things related to forensics. Witness interviews and following leads were the homicide detectives' domain—a job they guarded like attack-trained police K-9s.

It was common knowledge that professional rivalry existed between units within the police department. It was a case of "mine is bigger than yours." The homicide dicks—no pun intended—thought theirs were the biggest of all.

Stone's captain had turned a blind eye every time he put the same effort into other less notable cases, bending the official departmental directives—and solving a good number of them.

None of them rose to the level of these cases though. The media firestorm had caused a frenzy of fear with the citizens. The mayor's office reacted by applying enormous pressure on the NYPD. The administration at the NYPD reacted as expected, managing the problem with spin.

No commander sought the cases, considered political hand grenades. Stone did. He was confident he could solve them.

He knew he had a better chance winning the mega-millions lottery than getting the nod to continue his investigation. His captain had made it clear: he was to follow orders. He'd ignored that command and ended up on the rubber gun squad, a step closer to termination. That meant no gun and no crime scene work—his assignment shuffling paperwork for a month or so was a subtle reminder of who held the power.

Even an official reprimand—called a rip—from Inspector McFarland, and his temporary restricted duty, failed to dissuade him. Stone was nothing if not tenacious—resolute to a fault if he believed he was right, and throughout his career he'd been right a hell of a lot more than wrong.

He was fearless in the face of danger—with the scars to prove it. To his detriment, he made no distinction between the garbage he dealt with on the street and the people in the department who kissed ass to gain promotions. In his opinion, both endangered the citizens he'd sworn to protect. That was what got him his current assignment: the Sergeant Detective Specialist in Charge of Paper Pushing.

Until now, Stone's was a celebrated career. He'd received three Purple Shield Medals for gunshot wounds sustained saving other officers and a knife wound he got making an arrest. Two times, he'd used deadly force to save his own—and another officer's—life.

The NYPD had presented him its three most prestigious awards: the Medal of Honor, three Police Combat Crosses, and two Medals of Valor, along with a chest full of other decorations, none of which meant a hell of a lot to him. The NYPD was award crazy in his opinion, as evidenced by all the uniformed officers with colorful fruit salad adorning their chests.

He had his choice of assignments upon obtaining his detective's gold shield, presented by the police commissioner himself. That meant the commissioner had monitored his career and, if he wanted, Stone could've used the relationship to garner favor and promotions.

However, the NYPD had too many cops who promoted up the chain by tying their careers to a superior's coattails. These were the people Stone saw as the problem. Some were in positions of authority—but clueless how to do real police work. Inspector McFarland, in Stone's opinion, was the poster child of unbridled ineptitude.

Stone had decided against the Homicide Unit. It was already busting at the seams with proficient, but pugnacious, detectives. Instead, he chose the Crime Lab because of a love for all things forensic and its team approach. His storied career and promotions continued, not because of his relationships, but because of his successes.

All the same, if not for his reputation and the high regard the commissioner had for him, Stone believed McFarland would've already fired him. Exceptional actions provided a level of protection, and the previous year, he'd received official recognition for solving a difficult case. The commissioner had called him an exemplary officer—and gave him another ribbon.

Celebrated or not, Stone knew he'd flirted with disaster by refusing to follow orders. Some sins were unforgivable. Ignoring direct orders fell into that category.

He hoped reviewing the cases at night and on weekends would

allow him to continue his surreptitious investigation. He'd poured over the reports and photos, certain an obscure—but important—detail awaited his discovery. If he failed to catch a break, he would have no choice but to expand his investigation—at his own peril.

Even though ordered to stop investigating the cases, Stone had risked contact with the assigned homicide detective, a cop named Phil Burnside. They had been police academy classmates—like that carried any weight. Stone suggested Burnside compare the FBI's profile of the suspect against the violent offender arrests for the month the murders stopped. Burnside hadn't warmed to the idea.

His response, with unmistakable annoyance in his tone, was that he lacked the manpower. Stone guessed Burnside's real reason for nixing the idea was that he hadn't thought of it. Either that or the brass had tied up the department's resources by chasing their tails. Regardless of the reason, Stone's rank restricted his supervisory duties to Crime Lab personnel. He couldn't order Burnside to blow his nose.

Stone told Burnside he understood, although that was a lie. They had ended the call promising to keep in touch—another lie.

He knew his idea had merit and enough anecdotal evidence to support his theory. Serial killers didn't take sabbaticals. One could interpret that to mean the killer was dead or incarcerated, since no other jurisdiction had reported similar types of murders. He'd broken cases using less deductive reasoning.

Maybe he would skirt Burnside and try to get the records himself from the Department of Corrections. What was another violation if it would help him catch a serial killer?

Especially this one—because this was personal.

Chapter 2

STONE PUSHED AWAY FROM HIS desk and leaned back, the springs of his desk chair squealing in protest. He rubbed at the hint of a headache nagging at his temples.

The garbage he dealt with on the streets—and at the NYPD—wore on him more each day. An axiom he'd heard popped into his head. "I can handle the crap on the street; and I can handle the crap in the department; but I can't handle both at the same time." Yet, here he was—the meat in a shit sandwich.

His gaze shifted to a small framed photograph on his desk. He leaned in and took hold of it, his chair complaining again. He tilted the picture to get a better look under the glare of his gooseneck lamp.

The photograph showed a younger version of himself in a deputy marshal uniform, standing in front of the marshal's office in the small Colorado mountain town of Silver Lake. The stresses of police work had yet to encroach upon his youthful appearance. His arm rested on the shoulders of a beautiful young woman at his side—Molly. She gazed lovingly at him. Lately, the photograph seemed to draw his attention more than it used to. He thought back on what had led to his decision to leave Colorado and move to New York. A degree in criminal justice and two years as a deputy marshal under his belt, he'd tired of small-town law enforcement. He yearned to be a big city cop.

At least that was what he told himself.

Stone had switched majors from physical science to criminal justice after his parents died—forced off a mountain road by an unknown vehicle during his sophomore year of college. He'd sworn a secret oath to catch their killer—and failed. His life in Silver Lake a constant reminder, he decided it was time to fulfill his desire to be a cop in a large city—or run away to bury his sorrow, depending on how you looked at it.

Molly had disagreed. She wanted to stay in Silver Lake, their hometown. She told him she didn't feel the same pull he did. Their discussions often spiraled into arguments, resulting in cooling off periods that lasted days with little or no contact. Still, he refused to divulge his true feelings—as if to say the words was to admit the failure.

A few close friends had attempted to dissuade him from moving. As pressure mounted for him to stay, his determination to leave increased exponentially.

Realizing Molly would never change her mind or see things from his perspective, he made the decision to leave—leave his friends, his deputy marshal's job, and Molly—the woman in the photograph. He'd chosen not to announce his departure to anyone. He quit his job, packed his belongings, and left like a thief in the night. To this day, he wished he'd tried harder to convince Molly to come with him.

In New York and through the police academy, he'd refused to look back, and dedicated himself to being the best cop he could be. Over the last nineteen years, he'd worked his way to the rank of sergeant detective specialist, a unique position appointed by the police commissioner. He was the most experienced person in the Crime Scene Unit and one of the most decorated cops in the NYPD.

His naiveté from his days in Silver Lake was long gone. If asked to describe himself, he would say that although he wasn't a cheerful person, neither was he morose. As the years had slipped by, he'd come to accept that his chosen profession was as much a part of him as it was his vocation. Like many cops with years on the job, he existed in a world of brutality and cynicism, with occasional moments of selflessness and sacrifice: a world he saw as black and white, or more accurately—right and wrong.

Stone sighed and looked at the photograph again as he placed it back on his desk. His gaze shifted to the bullpen, where his and the crime scene investigators desks filled most of the space. He sighed again and shut off his computer. Done for the night, he turned his chair, stood, and stretched until his lower back popped. He reached out and clicked off his desk lamp.

As he grabbed his coat off the back of the chair, he glanced at the darkened captain's office in the back corner of the cavernous room. He liked his boss, Captain Sam Baxter. The man was one of the cops who'd risen through the ranks on his own merit. Stone figured his refusal to follow orders had resulted in Baxter catching a lot of grief. Regardless of his respect for Baxter, he believed he was right—and Inspector McFarland was unquestionably an asshole.

Stone knew some of the command staff saw him as cocky. Maybe he was—a little. Was it being cocky if you were right most of the time? His successful career came from solving cases, not by doubting his abilities or by being a milquetoast.

As he started toward the elevator, his eye caught a manila envelope sticking out of his mail slot. He veered toward the mailboxes, a large wooden box divided into cubbyholes, located on top of the gangrene-colored industrial file cabinets that lined two of the room's walls.

As he weaved his way through the face-to-face two-desk islands covered with assorted detritus, he shook his head. The place was a pigsty. He would have to address that. His eyes passed over the windows that dominated one of the walls. Even though it was dark outside, there was nothing to see through the filthy glass anyway—nothing but the side of the adjoining parking structure.

He snatched the envelope from his mail slot. It had his rank and name hand printed on it and the word "Confidential" stamped in red ink. He stared at it, shaking his head. He ripped open the envelope and yanked out the single sheet of paper. The official document directed him to report to Inspector McFarland's office at ten the following morning: no explanation included—and none needed.

Stone dropped the envelope into the trash and headed for the elevator, folding the paper and shoving it into his pants pocket. More McFarland crap headed his way. As he waited for the elevator, he examined his reflection in the full-length mirror mounted to the wall with a sign above it that read, **LOOK PROFESSIONAL - BE PROFESSIONAL**

What he saw staring back was a tired face, devoid of innocence and showing the hint of worry lines creasing his forehead. At least his steel blue eyes were clear and sharp, even though they had witnessed too much of man's inhumanity to man. He still sported a head full of dark, wavy hair, and no trace of gray had invaded his temples.

Waiting an interminable length of time, he reached out and stabbed the lighted elevator button several times. The elevator dinged, and the doors slid open. Stone shuffled in and pushed the button for the first floor. A long day behind him, he looked forward to a glass of Maker's Mark Bourbon and water—one of his few indulgences.

As he walked to his vehicle, Stone nodded to the officer assigned to guard the parked patrol and personal vehicles because of constant theft and vandalism. Even though spring had unofficially arrived, the air held the dying breath of a winter taking a last shot at New York. He pulled his coat tighter and shivered. He wondered if the chill had caused the shudder.

As he approached his Chevrolet Tahoe, he pressed the unlock button on his key fob. The doors unlocked with a clack, and the vehicle's interior and exterior lights blazed to life, igniting the gloomy area. He opened the driver's door and pulled the paper from his pocket, unfolding it. He leaned in, read the order again by the glow of the interior light—and crumpled it into a ball. As he slid into his SUV, he tossed the wadded paper on the passenger side floor.

He pulled out of the garage and began the short trek home to his homogeneous Queens's high rise. Even though he was seething, a small knot had begun to tighten in his gut, as he thought about what he faced come morning.

CHAPTER 3

STONE ARRIVED AT ONE POLICE Plaza, or 1PP in common police vernacular, and announced himself to Inspector McFarland's secretary. He noticed she was an attractive brunette who knew how to dress to emphasize her assets. She smiled and directed him to a row of straight-back armless chairs in the reception area—chairs designed to be uncomfortable.

Settling into one of the torturous chairs, Stone noticed the secretary stealing quick glances at him. He had what people called rugged good looks but doubted that was her reason for the surreptitious peeks. He suspected she knew what awaited him on the other side of McFarland's door.

At the stroke of ten, the secretary answered her phone, called his name, and motioned for him to enter the inspector's office. The look on her face at that moment convinced him she knew what awaited him.

As he entered, Stone noticed his captain, Sam Baxter, and Deputy Inspector Bussard occupied two of three tufted leather chairs arranged in a semi-circle in front of a huge, ornate wooden desk occupied by Inspector McFarland. A suit, unknown to Stone, leaned against a wall festooned with awards and photographs of McFarland with assorted dignitaries. McFarland, a short man with a receding hairline, puffy eyes, and a dusty voice, reminded Stone of the old actor Edward G. Robinson—at least his looks did. He waved Stone to the empty chair.

"Sergeant Stone," McFarland said in an officious tone, "this is an official inquiry." He pointed to the suit and added, "This is Lieutenant Moody from Internal Affairs."

Stone glanced at Moody, a tall skeleton of a man with an unfriendly air about him, a ruddy complexion, and a military-style crew cut that emphasized his protruding ears. Stone thought the buzz cut made him look like a taxicab with the back doors open. His suit looked like a custom Savile Row, but on him it was lipstick on a pig—again, no pun intended.

Moody glared at him with accusing eyes, remaining frozen in place. "You want your PBA rep?" Moody asked. His tone made the question sound like an accusation.

Stone knew he was in deep trouble, because Moody had asked if he wanted his union rep. He looked at Captain Baxter and asked, "What's going on?"

Moody pushed away from the wall and said, "Your captain's here as a courtesy, Sergeant. You'll address your questions and answers to the inspector, the deputy inspector, or me. Understood?"

Stone stared hard-edged at Moody. He had no love of Internal Affairs. Every cop knew of the scandal in the 1990s that embarrassed the NYPD and showed how ineffective the Internal Affairs Bureau was. The pendulum had swung the other way and—in his opinion—the IAB had become overzealous along the way, burning good cops along with the bad with their scorched-earth approach to investigations.

"Fine," Stone said, returning Moody's unfriendly look. "Why am I here?"

"Are you waiving your right to your PBA rep?" Moody repeated.

"For the moment."

"Okay. Would you like to start, Deputy Inspector?" Moody asked, resuming his position against the wall.

Bussard, a portly man with a perpetually red face and runny nose he wiped all the time, cleared his throat. "The Forensic Investigation Division assistant chief received another complaint about you from the Central Investigation and Resource Division assistant chief, who heads the Homicide Analysis Unit."

He stopped long enough to blow his runny nose and catch his breath before continuing. "The complaint relates to a series of active homicide investigations and your continued interference in those investigations beyond your authority—cases in which you received a direct order to stop investigating and were then placed on modified duty because of your refusal to obey that order."

Scrubbing his handkerchief back and forth under his nose again, Bussard added, "You know what cases I'm referring to, don't you, Sergeant?"

"I do," Stone said. "All I did was call Detective Burnside with a suggestion." *A suggestion to a backstabber,* he thought.

"Don't feed me that crap," Inspector McFarland snarled, smacking the flat of his hand on his desk. "You received a direct order to cease all your activities relating to these cases, and you disobeyed that order. Do you think I don't know you've continued your review of the case files?"

His lips pressed tight, Stone remained mute. His emotions crammed behind a wall of determination, he didn't want to make matters worse. He chanced a look at Baxter. His boss's typically darker complexion was waxy. His thick, dark mustache and dark hair accentuated the pallid look. A frozen grimace had replaced his smile, indicating he'd already received his ass chewing.

Stone decided he wasn't going to allow the likes of McFarland, a man who kissed ass to gain promotions, to speak to him as if he were a common criminal. He took a deep, calming breath and said,

"As the deputy inspector stated, *and* for the record, the order was to stop my *investigation,* which I did. No one ordered me to cease all activities. Calling Detective Burnside with a suggestion doesn't constitute a violation of that order. Neither does my reviewing the case files—on my own time."

"Semantics," McFarland shouted, banging his fist on the desk this time. "Don't try to play that game with me, Sergeant. If it were my decision alone, you'd be out the door. It seems the commissioner sees something in you I don't. That's the reason you still have a job."

His anger exploding through the wall, Stone shot back, "Nice to know being a real cop has value at the NYPD."

Infuriated, McFarland's ears glowed red, and the veins stood out on his neck. He glared at Stone and through gritted teeth hissed, "I don't think I'm getting through to you, Sergeant. Effective immediately, I'm ordering a two-week suspension without pay for continuing to violate a direct order and for lying about it. Is that clear, *Sergeant?*"

Stone knew he could fight the suspension but had little chance of getting it overturned. In that moment, he decided that if McFarland intended to suspend him, he might as well speak his mind—so the suspension was for legitimate reasons.

"I asked you a question, Sergeant," McFarland growled.

"I heard you. I was just wondering if a two-week suspension was the maximum the commissioner authorized you to give?"

Enraged, a flush of red climbed the inspector's neck and blossomed across his face as another vein in the middle of his forehead bulged and pulsed. "That's it," McFarland bellowed. "You've crossed the line, Sergeant. That's insubordination, so let's make that a four-week suspension."

Stone shot out of his chair, and Moody pulled away from the wall, taking an aggressive step toward him. Baxter looked at Stone and said, "That's enough, Stone."

"No," Stone hissed through clenched teeth shifting his glare from McFarland to Moody. "I'm. Not. Finished."

Except for Bussard's sniffling, the room fell as silent as a homicide scene, as Stone and Moody glared at each other. Moody broke eye contact and retreated back to his place against the wall.

Stone shifted his attention back to McFarland. "I can solve these cases, but it's obvious you don't give a damn about that—or the victims—because you're too busy playing politics. If you knew anything about criminals or investigations, you'd know this guy isn't done. So, when he starts killing again—and he will—it's on you. And you can bet your ass I'll make sure the commissioner knows who to talk to."

Stone spun and headed for the door. McFarland barked, "I didn't dismiss you, Sergeant. Get back here."

Stone ignored McFarland's order and yanked open the door.

"I said you're not dismissed," McFarland shouted as Stone exited the office, slamming the door so hard he thought the etched glass panel might shatter.

The receptionist and several waiting visitors looked on in surprise. Their stares followed him to the elevator.

***

Stone drove from One Police Plaza back to the Crime Lab, his anger boiling under the surface like a volcano that was ready to blow. He knew the suspension would stick. As the old saying went, "The size of the spank depends on the rank." If you pissed off the brass, they bit back—hard.

Still, he wasn't the least bit sorry for what he said or for walking out. McFarland was a pompous ass, and it was time someone called him on it. What concerned him was that, while on suspension, he couldn't work the cases.

All Stone could do was hope that whatever had stopped the killer for over three months would continue to keep him at bay until he was off suspension.

Chapter 4

EVEN WITH A STOP AT the lab to grab some personal items, drop off the departmental car, and retrieve his SUV, Stone was home a little past one. His Fresh Meadows Apartment was a twenty-minute drive from the lab on Jamaica Avenue in Jamaica Queens, but for the next four weeks, it might as well be on another planet.

Stone flopped on the couch in his living room, anger knotting his stomach. Time off work was foreign to him. In the past nineteen years, he refused to take time off unless he was sick or injured. In fact, he worked overtime most weeks. However, for the next month, he could forget any overtime—or a paycheck.

The suspension would hardly put a dent in his savings. He still disliked the idea of spending the money, even if he could afford it. At his rank and with overtime, his income was north of a hundred grand a year. With no friends or life outside work, he hardly spent any money. All he'd done for the last nineteen years was invest it.

He eyeballed his Spartan apartment from his seat on the couch. To his right was his combination kitchen/dining area—to his left his bedroom and a bathroom. He'd purposely chosen a miniscule apartment. It made cleaning quick and easy. He never considered how he would handle being a prisoner in it for an extended period of time. At least it was in a building with a laundry room, elevators, and underground parking.

Stone decided to put his worry on hold. Dulling his senses with good bourbon sounded like an excellent idea, and he knew just the place to go. He cleaned up and headed out for a night of wallowing in self-pity.

***

Waking from a booze-induced sleep, Stone slid his feet over the side of the bed and sat on the edge. His temples throbbed with a series of painful explosions. The morning light streaming through the bedroom window stabbed at his eyes like slivers of flying glass. Nauseated and dizzy, sweat prickled his forehead, and the back of his neck and his mouth tasted like a cat's litter box. *At least I managed to find my way home.*

He swallowed back bile trying to force its way out and stumbled into the bathroom, hanging his head over the toilet. After a few minutes of wishing he could vomit so he would feel better, he stood and stared at himself in the mirror, blinking at the fatigue staring back. He looked like shit—red, puffy eyes, and he needed a shave. He smelled like a mixture of booze and perfume. The smell caused his stomach to lurch again.

His gut settling, he tried to remember what had happened the previous night. He must have had a hell of a good time. It was too bad it was all such a blur. He turned on the cold water, rinsed out his mouth, and splashed water on his face. He drained his bladder and flushed the toilet, wincing at the noise.

Intent on crawling back into bed, he staggered back into the bedroom. A feminine-shaped lump shifted under the covers, and a long, sensuous moan floated out from the bulge. Shocked by the apparition, Stone forgot his hangover and searched for his pants. That was when he noticed the tangled array of men and women's clothing scattered on the floor.

He grabbed his pants from the jumbled pile and slipped into them. As he tugged on the zipper, the covers on his bed flew back, exposing a beautiful young woman wearing a big smile—and nothing else. Stone swallowed hard, damn near choking at the sight. He couldn't help himself and stared in admiration.

"Mmmm, good morning. Why don't you come back to bed?" she said, stretching and patting the mattress.

She was the embodiment of sexy. Firm, round breasts, neither too small or large, accentuated by a narrow waist and erotically curved, but narrow, hips. Her legs were long and shapely and Stone noticed she was a natural blond—that is, if you could believe the landing strip of pubic hair.

As he moved toward the bed, he wished to hell he could remember the previous night. He remembered going to Lucky's, a bar frequented by cops and assistant district attorneys. A bit at a time, the fog began to lift.

By the time she came in with her girlfriend, he was close to shitfaced. They flirted and found their way to his apartment. After that, everything went fuzzy. Even worse, for the life of him, he couldn't remember her name.

"Are you okay?" she asked, as he sat on the edge of the bed.

"I'm hungover." Then he remembered, Bridgett ... Bridgett Farnsworth. One of the new ADAs.

"Do you remember last night?" Bridgett asked, running her hand over his bare chest, her fingers stopping over one of his scars.

"I wish to hell I did," Stone admitted, his eyes admiring the curves of her body again. "It looks like I had a hell of a good time."

Bridgett laughed and slid her hand to the waistband of his trousers. "I was pretty out of it too," she admitted. "Why don't we try it again, since we're both sober?"

"I need a shower first."

"What a wonderful idea," Bridgett said, bounding out of bed. "I'll join you."

She moved close, pressing her breasts against him as she worked the button and zipper of his pants. As she leaned in, she brushed her lips across the scar. Stone shuddered at her touch. By the time his pants slid to the floor, he was ready to go. She took his hand, and they moved toward the bathroom.

They faced each other in the shower. As warm water cascaded over their bodies, Stone soaped the curves of Bridgett's breasts, feeling her nipples harden. He slid his hands along the curve of her body and slipped his fingers between her legs. Bridgett tilted her head back and moaned.

She stroked him as they kissed. Turning her back to him, she bent over and reached back, guiding him into her.

They made love slowly at first. Stone held her hips, moving rhythmically as she held onto his wrists. Each nearing a climax, their lovemaking became faster, more desperate. Bridgett cried out, tightening her grip on Stone's wrists as he climaxed. Exhausted, they finished showering and took their time toweling each other dry.

As they dressed Bridgett said, "I have to get home and change for a deposition."

"You want some breakfast first?" Stone asked.

"Thanks, but I'll be late if I don't get going."

Stone walked her to the door, and they kissed goodbye. "I hope I see you at Lucky's again," she said.

"Same here." Stone unlocked and opened the door for her. He watched her walk down the hallway. They waved to each other as she stepped into the elevator.

He closed the door, turned, and leaned back against it. It had been a long dry spell.

If the way the morning started were any indication, today would be a great day.

Chapter 5

STONE'S GREAT DAY TOOK A nosedive upon returning home from breakfast at a local bistro.

His smartphone chirped. He dug it out of his pocket and checked the screen: Captain Baxter. His captain never called him unless it was work related. His good mood began to fade.

"Stone," he answered.

"How're you doing?" Baxter asked.

Stone knew Baxter had an ulterior motive for the call. Following a brief lull, he said, "I'm fine. What's up, Cap?" His mood dropped another notch. It must have been evident, because Baxter got to the point.

"I thought you should know Inspector McFarland and a couple of IAB henchmen came to the lab." Stone heard concern in his boss's voice. "They tore apart your desk. Went through papers and even pulled out the drawers and dumped them on the desk. They copied your computer hard drive too. They ransacked your locker in the change-out room too."

Instead of anger, Stone's mood lifted, and he smiled. "They find anything interesting?" he asked. He knew the answer.

"They were pretty secretive, but I saw them put something in an evidence envelope," Baxter said.

"I guess they must have found something of interest." Stone couldn't keep himself from grinning.

"Look, Stone, McFarland's out to find something on you—anything he can use to fire you. Do you have anything you want to tell me ... before things get out of hand?"

"Nope. Nothing, Cap." It was all he could do to keep from laughing. "Don't sweat McFarland. He'll spin his wheels and find nothing."

Stone gave Baxter additional assurances he need not concern himself and ended the call. As he disconnected, he fist pumped the air. "Gotcha, asshole!"

What Stone held back from Baxter was that following his confrontation with McFarland, he suspected the man would pull some stunt. He knew McFarland was vindictive and a back stabber. As a patrol officer, his fellow officers had tagged him as a spineless coward. Other cops even started referring to him as McFaraway, a name that stuck because whenever hot calls came in, McFarland was never available.

Stone had challenged McFarland and embarrassed him in front of his subordinates. It was easy to figure out what might happen. He'd stopped by the lab to collect his sensitive files and decided to leave some clues for McFarland—to keep him occupied.

He found an old key in his desk, its use long forgotten. That had given him the idea. He taped the key to the bottom of his center desk drawer. He scribbled a couple of cryptic notes. On one he printed BIRDWATCHER CNTRL PK 4P and stuffed it under some papers in one of his desk drawers. He hid the other note in his locker. It read CNB KY 345.949.4655.

The note in his desk could mean anything, maybe a date to do some bird watching in Central Park at four. Stone knew McFarland would read something nefarious into it and begin chasing windmills. The note in his locker would send McFarland right off the deep end. CNB were the initials for the Cayman National Bank, and KY was the symbol for the Cayman Islands. Because McFarland had little investigative experience, Stone had helped him by including the bank's telephone number.

From an old case, Stone remembered that the banks in the Cayman Islands were secretive and refused to divulge information to anyone. People opened offshore accounts in the Cayman Islands to hide money from the taxman. McFarland would go crazy trying to tie Stone to some nonexistent offshore bank account. The key would send McFarland off the deep end.

Good luck finding what it opens, Stone mused.

The best part: since McFarland's search of Stone's desk and locker violated departmental policy and was an illegal search, he couldn't mention what he found or use it to harass Stone. His bogus investigation would keep him occupied. It might help keep him out of Captain Baxter's hair.

It *had* turned out to be a great day.

His cheerful mood back, Stone decided to change and go to the health club for a workout. Because of his obsession with the Blood Letter Killer cases, he'd spent too much time sitting on his ass.

Part of his commitment to being the best cop he could included keeping his six-foot-three-inch, two-hundred and twenty-pound frame in superb condition, through a damn near religious exercise regimen of running and weight lifting. He'd put on twenty pounds of muscle over the years and was as hard as *quebracho* wood.

To keep himself limber and agile, attributes needed to protect himself and apprehend suspects, he trained in a variety of martial arts and took advantage of police tactics taught by the department. One of the best programs he'd participated in was a military hand-to-hand combat program (ironically called SCARS.)

If nothing else, his suspension provided him the opportunity to get back into a rigorous workout routine.

***

Stone drove to Lucky's once the courts closed. He spent several hours nursing a couple of Maker's Mark and waters and talking shop with cops he knew. Disappointed the lovely Miss Bridgett had failed to make an appearance, he headed home.

Frustrated by a failure to connect with Bridgett, Stone sat on his couch in the dark. He'd wanted to end his first full day of suspension on the same high note it had begun. He'd forgotten to ask for her phone number, and she hadn't asked for his. He suspected her failure to ask was intentional. He, on the other hand, stunk at the social rules of hooking up, as young people called it. In nineteen years, he rarely engaged socially with women—no girlfriends, let alone anything more serious.

His suspension clawed its way back into his thoughts. What was he going to do for four weeks? Working out every day and going to Lucky's, hoping for another interlude with Bridgett, didn't strike him as an acceptable plan.

On a personal flash drive, he had copies of all the Blood Letter Killer case notes, diagrams, and crime scene photographs. He could work the cases from home, but he was persona non grata. No one working the cases would welcome his interference, and word of his involvement would get back to McFarland. He would play right into McFarland's hands—and it would cost him his career.

Stone sighed and stretched out on the couch, draping an arm over his eyes. His mind drifted, his thoughts turning to his life and career.

The last nineteen years had flown by. He was middle aged with little to show for it. No friends. No love interest. No hobbies. Even his workouts focused on staying in shape for the job. His career had superseded everything in his life—and that had just taken a significant hit. What others might call a speed bump in his career, Stone saw as a roadblock to his future at the NYPD.

The allure of the big city that had drawn him to New York had lost its shine. He no longer pictured New York as The Big Apple. It was closer to a rotten apple.

Stone believed in justice for the victims of crime, but the purpose of the criminal justice system wasn't to mete out justice. He called it what it was ... the criminal-legal system. Its focus was the application of law, not justice.

He saw himself growing cynical. Too often he saw the victims of crime as little different from the perpetrators. He was a garbage man, except he dealt with the human refuse left behind by the underbelly of society.

Stone's thoughts verged on the morose.

Now's not the time to make decisions, he thought. He headed for the bedroom.

He would figure it out tomorrow.

Chapter 6

STONE SLEPT FITFULLY. HE DREAMT of times past, his years in Silver Lake—and of Molly.

He awoke and saw it was dark outside. Wide awake, he knew further sleep would evade him. At least his dream helped him decide what to do with part of his suspension days.

The idea of getting out of New York resonated within him. For the last nineteen years, New York had been his whole world. The only other place he knew was from his past—Silver Lake. At least it had been familiar a long time ago.

Being analytical by nature, Stone examined his motives for returning to a place he'd been so anxious to escape. Was it for the change of scenery, the remembered familiarity—or was something else drawing him back?

He decided the reason was of no consequence. After nineteen years, he doubted there was anyone left who'd even remember him.

Stone knew that if he continued to question every thought and idea, he would spend his suspension going nowhere. He would re-involve himself in the Blood Letter Killer cases to his own detriment.

He powered on his computer tablet and checked the airline schedules.

***

Stone waited for the gate to announce the boarding call for his flight. Although JFK was closer and had earlier flights, they had no direct flights to the Denver International Airport, and he had no interest in stopovers in Washington DC or Detroit. It was bad enough connecting to a small commuter plane in Denver to get to Aspen and rent a car to drive to Silver Lake. With no other options, he'd endured the morning rush hour drive to LaGuardia.

As he sat in a concourse snack bar near his gate, he watched other travelers scurrying about like ants, carry-on suitcases trailing behind them. Excited to begin his long overdue vacation, he sipped a cup of coffee and ignored the hunger pangs gnawing at his gut. By indulging in a first-class ticket, a gourmet meal would come with the flight.

The announcement for early boarding blared from a loudspeaker. As he walked toward the gate, his smartphone chirped. He pulled it from his pocket and checked the caller ID.

The screen identified the caller as Captain Baxter. Stone stopped, standing motionless in the surging sea of travelers, and stared at the screen.

He grappled with his emotions. If something had happened, he wanted in on it. Then he remembered McFarland's admonition. They were never again going to allow him near the Blood Letter Killer cases. Baxter knew that, so the call had to be for another reason. It was likely more handwringing over McFarland's search.

Stone turned the smartphone off and slid it back into his pocket. Whatever it was, he refused to make it his problem. He was on suspension.

***

The meal was good—even for airline rations. With a full stomach, the drone of the jet lulled Stone into a lethargic daze as it sliced westward through the clear sky. He reclined his seat and stared out the window. An alert flight attendant provided him with a small pillow and a blanket.

"Thanks," Stone said, smiling at the woman. His eyes followed her receding figure, admiring the firm butt pressing against the fabric of her skirt. He turned back to the window, smiled at the tranquil view, and relaxed. His eyes slid closed as he drifted toward sleep.

He awoke from his restless nap over eastern Colorado and realized that although he'd chosen to avoid thinking about things, his subconscious had other ideas. He'd taken the time to examine his existence at home. The conclusion: his life was as hollow as a base drum—and his career was in the toilet. Apparently, there was more roiling about the fringes of his mind, awaiting examination.

The pilot announced their descent into Denver and recited the obligatory landing instructions, pulling Stone from his thoughts. Returning his seat to its full upright position, the sexy flight attendant relieved him of his pillow and blanket. Stone stared out the window at the much-changed skyline of a city he'd not seen in too many years, his psyche tingling with excitement.

He made his way into the terminal and learned he had a two-and-a-half-hour delay prior to the departure of his connecting flight to Aspen. That gave him time to get a snack at a concourse restaurant and wander the airport. Not that airports were citadels of fun, but this one looked like a giant circus tent. An antique airplane exhibit was on display in the main terminal. He walked the displays until it was time for his flight.

Airborne and headed west into the Rockies, Stone stared out

the window. His thoughts, interrupted by the earlier landing announcement, crept back into his mind. As he watched the mountains slide by below, he realized that deep inside he harbored doubts as to whether he wanted to return to the NYPD.

At twenty years on the job, he would attain retirement eligibility, which included free medical for life. If he opted for early-out retirement, he wouldn't get retirement or benefits for a year. Stone believed his career in law enforcement was as much a calling as a career—and he wasn't ready to walk away. Besides, he was too young. What would he do if he retired?

His reflection led to a decision: ride out the suspension and return to work. Focus on the job and avoid getting involved in anything outside his authority. McFarland could be vindictive, but Stone had a level of protection from the commissioner. He could revisit how he felt in a year.

As long as he kept his nose clean, McFarland should leave him alone.

Chapter 7

STONE PULLED OPEN HIS MOTEL room door. The rising sun blinded him. He squinted at the brightness of a clear, crisp mountain morning. The chirping of barn swallows welcomed the new day. Eyes closed, he took a deep breath as the morning sunlight cut through the chill, evaporating the dew that coated everything. The smell of fresh air, rich earth, and fresh pine triggered a flood of pleasant memories. Melting bits of snow clung to life on the ground in the shadows cast by pine tree boughs.

Because of his late start, the flight delay and drive from Aspen, he'd arrived in Silver Lake at dusk. Drained, he checked into the Lakeview Motel and went straight to his room, foregoing any sightseeing or food. He'd slept over eleven hours, uncertain if from exhaustion or the release of tension.

Rested, his priority was food.

Stone decided to walk to see if he could find an open restaurant. It would afford him an opportunity to see what changes Silver Lake had undergone over the past nineteen years. As he set out toward the main part of town, he heard a raven cawing and the faint sounds of traffic in the distance. He reached the main street—Dowd Street—he remembered, and glanced left and right. None of the stores appeared open. The tranquility brought a smile to his face.

He strolled along the covered boardwalk fronting the retail

shops along the thoroughfare. Silver Lake radiated the ambiance of an old western town. They had chosen to maintain the longstanding structures instead of replacing them with modern architecture. Even the newer buildings added since he'd left exhibited a style befitting the town's old west image.

Stone saw many of the stores still sold tee shirts and other memorabilia. Silver Lake had grown a little in his absence, but it remained a small mountain hamlet. Based on the trinkets displayed in the shop windows, it was still dependent on tourism for its survival. *Same as nineteen years ago,* he mused.

He remembered that with the arrival of spring, the current trickle of tourists would turn into a flood of vacationers. By luck, he'd picked an ideal time to visit. Any sooner and he would've arrived during the mud season, as locals called it, a miserable wet period spelling the end of winter. If he'd waited much longer, no motel rooms would've been available.

Ahead and across Dowd Street, Stone saw an open restaurant. At least it appeared open because of a number of pick-up trucks (local folks' vehicles, based on the dented and dirty look of them) parked in the diagonal parking spaces in front. He cut across the empty street to the restaurant. The name painted on the window announced it as the Silver Nugget Café. He thought he remembered the restaurant, but the name was unfamiliar.

Stone pulled open the door and stepped through into an alcove. It smelled great ... fresh coffee, pancakes, eggs, and hash brown odors saturated the air. To his right, he noticed a woman at the cash register ringing out a customer. Tacked to the wall in front of him a sign ordered, ***PLEASE WAIT TO BE SEATED***. He dutifully obeyed.

Finished with her customer, the woman grabbed a menu and silverware rolled in a paper napkin and indicated he should follow.

As they rounded the corner, Stone saw a few people seated along a row of faded, red vinyl-covered booths with old speckled Formica tabletops that lined the wall to his left. Paintings of the local scenery, some professional and others amateurish, all adorned with yellowed price tags, decorated the wall above the booths.

To his right, he saw a long counter dotted with old swivel stools with cracked red vinyl seat cushions. What looked like locals, older men wearing worn blue jeans, flannel shirts, dusty cowboy boots, and sweat-stained cowboy hats, sat at the counter reading newspapers, sipping coffee, and shoveling assorted breakfast foods into their unshaven faces.

Stone glanced at the people in the booths, and at the counter, as the woman led him deeper into the restaurant.

They were unfamiliar faces, and no one took more than a passing interest in him. The woman stopped at the last booth toward the back of the restaurant. An entrance into what Stone thought was the kitchen and the bathrooms lay deeper along a narrow hallway. He sat facing the front.

"Someone will be right with you," she said, and scurried off to attend to other customers. The counter stools appeared reserved for the locals, with tourists relegated to the booths. *Segregation in the form of seating arrangements*, he thought.

His position provided him a view of all the customers. Any cop with a sense of self-preservation sat at the back of restaurants—facing the front—these days. It surprised Stone the woman chose to seat him in the booth he would've selected.

He began scanning the plastic-coated menu. Out of the corner of his eye, he caught movement as a woman approached from behind and asked, "Would you like coffee?"

"Yes, please," Stone said, as he looked from the menu—right into Molly's eyes.

Shocked, Stone stared, speechless. It appeared that seeing him had stunned Molly too. They stared at each other with recognition and disbelief.

Molly was older, but no wrinkles had invaded the corners of her eyes. If possible, she was more beautiful then he remembered. Not the contrived beauty of a New York sophisticate or Broadway showgirl, hers was a natural beauty ... high cheekbones, full and inviting lips, and silky skin that radiated a healthy glow—no makeup required. Her golden hair was longer and tied back in a ponytail, and her eyes mirrored the color of a clear Colorado sky.

Stone broke the silence and said, "Molly, how are you? It's been a long time."

The silence that followed bordered on awkward. Molly blinked, broke her stare, and said, "Yes. It has been a long time."

Her coldness could've chilled the coffee in the pot, Stone thought. Taken aback by her indifference, Stone said the first thing that popped into his head. "Are you working here?"

As the words escaped his lips, he realized it was a stupid question to ask. What was she going to say? No. She just stopped in every day for the last nineteen years in case he dropped by for coffee.

"I own the restaurant," Molly replied, as though speaking to a stranger. She held the pot out and repeated, "Coffee?"

Stone righted the white ceramic mug on the table, and Molly filled it with coffee as Stone stared at her.

"Someone will be right out to take your order," she said, avoiding eye contact.

She spun and hurried back through the kitchen door by the hallway. Stone noticed she looked fit—very fit.

The encounter had staggered him. He'd expected that anyone he knew had moved long ago, and Molly's appearance had caught him off guard. He could tell the encounter had rattled her too.

He wondered if he should stay or go. Would Molly come back and talk to him? Was he ready to see her again ... or she him? He decided to stay and let her make the decision. Maybe it was the shock of seeing him that caused her reaction.

Stone had his answer once he'd finished breakfast, paid his bill, and was back on the street. Apparently, Molly decided not to interact with him any further. She'd entered the kitchen and hadn't reappeared.

He walked along the boardwalk, his hands in his pants pockets and his head down. If he'd known he would bump into Molly, he sure as hell would've chosen a better way. He wondered if he should check out of the motel and hightail it back to New York. Run—like he did nineteen years ago. The thought made him feel like a coward.

He hadn't expected to see anyone from his past, least of all Molly. Maybe deep inside he suspected there was a remote possibility; maybe deep inside he'd hoped he would see her.

Maybe.

For the first time in a long time, he had no idea what to do.

Chapter 8

STONE WANDERED ALONG DOWD STREET in a stupor. As he passed one of the numerous gift shops, his eye caught a tee shirt on display stenciled "My Mountain Man" with a bespeckled, sideways-pointing arrow under it. The memory of buying a shirt like that for Molly many years ago plucked at a raw nerve deep inside him.

Aimless wandering took him by Silver Lake's popular lakeside beach. This was another place of once-pleasant memories. He sat on a bench and stared across the water as a lone sailboat glided across the lake's seductive surface, cutting a ribbon through the water.

What the hell did I expect? he thought. He was the one who ran away, leaving Molly without even a goodbye. He was nothing but an unpleasant footnote in Molly's history at this point.

The clear, sunny day had taken on a dimness, as though looking at everything through a smoky haze. Whatever his rationale for coming to Silver Lake, it had evaporated like the morning dew.

Stone pulled himself out of his funk. He wasn't the kind of person to crumble because of a chance encounter. His job had put him in a lot tougher spots. *Molly wouldn't have acted so cold and been evasive if she had no feelings for me,* he thought.

He needed a plan. What would he do if he chanced upon a suspect back in New York? Not that seeing Molly was the same as encountering a suspect, but the principle was the same. Use the element of surprise to make your move, since you have the advantage of having the other person off balance.

If he gave Molly time, she'd harden to the idea of seeing him again. He needed to go back to the restaurant and ask to see her, so they could talk—so he could get a sense of how bad things were between them.

Stone set off like a man on a mission. As he approached the restaurant, he slowed ... and stopped. *Charging in the place like I'm pursuing a suspect might be the wrong approach,* he thought. He gathered himself and stepped through the door. Like the last time, a woman working the cash register as a customer put several bills on the counter looked at him, smiled, and said, "I'll be right with you."

He looked past the partition and spotted Molly taking an order near the back of the seating area. He didn't wait. As she stepped away from the table and turned, they came face to face. Molly's surprised look darkened.

"Before you kick me out, at least listen to me for a minute?" Stone asked. "Please?"

The stern look on Molly's face softened a bit. She turned and motioned for him to follow. She walked to the end of the narrow hallway at the back of the restaurant and spun to face him, crossing her arms. "Why're you here?"

Stone sighed and said, "I didn't seek you out, Molly. In fact, I had no idea I'd run across anyone from my past."

"That doesn't answer my question."

"I'd like to explain if you'll give me the chance ... but it doesn't look like a good time," Stone said, glancing back over his shoulder.

He could see her mulling it over. Molly uncrossed her arms, and as she shouldered past him said, "I'll consider it. Come back at dinnertime, and I'll let you know."

***

Dinner behind him, the day seemed to have brightened. Molly had agreed to meet him after closing the restaurant. Stone walked with a newfound bounce to his step. Elated, he felt a little nervous too.

Okay, a lot nervous.

As he ambled along Dowd Street, a smile glued to his face, he noticed traffic stopped in both directions ahead and a few people loitering on the walkways. A Silver Lake Marshal's Office patrol SUV, stopped in the street, was at the head of the stationary traffic. The overhead emergency lights flashed, and the driver's door was open.

As he approached, he could see three hogs (the nickname for Harley-Davidson motorcycles) stopped in front of the police SUV, leaning on their kickstands. The bikes had low-slung saddles, extended forks, and ape-hanger handlebars.

Even prior to seeing the players, Stone knew the cop had stopped outlaw bikers. As he moved toward the scene, he witnessed the trio of bikers confronting the town marshal in the space between the patrol car and the bikes.

Burly, dirty, tattooed, and dressed in leathers showing their colors, with the name "Disciples of Hell" embroidered on the rocker sewn to the back of their patch littered vests, the bikers had gotten the better of the cop. One shoved the marshal and stuck a finger in his face.

Stone was too distant to hear the exchange, but body language told him all he needed to know. The cop was afraid, and the bikers knew it. They pressed their advantage, as the marshal backed away.

Stone had dealt with many bikers in New York. The knife scar on his side was a permanent reminder of one encounter.

He knew two things. A show of weakness served to embolden them and—like cockroaches—if you failed to squash the first one you came across, you wound up with an infestation.

Without hesitation, Stone moved in. "Hey, asshole," he called as he walked into the street near the bikers. "Shoving an officer of the law is an assault."

The bikers shifted their focus from the cop to Stone. "The fuck?" the one who'd shoved the marshal said.

The largest of the three said, "You better walk, bitch. You don't want no part of this—unless you lookin' for a beat down."

Stone's martial arts training had taught him several things.

Never be the second to strike.

Never use your fist if you can avoid it.

Throw every blow for maximum effect and—never announce your intentions.

As Stone circled, the bikers turned to track him. His movement put the first biker between him and the other two. They looked tough ... thick necks and meaty arms, but they looked out of shape too. All three had flabby guts hanging over their belts. Gang life had made them fat, lazy, and overconfident.

Stone continued to maneuver, positioning himself. Out of the corner of his eye, he saw the marshal grab the patrol vehicle's radio mike. Stone stopped moving, dropped his arms to his sides, flexed his knees, and let all emotion slide from his face. He lowered his chin a couple of inches. The closest biker moved in, cocking his right arm to deliver a blow.

He never got a chance. Stone launched himself and slammed the top of his forehead into the biker's face. The biker's nose snapped, and blood flowed as the dazed man stumbled back. In pain, the biker's reaction was to cover his broken nose with his hands. Stone followed with a sidekick to the biker's left knee before he could recover. The leg hyper-extended backward. Stone heard another snap as the biker screamed and fell.

Stone moved past the downed biker and struck the second biker in the side of the head with a vicious elbow strike before he could recover from his surprise. The blow stunned the biker, and he staggered backward, trying to stay on his feet. Stone followed with another sidekick, snapping the second biker's knee. The man crumbled, writhing in pain.

The third—and largest—of the three bikers backed away and pulled a hunting style knife from a scabbard on his belt. "Come on, motherfucker," he said, flipping the knife from hand to hand, as if playing a movie role. "I'm gonna cut you up."

"You talk too much," Stone said, moving in.

The swing was wide and slow, and Stone stepped away from the attack. The knife passed by with inches to spare. Stone faked a charge, knowing the man would throw a backswing. The biker swung his arm back, exposing his head and body. Stone moved in and blocked another swing with his left forearm. He slammed the heel of his right hand into the point of the biker's nose. The snap was loud. He followed with a vicious front kick to the lower abdomen and groin, which caused the biker's legs to fly backward into the air, dropping the man on his damaged face.

Stone kicked the knife out of the biker's hand and grabbed him by his ponytail. He lifted the injured man's head and leaned in. "Listen to me. Get on your chopper, get out of town, and don't come back. You can recover your friends' bikes at the town line and collect your buddies from the hospital. You hear me," Stone spat, yanking the biker's ponytail for emphasis.

"Yeah," the man rasped, blood pouring from his ruined nose.

"I wouldn't tell anyone one person kicked all your asses," Stone added. "Not if you want to keep your colors. Your club needs to move on ... pick another place. You come back, there'll be lots of cops waiting to deliver more of the same."

Stone watched the biker get to his feet, stumble to his bike, and ride out of sight. He could hear the faint wail of sirens in the distance and a smattering of applause from the people watching from the walkways as the motorcycle faded into the distance.

He turned toward the marshal, who stood shamefaced at his patrol vehicle.

Chapter 9

AN OLD LOG STRUCTURE, LOCATED on a side street a few blocks off the main drag, displayed a carved wooden sign over the door, announcing it was the Silver Lake Marshal's Office. A gravel parking lot in front, and two giant blue spruce trees flanking the building, added to its antediluvian appearance.

Stone sat at a small handmade wooden table pushed against one of the walls. Excessive use over time had resulted in scratches, pot marks, and initials carved into the table's surface by the temporary summer deputies who used the table as a desk, lunchroom, or for any other purpose needed. Seated in one of the three worn wooden chairs tucked under the table, he worked on his official statement.

In all the years that had passed, the marshal's office had changed little. The small rustic buildings focal point, an antique black pot-belly stove sat dormant in one corner.

The marshal's desk, on the other side of the miniscule office, was different than he remembered. The computer and combination printer, scanner, and fax located on the work center peninsula—that gave the desk area an L shape—was a jarring add-on. It no longer fit the bucolic decor. Four portable radios in a charger on top of the scratched and paint-chipped, black metal file cabinet in the corner by the desk was another addition inconsistent with the pastoral ambiance.

Stone remembered the back room hid a holding cell, bathroom, and a uniform and equipment storage closet. The building's design was compact and functional.

As he reviewed his statement, the front door flew open, and a sergeant from the Pitkin County Sheriff's Department rushed into the office. Stone looked at the man, noticing that his brown uniform seemed loose on his thin frame. Balding, he bore a serious mustache that compensated for the lack of hair on his head. He had a harried look in his sepia eyes.

The sergeant pulled out the chair across from Stone and flopped into it as though he weighed a ton. "Shit," he exhaled.

"You okay?" Stone asked, placing the pen on the table.

"Yeah," the sergeant said. Remembering his manners, he added, "Oh, sorry." He proffered his hand and said, "Sergeant Rick Fowler, Pitkin County Sheriff's Department."

Stone shook the man's hand. Puzzled by the dramatic entrance he said, "Hunter Stone. You sure you're okay?"

The sergeant waved off Stone's concern. "Hell of a day, that's all. Would you believe the tourists who witnessed the ass whupping you gave those punks thought you staged it? For their entertainment!"

"You're kidding?" Stone said, surprised.

"Tourists. What can I say? Can't shoot 'em—'cause we need the money." He grinned lopsided at Stone.

"Glad to hear it, since I'm one of them," Stone pointed out, returning the smile.

"Not from what I've gathered. You're an ex-local and ex-deputy marshal is what I hear."

"A long time ago," Stone said.

"Yeah. Heard that too. Nineteen years NYPD. An exemplary career and a decorated sergeant. What brings you back?"

"If you know all that," Stone said, surprised at the speed the sergeant had obtained his background, "you've checked and know it's not that exemplary. I'm on suspension. So, I decided to visit some old haunts since I had the time off."

"We've all been there. One day you're the pigeon and the next you're the statue."

Stone liked the sergeant's interview technique. However, the friendly approach was a common police tactic. "Where're we going with this, Sergeant? Do I need an attorney?" he asked.

"Hell no! You're the hero du jour. My job's to match all the accounts to clean this up."

Stone started to respond, but the sergeant cut him off. "By the way, nice touch with the motorcycles. The Disciples will accept three of their own getting their asses kicked since it was three on one. But their bikes symbolize some serious mojo for them. I had them moved to the town limits—like you promised."

"Thanks. How're the two I took out?" Stone asked.

"In the hospital over in Aspen. Both had surgery to put their knees back in place. Nose too on one of 'em. Doc said they'd both walk again, but with limps. That'll make 'em easier to ID and catch when they go back to the life."

"Think they'll retaliate?" Stone asked, hoping his actions wouldn't result in additional problems.

"Nah. They're gone—out of the county. Looking for an easier place to terrorize, I suppose."

"Can't say I'm sorry," Stone said. "I saw them pushing the marshal around. It looked like he needed help."

"He did. He was in trouble and knew it. He's pretty rattled. Most all the town's residents are thankful, including the mayor. Course you can always count on one whiner. In this case, it's one of the town fathers."

"Uh, oh. Did I cause a problem?" Stone asked. He had no idea what a town father was, but it sounded like a position of importance.

"Nah. The Sheriff'll straighten him out." The sergeant pointed to the statement and asked, "You 'bout done with that?"

"I need to sign and date it." Stone finished and handed over his statement. Sergeant Fowler gave it a quick scan. He stood and proffered his hand again. "It's been a pleasure, Sergeant Stone. Enjoy the rest of your stay." He pulled a business card from his breast pocket and handed it to Stone. "You need anything, anything at all, give me a call." Before Stone could reply, he rushed out the door with the same flourish with which he'd entered.

Stone checked his watch and saw it was close to closing time at the restaurant. He slipped out of the Marshal's Office and walked back to the restaurant, anonymous in the darkness of the side streets.

Molly waited inside the door. As he approached, she pulled the door open and motioned him to enter. "You want coffee?" she asked over her shoulder as she headed behind the counter.

"If it's no trouble," he said, sliding into a booth. Although the fight with the bikers was the talk of the town, Molly made no mention of it. Apparently, small talk was out.

Molly placed coffee laden mugs on the table and slid in the seat across from him. Stone avoided eye contact by staring into the coffee mug cupped in his hands.

"I asked you a question this morning," Molly said, her tone neutral. "You never answered me, so I'll ask it again. Why're you here?"

"Like I said this morning, I didn't come back to find anyone. I didn't think any—"

"Why're you here?" Molly repeated, cutting him off.

Stone sat mute for a moment. He had no answer. He looked from the mug into Molly's eyes, knowing nothing he said would satisfy her, and said, "I'm not sure."

"Did you think you could waltz back into town like nothing's changed? Like your decisions didn't hurt other people?"

Stone heard the pain in Molly's voice, and the sorrow her eyes held broke his heart. "No, I didn't think that," he said, a deep sadness in his voice. He shifted his gaze back to the inky liquid in his mug. "I guess I didn't think things through or consider how my coming might affect others. I'm sorry." Stone released the mug and began to slide out of the booth.

"You don't get off that easy," Molly said, stopping him. "I had to work a long time to get past what you did to me. Since you decided to come back, you owe me the courtesy of an explanation."

Molly was right. She did deserve an explanation—and an apology. Stone sighed and looked into Molly's eyes again, seeing the look of determination on her face. "I made a mistake leaving the way I did and for that I'm sorry. I meant to call you, but days turned into weeks, then months, and then years. The longer I waited the more difficult it became." Even as he said it, Stone realized how self-serving his excuse sounded.

Molly sat staring, unresponsive ... waiting.

"I don't know what else to say," Stone said. "I didn't think I'd see anyone I knew from my past. It might not matter to you, but I'm glad I got to see you, if for no other reason than to apologize."

Molly failed to respond, so Stone added, "I'm heading back to New York in a couple of days. I'll never be able to find the words to tell you how sorry I am, Molly. Please believe me, you hold a special place in my heart—and you always will."

Stone slid out of the booth and stood, looking into her eyes. "I hope someday you can find it in your heart to forgive me."

He turned and walked out of the restaurant.

Chapter 10

A RESTLESS NIGHT'S SLEEP BEHIND him, Stone decided to avoid the Silver Nugget Café. He doubted Molly wanted to see him. Besides, what else could he say to her?

He ate breakfast at a hotel restaurant, the Summit Inn located on Dowd Street not far from his motel. Staring at his uneaten breakfast, he wondered if his recent difficulties at work had triggered some long held suppressed desire. On the other hand, maybe he'd subconsciously sabotaged his career to force himself to examine his life.

Stone pushed his plate away and drained his coffee mug. No matter. He'd made the decision to finish his career at the NYPD. He would revisit it in another year—with a full twenty years under his belt.

He paid the bill and resumed his exploration of Silver Lake. He cut through a side street to the lake and ambled along the boardwalk toward the south end of town. As he looped away from the lake and back to Dowd Street, he spotted a large boulder with a blackened bronze plaque affixed to it at the dead end of the street.

Anchored in that spot for as long as he could remember, it extolled the towns founding in 1860 by a prospector named Benjamin Dowd. Stone remembered a ghost story told to him as a child. Trails dotted with abandoned silver mines crisscrossed the mountains surrounding town. The story told was that Benjamin Dowd's ghost wandered the mines, seeking vengeance for his murder and the theft of his fortune. Stone had been so frightened he refused to go near the mines.

Stone smiled at the childhood memory and resumed his walk. He gazed at window displays as he strolled along. One caused him to come to an abrupt stop. He stared at the window, festooned with photographs of properties for sale. They surrounded a gold leafed name painted in an arc on the glass.

"Damn. Stemple Realty," Stone mumbled.

Will Stemple was a local realtor. They had been friends through Stone's college years and his years as the deputy marshal. More than friends, as a matter of fact. Will had filled a gap in Stone's life after his parents' deaths. He was older and had taken on the role of mentor. The office was still in the same location. A sign hanging inside the door glass read, "Closed." Stone decided to stop back by. He turned to leave and heard a voice call from behind, "See anything that interests you?"

Stone turned and came face to face with Will Stemple. "Hi, Will," Stone said, smiling and extending his hand.

"My goodness. Hunter Stone," Will said, grabbing and pumping the proffered hand. "After all these years." A broad smile creased Will's friendly, round face. "Let me get this door open so we can visit."

As Will unlocked the door, Stone noticed the years had added a few pounds to his friend's squat frame. His obsidian hair had receded and faded to a smoky ash that encircled his baldpate. It had been a long time, and time changed things and people—including him.

A bell at the top of the doorjamb jingled as Will pushed the door open and ushered Stone inside. "Have a seat, Hunter," Will offered, gesturing toward a chair. "Give me a second to get these lights on," he added, disappearing through a back-room curtain.

Stone remembered Will refused to call him by other than his first name. As a child, Stone had one day announced to his parents that he hated his first name. They were unhappy by the pronouncement but had eventually agreed to call him what he wanted—Stone. Will had refused for some odd reason.

Stone perused the office. He would swear that, except for the addition of a current wall calendar showing scenic photographs with outhouses in the foreground, the office appeared unchanged. A paper-laden desk with a swivel chair, both made of sturdy oak, and two straight-back visitor chairs of equal brawn, filled the small office.

Will returned, smoothed his brown corduroy slacks, and tugged at the open collar of his white dress shirt as he eased into his desk chair. He smiled and said, "It's a pleasure to see you Hunter, although I heard you were in town." Will's smile faded, and he added, "You made quite the entrance, for which the town is grateful. I'm sorry it became necessary for you to become involved in such an unpleasant matter."

It surprised Stone that Will knew he was the person who'd assisted the marshal. "I guess I made the local gossip column. How'd you know it was me?"

"As mayor, I get certain information from the police."

"You're the mayor?" Stone asked, surprised. "When did that happen?"

"Ummm ... close to eleven years ago. No one else wanted the job because of, ummm ... certain challenges, but that's unimportant. We're all grateful for your assistance."

"No problem," Stone said. "It's not the first time I've dealt with bikers. If you don't put a quick stop to them, they'll move in and take over."

Will nodded his understanding. "Enough of unpleasant subjects. So, tell me what you've been up to all these years. Did you go to work with the New York Police?"

Apparently, the sheriff's department had neglected to reveal everything they had learned. "Yes, I'm with the NYPD. I'm a sergeant assigned to the Crime Lab but worked my way to the lab via patrol, vice, narcotics, and the gang unit."

"That's an impressive résumé," Will said. "You must love what you do."

"Truth is, with nineteen years on the job, I'm close to burned out. I could retire, but it would delay my retirement pay and health benefits for a year."

Surprised, Will said, "You're a young man. What would you do if you retired?"

"I've considered that. I think I'd like to stay in law enforcement. Maybe move to a smaller department with less … everything … I guess."

Will leaned back in his chair, laced his fingers, and rested his hands on his rounded belly. "What does that mean?"

Stone hesitated a moment in thought and said, "Fewer crimes. Lower stress. Above all, no politics."

Will's brow furled as he pursed his lips. "I can understand your desire to work in a low-stress environment, but you'll encounter politics no matter your location, or what you choose to do."

"I know," Stone said, noticing Will had slipped back into his mentoring role without realizing it. "I can handle political input for the purpose of bettering a community. It's the interference that impedes criminal investigations I want to avoid."

"Is that what brought you back? Are you trying to determine if small-town life is something you might want to try again?"

Stone smiled and said, "You're the second person to ask me my reason for coming."

"I know. I'm late this morning because Molly asked to speak to me."

Surprised, Stone's smiled faded. He stiffened in his chair and asked, "How come Molly discussed our meeting with you?"

"Molly and I became close after you left. She confides in me—like you used to." Will cleared his throat, unlaced his fingers, and tilted his chair upright. His smile gone, he added, "I don't know if you noticed Molly was—conflicted about seeing you again."

"I guess it was a mistake coming back. I didn't expect to see anyone from my past, including Molly. I didn't mean to cause any problems."

Will leaned in, resting his forearms on the desktop. He looked into Stone's eyes and said, "I won't lie and tell you Molly hasn't carried mixed feelings all these years. Your leaving and the way you left … devastated her. It hurt us all."

Stone shifted his eyes away. He met Will's eyes after a moment's thought and said, "Of all the poor decisions I've made in my life, the one I regret the most was the decision to leave Silver Lake ... and Molly ... and everyone close to me the way I did. That decision's haunted me for the past nineteen years."

Like an unseen weight, an uncomfortable silence settled over the office. At length Stone mumbled, "I shouldn't have come back."

Will reached across the desk, placing his hand on Stone's arm and said, "Whatever your reasons for coming home, Hunter, I'm glad you did, and I'm happy to see you again. You're a part of our lives and the town. No matter your whereabouts or how long you're gone, this is your home, and you'll always be welcome."

"Thank you, Will," Stone said, embarrassed by the sentiment.

They chatted amicably for another hour or so. As the conversation slowed, Will asked, “How long are you staying?”

“Another day. I want to do some sightseeing. Play tourist and see the highlights in Aspen and Glenwood Springs.”

Prior to parting company, Stone and Will exchanged addresses and telephone numbers and promised to stay in touch.

As Stone wandered town for the last time he thought of the old adage—”You can’t go home again”—and wondered if it might be a truthful proclamation.

Chapter 11

WITHIN AN HOUR OF ARRIVING back in New York, Stone waded through a wall of discourteous people from the concourse to the luggage carrousels. The polluted odor that hung in the air assaulted his nose as he walked to the parking structure.

He refused to turn on his smartphone until he was in the long-term parking garage at LaGuardia. He had no interest in speaking to anyone. Nor was it anyone's business what he did on suspension—as long as it was legal. As he approached his SUV, he turned on the device and saw five voicemails.

Seated behind the wheel, Stone listened to the messages, all from Captain Baxter. Each sounded more desperate than the last, pleading for Stone to call him. Even so, his captain had avoided divulging the reason for the calls. Tomorrow was soon enough. Stone shut off the device.

***

"It's Stone, Captain. You left me a message."

"I've left messages for the last couple of days," Baxter snapped. "I'm sorry, Stone," he added. "I've had McFarland on my ass, demanding I get ahold of you."

"I've been on vacation and had my phone turned off." Stone sagged onto his couch as his stomach knotted in anticipation. The name McFarland didn't invoke warm fuzzies.

"I hate doing this on the phone," Baxter said. "McFarland's opened an official investigation relating to your actions in that Colorado town you visited."

Shocked at the news, Stone at first wondered how McFarland was even aware of it. Then he remembered the Pitkin County Sheriff's Department had checked him out with the NYPD. Someone had clued in McFarland. Apparently, McFarland had eyes and ears throughout the department. Irritated, he asked, "An investigation? For what? All I did was assist the town marshal."

"I know that," Baxter said. "I've read the reports. Some ambulance-chaser lawyer representing the two bikers you put in the hospital threatened to sue the NYPD."

Stunned mute, myriad thoughts swirled through Stone's head. Finding his voice, he said, "I didn't identify myself as a police officer."

"Regardless, McFarland's position is that he's acting to protect the NYPD," Baxter said. "The official charges include use of excessive force, acting beyond the scope of your authority, and bringing the NYPD into disrepute."

Upon hearing the charges, Stone went from stunned to angry in a flash. "That's a load of horseshit. Three bikers attacked me. What was I supposed to do, buy 'em a beer?"

"I didn't say they have a case," Baxter explained, "but McFarland's using the threat of a lawsuit as his reason for launching the investigation."

"Christ," Stone spat.

"Hold on a second," Baxter said.

Stone heard footfalls, heard a door close, and Baxter was back on the phone. "This part of our conversation never happened, okay?"

"Okay," Stone mumbled.

"You embarrassed McFarland in front of his subordinates. He means to have your badge any way he can get it—legally or ... you know. And you know he doesn't give a damn about ethics," Baxter whispered, sounding as though he thought someone might overhear. "He's vindictive as hell, and he told me he's pretty sure you put stuff in your desk and locker to send him off chasing false leads. If you have any way of getting help from the commissioner, you might want to ask."

Stone knew the commissioner liked him and had watched his career, but he couldn't—no—wouldn't—stoop to McFarland's level and ask the commissioner to intercede on his behalf. He could fight fire with fire, but it was unethical.

McFarland represented everything Stone saw as wrong with law enforcement. Using the same tactics to try to protect himself from McFarland's attack would make him no better. Stone said, "No. I can't do that."

"I didn't think you would."

"So, what should I expect?" Stone asked.

"Your suspension remains in effect. At some point, the IAB will contact you to come in for an interrogation and statement. I'd suggest you contact your PBA rep and get yourself a lawyer."

Stone knew his captain had helped all he could. If Baxter continued to offer help or injected himself in McFarland's investigation, it would look like favoritism. He would be jeopardizing his own career.

"Thanks for the info and your help, Cap," Stone said.

***

The following day, Stone hired the law office of Branski, Ludlow, and Stein. They represented police officers in both criminal and civil cases. He sat at a huge wooden table in a conference room, embellished with rich wood details, for his initial meeting with Harold Stein. Stein sat across the table and poured them each a cup of coffee from a silver carafe.

"No need to worry about criminal charges," Stein said, handing Stone a steaming cup. "The sheriff's department in Colorado didn't determine any criminality, and I've learned their local district attorney's office has declined to file any criminal charges."

A civil tort was another matter. Stein felt the biker's attorney had threatened a lawsuit to force the NYPD into self-protection mode—and that meant charging Stone with violations of departmental directives.

"He's waiting for the outcome of the internal investigation before deciding who to file against," Stein said, taking a delicate sip from his cup.

"What does that mean?" Stone asked. "He might sue me!"

Stein explained, "If the department fails to sustain any of the charges against you, the attorney could sue them. If they sustain even one of the charges, the attorney could file against you, because you have insurance coverage provided by the PBA. It's a typical squeeze play. He's seeking anyone with deep pockets to make him a quick settlement offer."

"Great," Stone said, disheartened. "On top of having an inspector out to bury me, their attorney has given him additional incentive to make sure he succeeds."

"Don't worry," Stein said. "I've handled other cases like this. Because no one in Colorado saw any wrongdoing, you don't need our representation for any criminal charges. It's unlikely the NYPD can sustain any of the internal charges at this point, but if they do, the PBA will assign you an attorney. If you'd rather use our services, call me, and we'll represent you."

Stone wasn't as confident as Stein. He was unaware how vindictive McFarland was. Nor did he know how close Stone came to putting the IAB lieutenant's lights out in McFarland's office. Both had plenty of incentive to hang him out to dry.

The meeting over, Stein ushered him from the conference room. The brief meeting cost him four hundred and fifty dollars.

Stone drove home, numb. He'd felt anesthetized since the conversation with his captain. As he pulled into the underground parking garage at his building, his smartphone chirped. *What now,* he wondered looking at the caller ID. It was Sergeant Tom Wilkerson, his PBA rep.

"Hey, Tom," Stone said, sounding defeated. Stone had known Tom Wilkerson most of his career and knew him to be a superb cop and a tenacious PBA rep.

"Chin up, man," Tom said. "A little birdie told me the saga of McFarland and Moody. I can assure you neither of them will have anything more to do with your case."

"Well, that's something positive. Thanks, Tom." Stone suspected Captain Baxter was the birdie but had no intention of asking.

"No sweat, my friend. Here's the status to date. I've gone ahead and challenged the charges. One PP has amended them, dropped the excessive force and acting beyond the scope of your authority charges. They couldn't justify either, based on the police reports. That leaves the charge of bringing disrepute to the NYPD, which is subjective at best."

If One Police Plaza sustained the final charge, Stone would find himself on the business end of a lawsuit, according to Stein. He wondered if he might face additional punishment from the NYPD too, since he was on suspension.

"I assume you've spoken to an attorney," Tom asked.

"Yeah. Harold Stein of Branski, Ludlow, and Stein."

"Great," Tom said, sounding cheerful. "If IAB calls you in before you hear from me again, you don't appear without me. Clear?"

"I got it," Stone said and disconnected. He sat in his SUV, staring out the windshield at the garage wall, feeling like fruit in a blender.

Chapter 12

STONE CRAWLED OUT OF BED. A restless night of tossing and turning had left his eyes red and scratchy and his mind foggy.

A vigorous workout at the health club, followed by a hot shower and healthy breakfast at a local eatery, helped lift the haze.

Back home, he loaded the hopper on his coffee pot with fresh-ground Caribou Coffee. The brewing process complete, he sat on his couch with a steaming mug.

His night of brooding had helped clarify things. No way would he survive another year. Not with McFarland circling like a hawk, waiting for the opportunity to swoop in and snatch his badge. No matter the outcome of the internal investigation, McFarland would keep gunning for him—until he found a reason to fire him or drive him into retirement.

If he terminates me, I'll lose my pension and benefits. That made the decision a no brainer.

Thoughts of taking early retirement brought back memories of his career and the many cases that had brought him to this point. He believed he could solve the Blood Letter Killer cases too ... if they would let him. But no way was that going to happen—not today—or ever. McFarland would make sure Captain Baxter kept him away from the cases.

Stone's anger swelled again as he thought of the oath he'd taken so many years ago. It was at the core of his belief system, yet no one could accomplish the impossible with McFarland in the way. His chances of ever working the cases again were long gone. So was his career.

It was time to seek other employment. Stone knew several websites that listed law enforcement job openings all over the country. He turned on his laptop and began the arduous task of updating his résumé.

Several hours and four cups of coffee later, he reviewed his updated résumé and the completed applications for the jobs culled from the law enforcement websites. He sat back on the couch, satisfied with his progress. All he had left to do now was submit the applications and his résumé.

Stone clicked on the website of the first department on his list. He attached the completed application and his résumé.

Finger poised over the enter key, he hesitated.

"No choice," he said to the empty room and tapped the key.

At six-ten, he sent the last application and résumé and shut off his computer. He sighed, stood, and stretched, popping his lower back.

Tonight was a good night to buy some Chinese take-out and spend the evening in front of the TV, watching a mind-numbing movie. Maybe he would be able to get a decent night's sleep.

***

Pulled from a deep sleep by the chirping of his smartphone on the nightstand, Stone reached for it as he squinted at his alarm clock. Nine-twenty. He yawned and answered, "Lo."

"Tom Wilkerson, Stone. Did I wake you?"

"That's okay, Tom."

"Christ, it's past nine," Wilkerson chided. "You gonna sleep all day?"

"Catching up." Stone sat on the edge of the bed, yawned again, and rubbed the sleep from his eyes.

A little too jubilant for Stone, Wilkerson said, "Shake the cobwebs, pal. I've got good news for you."

"I could use some," Stone muttered.

"You're off the hook on the last charge," Wilkerson said.

The news catapulted Stone from half asleep to wide awake. Surprised by the speedy resolution of the investigation, he said, "What? How's that possible?"

Wilkerson laughed and said, "Oh ye of little faith. It would appear the case landed on the commissioner's desk this morning. Right after he received it, he dismissed it."

Relieved the investigation was behind him, Stone was unhappy political favoritism had come into play to end it. He didn't want Wilkerson to think he was ungrateful, so he tried to sound happier than he was. "That's great, Tom. I can't thank you enough."

"Glad I was able to help," Wilkerson said. "So, get your ass out of bed, and go out and enjoy what's left of the day."

Stone no sooner ended the call than his smartphone chirped again. The caller ID showed the caller to be Captain Baxter.

"Stone," he answered.

"I hear congratulations are in order," Baxter said without preamble. "It's over, so all you have to do is ride out the rest of your suspension and come back to work."

"Speaking of that, do you have time to meet this morning?"

"Sure ... if you need to," Baxter said. "My office okay or do we need some privacy?"

"Your office," Stone said. "Is eleven convenient?"

"Sure," Baxter said, sounding confused.

As Stone dressed for his meeting, he wondered the best way to approach Baxter with his pending departure from the NYPD. He decided to make it as quick and painless as possible ... like ripping off an adhesive bandage.

***

Baxter's jaw dropped at Stone's retirement news, and he worked hard at talking him out of leaving. In the end, it was impossible to argue with Stone's logic. "I hate to see you go, but I understand," Baxter said. They talked for a while, and before they parted company, Baxter gave Stone his personal phone number and said, "If there's *ever* anything I can do for you, don't hesitate to call."

Stone wasted no time clearing out his desk and locker. He noticed that after nineteen years on the job all his accumulated possessions and mementos fit into a single evidence box, pilfered from the property room. He turned in his equipment at the precinct and drove to One Police Plaza to file his retirement paperwork—an entire career undone in a couple of hours.

He was home by mid-afternoon, an unemployed civilian with no income and an uncertain future.

***

The weekend passed with Stone sulking in his apartment.

Restless, he waited for Monday in the hope he would begin receiving some job offers. Monday came and went, as did Tuesday and Wednesday. No calls. For Stone, the days moved as slow as a three-toed sloth. He wondered if the lack of calls might be because McFarland had become involved in the background checks police departments did prior to making an offer of employment.

Thursday evening, as Stone stood in his compact kitchen, chopping vegetables for a stir-fry dinner, his smartphone chirped. He grabbed a dishtowel, wiping his hands, and raced into the living room to snatch the phone from the coffee table.

"Hello."

"Hunter?" a remote voice asked.

"Yes. This is Hunter Stone," he said, unable to identify the distant voice.

"It's Will, Hunter. Will Stemple."

Shocked at receiving a call from Will Stemple, Stone lapsed into a stunned silence.

"Are you there, Hunter?" Will asked.

"Uh—yes. Sorry, Will. Your call caught me by surprise. Is everything okay?"

"That would depend on one's point of view," Will said.

"What does that mean?"

"After you left our marshal resigned. So, we're looking to replace him," Will explained. "I remember you said you wanted to stay with the New York police for another year before looking for a smaller community in which to continue your career. Would you consider making that change early by trading in your New York badge for a Silver Lake star?"

Stone wanted the job and came close to blurting out his answer. He managed to hesitate as a profusion of questions exploded in his mind. Instead, he said, "You caught me off guard, Will. I wasn't expecting to hear from you."

"I'm sure you weren't," Will said.

"I hope you can understand that I might have some, uh—questions," Stone said.

"I can. However, let me assure you, this wasn't a snap decision.

A great deal of discussion preceded the decision to make you the job offer. I can offer you a starting salary of fifty-five thousand and benefits, including medical, if that answers some of your questions."

"Uh—some," Stone said.

"Perhaps I can answer another by telling you I've spoken with Molly, and she has no objection to you coming back."

Stone smiled. He accepted the job, and they agreed on a start date. Disconnecting, Stone sighed and whispered, "Thank you."

Although relieved, a small knot of apprehension continued to linger. He forgot dinner and poured himself a large Maker's Mark and water.

Chapter 13

STONE KNOCKED ON THE APARTMENT building superintendent's door, but no one answered. That was typical. The guy called himself the manager but did little to earn the title. Stone knocked harder and rang the bell several times.

The superintendent, a small, mean-spirited man with a ruddy complexion, thinning, slicked back, greasy black hair, and a pencil-thin mustache yanked the door open. Upon seeing Stone, he frowned, pulled out the stub of a cigar stuck in the corner of his mouth and exhaled a cloud of blue smoke in Stone's direction. "What?"

Stone leaned back and waved the noxious cloud away from his face. He handed the superintendent a written notice to vacate. "I've accepted a position in another state, Mister Crespo, so I'm vacating my apartment on the date indicated. Could you please send any deposit refund to me at the marshal's office address on my notice?" he said, pointing at the note.

The superintendent glanced at the notice, grunted something unintelligible, and slammed the door.

"I'll miss you too," Stone said, shaking his head.

He posted a moving sale notice on the lobby bulletin board and rode the elevator to his fifth-floor apartment. As usual, the elevator stopped on every floor. The kids again. They thought it was funny to run downstairs, stopping long enough to push the call buttons on each floor. He would miss that like a bullet to the brain.

It took two harrowing days to sell off all his furniture. Like sharks, the tenants circled, waiting to strike as soon as he dropped the prices. He knew their intent was to get whatever they could for free or as close to it as possible. *Typical*, he thought.

Stone knew some of these people from seeing them in the halls and on the elevators on and off for years. None had ever taken the time to try to befriend him. Communication consisted of a quick nod or hello. However, post a for sale notice and they acted like your best friend—as long as the price was right.

Prior to packing his computer, Stone typed a lengthy email to the commissioner, detailing the events that resulted in his early retirement. He held nothing back, placing the blame squarely on McFarland's shoulders for both his premature departure and the failure to solve the Blood Letter Killer cases. He hoped the commissioner would hold McFarland accountable for his actions but guessed the email was a waste of time. Departmental politics being what it was, he suspected nothing would come of it. At least he felt better. It was as though a weight lifted off his shoulders as he pushed the send button.

As he continued to pack, he removed the single photograph displayed in his apartment from the living room wall. Over eight million people lived in the five boroughs of New York and for nineteen years, he'd been a member of that clan. With all those people, and in all that time, he'd chosen to memorialize only his dead parents on his apartment wall. The other walls remained barren, his décor a testament to his life.

In his bedroom closet, Stone found a cardboard carton stored in a back corner. "My old memory box," he said to himself, surprised, as he pulled it out of the closet. He'd forgotten about it. Hidden in the corner for the better part of his career, a layer of dust coated the flaps.

Stone carried the box to the living room and sat on the floor with the box in front of him. He blew the dust off the top and—with reverence—opened the flaps. Inside, he first saw his parent's photo album, his high school and college yearbooks, and a trophy he'd won as a youngster for some long-ago forgotten event. As he removed the items from the carton, handling each as though he was a museum curator and his memories priceless antiquities, he took his time and examined each item.

Upon reaching the bottom, he spotted something tucked into the corner.

It was a small, black, velvet-covered ring box. He lifted it out of the carton and opened it. Inside was a one and a half-carat, round, solitaire diamond engagement ring—his mother's—the same ring he'd intended to give to Molly when he asked her to marry him. That is, before everything fell apart—and he ran. Stone stared at the ring, memories flooding his mind. Coming back to the present, he sighed, snapped the lid closed, and returned his memories to the box—and to the depths of his mind.

As he continued to pack, Stone's thoughts turned to his life. He reduced it to bite-sized pieces and turned over the fragments, examining them in infinite detail. Even though he wanted to blame others for being distant, he'd made the decision to keep people at arm's length.

His life was a train wreck.

He systematically disentangled his life in New York, waiting to feel a sense of loss. Instead of melancholy, the excited anticipation of a fresh beginning energized him. He was eager to put this chapter of his life behind him and begin a new one.

Relegated to sleeping on an inflatable mattress and using packing boxes for tables and chairs, he wanted to get going.

It took two days to transfer his bank accounts to a Wells Fargo Bank in Aspen, Colorado and collect a sizeable check from police headquarters for his unused sick leave.

With his SUV packed and three days left to reach his destination, he headed out, eager to put New York in his rear-view mirror.

***

Stone arrived Friday evening and checked into a room reserved for him at the Lakeview Motel, the same place he'd stayed on his vacation. He decided to wait until morning to call Will. It would give him an opportunity to wander the town anonymously, perhaps for the last time.

Unpacked and settled in his room, he ate a late dinner at the Summit Inn's restaurant, the same eatery where he'd had breakfast the day after his uncomfortable run-in with Molly at the Silver Nugget Café. He wanted to avoid any additional surprises. After sunset, he took a quick walking tour of town to work out the kinks of a long drive. Back in his room, he cozied down for the night.

In bed, Stone thought back on his years of fighting the worst of the worst criminals and how it had chipped away at his soul. Like a cancer, it had insidiously eaten holes in his humanity. He'd lost faith in everything and everyone, including himself. Some people compared it to going to war. Except at the end of most days, he could go home. He knew he'd reached a tipping point in his life. His hope was that he'd escaped New York with enough of his soul intact to salvage his humanity.

Stone drifted into a deep sleep. He dreamt of his cross-country journey, of the inkling of hope he'd begun to feel as he started his climb into the Rockies. Upon exiting the Eisenhower Tunnel on Interstate 70, with the tree line below him, he'd had an unobstructed view for hundreds of miles. White-capped chains of Granite Mountains, punctuated by cavernous, undulating valleys, crowded with carpets of deep green trees, stretched to the horizon. The sky, a broad expanse of brilliant azure, held no clouds to obscure the sun.

For the first time in many years, he'd felt the weight of his past life begin to lift.

Chapter 14

STONE'S EYES FLUTTERED OPEN TO sunlight that seemed to bend past the closed window curtain into his room. He stretched and yawned. He couldn't remember the last time he'd had such a sound night's sleep. Rested, he felt refreshed.

He sat on the edge of the bed and checked his watch on the bedside table. It was past ten. *Damn*, he thought, grabbing his smartphone. He'd slept close to twelve hours.

"Stemple Realty. Will Stemple speaking."

"It's Stone, Will. Sorry I'm late calling. I got in last night and didn't want to disturb you. Looks like I overslept."

"That's okay, Hunter. I'm glad you're here," Will said. "Was your room waiting at the Lakeview Motel?"

"It was. Thanks for making the reservation."

"My pleasure. Why don't you take the rest of the weekend to relax and meet me at the marshal's office at eight on Monday morning?"

"You sure? I'm okay working the weekend," Stone said.

"What we have to do can wait."

They said their goodbyes and disconnected. His schedule clear, Stone took his time and shaved, showered, and ate a leisurely breakfast at the Summit Inn. With time to kill, he wandered through town and found himself on the boardwalk along Silver Lake's beachfront.

Sunny and warm, it was a drop-dead gorgeous day—at least as warm as it got at 8,936 feet in the Rocky Mountains. Since his vacation visit a short time ago, the mud season had vanished, and the short summer had taken a firm, albeit temporary, hold. Silver Lake made the most of capturing tourist dollars through the three or so months of warm weather.

He sat on a bench and stared across the water at the speedboats thundering across the lake pulling wetsuit-clad skiers as small fishing boats swayed in their wake. Deep mountain lakes like Silver Lake, located high in the mountains, were bitter cold, so no one skied without a wetsuit—unless they had a death wish. The lake was so cold the local souvenir shops sold stuffed and mounted fur-covered trout they touted as a unique species, only caught in the frigid depths of Silver Lake.

Concentrating, Stone tuned out the happy babble of children as they pumped their legs, propelling paddleboats in the roped area near shore and the orders barked to his crew by a tour boat captain, readying his dockside vessel for a tour.

What occupied his thoughts was his dishonesty with Will. No, not dishonesty—but not the complete truth either. The sin of omission. He'd told Will he wanted to get away from the NYPD and work in a smaller department with lower stress. He'd withheld what was at the core of his need to get away. He decided that if he intended to rebuild his life in Silver Lake, he needed to be honest. If he refused to trust or be honest with the people who at one time meant everything to him, people with whom he hoped to reconnect, how could he ever expect to heal the tear in his soul?

It was time to cast off the NYPD Sergeant Detective Specialist Stone façade—let go of his reluctance to trust—let go of choosing to be a loner—let go of his repressed anger and depression. This was his opportunity to heal, and he meant to make the most of it.

A shriek pulled Stone from his reverie. The cop kicked in as his eyes sought the source of the scream. A woman standing near the shoreline pointed out into the water, yelling for someone named Kathy.

Stone's eyes shifted, following the line of her outstretched arm. A paddleboat sat empty, bobbing on the water, an empty lifejacket floating near the watercraft. He knew what had happened and launched off the bench. He kicked off his shoes and pulled his wallet and cellphone from his pockets, dropping them as he sprinted toward the water.

The coldness of the water shocked him as he dove into the lake. He shivered as he swam to the area near the life vest, took several deep breaths, and dove beneath the surface. Stone remembered the lake bottom dropped off precipitously into the deep recesses of the lake close to shore. If he was lucky—very lucky—he might have a chance of finding the girl.

He swam in a descending spiral in the murky water, praying he would find the child. His lungs began burning as a vague form appeared below him. He reached out and grabbed an arm, kicking for all he was worth toward the surface.

Stone's head broke the surface a moment before his need for oxygen forced him to suck in lake water. He pulled the girl's head above the surface and swam toward the beach, his numb limbs slowing his progress. His feet found purchase on the sandy bottom. He cradled the girl in his arms and staggered to the boardwalk. The girl's mother followed him yelling, "Help her! Help her, please!"

As the crowd stared in shock, Stone yelled to no one in particular, "Call 911." He laid the girl on her back on the wooden walkway. His mind, re-oxygenated, kicked into high gear. He remembered from his training that water rescues in temperatures below sixty-eight degrees, called near-drownings, allowed the drowning victim to survive longer. The cold water caused a diving reflex in which the body slowed the heartbeat and sent blood from the hands, feet, and intestines to the heart and brain.

Stone had no idea how long the little girl was under water prior to reaching her. He felt her neck for a pulse and found one. He tilted her head back to open her airway, pinched her nose closed, and put his mouth over hers. After blowing several breaths into her, the little girl began coughing, spurting water. Then she began wailing. Thankful, Stone rolled her onto her side. If she could cry, she could breathe.

Her mother rushed in crying, thanking him and trying to comfort her daughter at the same time. Someone appeared with a blanket and draped it on the little girl. Stone took one of the little girl's hands and began rubbing it, trying to get her circulation going again, but his hands were too cold to do any good. He directed her mother and several bystanders to assist as he rubbed her back through the blanket.

As bystanders attended to the girl, Stone heard the wail of the ambulance coming from the volunteer fire department located across the street from the marshal's office. Someone draped another blanket over his shivering shoulders.

The ambulance whisked the girl and her mother away to the hospital in Aspen. Stone retrieved his wallet, phone, and shoes. As he sat on the bench, peeling off his soaked and sandy socks, a teenager approached him.

"Thanks, mister. That was close," the kid said.

Stone looked inquisitively at the teen, wondering at the young man's odd approach. "Who're you?" he asked.

"Oh, yeah. I work at the dock." A moment later he added, "I rented the paddleboat to that little girl's mother."

Stone gave the kid a stern look.

"I didn't do nothin' wrong," the teen said in a whiny voice. "She was old enough."

He glared at the young man and asked, "And you thought an adult life vest was appropriate for a girl her size?"

"Hey, I just do what I'm told," the kid whined. "Besides, who're you to tell me I did somethin' wrong?"

As Stone stood, he turned and faced the teen. "The name's Stone. I'm the new marshal."

Chapter 15

STONE EMERGED FROM A LONG, hot shower, the chills gone. He toweled off and started to dress. His smartphone chirped, and he grabbed it off the nightstand. "Hello."

"Hunter, it's Will."

"Figured I'd hear from you at some point."

"That was a dramatic introduction you made to the townsfolk," Will said. "I'm thankful you were close by, or the outcome would've been tragic."

"Have you heard anything on the little girl's condition?"

"The hospital's keeping her overnight to make sure no complications develop, but she seems fine," Will said.

"I guess I need to speak to whoever controls the business licenses about that paddleboat rental place," Stone said. "I saw some obvious negligence. The kid who rented out the paddleboat was pretty defensive."

"I heard. I've suspended their license," Will said. "They're closed until we can look into it a bit further. One of the town fathers owns the dock area and attractions, and he's unhappy with my decision."

"He should worry that he might get sued. What kind of man put profits ahead of peoples' lives?

"Do you remember back when you were the deputy marshal, making a drunken-driving arrest on a wealthy local, William Hendrickson?" Will asked.

"Can't say I do. That was a lot of cases ago."

"I'm sure he hasn't forgotten you or the arrest. I suspect that explains his reason for being the sole holdout on hiring you," Will said. "Neither of the other town fathers, Leo Feldman and Douglas Langford, agreed with him."

"So, what does this have to do with the rental shop?" Stone asked. This was the first he'd heard of someone objecting to his hiring.

"William Hendrickson owns the dock and businesses."

"Oh, shit. So, this guy doesn't like me because of an old arrest and now he's pissed at me—and I haven't even started?" Stone asked.

"No, no. Everyone's grateful for your quick actions, but Hendrickson can be a difficult man at times. I'm just giving you a warning—in case you bump into him."

You're back mentoring me, Stone thought, a smile creasing the corners of his mouth.

"Since you can't seem to wait to start, let's meet at the marshal's office in the morning instead of Monday," Will said.

"That's okay with me."

They disconnected, and Stone sat on the bed, putting on his shoes. With time on his hands, he wondered what he should do. He decided to check out the town from a cop's perspective. Afterward, he might stop by Molly's restaurant to test the waters, so to speak. He prayed his reception would be warmer than the frigid lake water.

Stone walked the town, making observations. Done, he stopped by the Silver Nugget Café for dinner. This time Molly was at the cash register upon his entry. "Hi, Molly."

"Stone," she said as she led him to the same booth he sat in on vacation.

As he slid into the booth, he asked, "Can I buy you a cup of coffee?"

Molly looked at her watch and said, "I'm off in half an hour. Can we take a walk instead of coffee?"

Stone agreed, and Molly left. He thought she sounded a little friendlier. Then he remembered their last meeting.

***

Stone and Molly walked along the boardwalk by the lakeshore. His hands stuffed into his pants pockets, Stone walked along, focused on the wooden slats of the walkway as though inventorying the boards. Molly walked alongside, looking straight ahead. Stone found the awkward silence unnerving.

Molly broke the ice. "The talk of the town is your rescue today. People said it was your quick thinking that saved that little girl's life."

"It felt good—doing something positive for a change," he said, thankful Molly had taken the initiative.

Molly came to an abrupt stop and looked at Stone. "You know, you haven't said what your reason for coming back was. Is it a secret?"

Stone thought for a moment. He looked at Molly and said, "I don't know. Other than New York, Silver Lake was the only other place I knew. Maybe that's the reason I chose it."

Stone shifted his eyes away, knowing he'd dodged the truth again. He'd seen in Molly's face that she knew it too. It was foreign to him to show weakness or vulnerability. But if he intended on healing himself, he needed to be honest—express his feelings—even if it made him feel uncomfortable.

He reminded himself of the commitment he made as part of that healing process. *No time better than the present,* he thought. He looked back into Molly's eyes and said, "Okay, the truth. I needed to get out of New York because I was on suspension from the NYPD, and I knew if I stayed, I'd make my situation worse."

"Shut the front door. How come they suspended you?" Molly asked. She appeared surprised but interested.

He looked away again and said, "I haven't told this to Will, so please don't repeat it until I have a chance to tell him myself. Will's job offer couldn't have come at a better time for me."

"What do you mean?" Molly asked.

"An inspector out for my badge suspended me for working a case my boss ordered me to drop. Because of the incident with the bikers here, the inspector filed internal charges against me. It became obvious he wasn't going to quit coming for me until he got my badge. And he didn't care how he got it. So, I retired to save my retirement and benefits a few days prior to Will's job offer. I'd started looking for a job at a smaller police department when Will called and made the offer."

"I understand you hesitated to take the job until Will told you I was okay with it," Molly said with a wisp of a smile.

It was Stone's turn to look surprised. He'd forgotten how hard it was to keep a secret in a small town. He directed Molly to a bench and they sat. He looked into her eyes again and said, "Molly, I want you to know that I've regretted the way I left every day for the last nineteen years. I can't tell you how sorry I am for hurting you."

"How come you left like that?" Molly asked, a confused look on her face and a touch of anguish in her voice.

"I wish I could give you a rational explanation. I can't." Stone took a deep breath. He looked away, then looked back at Molly and said, "Do you remember the accident that killed my parents?"

Molly nodded but remained silent.

"Remember how I changed my major to criminal justice? I did that because the day they died, I made a promise to them. I promised to find out who killed them. I failed, and every day became a painful reminder of that failure."

"Oh, Stone," Molly said, a profound sadness in her voice. "That wasn't your fault. No one could solve it."

Stone continued, the floodgates open, "I couldn't face my failure. I was angry, I think with myself. I buried that anger by convincing myself I wanted to leave, become a big city cop. The longer you and others pressured me to stay, the more determined I was to go. I didn't think I could change your mind, so I left, snuck out like a coward to seek what I'd convinced myself I wanted. And I sure as hell got what I wished for."

"What does that mean?"

Stone shifted his gaze to the boardwalk between his feet.

"It means I came close to losing myself and my humanity in the process of living my so-called dream."

"I don't understand," Molly said.

Stone hesitated again, looked deep into Molly's eyes, and with a palpable sadness in his voice said, "I have a hole in me ... a hole I don't know I can ever fill again. Maybe that was my reason for coming back—to try to find myself again."

Stone saw concern on Molly's face. He looked away and they sat, neither speaking for a few moments. Molly broke the silence again and said, "I don't think you've lost your humanity. You risked your life to save that little girl today."

Another brief moment of silence followed. Stone looked into Molly's eyes again and said, "Thank you for that. I hope you're right, and I can start my life over."

Another uncomfortable gap in the conversation followed. Molly broke the silence and said, "Stone, I can't—"

"I know," he said. "I want the chance to rekindle our friendship. If more's to come, it'll come in time."

"I can do that," Molly said, giving him a warm smile.

Stone and Molly resumed their walk. Stone felt as though a boulder had lifted from his shoulders. Telling Molly the truth had been difficult, but cathartic. He felt relieved they had breached the invisible wall between them too. Maybe one day they could be more than friends—because—he realized she was his one true love.

Chapter 16

STONE ATE BREAKFAST AT THE Silver Nugget Café, enjoying a pleasant but brief chat with Molly. Ready to begin a new chapter of his life, he drove to the marshal's office. He pulled in beside a newer model white Ford F-150 parked in front of the office. As he exited his Tahoe, he noticed two other vehicles parked alongside the building. One was the newer model Chevrolet Suburban he'd seen the previous marshal driving, and the other was an older model Chevrolet Tahoe. Both vehicles, painted black and white and adorned with numerous antennae jutting from their roofs, displayed large six-point gold star logos surrounded by the name Silver Lake Marshal's Office on their doors.

As he approached, the door swung open and a beaming Will Stemple greeted him.

"Welcome back, Hunter. Come in. Come in."

"Hi, Will." Stone smiled, shaking the proffered hand. "It's good to be back."

"Wonderful. Are you ready to get started?" Will asked.

"Ready, willing, and eager. What's first on the agenda?"

"Swearing you in," Will said. "You'll need to go to the Pitkin County Sheriff's Department so the sheriff, Roger Davis, can swear you in too. We have the same reciprocal agreement with them we had back when you were the deputy marshal. They'll assist by patrolling town as needed, and we assist if a deputy calls for assistance near town or they need help with search and rescue."

Stone remembered the agreement. He knew the Sheriff's Department had jurisdiction throughout the county, including within the Silver Lake town limits. His jurisdiction as the town marshal stopped at the town limits. As a sworn deputy sheriff, his jurisdiction would expand to include the entire county.

Will swore Stone in and presented him with the marshal's badges. Will explained the upgraded and expanded radio system. "Silver Lake has one channel, four, for our exclusive use. Your call sign is Silver Lake One. Your deputy marshal, Harry Field—you'll meet him tomorrow—is Silver Lake Two. The sheriff's department uses the first three channels. Channel Five is the clear channel for car-to-car communication between Silver Lake and the Sheriff's Department. All communication goes through their dispatch center."

Will motioned for Stone to come to one of the two windows located on both sides of the front door. He pointed toward the two-story, three-bay volunteer rescue and fire department building across the street and said, "The town fathers have an office on the upper floor. Monday through Friday their secretary, Emily Pritchett, occupies it. Be careful what you do and say within her sphere. She's the eyes and ears for the town fathers and reports *everything* she sees and hears to them."

This was the second time Will had spoken of the mysterious town fathers. "Ever since you mentioned that guy Hendrickson, it's been on my mind. I get the town fathers are important, but who and what are they?"

A surprised look on his face, Will said, "I'm sorry, Hunter. I guess I got ahead of myself. You couldn't know, because you left prior to the change."

"Change?" Stone asked.

"Twelve or so years ago, the town voted to change the form of government from a town manager and council system to a mayoral system of management headed by the town fathers," Will said.

"So, *they* run the town?" Stone asked.

"No. It's my job to manage it," Will said. "The town fathers assumed the role of the council."

"Can you fill me in on them?" Stone asked. If he intended to make a life in Silver Lake, it was important he avoid potential issues should he have contact with any of them.

"I should've done that first thing," Will said. He seemed to think a moment, organizing his thoughts. "The town fathers are a group of three wealthy businessmen who own many of the buildings and land in town. Douglas Langford and William Hendrickson are joint owners of an exclusive and expensive resort, the Lake Lorraine Lodge. It's located off Highway 82, on the other side of Independence Pass in Lake County. It's about nineteen miles or so east of the Route 138 cutoff.

"I remember seeing the sign," Stone said.

Will nodded and continued. "They're involved in numerous other business ventures, and each serve on the boards of several multi-national corporations. With all the traveling they do, it's rare to see them.

"The third city father, and the liaison with whom I have most of my contact, is Leo Feldman," Will explained. "He owns three of the motels in town including the Lakeview, some other buildings, and a string of successful restaurants located nationwide, the Tuscany Renaissance."

"I've eaten at one of them," Stone said, surprised. "Great food."

Will paused, lowered his voice, and continued. "The most contentious and difficult one to deal with is Hendrickson," Will said. "I told you he was the no vote on your hiring."

"I assume you're telling me to avoid him?" Stone said.

"As long as the tourist dollars keep pouring in, and they don't receive any complaints, I doubt you'll ever see or hear from them. They pass things on to me to handle," Will said.

"That's fine with me," Stone said. If he could avoid dealing with them, he could avoid the politics.

"It might be a good idea to at least familiarize yourself with their faces. I'm sure I can find something in my office with their photos."

They got back to work, and Will provided Stone the marshal's office and vehicle keys and the computer password. As Will filled out the necessary paperwork, Stone rummaged through the storage closet in the back room and found some serviceable uniform shirts. He had his bulletproof vest, leather police belt, his Heckler and Koch, Mark 23, forty-five caliber ACP semi-automatic pistol, and his holster. He would need to buy a black western style hat, black jeans, and boots to complete the uniform. After Will finished with him, he would do some shopping at the local western-wear stores.

As Stone returned to the front office, Will finished the paperwork. "So, any advice for the new guy?" Stone asked.

Will seemed to ponder the question, then said, "The town and job haven't changed a great deal since you were the deputy." He paused, thinking, and added, "The best advice I can give is to keep your wits sharp, your heart open, and your powder dry."

No mistaking the meaning of Will's metaphorical advice, Stone thought. Stay on your toes and learn who your friends are. Be fair with people, but don't lose sight of the town's needs and—prepare for anything.

"I need to confess something to you, so there're no secrets or surprises," Stone said. He explained the confrontation with his old inspector, the subsequent suspension, and his premature retirement upon returning to New York—prior to Will's offer of the marshal's job.

Will smiled and said, "Politics. You can't get away from it." He chuckled and added, "If I'd known your employment status, I might have offered you a lower salary to start."

Stone laughed. "Why do you think I waited to tell you?"

It was Will's turn to laugh. "It doesn't change anything, but I appreciate your honesty." Changing the subject, Will said, "I have what I hope will be a pleasant surprise."

"Oh." Stone wasn't fond of surprises. He hoped he hid his displeasure. "What's that?"

"I'd rather show you, if you'll bear with me. We'll need to take a short drive."

Chapter 17

MONDAY MORNING, STONE ARRIVED AT the marshal's office, dressed in the requisite police uniform. Both Will and Stone's deputy, Harry Field, would arrive in an hour or so.

He unlocked the door and carried in a small handmade rustic wooden table, a fourteen-cup coffeemaker, and all the trappings to make and doctor coffee. He assembled the items into a coffee station under the window closest to his desk, loaded fresh grounds, and filled the pot with water from the bathroom sink.

As the coffee brewed, Stone sat at his desk. The swivel chair squealed in protest at his movement. He grimaced at the irony, promising himself to fix it or replace it.

An old habit, he filled his coffee mug as water continued to drip into the grounds funnel. As he sipped the fresh-brewed coffee, he thought back on Will's surprise.

Will had driven him to a semi-isolated log cabin near the edge of town. Confused, he'd questioned Will. Will had scolded him and said that as the new marshal, it was "un-marshal like" to live in a motel—like a tourist.

The cottage was a furnished, new listing. Stone liked everything about it, including the home's warmth. The price was right, and the owners wanted a quick closing. Will had called a friend at the Wells Fargo Bank in Aspen who handled mortgage loans. Stone had told him he had to swing by the bank in Aspen to get some checks and deposit his sick-leave check, so Will had arranged to have the mortgage application packet ready to go.

By the time Will arrived at eight o'clock, Stone was on his third mug of coffee. Will nodded toward the table and coffeepot and said, "I see you're making yourself right at home. Smells good."

"It's Caribou Coffee, my favorite. Help yourself."

As Will poured himself a cup, Stone said, "So, fill me in on Harry?"

Will carried one of the chairs from the deputies table over near the desk. He took a sip of coffee. "Excellent." He sat, seemed to think for a moment, and said, "Let's see ... Harry. Harry's worked as Silver Lake's summer deputy for the past four years. He lives in Wescott, and he works over in Lake County as a reserve deputy too."

"I can't wait to meet him," Stone said.

"I think you'll like him. He knows the town, and the locals like and respect him."

As they awaited Harry, Stone drained his mug and stood to refill it. His chair squealed again. He shot a nasty glance at the chair as he grasped the coffee pot.

The sound of a vehicle pulling onto the gravel lot drew his attention to the window. A rust-colored and dented pick-up truck parked by Will's truck. A tall, thin man wearing a uniform that matched Stone's slid out of the driver's seat.

"I assume that's Harry," Will said from his seat.

The door swung open, and Harry shuffled into the office. He looked from Will to Stone, removed his black cowboy hat, and approached Stone extending his hand. "Howdy."

Stone shook the proffered hand. As they shook, Will made the introductions. "I'm going to leave you two to get acquainted. You have a ten o'clock appointment with Sheriff Davis. Harry knows the way, so he can guide you," Will said, standing and moving to the door.

They said their goodbyes and Will left. Harry flopped in the vacated deputies' table chair and said, "We'll need to saddle up soon to get to the sheriff's department on time."

Stone noticed Harry was tall and lanky. His face had a chiseled look, with a square chin and warm hazel eyes. His facial features combined with a disheveled mop of medium-length brown hair gave him the appearance of a beardless Abraham Lincoln.

"Okay. You want some coffee before we go?"

"Yup, sure would," Harry said, helping himself. "Thanks," he said, sipping the coffee.

Harry finished his coffee, and they headed for the Pitkin County Sheriff's Department with Harry driving the Silver Lake Police Suburban. As they headed toward Aspen, they chatted. Stone liked his deputy. He deduced that Harry might come across as a laid-back good old boy, but—in fact—was razor sharp with a quick wit.

Stone learned that in addition to his police work, Harry and his wife owned a supply store. "Got to have another career," Harry quipped. "When it comes to police pay, they're tighter'n the bark on a tree."

That made Stone laugh.

Stone stopped laughing as they crested a hill on Highway 82 and came face to face with a car heading straight for them. Harry swerved to the shoulder and slammed on the brakes as the approaching car swerved back across the double yellow line, just missing the front end of the tractor-trailer it had passed.

"Son of a bitch," Stone said, turning and looking through the rear window at the car receding into the distance. "Go get that asshole."

Harry whipped a U-turn in the Suburban that would've made a racecar driver proud. He turned on the emergency equipment and floored the SUV in an attempt to catch the car. As he passed the truck, which had pulled over as far as possible to give them room, they could see the car speeding over the crest of another hill. Harry pushed the Suburban to over one hundred and closed the gap. They pulled the car over a couple of miles east of the Silver Lake turnoff.

As they exited the Suburban, Harry looked at Stone over the hood and whispered, "I know that car. It's Mister Hendrickson's."

It was a dark blue Bentley Continental with designer Colorado license plates. Harry and Stone switched sides in front of the Suburban. As Stone approached the car, the driver's door flew open, and a man exploded from the car with an angry look on his unpleasant face.

"What the hell do you think you're doing?" the man shouted, pulling himself to his full six feet and sticking his chest out over his stomach paunch.

He's puffed up like an adder ready to strike, Stone thought. The man had a balding pate and brown eyes that radiated hatred. Based on the make of car and the expensive-looking suit he wore, Stone was certain this would be his first contact with the worst of the town fathers. *So much for avoiding political conflict,* he thought.

Stone approached and said, "Good morning, sir. We stopped you for passing in a no-passing zone and careless driving. May I please see your license, registration, and proof of insurance?" He wanted to keep this as civil as possible.

"You may not," Hendrickson spat. "You have no jurisdiction outside of Silver Lake, Marshal."

As Hendrickson turned to return to his car, Stone placed his hand on Hendrickson's upper arm, stopping him. Hendrickson pulled his arm free and shouted, "Who do you think you are!"

"I'm sorry, sir. You aren't free to go," Stone said with a calm in his voice that was unfelt. "And you're correct, sir. I don't have jurisdiction outside of Silver Lake—but he does," Stone said, pointing at Harry.

Harry swallowed hard, his Adam's apple bobbing like a fishing bobber with a fish on the hook.

The tractor-trailer they had passed in pursuit of Hendrickson rumbled past them. The driver gave two quick blasts of his air horn and waved.

"Sir, I'll ask you again. May I please see your license, registration, and proof of insurance? If you refuse again, you'll force me to instruct my deputy to place you under arrest." Stone stared at Hendrickson with a neutral look, but they both knew Stone had challenged him to a test of resolve.

"Fine," Hendrickson said, pulling out his wallet and removing his license and registration and shoving them at Stone. "My proof of insurance is in my glove box. Do you object to me getting it?"

"Go right ahead, sir," Stone said. As Hendrickson rummaged through his glove box, Stone thought over the ramifications of his run-in with the man. He might be able to mitigate the firestorm if he let Hendrickson go. But what kind of message would he send Harry as to the manner of man he was? The law applied to everyone, and no matter what Hendrickson said or did, as long as Stone was marshal, he intended to apply the law—the same way—for everyone.

Back in the Suburban, license, registration, and proof of insurance in hand, Harry asked, "What do you want me to do?"

Stone looked through the back window of Hendrickson's car. He could see Hendrickson engaged in an animated conversation with someone on his cell phone. Stone sighed and said, "Stopping someone for traffic code violations is usually sufficient if they understand and admit what they did was wrong, and they learn a lesson. Does it appear to you Mister Hendrickson thinks he did anything wrong or has learned any lesson?"

"Uh, no. He isn't that kind of person," Harry said.

"Sounds like you have your answer. Write him for both violations."

Chapter 18

SHERIFF ROGER DAVIS WAS A gracious, soft spoken, and likeable man in his mid-fifties. He was on the short side, a little thick in the middle, and had a head full of short brown hair, tending toward gray. His kind sienna eyes, whimsical smile, and snub nose gave him a friendly look. The swearing in completed, giving Stone police powers in Pitkin County, the sheriff gave them a tour of his department. It surprised Stone that in a county rivaling the size of Rhode Island, the sheriff's department only had a staff of thirty-eight patrol personnel and two detectives. Compared to New York, it was miniscule, with fewer people than he'd supervised in the NYPD Crime Lab. Then again, he was the marshal of Silver Lake, which encompassed a whopping one-point-two square miles and had a staff of two—himself included.

Funding for services was an issue in all the sparsely-populated counties of Colorado. Even though Pitkin County was large, forest dominated the landscape under the jurisdiction of the Bureau of Land Management or the National Forest and State Park Services. Regardless of its size, Stone saw that the sheriff's department had some nice toys. Lots of specialized S.W.A.T. equipment and even an armored response vehicle, no doubt funded through Homeland Security dollars the Fed had thrown at police departments all over the country.

What it lacked was forensic equipment and personnel. Sheriff

Davis explained that most of the rural counties and small towns relied on the Colorado Bureau of Investigation for their forensic needs. CBI was a full-service state-run lab in Denver, staffed with crime scene investigators and all the requisite specialty sections and equipment for handling DNA, latent prints, chemistry, ballistics, questioned documents, and trace and digital evidence. It had satellite offices in several other large Colorado cities.

The tour complete, the sheriff took Stone and Harry to lunch at a local Aspen restaurant. Stone enjoyed both the food and the company. At lunch, Sheriff Davis told Stone and Harry of a phone call he'd received. "I got a call from a pissed off motorist," he said.

"I can't say I'm surprised. What was Hendrickson's complaint?" Stone asked.

"He didn't like you stopping him. Seems to think laws shouldn't apply to him like they do other people. Tried to throw his weight around by intimating that he could shift his support and money to someone else in the coming election if I didn't get behind him on this."

"What'd you tell him? Stone asked.

"I recited the Colorado Revised Statute 18-8-306. It says that attempting to influence a public servant is a Class 4 felony."

"How did he take that? Stone asked, unable to hide the grin on his face.

"He hung up on me."

Stone and Harry laughed as Sheriff Davis' feigned emotional pain at Hendrickson's actions.

"What'd you write him for?" Davis asked.

"Careless and passing in a no-passing zone. He passed a tractor-trailer on a hill and damn near hit us head on. If Harry hadn't reacted as quick as he did, instead of enjoying lunch, you'd be out on 82, scraping us off the pavement."

"Sounds like he got what he deserved," Davis said.

"Yeah, but I'm sure I'll hear from Will when we get back to Silver Lake. For reasons I don't understand, Hendrickson has a distinct dislike for me. The mayor said I arrested him for DUI over twenty years ago, but that's a long time to carry a grudge."

"If Will has any questions as to the legality of the stop, have him call me," Davis said.

Lunch over, Stone and Harry swung by the Wells Fargo Bank, then began their trek back to Silver Lake, continuing to become acquainted. They patrolled town, and Harry pointed out the hot spots and explained the various issues Stone could expect to encounter. Will had been right. Harry seemed to have his finger on the pulse of the town.

Close to four, Stone asked Harry to follow him to the Lakeview Motel, so he could drop his personal SUV. Back at the marshal's office, they planned a work schedule. A full day behind them, Stone sent him home for the day.

Alone in the office, Stone called Will. As the phone rang, he sighed and braced for what he suspected might come.

"Stemple Realty. Will Stemple speaking."

"It's Stone, Will. Did you happen to hear what transpired out on Highway 82 today?"

"Hear about it," Will said. "My phone hasn't stopped ringing all afternoon. Did you have to give him a ticket?"

Stone explained the events that had taken place and told Will he could call Sheriff Davis if he needed information on the legalities. "Believe me, Will, the last thing I wanted was to run into any of the town fathers this way," Stone said.

"Let me tell you, if Mister Hendrickson didn't like you prior to this, his feelings have escalated from dislike to absolute loathing.

He ordered me to fire you, but it takes a majority vote of the town fathers and me to make that happen. The rest of us wouldn't entertain the thought. So, he ordered me to fire Harry because he wrote the tickets. I reminded him that the city charter gives the power to hire and fire deputy marshals to the marshal."

"I'm guessing none of that sat too well with him," Stone said, a sour knot forming in his stomach.

"It didn't, but there's nothing he can do—which doesn't mean he won't look for reasons to cause you trouble."

Great. I've gone from McFarland looking for a reason to fire me to Hendrickson carrying a vendetta, Stone thought. "Fantastic. Where do we go from here?"

"Nowhere. It's done," Will said. "The odds on you even seeing Mister Hendrickson again are slim, and he's too busy to spend time focused on you or what you do. The town fathers focus is on profit and people enjoying themselves. Make that happen, and you won't hear a disparaging word from any of them."

"I'll do that," Stone said. "I'd like to stay."

"Don't worry," Will said. "I've got your back, and the other two town fathers know what Mister Hendrickson's like. They don't put any credence into his rantings. Do your job and this incident will fade into the past."

Stone ended the call feeling a little better. He wondered if he could've handled it any differently than he had. He decided Hendrickson had determined the course of events, and Stone refused to spend any more time hand wringing over it. *I'd handle it the same way if it happened again,* He thought. He decided to focus his thoughts on his new life in Silver Lake.

He drove to the Silver Nugget Café for dinner—and a chance to see Molly again. Molly invited him to drop back by after closing for coffee, pie, and conversation.

As he paid his bill, Molly told him everyone had heard of the incident with Hendrickson. "It's time someone put him in his place," she said, laughing.

Jesus, Stone thought. It was the small-town gossip network again. News leaked like a sieve and spread like wildfire.

Stone drove back to the office to begin filling out the myriad papers required to obtain a mortgage and await his rendezvous. As he settled into the desk's wooden swivel chair, it squeaked in protest again. *You're history,* he thought.

Past nine, the last residue of light having slipped behind the western peaks, Stone locked the office. As he walked to the police Suburban, he noticed the sky and land had melded into an onyx void, bespeckled with twinkling points of light above. As he stared, a shooting star cut across the sky, its tail fading as it sped beyond the horizon. A line from an old John Denver song, "I've seen it raining fire in the sky," popped into his head and he hummed a few bars.

He climbed into the Suburban and started the engine. A smile on his face, he resumed humming the familiar song. For the first time in a long time, he was happy and beginning to feel at peace, the vice-like grip on his soul loosening another notch.

PART II

HIDE AND SEEK

CHAPTER 19

BILLY RAY HATCHER SAT ON the bunk in his overcrowded and dingy cell at the cesspool known as the correctional facility at Riker's Island. He despised the place. Forced to associate with all manner of sub-specie races, it went against his belief system and disgusted him.

Not that he was a bigot. He saw himself as a patriot who believed in a white America—free of anyone whose pigmentation, language, or religion differed. He hated Mexicans most of all. They contaminated the country, breeding like cockroaches, stealing American jobs, and ripping off the system.

Incarcerated for over three months—and no trial. He wondered what in the hell had happened to that pissant attorney of his. It was close to a month with no word from him. It had been a stupid bar fight. The punk had drunk himself into a stupor and bumped Billy Ray's arm as he took the winning shot. It cost him a hundred bucks and the pissant had refused to apologize—or pay back the money.

Billy Ray believed the best justice was instant justice, which he'd administered with the thick end of his pool stick to the side of the pissant's head. Word was he fractured the guy's skull.

To keep occupied and avoid the pissants in the jail, he worked out in the exercise yard and his cell every chance he got. A solid one hundred and seventy-five pounds of muscle on a six-foot frame, he wanted to be in the best shape of his life when he took Stone out.

No mistakes. Nothing left to chance. Stone was an old man who spent his time sitting on his ass at the police station. Billy Ray was young, in his mid-twenties, schooled in fighting and in great shape. One on one, Stone had no chance.

***

In line at the prison cafeteria for the mid-day meal, some whiny little fence fairy slowed the line because he felt the urge to bitch. Something to do with the shitty food.

He's right, Billy Ray thought. *But whining ain't gonna change nothin'.*

"Shut yer pie hole and move, roach," Hatcher ordered, pushing the little man in the back.

The Mexican spun to face him and said, "Hey, stick it in your ass, *pendejo*."

No one talked to him like that, including a low-life taco jockey. If the pissant had done as told, he would've had no trouble. Billy Ray did a quick scan of the cafeteria: two guards on duty and both of them busy with the start of a fight at a table across the room.

"I'm gonna stick it in *yer* ass, you fuckin' greaser," Billy Ray snarled, moving closer. He swung the corner of his industrial plastic food tray into the Mexican's temple. The edge of the tray made contact with an audible thunk, and the con crumpled to the floor like a building had fallen on him. Billy Ray stepped over the unconscious man as the line moved.

***

Back in his cell, Billy Ray heard the announcement over the public-address system as he sat on his bunk. "Prisoner 14-R-3260 Hatcher, you have a visitor. Report to the Pod C Control Room."

Clad in his orange jumpsuit, rubber flip-flops, and a pair of handcuffs, Billy Ray sat on one of the visitor section's window stools. He hated the visitor section. It looked and smelled like the toilet the whole place was.

Hard metal stools bolted to the floor, like soldiers at attention, in arrow-straight rows. Prisoners sitting side by side on one side of thick Plexiglas windows; visitors subjected to the same seating arrangements on the other. Being this close to some of the other prisoners made his skin crawl.

The telephone receivers mounted by the windows provided the sole means of communication. Shoulder to shoulder with the person on the adjacent stool, private conversation was impossible.

Billy Ray watched stone-faced as his attorney swaggered into the visitor's section, glad-handing the guards as if they were old pals. He schmoozed his way to the window. At six-foot-four, with a slim build accentuated by a custom-made suit, handsome face, and styled sandy hair, he looked like a politician, as opposed to a criminal defense attorney.

Billy Ray had chosen his attorney by picking the most professional-looking business card tacked to the bulletin board in the booking area of the jail. His lawyer had demanded a substantial upfront payment with no refunds, Billy Ray later learned.

So much for fancy business cards.

At their second meeting, Billy Ray began to develop a dislike for his attorney. The pissant was rude and tried to tell him what to say and do. No one got away with that.

However, as long as he was in jail, he had no other choice but to use him. He couldn't afford another lawyer. As their relationship deteriorated, Billy Ray came to believe this prima-donna-in-a-suit was more interested in controlling his clients than defending them.

His attorney sported a large gold ring on the pinky of his right hand with the initials JJ, for Jack Jordan, set in diamonds. He should've guessed right off that anyone who needed to wear his initials was an asshole. He wanted to cut that finger off and ram it down Jordan's throat, ring and all.

Although to all outward appearances Billy Ray seemed calm, inside he roiled with anger. He sat rigid, his angry eyes tracking Jordan as he approached the window and sat on the stool across from him.

Jordan avoided eye contact as he placed a folder in his lap, shot his cuffs, and disinfected the telephone with an alcohol wipe. He brought the receiver to his mouth and raised his eyes.

"How're you doing, Billy?" Jordan asked into the receiver, flashing a disingenuous grin.

Billy Ray glared at Jordan with the same warmth he would a bug stuck on a pin but remained mute. As he continued to stare, Jordan's smile faded and morphed into a look of annoyance.

"The name's Billy *Ray*," he spat. "And how you think I'm doin'? Over three months in this shithole 'cause of you. Where you been?"

"Look, because I haven't been to see you doesn't mean I'm ignoring your case," Jordan said. "And the reason you're in jail is because you had no permanent local address and the judge considered you a flight risk."

Not waiting for another outburst, Jordan placed the telephone on the window shelf and shifted his gaze to the folder in his lap. He removed a sheet of paper, held it with both hands, and snapped it taut. He slapped it against the glass, so Billy Ray could read it.

Billy Ray leaned in to try to decipher the document. The truth was he could barely read, and the paper made no sense to him. "What the fuck is this?" he asked, jutting his chin in its direction.

Jordan couldn't hear him. However, the confused look told him what Billy Ray wanted to know. He retrieved the telephone handset and said, "This is a motion for another continuance."

Billy Ray went red in the face as Jordan placed the paper back into the folder. He opened his mouth to argue, and Jordan held out a hand stopping him. "Let me go over this again. You assaulted a man."

Billy Ray started to argue again. Jordan cut him off. "I know you felt justified in your actions. The police and district attorney disagree. Because you used a pool stick and the victim may have a permanent brain impairment, the DA charged you with the class B felony of first-degree assault."

"What's that mean?" Billy Ray asked.

"It means that if we go to trial and you lose, the judge can set any minimum sentence he wants, with a maximum of twenty-five years. And trust me, this judge isn't your friend."

"I can't do no quarter," Billy Ray said, at last realizing the seriousness of his predicament.

"And I'm working to make sure that doesn't happen," Jordan said. "The DA's lost the two witnesses to the assault, the guy playing pool with you and another guy watching from the bar. They both seem to have disappeared. No witnesses, no testimony."

Billy Ray smiled and asked, "So, what'm I doin' in here?"

"I delayed the trial in the hope the witnesses might decide to move on. Now that it's happened, all the DA has is the victim. He's been unable to give a statement, because he can't remember what happened to him."

"Then get me out," Billy Ray said.

"Soon," Jordan said. "The DA's office has an overload of cases. By asking for another continuance, I'm forcing the DA's hand. With no witnesses and a victim who can't remember the assault, I'm hoping to work a deal in which you plead guilty to misdemeanor assault and the DA agrees to ask for no more than time served."

"Okay," Billy Ray said, grinning. "I can wait 'til you make that deal."

Chapter 20

TWO WEEKS LATER, BILLY RAY stood in front of a judge with his attorney. As promised, the DA accepted the time served as sufficient punishment. The judge verified that the prosecution and defense agreed to the deal made and determined that Billy Ray understood the ramifications of pleading guilty to misdemeanor assault. Satisfied, the judge accepted the plea and released Billy Ray.

The Department of Corrections transported him back to Riker's Island to process out of the jail. He was ready to get out of this place and get on with his plans. If he stayed any longer, he would kill someone.

An officer returned his personal effects, secured in a giant plastic bag. He checked to make sure no one had taken any of his money, signed for his possessions, and shed the jumpsuit, changing into his street clothes. After what seemed an interminable length of time, they released him. A guard directed him onto a white DOC bus. Packed with other released prisoners, they waited for a final ride from the jail to a parking lot on Hazen Street in Queens, near the Riker's Island Bridge.

As they rumbled over the bridge's expanse from the detention center toward Bowery Bay, the smell of warm, moist air infused with the faint stench of polluted saltwater invaded the bus. Billy Ray tried his best to avoid inhaling the malodorous stench. The hypnotic thrumming of the tires passing over the bridge's expansion joints lulled Billy Ray into a relaxed state, which brought back fond memories of his kills.

The motion of the bus exiting the bridge and turning into a parking lot jostled him back from his reverie. The driver pulled a handle opening the bus door and said, "This is your stop, gentlemen. Off." Just like that, the system unceremoniously spit him out like a used piece of gum.

He walked a short distance, spotting a hole in the wall that served all things Italian. His clothes were loose from weight loss, because the prison food was close to inedible. The rich aromas of pizza, sauces, and Italian cold cuts made his mouth water. He took a seat in a booth and ordered an antipasto, a pasta dish laden with primavera sauce and a tall, cold beer. He smothered the pasta with parmesan cheese.

Woofing his food like a starving man, he sat back stuffed, and let loose a loud belch. He ignored the looks he got from other patrons and the waiter. He ordered a second beer, drained the bottle in one swig, and—to add emphasis to how little he cared what others thought—belched again as loud as he could.

It felt good to be free—free to eat what he wanted, go where he wanted, and do what he wanted to do. Best of all—he was free to pursue Stone again.

He paid the bill and walked to a bus stop close by. Enduring a labyrinth of transfers, he reached the Bronx, where his car waited in a long-term self-storage lot. The only real help his attorney had provided was to have his car towed to the lot. Even that was a fight. He had to pay for the tow and six months of storage fees before the pissant would do it.

Billy Ray located his dirt-covered, older model gray Ford Taurus. He noticed it had a low tire. It also held his special backpack in the spare tire well. He shoved the key into the ignition and cranked the engine. The car complained, coughed, and caught. The gas gauge needle indicated a near-empty tank. He limped the car to the nearest gas station to take care of its needs.

It was time for Billy Ray to disappear. In the same bar where he'd smashed the pissant in the head, he'd met a guy who said he could get you damn near anything you wanted. At least that was how he put it. As fate would have it, the guy was at the bar having a beer when Billy Ray walked in. The pissant with the dented skull was absent.

In a few hours, Billy Ray was the proud owner of a phony Social Security card, a genuine fake New York State driver's license, a New York license plate with stickers, a matching vehicle registration with a phony name and address, and a vehicle safety sticker for his windshield. He negotiated the price from fifteen hundred to twelve hundred and fifty bucks.

Lucky for him, money wasn't an issue. Between his savings: what he'd been able to scrounge prior to setting out on his quest, several armed robberies on his way to New York from Texas (one providing a big payday), and relieving his dead victims of whatever cash they had, he had a sizeable nut.

Between attorney fees, car storage, stuffing his face, and gassing his car, he was low on pocket cash. He'd retrieved a wad of money hidden behind the lining of his suitcase in the trunk of his car. Good thing he had the cash. The phony ID cost more than expected.

Finished with his business, he switched plates and added the safety sticker to the windshield. He drove to East Brooklyn, found another parking garage, and rented a space for his car. With its bogus plates and stickers and all the crime in the area, it was smarter to keep it off the streets and away from prying eyes. It was a short hike to the Brownsville neighborhood of Brooklyn where he'd found a place to stay. He pulled his suitcase from the trunk and his knife from his hidden backpack.

It could be a dangerous walk because of gangs and rampant crime.

A plethora of sleazy joints dotted this part of town. A person could disappear in a place like this. Even better, it was close to his chosen hunting ground. It was the perfect location.

Billy Ray glanced down the street at the collection of riffraff. Homeless people, dressed in baggy clothes with oversized shoes flopping on their feet, pushed shopping carts full of all manner of crap. Bums tucked into every crevice afforded by the rundown buildings begged the few passersby for spare change. Drug dealers sold their illicit wares right in the open.

That meant the cops avoided this part of town.

He walked into the seedy hotel he'd selected. The acrid odor of body sweat mixed with urine assaulted his nose as he entered the foyer. Light filtered in through grimy windows and seemed to hang in the stale air along with smoke and suspended dust particles. A fly, its buzzing the lone sound in the lobby, beat against a window trying to escape—or maybe commit suicide.

An unkempt man, sitting on a threadbare couch with a cigarette dangling from his lip, peered at him over a pornographic magazine that displayed a full-page photograph of a spread-legged, nude woman on the cover. Billy Ray turned toward the empty registration counter and rang the tap bell.

"I'm comin'," porno man said, dropping the magazine on the couch and shuffling to the counter. The long ash on his cigarette fell to the grotesque carpet. "Forty a night, cash—in advance."

The man looked like an unkempt weasel. Billy Ray glowered at him. "I want clean sheets, no cockroaches, and my own bathroom."

"We ain't got no cockroaches," porno man said, acting insulted. "You want a suite, huh? That's fifty a night—and the sheets'll cost you another ten."

Billy Ray fished the fresh wad of money out of his pocket and counted out three hundred dollars in used twenties and tens.

"Six nights *and* clean sheets. I might stay longer."

The man swept the money off the counter without arguing and stuffed it in his pocket. He turned to a board with keys attached to plastic fobs and grabbed one from its hook. As he dropped the key on the counter, he said, "Want to fill out the registration book, Mister—"

"Smith." Billy Ray ignored the invitation and grabbed the key. The faded room number—348—imprinted on the fob, was close to unreadable.

"Up the stairs to the third floor, turn right. Elevators busted," the counter man added with a black-tooth grin, "Cause we ain't got none." He chuckled at his own joke.

Billy Ray glared at the clerk until he quit laughing and turned away. As he climbed the creaking stairs, he noticed mismatched paint crisscrossed on the stairwell and hallway walls obscuring graffiti—or at least trying. He walked to his room on a dirty threadbare carpet. He unlocked the room door, pushed it open, and scanned the interior from the threshold.

Not bad for a fleabag hotel. A cleanish bed, overstuffed chair, and a dresser with a television on it. A set of rabbit ears perched like a treasured antique on top of the television. The ceiling light lit upon flipping the switch, revealing the shadows of long-dead insects inside the cracked glass shade. The bathroom was halfway clean, and two towels hung from a towel bar by a cracked full-length mirror mounted to the wall. As promised, no cockroaches. He hoped no bedbugs either.

He slid the shabby window curtain open and looked out. A fire escape provided a means of egress and ingress. His view was the side of a brick and broken cement building across the alley.

Billy Ray slid his suitcase under the bed and hung his jacket on a bent wire hanger in the clothing cubbyhole. He burned his Billy Ray Hatcher identification in a metal trashcan he found in the bathroom and flushed the ashes.

Satisfied, his focus shifted to the next order of business.

It was time to let Stone know he was back.

Chapter 21

BILLY RAY SPENT A COUPLE of days scouting part of the area's urban decay to find the perfect location to announce his return. Discarded syringes and used condoms scattered in various rooms of an abandoned building with access off an alley were a sure sign prostitutes used the place for sex and drugs. He found places to hide to wait for a hooker and a john. He would use them to leave a message for Stone, announcing his return.

***

Near dark, he exited his window and descended the fire escape to the alley. He had no particular reason for hiding his movements, yet he saw no reason to let the hotel clerk or anyone else see him coming or going.

As he approached the end of the alley, a vagrant sitting on a flattened cardboard box in the shadows pleaded, "Got any spare change, Mister?"

"Get a fuckin' job," Billy Ray snapped at the beggar.

"Bite me," the bum spat back.

Billy Ray kicked the tramp in the head. The homeless man fell onto his side, moaning. Billy Ray followed with several body kicks. "Get out'a here. I won't be so nice, I see you again."

He retrieved his car and parked it a few blocks away from the abandoned building he'd chosen. His backpack cinched over his shoulders, he walked into the alley adjacent to the building. Night had cloaked the dilapidated structure in obscurity by the time he entered the door off the alley. He found a room deep inside to change.

Safe in his hide, he opened the backpack and removed his stygian hunting attire—the same clothing he'd worn for each of his attacks. He changed into the raven-colored hooded jumpsuit and added his ski mask and black gloves. His obsidian eyes were all that remained exposed.

He had his favorite weapon out—purchased long ago from a military surplus store, it was a non-glare, old military-style knife that molded to his hand. Ready, he moved from the deep recesses of the building to a room closer to the entrance off the alley. He settled in to wait.

Alone in the darkness, Billy Ray allowed the intoxicating thrill of the hunt to wash over him. In all his years as a hunter, he'd come to enjoy the hunt as much as the kill. What he hunted was unimportant to him. Billy Ray saw himself as a predator. However, unlike the wild animals that hunted for food, he pursued his prey for other purposes. The comparison made him smile under his mask.

Billy Ray willed himself to relax. He knew part of hunting included patience and the ability to remain motionless until the time came to strike. He closed his eyes and allowed part of his mind to drift.

His thoughts wandered at first but soon crystalized. The face of the man he'd loved and idolized, who meant everything to him materialized in his mind's eye—the man Billy Ray had come to New York to avenge, his older half-brother, Arnet Gantz.

Billy Ray's father was a long-haul trucker. He was on the road most of the time, which was good because when he was home he brutalized Billy Ray and his drug-addicted mother. At the age of five, Billy Ray's father left on a trip and never returned. His mother, hooked on heroin, died a year later from an overdose. If not for Arnet, his father's son from a previous marriage, he would've bounced from one foster home to another. Arnet had taken on the job of raising him.

Arnet had taught him everything, from hunting wild hogs in the Texas underbrush to mentoring him in the ways of the White Brotherhood of Texas, a self-proclaimed violent group of extreme racists reputed to be responsible for many minority deaths. The brotherhood, and as such Arnet, who was one of the five generals in the wheel, or steering committee of the organization, taught him to hate all non-Christians, gays, and non-whites. Billy Ray had further emulated Arnet by developing a particular loathing for Hispanics, illegals in particular.

Arnet had brought Billy Ray into the fold. On Billy Ray's thirteenth birthday, Arnet sponsored him for provisional membership as a prospect. By his sixteenth birthday, Billy Ray was ready to earn his bones and become a full member.

He remembered the night a senior lieutenant of the White Brotherhood guided him to an area where illegals camped to witness his initiation. He couldn't tell if he was more excited or nervous. A proficient shot, this would be his first human kill.

They had spotted the fire in the distance and made their way to a stand of trees close to forty yards away. His targets, suspected illegals, were a Hispanic man and woman following the cotton-picking season, working their way north. As he positioned himself and readied his rifle, the lieutenant had instructed him to shoot the man first, because the woman would be slower to react to the shot—advice he would follow from that day on. The rifle steadied, he'd peered through the scope, and sighted in on the man's back.

He remembered the feel of the rifle bucking in his hands as he squeezed the trigger. The shot was true, and the man's back arched as the projectile struck. As the man slumped to the ground Billy Ray had shifted the sight to the woman, who was on her feet screaming, and shot her in the chest.

Pulled from his reverie as the door off the alley creaked open, Billy Ray focused on the sounds. Distant voices announced a man and a woman had entered the abandoned building.

In the near total darkness, Billy Ray made his way toward the voices, careful to avoid kicking or stepping on any debris. He stopped outside a room near the alley door. Their voices were clear.

"What you want?" the hooker asked, determining the service wanted and negotiating the price. Billy Ray strained to listen, gauging the right moment to strike. He chanced a peek upon hearing heavy breathing. They were across the darkened room, the man's back to him, blocking the whore's view of the room.

Billy Ray moved with purpose, closing the gap. Before they could sense his presence, he reached out and slashed the knife across the man's throat. As his victim uttered a gurgling sound and grasped at his neck, Billy Ray shoved him to the side. Confused, the woman—who was on her knees—looked at the shadowy figure standing over her. Billy Ray raked the knife across her throat. He stepped back and kicked her in the chest, knocking her back into the wall. She slid sideways to the filthy floor where the john had fallen, writhing in a death throe.

His victims dead, he relieved them both of their cash. He cut off the man's penis, dipped it in the pool of blood, and printed a message on the wall above his victims.

YOU FUCK INOSENT PEOPLE STONE.

***

The city of New York awoke to the news that the Blood Letter Killer was back.

“Where you at, Stone?” Billy Ray growled at the TV in his room. He pulled, pushed, and bent the rabbit ears, attempting to clear the picture. The different news stations had live feeds from satellite trucks positioned close to the crime scene. Stone wasn’t on any of the broadcasts.

Billy Ray released the antenna when he got a halfway decent picture. He sat on the bed to watch the news. Maybe he could catch a glimpse of Stone.

A reporter interviewed a sergeant who admitted the presence of a bloody message at the scene. The sergeant refused to provide further details. That was no surprise. Stone’s absence was. He wondered if they had pulled Stone off the cases because they saw the truth of his messages.

Billy Ray sat on his bed and thought through his options. He decided it was time to stop leaving messages and complete his retribution by putting an end to Stone. Killing him would require careful planning.

It would be suicide to attack him at the police station, and he had no idea what Stone’s address was or the places he frequented. No way would the NYPD give out any information. He could check the borough telephone books, but cops never listed their telephone numbers.

Then he tumbled onto the answer. Public records. You could

locate anyone through public records. As he thought it over, he realized he couldn't do the research himself. Someone might remember his face—or worse, government offices used video surveillance systems. The chance of exposure was too great. He decided his best option was to hire a private investigator to do the legwork.

Even though the hotel had a pay phone, Billy Ray knew better than to use it—*do nothing that can lead back to you*. He would need to purchase a prepaid cell phone he could use and discard. He'd watched TV cop shows and saw how they found people by pinging cell towers or something like that.

Chapter 22

BILLY RAY RETRIEVED HIS CAR and drove around until he spotted a supermarket with a pay phone attached to the outer wall. The phone itself was of no use to him—he needed the phone book attached to the station by a chain. Inside the store, he purchased a prepaid cell phone, a pre-made sandwich from the deli, and a can of pop. He returned to the pay phone and flipped through the yellow pages, picking a private detective agency. The advertisement was a couple of lines long.

Small-time, Billy Ray thought, *the kind of person who'd jump at a cash deal.* He ripped out the page and returned to his car.

It took some time to find the address, a dilapidated building in a rundown neighborhood. Billy Ray parked a couple of blocks away from the address and punched the number into his cell phone.

A man's voice, sounding eager, answered the phone on the first ring. "Shield Security Services."

Billy Ray got right to the point. "I'm tryin' to find someone. You do that?"

"Sure," the man said. "It's a matter of knowing where to look. I get fifty an hour, and you pay all expenses."

Billy Ray was sure he heard hunger in the voice. "What'cha need from me?" he asked.

"A two-hour cash deposit and all the information you can give me on the person you're looking for."

“Gi’me ten minutes.”

“I’ll see you in ten, Mister—”

“Smith,” Billy Ray said.

“Mister Smith it is,” the man responded, a note of sarcasm in his voice.

Billy Ray walked to the building. On the second floor, he found a worn wooden door with a hand-printed piece of paper in a plastic sleeve tacked to it. The sign read “Shield Security Services—please knock and wait.”

He walked in without knocking. A short and stocky bull of a man with sagging jowls, droopy eyes, and a thick neck that gave him the appearance of a bloodhound sprang from a battered wooden desk and asked, “Mister Smith?”

“Yeah. Who’re you?”

“Sam. Sam Spade,” the man said, a grin on his K-9 face.

Billy Ray wanted to cut the sarcastic pissant’s throat, but he needed information first. He pulled a wad of cash out of his pocket and peeled off a stack of twenty-dollar bills. As he dropped them on the desk he said, “Two hundred now and another hundred if you get what I want quick.”

“What’s the name?” the gumshoe asked, hunger in his eyes as he stared at the pile of cash.

“Stone. Hunter Stone,” Billy Ray said as the PI took notes.

“What info you got on him?”

“He’s a cop. White guy. Tall but old—forty or forty-five maybe. Works for the Crime Lab.”

Spade had stopped writing and looked at Billy Ray. “Hold on. I don’t want to get in the middle of a beef with a cop.”

“No beef,” Billy Ray said with a disingenuous smile. Take another hundred for your trouble,” he said, peeling off twenties—”and another three when you get the info.”

"You sure?" the sleuth questioned, a note of distrust in his voice. His concern didn't stop him from snatching the bills off the desk like a man dying of thirst would grab a bottle of water.

"Yeah," Billy Ray said as he turned toward the door.

"Give me a couple of hours," the PI called as Billy Ray exited the office.

Billy Ray walked back to his car and reached under the driver's seat. He withdrew his non-glare knife and tucked it under his shirt. He sat behind the wheel, ate the sandwich, and downed the drink as he listened to the radio.

Two hours to the minute, he returned to the office. The private eye sat at his desk, drinking a Coca-Cola and eating salted peanuts from a can.

"Well?" Billy Ray said.

"Get your money out," Spade said, a smile on his wide, droopy face. He pointed to a piece of paper on the desk and said, "I got an address. That good enough for you?"

"Yeah," Billy Ray said, dropping a stack of twenties on the desk.

The PI snatched the bills and turned, exposing his back as he headed for a file cabinet. That was all the opportunity Billy Ray needed. The knife was out, and he was on the PI in a second. He ensnared the detective's beefy neck with his arm and plunged the blade into his back, twisting it side to side. Spade let out a strangled gurgling sound as his back arched, the knife blade penetrating his heart. Billy Ray released his stranglehold, and the PI dropped to the floor.

The wound made a sucking sound as Billy Ray pulled the knife out. He wiped it on the dead man's pants and grabbed the bills in his victim's hand.

No point wasting money.

He checked the gumshoe's pockets and found a wallet and a handkerchief. The wallet contained a lousy eight dollars. He took the money, wiped the wallet with the handkerchief, and dropped it on the floor.

Billy Ray opened the top file drawer using the handkerchief. Inside he found the other three-hundred dollars and a thirty-eight-caliber revolver in a worn brown leather holster. He pocketed the cash and stuffed the gun into the waistband of his pants.

He followed by ransacking the desk and file drawers, using the handkerchief to avoid leaving fingerprints. The piece of paper with Stone's information sat on the desk and drew his attention like a beacon. Billy Ray grabbed it and stuffed it in his pants pocket. He used the handkerchief to wipe the surfaces he might have touched. Satisfied the cops would think it was a robbery-homicide, he slipped out the door unnoticed and ambled back to his car.

Billy Ray drove back to the garage and parked. He returned the knife to his backpack but kept the newly acquired gun in his waistband. A smile on his face, he strolled back to the hotel.

The alley was free of bums. Word must have gotten out. He climbed the fire escape to his room. Back inside, he sat on the bed and stared at the paper with Stone's address on it.

***

As Billy Ray waited for night, he thought of the events that had resulted in him being in New York, ready to kill a cop. His half-brother, Arnet, had come to New York with several other members of the White Brotherhood. A nationally-advertised gay pride parade had provoked the White Brotherhood into sending members to make a statement. They gave the honor of leading the group to Arnet.

Arnet and three other White Brotherhood members had beaten two gay men to death with baseball bats in broad daylight—and in public. The NYPD caught them trying to escape. Stone had been the cop who interrogated Arnet. According to news reports, Arnet made a deal and rolled over on his associates.

Billy Ray knew in his heart the confession was bullshit. Arnet would never have cracked. And he would've sooner gouged his eyes out than make a deal with the cops to blame his brothers. That left one conclusion for Billy Ray to reach: Stone had lied. The confession was a lie. Arnet blaming his brothers was a lie.

Everything was a lie.

The system convicted them all the same and after landing in prison, someone had shanked Arnet, killing him. The White Brotherhood posthumously stripped him of his rank and membership.

They stripped Billy Ray of his membership too and would have nothing else to do with him. The rejection devastated him. The White Brotherhood was his family—his whole world. He was on his own again with no one. And this time there was no Arnet safety net.

A teenager left to fend for himself and stripped of everything he held sacrosanct, his despair turned to anger. He acted on that anger, attacking and robbing people and businesses to survive and show the White Brotherhood they were wrong. He survived on the street and his violence increased with each passing year. The police had arrested him several times. Liberal judges had given him probation most of the time. Billy Ray did do a six-month stint in the county lockup after he turned eighteen. Incarceration convinced him to plan his crimes and learn how to leave no evidence. Lessons from other inmates helped hone his skills.

As Billy Ray aged into adulthood, he continued to take out his anger on anyone he perceived did him an injustice or disrespected him. A plan to redeem Arnet's reputation and reingratiate himself with the White Brotherhood percolated in his mind until he figured out how to accomplish it. It would take money—lots of money—so he'd acquired it every way he could, all through illegal acts.

The plan had worked too, except for that little scrape involving the pool stick. The time had come to end the game. He needed to decide how he would kill Stone—after he got him to write a confession. He had a plethora of ideas, yet none seemed fitting enough for what Stone had done to Arnet and him.

One thing he knew for sure.

Stone's death would be slow and painful.

Chapter 23

BILLY RAY WAITED UNTIL DUSK to drive to Stone's address. He parked a block away, tucked the gun under his seat, and walked past the building, eyeballing the lobby through the glass door.

He backtracked and checked the building's buzzer directory. No listing for Stone. An "Apartment for Rent" sign taped to the glass panel framing the door gave him an idea. The directory showed the name Crespo/Superintendent, so he pushed that buzzer. After waiting what seemed an eternity, the electronic door lock buzzed. He pulled open the door and slipped into the building.

The lobby was empty, and no one had opened their door to see whom they had buzzed in. He checked the apartment doors off the lobby, locating the manager's apartment. The superintendent, Francis Crespo, yanked the door open after Billy Ray knocked numerous times.

"What?" the irritated runt of a man spat.

"Friend told me you have an apartment an—"

"Don't show apartments at night," Crespo interrupted, fouling the air with the smoke of a cheap cigar stub shoved into the corner of his mouth.

"Sorry," Billy Ray said, straining to mask his growing anger. As Crespo tried to push the door closed, Billy Ray stepped closer and held it open with his foot. He smiled and asked, "My friend's Hunter Stone. What apartment's he in?"

Crespo pulled the cigar from his mouth, waved it in the air as if for emphasis, and grunted, "He moved." He shoved the cigar back into the corner of his mouth.

Surprised, Billy Ray dropped the friendly pretense. As the smile slipped from his face, he demanded, "Where?"

"None of your business, that's where. And get your damn foot out'a my door," Crespo ordered, trying to shove the door closed.

The runt had pissed him off. He'd come too far to let a little grease ball thwart him. Nothing could stop him. He was too close to the endgame.

He glanced over his shoulder toward the lobby. With lightning speed, he delivered a savage punch to the side of the landlord's head. The cigar flew from his mouth and dropped onto the floor in a hail of bright embers. Unconscious, Crespo's limp body crashed to the floor, his face smacking the hardwood.

Billy Ray ducked into the apartment and closed the door. As he threw the deadbolt, he looked out the peephole. No witnesses.

He stepped on the cheap cigar, grinding it into the worn wood.

Then he stepped over the super's limp body, checking all the rooms to make sure no one else was in the apartment.

He closed the living room window shades, checking the windows in the building across the alley as he did. New Yorkers might avoid eye contact with each other, but they had no problem gawking at anything that caught their attention.

Billy Ray moved to the kitchen, found a pair of latex gloves under the sink, and slipped them on. A quick search of the kitchen drawers netted him a large carving knife and a roll of duct tape. He added an aluminum-framed kitchen table chair with plastic cushions to his arsenal and returned to the living room.

In a cheap entertainment center with sagging shelves, he turned on an old stereo system. He shoved a battered faux-leather chair across the living room floor with his foot to clear an area near the middle of the room and put the kitchen chair in its place. Satisfied, he returned to his unconscious victim.

He stripped the superintendent below the waist and dragged the unconscious man to the kitchen chair. He stuffed one of the super's socks into his victim's slack mouth and wound the duct tape around the landlord's head, being careful to leave his nose free. Further securing his victim, he taped the manager's ankles to the chair legs. As he wound tape around the chair and the super's torso, pinning his arms at his sides, Crespo began to wake, moaning behind his gag.

Billy Ray positioned himself in front of his victim. "Wake up, pissant."

As he watched with eyes devoid of all emotion, Crespo's eyes fluttered open and a look of panic registered on his taped and swelling face. Crespo began to struggle, trying to free himself. Billy Ray slapped him across the face hard enough to snap his head to the side. A small rivulet of blood, trickling from his damaged nose, flew across the room, landing on the floor. Crespo quit struggling and stared in terror at his assailant.

Billy Ray scanned the room, finding what he wanted. He unplugged a floor lamp and wrapped the cord around his gloved hand, yanking it from the base of the lamp. With the kitchen knife, he split the cord and peeled back the insulation covering the wires. As he worked he said in a flat voice, "You should'a told me."

Crespo tried to speak through the gag. Billy Ray slapped his face again. "Shut up, pissant. You talk when I tell ya."

Billy Ray ripped off two pieces of duct tape from the roll.

As Crespo watched horrified, his assailant taped one end of the bare wire to the inside of his thigh and the other to his abdomen. Crespo began to struggle and lost control of his bladder. Billy Ray grinned, a look so malevolent it made Crespo's breath catch.

Without another word, he plugged in the cord. The super's body shook, and he uttered indiscernible sounds. Billy Ray knew the electricity shooting through his victim spawned excruciating pain as it raced through his groin, legs, and abdomen. He pulled the plug and watched the manager sag in the chair. Crespo's breath huffed from his nostrils in hard bursts. It sounded to Billy Ray like steam puffing from an old locomotive.

"You ready to tell me—pissant?"

Crespo nodded his head as fast as he could. A mixture of mucus and blood flew into the air from the tape under his nose.

"I think you're lyin'," Billy Ray sneered.

Crespo shook his head no and Billy Ray saw the landlord pleading with his eyes.

"Liar!" Billy Ray hissed, pushing the plug back in. His victim went into spasms as electricity surged through him. Billy Ray pulled the plug after Crespo passed out.

He filled a pitcher with cold water from the kitchen sink. Crespo awoke with a start as the water cascaded over his head.

"You ready to tell me?" Billy Ray demanded.

Crespo nodded again, sending droplets of water arcing into the air.

"Maybe I still don't believe you," Billy Ray said, leering at his victim.

Crespo shook his head again and tried to utter a plea through the sock.

"Okay, pissant. You got one chance to tell me," Billy Ray said, reaching for the tape wrapped around his victim's head. "Don't say nothin' 'til I tell ya to talk. Ya got it?"

Crespo nodded.

Billy Ray worked the knife under the tape at the side of the superintendent's face until the tip emerged at the top. He twisted the knife and yanked it up, slicing the tape. The action caused the tip of the blade to burrow into his victim's cheek.

Crespo shrieked in pain through his gag as the knife punctured his cheek and blood began flowing down his face.

Billy Ray pressed the knife blade against Crespo's throat. He leaned close and ordered, "Shut it—or I'll gut you like a fish."

Crespo whimpered and fell silent. Billy Ray's merciless face inches away, he glowered into his victim's eyes with a cold, dead stare. Crespo shifted his eyes, shuddering.

Bent over for what must have seemed an eternity to Crespo, Billy Ray continued to glare. At last he stood and withdrew the knife from his victim's throat. He reached out and pulled the tape and sock from Crespo's mouth.

"Don't say nothin'," he commanded as the sock swung free, stuck to the flap of duct tape.

Billy Ray walked behind the chair and leaned in, his lips close to Crespo's ear. "Okay, pissant," he whispered. "Tell me where he's at."

Chapter 24

CRESPO CLEARED HIS HOARSE THROAT and whispered, "Colorado."

"Where?" Billy Ray demanded, flashing the knife in front of his victim's eyes.

"It's in the center desk drawer in my office," he rasped.

Billy Ray grabbed a handful of the superintendent's thinning hair and yanked his head back. He pressed the knife against his victim's throat again. "I think you're lyin.'"

"No, no," Crespo pleaded. "He wrote the address himself—so I could mail his deposit to him."

Billy Ray let go of the superintendent's head and flipped the knife from hand to hand, staring at his victim. Crying, Crespo shifted his eyes, unable to look at his tormentor. Tears and blood streaked his face, dripping from his quivering chin.

"Okay, pissant," Billy Ray said, tapping the flat of the knife blade against the top of Crespo's head. "Open your mouth."

He grabbed the sock and pushed it back into the superintendent's trembling yaw. He used another length of duct tape to secure it.

In the office, he found the notice to vacate letter from Stone with his new mailing address—the Silver Lake Marshal's Office in a town called Silver Lake, Colorado. He stared at the letter, grinning like a kid who'd found a hundred-dollar bill. His efforts had paid off. And no one would warn Stone, because no one would know of his clandestine search for him. His desire to get to Colorado dominated his thought process.

Billy Ray knew he needed to slow his mind and gain control of his emotions. It would do no good to rush and leave evidence behind. He wasn't finished staging the scene—and he had a live witness taped to a chair in the living room.

He wanted Stone to feel safe—to feel like he'd left his past behind. That way, it would destroy him when Billy Ray let him know he couldn't hide from his past misdeeds. He folded the paper and stuffed it in his pants pocket.

His emotions in check, he rifled through the desk. In the center drawer, he found an envelope that contained cash, checks, and rent receipts. He took the cash, scattered the checks and receipts on top of the desk, and dumped the contents of the desk drawers on the floor.

Billy Ray returned to the living room. He put a hand on the superintendent's forehead and pushed his head back. Without saying a word, he sawed the knife blade across his victim's neck. Crespo's throat and carotid arteries opened in a wide, red ribbon. The superintendent rocked in the chair, blood spurting from the gaping wound.

Billy Ray looked at the crimson-stained knife in his hand. As casual as a walk in a park, he strolled past the chair, spun, and slammed the knife to the hilt through the back of Crespo's neck. A full three inches of blade protruded through the slice in his throat.

As Crespo bled to death, Billy Ray washed the blood off the latex gloves at the kitchen sink. He returned to the living room, turned off the stereo, and wandered through the apartment, opening and ransacking closets and pulling out dresser drawers, dumping the contents on the floor. He rifled through a jewelry box that contained cheap trinkets.

Back in the living room, he pulled the wallet from the superintendent's pants, took the cash, and threw the wallet on the floor. He moved back into the kitchen, placing the gloves back inside the cabinet under the sink. Using a dishtowel, he wiped the sink dry. He worked his way through the apartment with the dishtowel, wiping away any fingerprints he may have left behind. At the front door, Billy Ray looked out the peephole again. The lobby was still clear. He opened the door and threw the deadbolt lock lever. With a final wipe of the doorknob and lock lever, he slipped out, pulling the door closed behind him.

***

Billy Ray parked his car in the alley. He was in too much of a hurry to park it in the garage and walk to the hotel. After he put the gun into his hidden backpack, he climbed the fire escape, being careful not to make any unnecessary noise. Back in his room, he kicked off his shoes, peeled off his clothes, and emptied his pockets. He shoved the dishtowel, his shoes, and his blood-spattered clothing into one of the grocery store paper bags used to line the dresser drawers.

Taking a quick shower, he positioned himself in front of the mirror and stared at his reflection. His malicious, ebony eyes scrutinized every inch of his body, from his dull-brown mop of hair to the soles of his feet, until convinced he'd scrubbed away every trace of the superintendent's blood.

Pulling his suitcase out from under the bed, he plopped it on the lumpy mattress. He popped the latches and opened the battered valise. From the pile of folded clothing, he pulled out fresh underwear and socks, a black tee shirt, a pair of blue jeans, and a pair of multi-colored sneakers.

He peeled back a corner of the suitcase lining under his clothing, held closed by Velcro strips, which exposed his hidden cash stash. He added the cash taken from the superintendent's apartment, withholding three hundred dollars in assorted bills, which he added to his wallet.

His prize, the folded piece of paper with the Silver Lake address on it, went into a pocket in his wallet. Ready to leave, he slipped into his black leather jacket. In the jacket pocket, he felt a lump. It was the cell phone he'd purchased. He removed the SIM card and broke the phone, making it unusable. Standing by the dresser, he surveyed the room, double-checking to make sure he'd left nothing behind.

Satisfied with the effort and eager to get moving, he climbed out the window and down the fire escape. He saw no one in the alley. Billy Ray threw his suitcase on the back seat. He put the grocery bag containing his bloody clothing, shoes, and the dishtowel in the trunk. Once he crossed into New Jersey, he would find a dumpster to discard the bag with his bloody clothing.

***

The bag discarded, Billy Ray continued his westward trek. Clear of the congested metropolitan areas, and into the New Jersey countryside, Billy Ray opened the driver's door window and threw the broken cell phone out the window and into a ditch paralleling the highway. Several miles further, he repeated the process with the SIM card. Other than the contents of his hidden backpack, he had nothing left to tie him to any of the New York murders.

As the miles rolled by with nothing to occupy him, Billy Ray's mind wandered. He thought of his half-brother, Arnet. Years ago, when he was a boy, Arnet had taught him three lessons:

Human life had little value.

Only the weak showed compassion.

And the best lesson of all: the flavor of revenge was sweet—its texture sticky. Life had taught him to live by that credo.

As the hours passed, Billy Ray maneuvered his car through the Pennsylvania countryside. The twin headlight beams pierced the darkness as desultory thoughts of how he would get his revenge occupied his mind. Many hours passed before he crossed from Pennsylvania through a finger of West Virginia and into the Ohio countryside.

After pushing himself and his car for over eight hours, the adrenalin had worn off. He began nodding off. Exhausted, he pulled into a rest stop along Interstate 70.

To keep out of the light cast by the tall light poles, he parked in a corner of the lot. He wanted to get away from the other vehicles parked in the lot, a couple of tractor-trailers idling side by side. Curled into a ball on the back seat, he draped his jacket over his head and fell into a dreamless sleep.

Chapter 25

UNINTELLIGIBLE SOUNDS PULLED BILLY RAY from the depths of his slumber. Half awake, he tried to figure out what could make such a God-awful ruckus. It sounded like a crow with smoker's cough. He wished it would stop so he could go back to sleep. Instead of quitting, it grew louder.

He craned his neck and looked out the window into the pale morning light. The trucks had gone. Another vehicle, a motor home, had parked in the lot. An older man moved toward the cinderblock building housing the restrooms. He wasn't the cause of Billy Ray's annoyance.

His bloodshot eyes searched the lot until he spotted her. An old woman, the man's wife he guessed, walking a white toy poodle with dark stains under its eyes. She cooed to the dog in a high-pitched, raspy whine as she approached the grass area near his car. Her big mouth was what had roused him.

Billy Ray rubbed the sleep from his eyes, yawned, and stretched. He crawled out of the passenger side of the car and gave the woman his nastiest stare. Thanks to her, he'd gotten fewer than two hours of sleep and that pissed him off. Under his breath he muttered, "Stupid cow."

Chilled by the morning air, Billy Ray watched the ugly little dog squat and leave a pile of steaming droppings near the front of his car. The dog scratched at the ground, trying to cover the offending mound. The old hag began her raspy clucking again as she walked away, pulling on the dog's leash.

"Hey, you gonna pick up that shit?" Billy Ray asked, pointing toward the offending mass.

"Mind your own damn business," the old broad growled.

Too tired to argue, he ignored her rudeness and walked to the driver's side of his car. Other priorities occupied his mind. As he opened the driver's door, he glanced over and saw the woman nearing the restrooms. She saw him look and flipped her middle finger at him. With a sharp yank on the leash, she dragged her mutt into the women's restroom.

The uncomfortable back seat and lack of sleep had done nothing to elevate his mood. Now this pissant thought she could be rude, flip him off, and get away with it. Over three months of incarceration, dealing with his jackass attorney and all the other pissants he'd endured, he'd overloaded his quotient of tolerance. Done with other people's crap, he slammed the driver's door and opened the trunk. He removed his gloves and favorite knife from his special backpack.

He jammed his hands into the gloves and marched into the women's restroom and right up to the old bag, washing her hands at a sink. She saw him coming and yelled, "Get away from me!" Her eyes widened as Billy Ray brandished the knife and she screamed, "Fraaaank!"

Those were her last words. Billy Ray slashed the knife across her throat. She sank to the floor, blood pumping from her gaping wound. Billy Ray hopped out of the way to avoid the spurting blood. He silenced her yapping dog next by cutting its throat. He returned to the woman and cut off her offending middle finger.

As Billy Ray backed away, Frank, he assumed, shuffled into the restroom. He stopped dead in his tracks upon seeing the carnage, his eyes wide in shock and his mouth gaping open in surprise. "Oh my God!" he cried. He looked from his wife to the dog to Billy Ray. "What've you done?"

Billy Ray attacked and buried his knife in the old man's chest. Frank sank to the floor like an actor in a slow-motion scene, the life fading from his eyes. He returned to the woman and dipped her severed finger in her own blood. Using the detached digit as a writing instrument, he wrote on the mirror:

BITCH ASK FOR IT.

Wasting no time, he threw the finger into one of the sinks and washed the blood from his gloves and knife in another. As he washed, he checked himself in the mirror. Although he'd tried to avoid it, a spot of blood spatter had landed on his shirt. He wiped the sink and faucet with a paper towel.

Billy Ray ran to his car, packed his killing paraphernalia, changed his shirt, and pulled back onto Interstate 70, afraid someone might come into the rest stop and see him. Too bad the old man had to get it. It was his nasty old lady's fault. Billy Ray wished he'd had time to relieve himself and wash the sleep from his eyes. All the activity had made him hungry too.

An hour and a half west, the bright sun hanging in the clear sky, he came upon a large complex with gas pumps, a souvenir shop, and a restaurant near Springfield, Ohio. He filled his gas tank, parked, and headed into the souvenir shop to pay his gas bill. From a huge rack of maps, he purchased a map of the United States and one of Colorado. In the men's restroom, he relieved himself and washed the best he could in a public restroom sink. Refreshed, he ambled into the restaurant.

As he ate, he reviewed the maps to plot his trip. If he could put in a full day today, he could make it to Kansas City, Missouri in a little over nine hours. Tonight, he planned to stay in a motel so he could get some decent rest and a shower. Another tiring day on the road would put him in the Denver, Colorado area. That would leave him within a few hours of his destination. He would crash in a cheap motel and review his plans prior to the final leg of the journey.

Satisfied with the plan, he folded the maps. His gaze shifted to the window. Two Ohio state trooper vehicles had stopped in the parking lot. The troopers wandered the lot, recording the license plate numbers of all the parked vehicles.

As Billy Ray enjoyed a fresh cup of coffee, the troopers entered the restaurant and began contacting the patrons. One of them approached him. "Excuse me, sir. Do you have a vehicle parked in the lot?" the trooper asked, pointing out the window.

"Yeah. It's that one, the Ford," Billy Ray said pointing.

"The gray one with the New York plates?" the trooper asked.

Billy Ray nodded and asked, "I do somethin'?"

The trooper ignored the question and pointing asked, "Did you stop at a rest stop on the interstate east of here?"

Billy Ray feigned surprise and said, "Didn't see one. Must'a drove right by it."

"Where're you headed?" the trooper questioned.

"West. I'm on vacation. Seein' the country," Billy Ray answered, smiling at the trooper. He knew the purpose of the questioning.

"May I see your license and registration, please?"

Billy Ray knew of no legal requirement forcing him to provide anything to the trooper. Nevertheless, if he wanted to avoid calling undue attention to himself, he needed to appear cooperative. "Sure," he said, reaching for his wallet.

The trooper copied information from Billy Ray's license and registration onto a pad of paper clipped to a metal storage clipboard. Done, he handed the documents back and thanked Billy Ray for his cooperation. Billy Ray felt relieved as the trooper moved on to another table.

He slid out of the booth and paid his bill. Wide-awake from a coffee buzz and the encounter with the cop, he drove back onto Interstate 70 and headed west. As he drove, he contemplated how he would announce his presence to Stone. The map indicated Silver Lake was a small town in the mountains. He would need to find a place to stay that would allow him the freedom to keep track of Stone. By imitating a vacationer, he could hide in plain sight. He could explore the town and learn the lay of the land ... take his time and determine how best to announce his presence.

It was important he determine Stone's habits ... what kind of work he did, when and where he worked, who he worked with, and what he did when he wasn't working: find Stone's strengths and weaknesses. Billy Ray realized it might take longer than anticipated to find out all he needed to know.

Maybe he could look for a job. The longer he thought of getting a job, the better he liked the idea. It would be hard to blend in for long. Aimless wandering was a sure way to call attention to himself, especially once he began leaving messages for Stone. In New York, none of that was important. New York was big, impersonal. In a small town, he wouldn't have the freedom afforded by anonymity for long.

He would need to find the best places to hunt too. Motels were too dangerous. Too many people present all hours of the day and night. Since Silver Lake was a small mountain town, there might be campgrounds near it. If the campsites were close to each other, he would avoid them. If he were lucky, some campers would seek the privacy of the forest. Private houses located in the woods would be ideal too.

As he thought through the challenges awaiting him, he realized he needed to take his time. A great deal of observing and planning would be necessary. He had to temper his emotions and not allow them to dictate his actions. He'd failed at that this morning—and was damn lucky to have gotten away with it.

Once he got to Silver Lake, he would evaluate the situation. It would be like his days of hunting wild hogs in Texas. Determine their habits. Set 'em up, let 'em get comfortable, and draw 'em in to go for the kill.

The thought gave him a sense of satisfaction.

Chapter 26

OHIO STATE TROOPER DAN DEEGAN, a tall, slender, and fit man with a clean-shaven youthful appearance, square jaw, narrow aquiline nose, and thin lips arrived at the Office of Investigative Services at the Cambridge District Post at ten-thirty. His supervisor, Sergeant Thompson, had called him in on a Saturday morning. He knew it must be something big as he walked into the office, because his intense, chestnut-colored eyes saw other investigators working at their desks. No sooner in the office he heard his name called. "Deegan, my office," Sergeant Thompson called.

The last three years in the investigative unit as a plainclothes investigator had been a fulfilling assignment change following nine years as a uniformed trooper patrolling the Ohio highways. It had afforded Dan the opportunity to investigate all manner of criminal activity other than traffic offenses—although never before on a weekend. Dan ran his hand though his short, semi-militaristic-cut brown hair and knocked on the doorframe, even though the sergeant's door was open.

"Come," his sergeant ordered as Dan stepped across the threshold. "I got a call this morning from Captain Adams. We caught a double homicide at the westbound rest stop on I-70, mile marker 163, Zanesville. I'm assigning you the case."

That surprised Dan. The Columbus District Post, with a larger compliment of plainclothes investigators, almost always handled cases this serious. Either that or the Ohio Bureau of Criminal Investigation would try to hijack it—even though it was within the OSHP's jurisdiction. Instead of questioning the order, Dan, a man of action and intense focus—as opposed to excessive verbiage—asked, "Any info?"

"Looks like an older couple. Motor home in the parking lot with Pennsylvania tags is likely theirs. Tourist discovered the scene in the women's restroom and called it in. Troopers closed the rest stop and detained the witness on scene for interview."

Dan knew the rest stop. He'd patrolled that part of Interstate 70 as a patrol trooper. It was thirty minutes away.

"Anyone en route?" he asked, knowing his Sergeant understood he meant the coroner and crime scene technicians.

"I notified the Muskingum County coroner. He said he'd respond when you're ready. Our lab's not equipped to handle this kind of scene, so I've notified the BCI lab, due to travel time."

Dan nodded his approval. He knew the closest Ohio Bureau of Criminal Investigation Unit was in London, an hour and a half away from the scene. The BCI had a full staff of personnel that had experience with homicides. He would've made the same decision. "Patrol sweeping rest stops and service centers?"

"First thing I set in motion. The info's trickling in to the other investigators," the sergeant said, pointing.

Dan looked back over his shoulder and counted four other investigators in the office. He looked at Sergeant Thompson, the unasked question obvious. Why so many people working the case?

"Captain told me to make this one a priority."

"Am I working it alone?" Dan asked.

"Take Trooper Lynbrook with you. Both of you're off case rotation. This is all you work on. Understood?"

"Got it," Dan said, turning and exiting the office. As he headed toward the exit, he motioned for Hal Lynbrook, a short bull of a man with bulging muscles from weight lifting, a square head sporting tiny ears, a crooked nose, full lips, and close-set blue eyes under heavy blond eyebrows that matched his crewcut hair, to join him. Lynbrook was a rookie in the plainclothes division.

En route to the scene Dan briefed Hal on the facts garnered from Sergeant Thompson. As they arrived on scene, Dan ordered, "Interview the witness. When you're done, join me in the restroom."

***

Dan saw the reasons the Columbus District Post and the BCI had pawned off the case on his office. No witnesses and no murder weapon—although a blind man could see what had been the weapon of choice. No obvious evidence other than a misspelled message on the mirror and what appeared to be the woman's middle finger in one of the sinks. The perp had even killed the victim's dog.

Dan figured the message on the mirror, along with the severed finger and the dead dog, indicated an angry perp. Angry people tended to act in the heat of the moment. That was good because crimes of passion were sloppy crimes. Sloppy crimes resulted in evidence left behind.

Hal joined him as Dan scanned the scene, thinking through the logical sequence of events. "The suspect killed the female first, based on the blood spatter and her body position," Dan said, pointing to the woman. "Since the dog's on a leash, wrapped around her wrist, I'd say it was next. Assuming the female yelled for help during the attack, the male victim came to her aid, resulting in his murder."

The hypothesis fit. While it might be only one possible scenario, it was the best one—unless evidence showed something else. That meant a possible confrontation on the road or in the parking lot prior to the attack. Dan made a mental note to order a detailed search for signs of a confrontation or possible evidence. Perhaps she'd flipped off the wrong person.

The BCI Crime Scene Technicians moaned upon learning the scene was a lavatory at an interstate rest stop. One of them told Dan public restrooms were cesspools of DNA and fingerprints. To their credit, they moved through the scene like the professionals they were, photographing, videotaping, swabbing for DNA, collecting blood samples, and dusting for prints. They followed that by completing a detailed sketch with measurements and began analysis of the blood spatter.

As the crime scene technicians finished the areas surrounding the bodies, Dan motioned Hal over and said, "Time for the coroner."

Hal called in the request as Dan contacted several troopers on scene and organized a detailed grid pattern search of the rest stop. By the time the coroner arrived, the search was complete. The evidence discovered—if you wanted to call it evidence—was a fresh pile of small dog droppings.

Dan and Hal watched as the coroner, Doctor Coopersmith from Zanesville, began his examination of the bodies. He first removed the man's wallet, which contained several hundred dollars in cash. The driver's license matched the registration of the motor home parked in the lot. A ring of keys recovered from the man's front pants pocket had one that fit the RV. A purse in the vehicle held the female victim's identification and additional cash. Robbery was out as a motive.

Coopersmith announced the obvious upon examination of the wounds. "He killed them both by use of a sharp-edged instrument.

I'd guess a knife with a single-edged blade. I assume it was the same weapon. I can't be sure until I complete the autopsies. Finger looks like hers too. The female victim's throats incised ... looks left to right," he said, probing and squeezing the wound. "The male victim has a deep penetrating wound, downward trajectory, left to right." The coroner looked at Dan and Hal and added, "Assuming the victims faced their killer, I'd say you have a right-handed suspect who's taller than the male victim."

"TOD," Dan asked.

The coroner flexed the victims' arms, legs, and necks and pulled what looked like a meat thermometer and a scalpel from his case. He made a small incision in the man's abdomen, circling the new wound with a black marker, and initialing the skin near the circle. He inserted the thermometer through the incision and pushed it deep into the core of the man's body. Finished with the male victim, he repeated the process with the female. Checking the victims' eyes and gums and pressing on their skin where the blood had settled he announced, "Based on rigor, lividity, and core temp, they both died close to the same time. Time of death would be this morning, say six-thirty to seven-thirty." The coroner added, "I don't see any signs of sexual assault."

That eliminated rape as a motive. The coroner believed the suspect cut off the finger postmortem. Having learned all they could from the victims, the coroner taped paper bags over the victims' hands, in case one of them had scratched the suspect, and wrapped each victim in a clean sheet to trap trace evidence before bagging the bodies. He bagged the finger in a small paper bag. With assistance from several troopers, he loaded the bodies into the coroner's van. As he prepared to leave, he advised Dan the autopsies would be on Monday, and he would call with the time.

The BCI Crime Scene Technicians had the victims' RV towed

to their facility for processing, although they had no indication the vehicle would provide any additional evidence. A cursory check had shown no exterior damage, so Dan had eliminated an accident as a motive for the attack.

Dan stood in the restroom and surveyed it one final time. He stared at the mirror and took a photograph of the message with his smartphone. He and Hal headed back to the office, each alone with his thoughts. As they pulled into the district office lot Hal asked, “Where do we go from here?”

Excellent question, Dan thought.

Chapter 27

SATURDAY NIGHT, DAN DEEGAN SAT alone in the Office of Criminal Investigation at the Cambridge District Post in Ohio. Everyone else had left, because there was nothing left to do. He stared at the paperwork, as though a clue might jump off a page.

The information gathered by the patrol troopers who swept the rest stops and service centers sat on his desk. Collated and cataloged it was useless until they uncovered new evidence that pointed toward a suspect. They had no way to know if the suspect had stopped anywhere. They assumed the perp was westbound, which was a guess. He could've gone east or exited Interstate 70 on any number of county roads or state highways.

The BCI Lab had called Dan a few hours earlier and advised him that—as suspected—they had collected a profusion of fingerprints and DNA. It would take days to run all the prints. They told him that due to the cost and time constraints, they would wait to process the DNA until he developed a suspect.

A bit of positive news was that the BCI Lab's analysis of the crime scene and blood spatter confirmed his hypothesis of the sequence of events. Even with the confirmation, the information wouldn't lead him to a suspect. The autopsies were still pending, but he wasn't expecting any additional useful information from them either.

As he stared at the case file paperwork and photos cataloged and secured into a murder book, something kept niggling at the periphery of his mind. Every attempt he made to pull it into focus failed.

He decided to go home. Maybe if he stopped trying so hard to capture the elusive thought, it would come to him.

At least he hoped. Because he had nothing else.

***

Sunday, Dan sat on his living room couch, his laptop resting on his thighs. His trick of avoiding focusing on what scratched at the periphery of his memory had worked. The memory had popped into his mind as he lunched on a liverwurst sandwich a short time ago. A few months back, he saw a news story detailing some murders in which the killer left messages in the victim's blood—like the message at the rest stop.

He opened a search engine and typed in the words. "Murders with messages left in blood." Numerous sites popped up, many with references that matched his search. As he read the stories of the multiple New York murders he whispered, "Shit."

The articles had too little information to determine if the New York and Ohio rest-stop killer was one in the same. Both used a knife and left messages. That was all he could glean from the articles—except the name the media had given to the killer—the Blood Letter Killer. From what he could tell, the police never disclosed the contents of the messages.

Dan typed NYPD into his search engine. He found a list of telephone numbers for the different divisions and copied the number for the Homicide Analysis Unit.

He turned off his computer and set it on his coffee table. As he stared at the telephone number, he prayed he would have his answer tomorrow.

***

Monday dawned clear and warm in Ohio. By eight o'clock, Dan was at his desk in the Office of Criminal Investigation at the Cambridge District Post. He plucked his desk phone from its cradle, pushed an open line button, and punched in the NYPD Homicide Analysis Unit's telephone number. Briefed by Dan, Hal listened in on another telephone.

A man with little patience for inefficiency, the NYPD tested Dan's determination by disconnecting him one time and transferring him numerous others. When he'd hit the end of his limited patience and was ready to quit trying, someone routed him to the correct extension.

"Detective Burnside."

"Detective Burnside, I'm Trooper Dan Deegan of the Ohio State Troopers Office of Criminal Investigation. Are you the detective assigned the Blood Letter Killer cases?"

Following a brief hesitation, Detective Burnside asked, "Who'd you say you were?"

Dan began to wonder how in the hell they ever solved anything in New York. "Deegan. Dan Deegan. I'm an investigator with the Ohio State Troopers. I'm investigating a double murder that appears similar to the Blood Letter Killer cases."

"That's a media tag," Burnside scoffed. "We don't use that reference to refer to the cases."

Dan heard the condescension in Burnside's voice and wanted to ask why in the hell it mattered, but he needed information, so he swallowed his growing frustration and said, "Sorry, detective. I got my information from the Internet. Are they your cases?"

"They are," Burnside said. "What can I do for you, Detective Deegan?"

"It's Trooper," Dan corrected, returning Burnside's rudeness. "I'm trying to determine a link between my case and yours. My perp used a knife with a single-edged, serrated blade and left a message in the victim's blood. I couldn't find any information on the messages left at your scenes."

"That's because we haven't released that information," Burnside said. "Look, for all I know, you could be a reporter trying to get information. If you're legit, you need to submit an official request through the proper channels. When I get it, I'll release the information to you."

At the end of his patience Dan said, "Detective Burnside, I'm trying to solve a double murder—not find a lost bicycle. You know how fast cases go cold. Can you find the Ohio Cambridge District Post number and call me back? Verify I'm legit?"

"Sorry. You'll have to go through the proper channels," Burnside said with cold finality.

Dan was over this pompous ass. "I understand. May I speak with your supervisor—please?"

"Hold the line." A dial tone followed a series of clicks.

"Asshole," Dan spat, banging the receiver into the telephone cradle. He looked at Hal and asked, "You believe it?"

Dan took a deep breath to calm himself. Composed, he opened the NYPD directory on his desktop computer and found the name and a photo of the Central Investigation and Resource Division assistant chief, listed as the head of the Homicide Analysis Unit.

Prepared for another round of pass the caller, he called the NYPD again and asked for Central Investigation and Resource Division Assistant Chief Brian O'Malley. It surprised him that he got right through to the correct office. He identified himself and explained his situation. The chief's secretary put him on hold. Dan raised an eyebrow, ever the skeptic, and waited to hear the dial tone again.

An unexpected voice broke the silence. "Chief O'Malley. How can I help you?"

Dan explained his investigation again to the chief and emphasized his urgent need for information. He told the chief the essence of his conversation with Detective Burnside and asked if someone could call his division to verify who he was.

"No need," Chief O'Malley said. My phone's digital display shows your number and identifies it as the Ohio State Trooper Cambridge Office. What is it you need?"

Dan wondered if Detective Burnside had a phone display. "I'm trying to determine if my perp could be the same person who committed the New York murders. I need whatever I can get on the cases."

"Give me a fax number, and I'll have the reports sent over today," Chief O'Malley said.

"Thank you, Chief," Dan said, reciting the division's fax line number.

O'Malley added, "The suspect addressed the messages to a specific sergeant detective specialist. His name's Hunter Stone, and he worked out of the Crime Lab."

Dan caught the past tense reference and asked, "Worked? Is he retired?"

"I heard he took an early out and got another job. I don't know where," O'Malley said. "Hang on a second."

Dan heard the rustle of pages, and Chief O'Malley was back on the phone. "Try Stone's captain. He might know Stone's whereabouts." O'Malley gave Dan the captain's name and number and wished him luck.

They disconnected, and Dan called the number provided by the chief. "Forensic Investigation Division. Captain Baxter speaking."

Dan went through all the particulars again. "I need to speak with Sergeant Hunter Stone, and Chief O'Malley said you might have his contact information."

"It's Marshal Stone now," Baxter said. "He's the town marshal of Silver Lake, Colorado. All I have is his cell number. His office number might be available online or through directory assistance."

Dan copied the number and said, "Thank you. I'll give him a call."

"When you do, don't call him Hunter. He hates that. He goes by Stone," Baxter said. "One other thing. You should know that he focused on our serial murder cases to the point of obsession. Be careful what you say, or you might have him in Ohio—investigating your case."

"No need for him to come this way," Dan said. "If this is the same perp, my guess is he's headed west—to Colorado."

"Shit," Baxter groaned. "I hope you're wrong, but if you're sure, Stone needs to know the killer's headed his way. Be damn sure, though. He left the NYPD to get away from shit like this."

"I won't call the marshal unless I'm sure the perp's headed his way. Okay if I call you back if I need help?" Dan asked.

"Sure," Baxter said. "I don't know what help I can give you but call anytime. Let me give you my cell number."

Prior to disconnecting, Baxter asked Dan to keep him updated. Dan said he would.

He sure as hell had no intention of providing *any* information to that asshole. Burnside.

Chapter 28

AS EXPECTED, THE AUTOPSIES IN Zanesville wasted Dan's time. Doctor Coopersmith was unable to provide much useful information. Examination of the male victim's chest wound indicated a blade length approaching seven inches. Therefore, the knife blade shape and length resembled an old military style KA-BAR fixed-blade weapon. Doctor Coopersmith said he would call with toxicology results, but he doubted anything useful would come of them.

The morning shot, Dan returned to the office. He found piles of faxes stacked on his desk. The reports from New York included a surprise report: the latest New York double homicide, which happened shortly before his double murder. Chief O'Malley had come through. Dan would've killed to be a fly on the wall when the chief ordered Burnside to cooperate.

He began amassing the pages into loose-leaf binders. The murder books assembled, Dan and Hal began reviewing the New York cases, looking for similarities to the rest-stop murders.

"The killer doesn't seem to have a specific victim type or geographical preference," Hal said. "He's all over the board."

Dan noticed the consistency in the choice of weapon, the knife with the single-edged blade. That and the notes left at every scene in the victims' blood. "Let's list the message contents in the order the perp left them."

In short order, the pattern became apparent. The killer had a personal beef with Stone. Each message was more accusatory, expressing in various bloody metaphors how Stone was a poor investigator and a murderer who lied to make his cases.

"It's obvious he's got a vendetta against this guy, Stone," Hal said. "But that doesn't help us. The message in the restroom doesn't match with these."

Dan wondered. The act of leaving a message in the victim's blood was so unusual; he thought it too coincidental to be a coincidence.

"Something else I'm seeing in these reports," Hal said, interrupting Dan's thoughts. "They recovered black polyester cotton fibers at some of their scenes. I don't remember the BCI Lab rats finding any fibers."

Dan figured the fibers came from something the killer wore as he committed his crimes. He had suspected the restroom murders were a spontaneous act. The fact that the BCI crime scene investigators failed to find similar fibers in the restroom served to reinforce that belief.

Approaching six, they had been at the reports for over five hours. Hal was antsy to quit for the day. They had reviewed everything and culled what useful information they could. There was nothing left to do. Dan called it a day, and they walked out, both looking dejected.

As Dan drove home, his gut kept telling him that somewhere the cases intersected, even though no definitive evidence of a connection had surfaced. He wondered if maybe his approach to the investigation was wrong. A glaring, unanswered question hung in the air like fog. If he could answer it, he would know if he was right or wrong.

***

Tuesday morning, Dan was back at his desk at seven o'clock ... eight o'clock New York time. A restless night behind him, he'd been impatient for morning to come so he could make the call. He yawned and punched in the smartphone number.

"Hello."

"Captain Baxter, it's Trooper Dan Deegan."

"Oh. I didn't expect to hear from you again. At least not so soon," Baxter said. "Did you call Stone?"

"No, sir. Not with what I have."

"And what've you found?" Baxter asked. His question sounded like a challenge to Dan.

"Anecdotal evidence. Nothing definitive." Dan winced, knowing what Baxter was about to say.

"Maybe that's because the cases aren't connected," Baxter said, stating the obvious.

Dan knew it. His boss would've responded the same way.

"That's one explanation. I think I can prove or disprove a connection with your help."

"I don't know what I can do to help. What do you need?" Baxter asked.

"I want to determine how the killer could've known Stone moved—and where." If he could uncover evidence that someone had obtained the information, he would have his proof.

"Hmmm. Interesting approach," Baxter said, sounding intrigued. "How would *you* find Stone?"

"I assume his address and telephone number weren't published or provided to anyone by the NYPD."

"It's departmental policy," Baxter said. "No one lists their address or telephone number. That's no guarantee some unscrupulous employee didn't leak the information, but the odds are slim."

"What if I checked public records?" Dan asked.

"That wouldn't tell you where he moved," Baxter said.

"Okay. Who would he give his forwarding address to?"

"He'd have to provide it to NYPD Personnel, so they'd have an address to send his final pay and retirement benefits," Baxter explained. "However, that information isn't provided to anyone unless they have proper authorization and a damn good reason to ask for it."

"Who else? Dan wondered aloud. "The post office? A landlord?"

"Both," Baxter said, a note of excitement in his voice. "If you could find his address through public records, you might get his forwarding address from his landlord. That's excellent deductive reasoning, Trooper Deegan."

"Would you—"

"No need to ask," Baxter said. "I have his old address. I'll check with the landlord and call you back."

They disconnected, and Dan tilted his chair back. He squeezed his eyes shut and pinched the bridge of his nose. He hoped this was the break he needed. It was all he could think to do.

***

Close to six hours later, Dan's desk phone rang. He snatched the receiver from its cradle. "Office of Criminal Investigation, Trooper Deegan speaking." Dan waved at Hal and held out three fingers, indicating which line he was on. Hal grabbed an extension to listen in on the call.

"Son of a bitch if you weren't right," Baxter said.

"What'd the landlord say?"

"We can't question him, because he's dead," Baxter said.

"Dead? How?" Dan asked, stunned.

"They listed it as a robbery/homicide. I've talked to the detective's assigned the case and reviewed the crime scene photos. I've got to tell you, it's the strangest damn robbery/homicide I've ever seen."

"What do you mean?" Dan asked.

"The suspect tortured the landlord—with electricity—then murdered him. Made it look like a robbery. You can bet your ass he gave the suspect Stone's forwarding address. And we had another robbery homicide the same day. My crime scene people worked the scene and attended the autopsy. A knife with a single-edged, serrated blade was the weapon used. Victim was an ex-cop/turned smalltime private investigator. The detective assigned the case ran his LUDs and found a call to the DMV the same day as his murder."

"What's a LUD?" Dan asked.

"Local Usage Details or LUDs. In simpler terms, his phone records," Baxter said. "As an ex-cop, he could've had a source at the DMV, who could've given him Stone's address by running his name through their vehicle registration database. We haven't been able to verify that, because we can't ID the person who took the call. And I doubt we will, because they'd get fired in a heartbeat." Following a brief pause, Baxter added, "My gut tells me this is all too coincidental."

"I guess I know where he's headed," Dan said. "I better make the call."

Baxter wished him luck, and they disconnected. Dan looked at Hal, a smile on his face. "I'll go brief Sergeant Thompson."

PART III

CAT AND MOUSE

Chapter 29

AS STONE STARTED TOWARD THE office door for his afternoon rounds, the telephone rang. He reached back and snatched the receiver from its cradle. "Marshal's Office, Stone speaking."

"Marshal Hunter Stone?" a voice inquired.

"Yes, this is Marshal Stone. Who's this?"

"Trooper Dan Deegan," the voice said. "Ohio State Troopers Office of Criminal Investigations."

The pronouncement caught Stone off guard, and he hesitated, then asked, "What can I do for you, Trooper Deegan?"

"I have some unpleasant news, Marshal."

Stone returned to his new desk chair and eased into it. "You have my attention."

"I believe the New York serial killer's headed your way," Trooper Deegan stated, as though it was an undisputed fact.

Stone stiffened as if shot by a stun gun and demanded, "How do you know that?"

Dan briefed him on his double-murder case and how it had led to his contact with the NYPD and to Captain Baxter. "Someone tortured and murdered your old landlord. The same day, someone murdered a private detective who contacted the DMV. No suspect's been ID'd in either case."

As the trooper's words pressed in on him, Stone found breathing difficult. It felt like a giant boulder had settled on his chest.

His pupils dilated, causing pinpricks of light to invade his brain in bright flashes, and he could feel the cloak of dread envelope his soul as though it was a living organ.

His new life in Silver Lake was less than a month and a half old. He thought he'd been successful at packing away his past. The trooper's words severed that myth as cleanly as a scalpel sliced flesh.

Myriad thoughts careened through his mind. Even though it was irrational, he felt immediate guilt. New York had over 34,000 sworn officers. Silver Lake had two. Even with all that manpower the NYPD had failed to catch the serial killer. If he'd found his way to Silver Lake, Stone feared the town would become a killing field—and nothing he could do would stop it.

The faint hiss of the open line marked his silence.

"Marshal?" Dan asked.

"I'm listening," Stone whispered. "Give me the details."

As Dan filled in the minutiae, Stone began to see holes in the trooper's reasoning. Or maybe he wanted to find gaps. "You don't have any actual proof, only conjecture based on two unconnected incidents."

"Common sense would—"

"I need more than speculation," Stone interrupted. His mind refused to accept the hypothesis without proof.

"I don't know what else you want."

"Proof. Definitive proof," Stone demanded. "The PI could've called the DMV for reasons having nothing to do with me. His call could've had nothing to do with his or my old landlord's death. You said you don't know the reason or even who he called."

"They were both murdered on the same day, and the perp killed the PI with a knife showing the same specifics as the serial killer's weapon of choice."

Stone knew that ten to fifteen percent of all murders involved the use of a knife. It was the preferred weapon of certain ethnic groups. "You said they listed both cases as robbery/homicides. That M.O. doesn't fit the New York killer. Did they find any messages in blood at either scene?" Stone asked.

"No, but if his intent was to find you, he killed them for a different reason. How else do you explain the torture of the landlord?"

"I don't—but you didn't have the pleasure of knowing my landlord. He was an asshole," Stone said. "I can see him giving robbers a ration of shit. His attitude and big mouth could've cost him his life."

Frustration evident in his voice, Dan asked, "So, you're unwilling to accept that the killer's headed your way?"

"Unwilling, no ... cautious, yes. Is it possible? Sure, there's a remote possibility. But we've had no indication of any problems in the area."

"He could be en route or waiting for some reason," Dan said. "I have authorization to travel to Silver Lake and coordinate a joint investigation with you."

"I'm sorry, Trooper Deegan—without something concrete, I can't launch an investigation. This is a small-town, dependent on tourism for its survival. Besides, you can bet your paycheck the powers-that-be would demand I have solid proof prior to authorizing anything that could in any way affect the tourist trade."

Following a brief silence Dan said, "Understood," the disappointment evident in his voice.

"This's what I will do," Stone offered. "I'll keep my eyes and ears open. If I get wind of anything of a suspicious nature, I'll call you, and we can coordinate an investigation at that time."

Stone copied Dan's smartphone and work numbers. They disconnected, and Stone sat at his desk, staring into mid-space. A jumble of unpleasant thoughts swirled through his head—thoughts of what was to come if Trooper Deegan was right.

Stone decided it was possible the trooper wanted to be right, so he'd used inductive reasoning—develop a hypothesis and find facts to support it—ignoring any that failed to support the hypothesis. That was how innocent people went to jail—and how small-town marshals got their life turned inside out for no good reason.

Stone tried to put the call out of his mind as he completed his afternoon and evening rounds, but the trooper's words stuck like gum on a shoe. He wondered if the trooper had jumped to conclusions or if, perhaps, he was in denial about any other possibilities.

The day's paperwork finished at ten fifteen, Stone decided to knock off for the night. The shops in town had all closed. Only the bars remained open.

Even though Harry was off tonight, Stone had no concerns. The marshal's office had a long-standing arrangement with the bar owners to arrange rides for those who showed signs of getting either too drunk or too rowdy. So, he knew there was little chance of any problems.

He yawned and clicked off his desk lamp. The chair's wheels rumbled on the uneven wooden floorboards as he stood, pushing it back. He retrieved his cowboy hat from the wall pegs by the office door and pulled open the door. The cool night air enveloped him, forcing its way through the opening on a light breeze.

Stone surveyed the office. Everything was tidy, and the coffee pot off. He flicked off the overhead light switch and stepped out into the night, pulling the door closed behind him.

As he walked to the Suburban parked on the side of the building, an eerie feeling struck him. The hair on the back of his neck and arms prickled to attention. He felt someone watching from the darkness. He froze, ears straining to hear any unusual sounds.

He tried to spot anything that appeared out of place, however, his vision hadn't adjusted to the dark. His eyes still searched, darting from shadow to deep shadow, trying to distinguish an out-of-place silhouette or the slightest movement.

Stone remembered that a few times every year, bears wandered into town seeking a trashcan treat; however, they were anything but quiet. They made enough noise trying to get the top off the can to wake half the town. And this didn't feel like the gaze of a four-legged predator.

Then he heard it. The faint whisper of a scrape. He snapped his head in the direction of the sound. No movement. Stone continued to stare, laboring to see movement or hear the slightest noise. Remaining frozen for what felt like eternity, he resumed moving toward the Suburban again.

He pulled the door open and slid into the inky interior, the dome light disabled long ago. As though he might see the source of his abrupt discomfort lurking in the darkness, he gripped the wheel, peering into the darkness again. Nothing. No movement.

Stone relaxed, concluding he'd terrorized himself. His jumpiness was residual concern from the call he'd received from that trooper. Everything was fine.

He locked the doors anyway.

Stone shook his head at his own folly. He started the engine and twisted the headlight switch. The darkness retreated in the twin cones of light.

As he backed out of the parking space, he watched the headlight beams sweep across the trees and bushes surrounding the marshal's office and shook his head again.

***

In a stand of aspen trees, couched low to the ground, a black-clad figure watched Stone drive away. Quiet and dark again, Billy Ray slipped away into the night.

Chapter 30

TROOPER DEEGAN'S CALL HAD LEFT Stone hyper-vigilant and uncomfortable. For the first few days, he'd watched the tourists as though examining a line-up of suspected killers. He'd decided to keep the trooper's call to himself. Time passed and as one week turned into two, his angst faded.

Foot patrolling the business section of town afforded him the opportunity to chat with the tourists and interact with the residents and shop owners. His relationships with his deputy, Harry Field, and the mayor, Will, grew stronger day by day.

He spent all the time he could with Molly, eating most of his meals at the Silver Nugget Café. Not that he had an agenda, but his relationship with Molly had started to change—evolving into something beyond a friendship.

He was back to working out and running, although at Silver Lake's altitude, he ran a little slower and for shorter distances. His motivation for staying in shape had changed too. It was no longer only work related. In an Aspen newspaper, he'd found a set of free weights, a heavy bag, and a cable-operated home gym for sale. They found a home in the garage behind his cabin, converted into his exercise room.

His cabin.

Will had surprised him with the house. Stone hated surprises, yet he had to admit he'd liked the cottage and location from the start and felt a sense of comfort in his new home. It was an old log structure located on the southeast corner of Fifth Avenue and Mountain Street on the east edge of town, and it sat on a large lot with no other homes close by. A craggy mountainside dotted with rock outcroppings, clumps of bushes, and stunted pine trees occupied the view across the hard-pack dirt road, Mountain Street.

The privacy it afforded suited him.

Two large blue spruce evergreens stood sentinel at the front corners of his cabin. The detached garage, set back from the cottage on the right side, appeared old and sturdy. Twin dirt tracks, with thick flora between them, ran from the garage to Mountain Street. Clumps of bushes encroached upon the garage and cabin.

The interior had belied the cabin's antique log exterior. Deer antlers mounted to the wall inside the front door served as a hat rack. In the southeast corner, a sofa and two overstuffed recliners, nestled around a coffee table, faced a moss-rock fireplace with a flat-screen TV mounted over the hearth, creating a comfortable sitting area. The northeast corner contained a cozy reading nook with two bookcases against the walls. A small table with a lamp on it separated two high-back leather chairs that filled the space.

Farther into the cabin, a breakfast bar with three stools separated a small dining area from the kitchen. A hallway alongside the kitchen led deeper into the cabin to a single bedroom and a hall bath. Log-crafted furniture added a sense of warmth throughout the cabin. A cellar door off the hallway provided access to the water heater, furnace, and a washer and dryer. At a bit over a thousand square feet, the size fit his needs to a T.

***

Stone had settled into a routine, spending a little time each day working his way through stacks of old reports found in the office file cabinet. Back from morning patrol, he sat at his desk, his coffee mug filled and at the ready, and untied another bundle of old reports. He began to sift through them. Partway through, he uncovered a manila envelope with the name **STONE** and a report number printed on its face. The sight of it hit him in the gut like a sucker punch.

Although he hadn't seen the report for twenty years, it brought back painful memories—including his failed promise. Stone lifted the envelope from the stack and stared at it. Even though it was thin, it felt weighty in his hands and electric to the touch.

Stone remembered this was a copy of the Hit and Run Resulting in Death" report he'd obtained from the sheriff's department when he was the deputy marshal. Because the incident was a county case, the sheriff's department had completed the investigation, so they were in possession of the original report.

No longer, he realized. The statute of limitations was long past, being five years for that particular crime. The sheriff's department would've purged and discarded anything to do with the case long ago.

The clasp broken, he opened the end flap and tilted the envelope on end, so the report would slide out. A smaller, sealed plastic evidence bag slipped out past his waiting hand. Stone's eyes tracked the evidence envelope as it fluttered to the floor.

"What the—" he blurted, upon realizing what it was. He retrieved it from the floor. Sealed with evidence tape, it contained scrapings and flecks of paint transfer from the hit-and-run vehicle. Someone must have sent the evidence to the marshal's office instead of destroying it with the case file.

For whatever reason, the sheriff's department had failed to submit the paint samples to the FBI for analysis ...

"That doesn't mean I won't submit it," he mumbled. Stone's mind began churning. The case was too old to prosecute, but he might have a chance of finding out what make and model of car had struck his parent's car. That was more than he had twenty years ago, and who knew what leads it might produce.

He'd submitted paint samples to the chemistry unit of the FBI's Laboratory Division in Quantico, Virginia from the NYPD Crime Lab and Paint Data Query (PDQ) of the Royal Canadian Mounted Police. The RCMP had a database of chemical compositions of paint from most vehicles marketed in North America post 1973, and those manufactured in Japan and Germany too.

As he turned the evidence envelope over in his hands, looking through the clear plastic at the red flecks, he realized that neither the FBI nor the RCMP would analyze a single sample from Silver Lake, Colorado. Neither agency levied a charge for analysis, but submitting agencies needed to supply a substantial number of paint samples a year. In addition, they would refuse because the case was beyond the statute of limitations.

Stone refused to let any of that deter him. For every obstacle, a solution existed. If his old captain was as good as his word, he could get the analysis done. He found Baxter's smartphone number and called him from his own smartphone.

"Hello, Stone," Baxter answered. "You calling because of Trooper Deegan's warning?"

"No, Cap. We've had no indication that the killer followed me, and I think Trooper Deegan's conclusion was premature. I am keeping my eyes open though."

"I'm guessing you haven't heard that we had another homicide after you left; a double by the same serial killer," Baxter said. "Left another message for you too. He wrote 'Stones a whore'—misspelling whore."

"No, I didn't know that." *Shit,* Stone thought. A rock came to rest in the pit of his stomach. "So, he's active again?"

"No. We had the one double, and they stopped again," Baxter said. "It was two days prior to the murders Trooper Deegan's investigating."

The rock grew heavier and more uncomfortable. "That doesn't mean he's coming to Silver Lake," Stone said.

"Denial's a powerful emotion, Stone. I know you couldn't wait to get away from all this crap, but don't discount Trooper Deegan's suspicions because you don't want it to be true."

The rock became a boulder. "I said I'm keeping my eyes open." Stone realized how defensive he sounded. "Sorry, Cap. Even if he's headed this way, what can I do unless—or until—I have some evidence he's in Silver Lake?"

"You're right," Baxter said. "I didn't mean to preach. I just don't want you to let down your guard."

"I won't and thanks for the advice," Stone said, hoping to end the serial killer conversation.

"So, if that isn't your reason for calling, what can I do for you?" Baxter asked, answering Stone's wish to change subjects.

Stone took a deep breath and refocused on the reason for his call. "You said if I ever needed anything, I could give you a call. I need a favor." Stone explained the incident that resulted in his parents' deaths and the evidence he'd found. "I need an analysis to ID the vehicle year, make, and model, but neither the FBI nor the RCMP will process it for a small mountain town marshal's office—plus, it's beyond the statute of limitations."

"Overnight it to me if you can," Baxter said, without hesitation. "I'll get the results back to you ASAP."

"I can't thank you enough," Stone said, relieved.

"Least I can do under the circumstances."

"What circumstances?" Stone questioned.

"The email you sent to the commissioner created a bit of a stir," Baxter said.

Stone thought he heard the lilt of elation in Baxter's voice and asked, "What happened?"

"I had a personal visit from the commissioner because of your email," Baxter said. "He was interested in the search conducted of your desk and locker."

"I didn't cause you any problems, did I?" Stone asked, concerned. "I had nothing but good things to say about you."

Baxter laughed. "No problems for me. I can't say the same for McFarland. The commissioner seemed pissed enough to lop off some heads as he left."

"I don't feel sorry for McFarland. If it wasn't for him, I'd have finished my career with the NYPD." *And solved the serial killer case.*

"I'm getting a kick out of sitting back and watching events unfold. An internal investigation followed the commissioner's visit, which led to an announcement that both McFarland and Bussard decided to retire at the end of this month. I'd bet a dozen donuts someone might've suggested it would be in their best interest. So, my life just got a lot easier," Baxter said.

"I didn't think anything would come of my email. I sent it to make myself feel better, but with politics and all ... you know."

"One never knows," Baxter said. "So, tell me, how's it going in the Wild West?"

Stone and Baxter continued to converse for a few minutes, then disconnected. Stone grabbed his hat from the wall peg and headed to the post office.

Baxter's words of warning had attached to his brain like a malignant tumor and shrouded him in a mantle of fear. So much for what little peace he'd begun to feel.

Chapter 31

STONE RETURNED FROM HIS MORNING run along one of the many mountain trails surrounding Silver Lake. Although he enjoyed the solitude of his runs, one of the local residents, a feisty squirrel, took exception to his presence and chewed him out from a tree branch whenever he ran past its territory. His jogs along the undulating and jagged paths provided a temporary reprieve from the pressure he'd felt since receiving the call from Trooper Deegan.

It was a beautiful, warm day, at least at Silver Lake's altitude. Summer would endure for another month and a half at least. Stone remembered that as summer faded to fall in the mountains, the indicator would be a subtle change in the Aspen leaves. The days would be warmish, but nighttime temperatures would begin to dip. As the temperature dropped, the quiet green palette of the aspen trees summer foliage would begin a slow transformation into the vivid splash of quaking autumn gold.

The tourist season would begin to wane come fall. He prayed the summer would pass without incident. Silver Lake would continue to have visitors in the fall, although they were fewer and farther apart. Winter would bring the diehard skiers, snowboarders, and ice anglers. By then, most of the shops would've closed for the winter, with the owners relocating to lower regions along the Front Range, like the Denver metro area and Colorado Springs. It would be a lot harder to hide as the tourists thinned out.

Shaved and showered, he outfitted himself in his Silver Lake police attire. He swallowed the remnants of his first cup of coffee of the day. Following an old routine, he emptied and washed the coffee pot and his mug.

As he strapped on his gun belt and snapped on the keepers, the leather retaining straps used to keep the gun belt in place over his pants belt, his smartphone chirped.

"Hello."

"Hey, Stone, it's Rick."

"Hi, Rick. What's going on?" Stone had liked Sergeant Rick Fowler since they first met following his run-in with the bikers while on vacation. They had become friends since his return.

"I'm out at a pretty bad scene," Rick said, the seriousness evident in his tone. "Sheriff Davis asked that I contact you and see if you'd respond."

"Sure, Rick. I'm headed out the door. What's your location?"

"We're at the Mountain View Campground on Route 138, two miles off Highway 82. One of our cars is at the entrance."

"I know the place. Give me fifteen." Stone disconnected and called Molly. "I won't be able to make it for breakfast. The sheriff's department called and asked for my assistance."

"Okay. Try to make it for lunch," Molly said. "I've got a new recipe I'm thinking of adding to the menu, and I need a guinea pig to try it on."

"I'll do my best," he said, smiling.

Stone grabbed his uniform hat from the deer antler hat rack on his way out. He hopped into the Silver Lake police Suburban parked in his dirt and grass driveway, tossed his hat on the front passenger seat, and backed out onto Mountain Street, spinning the rear tires on the cement-like dirt surface as he shifted from reverse to drive.

His intuition told him the call from Rick was bad news, and he felt an uneasy twinge in his stomach.

He maneuvered the Suburban north to the ninety-degree turn onto North Avenue, which he took at too great a speed. The rear wheels scuffed sideways on the hard-pack surface. He sped to Dowd Street—a.k.a. Route 138—beyond the town limits and made it to the campground in twelve minutes. The campground was close to seven miles outside of Silver Lake—and Stone's jurisdiction.

As he slowed to make the turn into the campground, a sheriff's car blocking the entrance moved to allow him access.

He drove a short distance on the gravel road and parked behind several sheriff's department cars. As he exited the Suburban, he saw Rick Fowler striding his way.

"Stone," Rick called as he approached. "Thanks for coming."

They shook hands and Stone asked, "What's going on, Rick?"

"Let's get to the scene," Rick said, motioning for him to follow. "The sheriff's waiting for us. He'll explain."

Stone's stomach twinge knotted at the news Sheriff Davis was on scene. "The sheriff responded?" Stone asked, a sense of dread beginning to envelope him.

Rick ignored the question as they walked a short distance and cut left through an opening in a stand of trees. Stone saw crime scene tape strung in a wide ring surrounding a campsite tucked back into the trees. A deputy stood guard inside the barrier tape, trying to avoid looking at a green dome tent tucked under the canopy of tree branches. He looked as green as the tent.

Sheriff Davis stood on the periphery of the scene, looking grim himself. As Stone and Rick approached, the sheriff rubbed the back of his neck and said, "Jesus. We've had some tough scenes—but never like this." Davis swept his arm toward the tent and added, "The victim's been eviscerated."

Stone swallowed hard at the news. The knot in his gut seemed to grow to the size of a grapefruit. He glanced at the tent and asked, "What can I do?"

"Take a look and fill us in," the sheriff said.

Stone got an uncomfortable vibe from how the sheriff had worded the request. He nodded, ducked under the tape, and headed toward the tent. Along the way, he noticed a couple of piles of vomit.

As he neared the tent, he slowed, focused his mind, and allowed his senses and experience to take control. At the tent entrance, he squatted and peered inside. The strong, coppery smell was overpowering, and what he saw was a bloodbath.

The victim, dressed in his underwear, was on his back on top of a sleeping bag, with deep incisions across his throat and lower abdomen. The suspect had pulled most of his victim's twenty-three-foot-long small intestine from his abdomen. The viscera serpentined like a bloody snake across the victim's body and throughout the tent interior.

Spattered on every interior surface of the tent, blood had flowed in rivulets on the walls, creating a psychedelic effect. Large, congealing pools of blood glistened in the diffused light. The warming air, mixed with the pungent odor, had attracted a large number of green bottle flies. They buzzed the blood pools, some alighting along the edges to drink their fill, and prepare to lay their eggs inside the victim.

Stone stood, backed away from the opening, and circled the tent, coming to a sudden stop at the back. He could feel the color drain from his face, and his knees weaken, as he stared at the cryptic message in blood.

NO GUTS STONE.

He looked across the expanse at the sheriff and Rick, and saw their eyes tracking him as he returned.

"Who'd do this?" Davis asked, as Stone approached. The sheriff looked ill.

Stone looked back over his shoulder at the tent. His eyes shifted to Rick and the sheriff, and he said, "I know who did it."

He explained the New York cases, the call from the Ohio state trooper, and his double murder.

"I didn't hear about any killings in New York," Rick said.

"Shit. I did," the sheriff said. "That was you?"

Stone nodded. "Unfortunately, yes," he said. "I didn't want to accept that he could find me, let alone follow me to Silver Lake."

"We've managed to keep a lid on it," Davis said. "Although I don't know how long we can continue the charade. The campground owner found him and called it in. We convinced him it was in his best financial interest to keep what he'd seen to himself.

"We've told the other campers it's an assault investigation, and we've kept it off the main police channels too, so the press doesn't have wind of it. But you can bet your ass that'll change. If they find the connection to Ohio and New York—and I'm afraid they will—it's going to turn my county—and Silver Lake—into a damn media circus."

Stone was thankful the sheriff avoided the blame game by accusing him of bringing the killer to his county. He already carried enough guilt to crush a lesser man. "I have to tell the mayor. And I guess he'll have to notify the town fathers," Stone said, as though apologizing.

"Follow your protocol," Sheriff Davis said. "I doubt they'll be eager to have this leak."

"I told the trooper I'd call if anything happened. He wants to fly out as part of a joint investigation."

Sheriff Davis seemed to think for a moment and said, "That might be a good idea. As long as you're both clear the sheriff's department is lead on the investigation, the three of you can form a task force and work the case. We can provide any resources you'll need, including help from CBI."

"I'm good with that," Stone said. Following a pause, in which each man stared at the tent, Stone added, "I'm afraid this is just the beginning. It's gonna get a lot worse unless we can stop him. And without a clue who he is ... or where he'll strike, it's gonna be a challenge."

"Let's get started," Davis said. "I've notified CBI, so they'll handle this scene. You two go and start your investigation, unless you need something else from the scene."

"Ask CBI to look for black nylon fibers," Stone said. "We found them at the New York scenes."

Rick walked with Stone back to his Suburban, and they agreed they would meet again when the trooper arrived.

As Stone drove back to town, he struggled with his emotions. He feared what having the killer in Silver Lake would mean. And he felt guilty ... guilty because he was responsible for the killer coming to Colorado. How many people would die if they failed to stop this monster?

By the time he parked the Suburban at the marshal's office, his guilt had morphed into anger. He wasn't responsible for the killer coming to Silver Lake. But he sure as hell intended to put an end to him.

At least this time no political impediments, like those he faced at the NYPD, would cause issues. Sheriff Davis, Rick, and the Ohio state trooper seemed as ready as he was to catch this sick bastard.

Chapter 32

"HE'S THERE?" DAN DEEGAN ASKED.

"Yeah," Stone said and briefed Dan on the murder and the joint investigation Sheriff Davis had authorized.

"I can be in Silver Lake by this evening."

"I'll make reservations for you at the Summit Inn," Stone said. "It's on Dowd Street, on your left, as you come into town. Get yourself settled in and call me."

After they disconnected, Stone called Will's office.

"Stemple Realty. Will Stemple speaking," Will answered in his customary manner.

"I need to see you," Stone said without preamble, hearing the urgency in his own voice.

Stone's abruptness caused a brief hesitation. "Okay ... do you need me to come to your office?"

"No. I'll come to you." Stone decided to walk to give himself time to organize his thoughts. He was unsure how Will would take the news—but was certain the town fathers would be apoplectic.

He called Molly first. "I'm sorry. I can't make lunch either. I'm helping the sheriff's department with that case I mentioned to you earlier. I don't know when I'll find the time to come by the restaurant."

"You have to eat sometime," Molly said, sounding disappointed. "You can fill me in at dinner."

***

Amid the throng cruising the covered boardwalks along Dowd Street, Billy Ray appeared to amble along with no particular purpose, blending with the masses. As he strolled from shop to shop handling souvenirs, only his thoughts distinguished him from the horde. His actual focus was on the man walking with purpose across the street.

What in the hell is Stone doing walking the town instead of investigating the offering I left him this morning? Billy Ray had heard no talk in town either. By this time, he'd expected some kind of buzz—or outright panic.

Someone should've found his bloody gift. The campsite was in the trees, yet visible. And Stone must have seen the message he left.

It was against his instincts to return to any scene. However, out in the sticks with no talk or media to spread the news, he had limited options. He had to drive past the campground on his way out of town so he could check it.

Billy Ray sidestepped a gaggle of vacationers and watched Stone stride along Dowd Street. He looked focused and—*Is he mumbling to himself?* Billy Ray guessed Stone's path would take him to the restaurant to see that woman he seemed sweet on.

Surprised as Stone walked past the restaurant and crossed the street, Billy Ray continued to follow, keeping a safe distance. Stone entered a real estate office. Billy Ray knew another of Stone's friends worked there.

***

They settled in the chairs at Will's desk. Will had locked the door and spun the sign to read "Closed" at Stone's request.

"I'm hearing some rumors from some of the shop owners. What can you tell me?" Will asked.

Even though Sheriff Davis had tried to keep the investigation under wraps, Will told Stone speculation had started flying through the shop owners' gossip network at warp speed. Word was with all the police activity, whatever happened at the campground was something other than an assault. No one seemed to have figured out the actual nature of the crime—yet.

Stone figured the small-town rumor mill would keep digging and questioning until something broke. A slip of the tongue or a discrepancy in the version of events would lead to the lid blowing off and the truth coming out.

Stone sat back in the chair, sighed, and said, "I have something to tell you."

Stone told Will everything, from the New York investigations to the Ohio murders and call from Trooper Deegan, to the tent killing and message found this morning. Finished, they both sat in silence. Stone watched the initial shock on Will's face change as the seriousness of the situation sunk in. The sudden sag in his shoulders and the troubled look on his face said it all.

With a slight tremble in his voice, Will said, "You know, I'll have to inform the town fathers."

"I know. And I hate to ask, but I think I'm going to need your help running interference."

"What do you mean?" Will asked.

"Once we start the joint investigation, we can't have the town fathers interfering. I know their focus'll be on making sure Silver Lake's reputation isn't tarnished and on keeping the revenue flowing. Assure them I'll do everything I can to keep that in mind, but I won't endanger the lives of the tourists or the residents. Their safety must be my first priority."

"Okay," Will said, following a brief pause. "I'll do what I can, as long as you promise me you'll keep me updated so I can keep them informed. If they feel cut off from what you're doing, they'll raise hell. At least one will."

"Fair enough," Stone agreed, unsure he could keep that promise. "My first order of business is to have a meeting tonight with Harry, Rick Fowler from the sheriff's department, and Trooper Deegan, so we can compare notes, collate evidence, and work on a game plan. Do you want to come?"

"No. I don't have any experience with this sort of thing," Will said. "Just let me know your plans."

***

Billy Ray broke off his surveillance and began walking back toward his car. Even though he'd heard no talk about the tent murder, his planning had paid off. By remaining invisible, watching, and listening, he'd gathered a wealth of information. He knew of the relationship between Stone and that woman at the café. By eating at the restaurant, he'd been able to get a good look at her. She'd make a tasty piece of ass. One day, he'd followed her to her house.

By playing the tourist, he'd identified the other cop who worked in Silver Lake. The guy seemed to be a layback country bumpkin. Texas had plenty of them, and they posed no threat.

The warm temperatures, blue skies, beautiful scenery, and shops full of delights cloaked a malevolent reality. No one in this mountain town was safe. And Stone could do nothing to protect them.

Billy Ray scolded himself for his hubris. He remembered a lesson taught to him by his half-brother: know your enemy. Knowledge is power—power to dominate.

With the announcement made, Stone would find the tent at some point. Billy Ray decided to let Stone twist in the wind for a few days. Let him wonder when and where the next attack would take place. Billy Ray decided it needed to be personal, hit closer to home. The woman might make a good target, or maybe that old realtor guy.

His eyelids began to flutter as he sat in his car. Exhaustion from the lack of sleep, he realized. He'd worked a full shift then driven to Silver Lake and spent hours stalking his prey. He was awake all night, waiting for the perfect time to attack.

He was off tonight and could get plenty of sleep, but he had to work the day shift in the morning. It was time to head back—checking the campground on the way, he reminded himself.

As he headed for Highway 82, driving north out of town on Route 138, his path took him past the entrance to the campground.

As he approached, he eased his foot off the gas, letting the car slow. As he prepared to turn, a police car came out of the campground and stopped at the intersection with the highway.

Billy Ray hit the gas, driving past the access road and police car. A quick glance in his rearview mirror showed the police car pulling out and heading in the opposite direction.

They must have found the tent. He looked in the rearview mirror again. Something struck him as odd. Then he realized what it was. The police car was a county sheriff's car.

"Shit," he said. No wonder Stone was unaware of his announcement. The county sheriff's department was investigating.

Billy Ray realized that for future targets, he would have to make sure he attacked them in town if he wanted Stone involved in the investigation. It made no difference in New York. Stone worked all five boroughs, so he was at every scene. It appeared that here, he worked inside the town limits, and the sheriff's department handled things outside the town.

That was the reason Billy Ray had heard no talk in town. The sheriff's department had kept the investigation under wraps for some reason.

CHAPTER 33

THE LAKE LORRAINE LODGE RESEMBLED a French chateau instead of a lodge, as its name implied.

Nestled in a valley formed by glaciers over millennia, its eight floors of elegantly decorated suites, all with majestic views of the surrounding sharp-toothed mountains, catered to the nouveau riche from all over the world. The **L L L** in gilded gold leaf atop the front doors announced to all they were about to enter a five-star resort of unparalleled service, gourmet dining, and regal elegance. A glacier-fed lake of sapphire beauty nestled among the surrounding mountains and adjacent to the lodge sparkled in the sun like a cerulean diamond tiara.

Billy Ray had been fortunate to land a job as a busboy at the lodge. With the low pay and hard work, the lodge had difficulty hanging onto summer staff. But it fit his needs by giving him ample time to surveil Stone and his friends, scout the area, and select his victims.

Because the lodge was nineteen miles east of Silver Lake, on the other side of Independence Pass, it provided him the anonymity he needed. Residents of Silver Lake seemed to avoid the lodge. He guessed it was too rich for their blood.

The lodge staff lived in ranch-style barracks with individual rooms provided as a part of the pay package. To reach the staff living quarters, employees had to hike along a wide, macadam sidewalk marked by a bold sign stating, "Employees Only." The staff quarters, tucked into the surrounding forest, was over a quarter mile from the lodge. The area was even invisible from the penthouse suites' windows and balconies.

Mid-level managers lived in small cabins near the barracks. A well-stocked supply store located in Slave Village—as the employees had dubbed it—provided for the employees' needs. Designed to keep nonworking employees out of sight and away from the paying guests, employees used a large parking lot for their cars with a separate access road that allowed them to come and go unseen. The same road permitted trucks to ferry in supplies for the lodge.

Billy Ray made a point of parking his car in the far reaches of the employee parking lot and making sure no one saw him come and go. He'd provided false information on his application, including his vehicle description and license plate number. It might not have been necessary to be so cautious, but it was in his nature to conceal personal information.

Billy Ray realized that once he started killing, Stone might start looking at any vehicles with a New York license plate. He'd decided to switch plates as a precaution. He knew most people failed to pay attention to their license plates. As long as their subconscious registered a plate on their car, they paid no further attention to it.

New York required one license plate. Billy Ray had witnessed an older couple from South Carolina loading their car one evening, he assumed in preparation for leaving the following day. South Carolina cars used a single plate too. He'd snuck back in the dead of night to switch plates.

The particular style of his New York and their South Carolina plates were close in look and color. The noticeable difference was the symbols. New York had a New York state symbol and South

Carolina's was a palm tree with a crescent moon. It was close enough to avoid attracting the owner's attention, Billy Ray thought.

Odds were, they would continue their vacation without noticing the switch. By the time they figured it out, they would have no idea when or where the switch had taken place. Even if they reported it to the police, and the police ran the tag on their car, it would register as a stolen New York plate. It was worth the risk of switching plates in a hotel parking lot.

The false name on his driver's license and social security card, which he had to produce for employment, was Bill Hatch. He'd chosen the name because he knew the best fake names were close to your real one. That way, if someone called you by name, you had a better chance of recognizing it.

Back in his room, a long day and night behind him, he kicked off his shoes and flopped onto the bed. He was too exhausted to undress. He rolled onto his side and let his mind drift back to happier times.

As he reflected, pleasant thoughts of his past life and his half-brother filled his mind, and he drifted into a deep sleep.

***

Stone briefed Harry on the day's events and plans and swore him to secrecy upon his reporting for swing-shift duty.

Harry left to patrol town, and Stone called Molly again to apologize. "I'm really tied up. I'm sorry, I can't make it for dinner at the restaurant."

"It must be pretty serious. I'm hearing rumors, but no one seems to know what's going on," Molly said, the question left hanging in the air.

"I promise I'll explain things to you when I can," Stone said.

"Whatever it is, be careful, okay?"

"I will. Talk to you in a bit," Stone said. Upon disconnecting, he realized Molly had expressed worry for him. He smiled in spite of the weight he carried for the town's safety.

By eight o'clock, Harry had finished patrolling the town and he, along with Pitkin County Sheriff's Department Sergeant Rick Fowler and Trooper Dan Deegan (who'd arrived in town an hour earlier), gathered in the small marshal's office for their first meeting.

Stone noticed that he and Dan Deegan were close to the same height. Deegan's youthful appearance surprised him. Stone guessed him at no older than thirty-five—if that old. His piercing chestnut eyes, deep set under a knitted brow, belied his youthful appearance.

Stone, Harry, and Rick were all dressed in their official police uniforms. Dan arrived wearing a blue polo shirt over khaki slacks and black loafers ... *Professional casual*, Stone noted.

The introductions complete, they settled at the deputies' table—with Stone at his desk—to begin the meeting.

Rick announced, "The Colorado Bureau of Investigation's out on other assists and can't make it until morning. We've got deputies sitting on the scene, and the county coroner took the body."

"It's out of our control," said Stone. He doubted CBI would find any useful evidence, based on the scenes he'd worked in New York. "At least we're all here now and can get started."

Stone started the meeting by providing a detailed account of the New York murders and the results of the investigations. Dan Deegan followed with the Ohio murders, and Rick Fowler finished with the details of the tent murder.

They each listened, asked pertinent questions, and began a list, Harry writing as each man made a point. They figured the killer:

- Was probably a white male, because most serial killers were.
- Was right handed, based on forensic evidence.
- Wore or used something made of black polyester cotton, based on the fibers found at many of the scenes.
- Preferred to kill up close and personal with his weapon of choice, a non-folding military style knife with an approximate seven-inch, single-edged, serrated blade.
- Showed a lack of formal education, based on the spelling used in the messages.
- Was an organized offender who carefully planned and carried out his murders, except for the Ohio murders, which appeared spontaneous and personal.
- Had a personal vendetta against Stone, based on a perceived wrong done to him or someone close to him.
- Believed Stone was unethical or lied to make a case against him or someone close to him.
- Was obsessed to the point of torturing and killing to locate Stone.
- Had stopped killing for over three months for an unknown reason.

Harry read back the compiled list.

Stone said, "None of that helps us identify him."

"No, but it's the beginning of a profile and shows us his MO and intent," Rick said.

With a hint of anger in his voice, Stone pronounced, "If his intent is to discredit me, it didn't work in New York, and it won't work in Silver Lake either."

"I'd guess he knows that," Dan said.

"Which means he could change his M.O.," Rick said.

"Do you think he'll come straight at me?" Stone asked the group. He hoped the bastard would.

"He might want to make you suffer," Harry said, "by taking out those closest to you first."

With Harry's words hanging in the air like a dying breath's premonition, the group decided to call it a night and meet at the office again first thing in the morning.

Chapter 34

BILLY RAY FELT REFRESHED AND revitalized upon waking. He'd slept straight through from yesterday afternoon until near four o'clock in the morning. He had the day shift today, and it started in the pre-dawn darkness, so he needed to get moving. Besides, he'd slept so long, he had an urgent need to use the john. He stretched and sat on the edge of the bed. Rubbing the sleep from his eyes, he shuffled to the bathroom.

His eyes locked on his reflection in the bathroom sink mirror. The smile slid from his face as he remembered his mission. "You ruined my life, Stone, and I'm gonna make you pay."

***

"That's correct, sir," Miss Pritchett said. "I can see a Pitkin County Sheriff's Department car parked in the lot. I see another car too, and I don't recognize the car or driver. "The way they're sneaking around and having closed-door meetings, I'm sure they're involved in something underhanded."

William Hendrickson had Miss Pritchett provide the vehicle and stranger's descriptions. "Thank you, Miss Pritchett," Hendrickson said, and disconnected without further comment. He'd heard rumors of some investigation in the county and had ordered Miss Pritchett to keep a sharp eye on the marshal's office. As he suspected, it looked like the marshal had involved himself in matters having nothing to do with Silver Lake.

***

Summoned by a curt phone call, Will drove over Independence Pass to the Lake Lorraine Lodge to meet with William Hendrickson, the most belligerent of the town fathers. Hendrickson had refused to disclose the nature of the meeting. Will suspected he knew.

Hendrickson avoided venturing into Silver Lake, as if the town and residents were beneath him. That meant if he had information pertaining to the investigation, it could only have come from one source. With an intrusive eye and a snitches's mouth, Miss Pritchett was the town father's eyes and ears in Silver Lake. If someone had fed Hendrickson information, it was she. No one else in town, even the tenants of buildings he owned, associated with him on the rare occasion he graced the town with his presence, because he was so unpleasant and arrogant.

Will had tried to contact either of the other two town fathers, but they were both away on business. Against his better judgement, he'd decided to wait until all the town fathers were back prior to informing them of the joint investigation. That might have been an error in judgement.

As he drove along Highway 82, he saw numerous diamond-shaped yellow warning signs with deer silhouettes on them. Most had bullet holes or dents in them. He hoped they weren't omens, foreshadowing what was to come.

Will pulled his car to the employee entrance door at the rear of the Lake Lorraine Lodge, avoiding the red-vest-clad valet parking attendants outside the main entrance. Inside the employee door, lodge staff moved along a vascular system of hidden corridors as efficient and silent as blood coursing through the vessels of the body. Signs posted in strategic locations helped them avoid aimless wandering. Will followed the signs directing him to the general manager's suite of offices.

As Will neared the offices, an employee startled him as he whisked around a blind corner on a collision course. An athletic and quick pirouette by the staff member saved them from a collision. Will mumbled an apology and kept walking.

***

The employee came to an abrupt halt and stared at Will's receding form in disbelief. *What's Stone's friend doing at the lodge—and in the back hallways*? Billy Ray felt exposed.

"You lost, Hatch?" a voice barked from behind him.

Billy Ray spun and faced his supervisor, a self-serving asshole who enjoyed running roughshod on his subordinates. "Uh, sorry, Larry ... Mister Stisick," he said, hoping his supervisor missed the flicker of hatred in his eyes. "I got sidetracked for a second."

"I don't want to hear excuses. You've got clean-up duty in the main dining room. Chop-chop," Stisick added with a superior grin, slicing his hand through the air, as though chopping wood with it.

Billy Ray wanted to chop off the offending appendage and shove it up the pissant's ass. Instead he said, "Yes, sir," and moved away. Out of sight, he ducked into a supply closet and waited until his supervisor moved on to harass other employees. The coast clear, he edged his way toward the general manager's offices where Stone's friend had gone.

Outside the office door, he hesitated, unsure what to do. He needed to find out the reason Stone's friend had come. Prepared to wing it with anyone who might challenge him, he opened the office door and stepped inside.

A woman of some dimension filled the space behind a large mahogany desk inside the door. By her hand, a can of sugar-laden pop sat at the ready. Round chocolate balls dumped out of a family-sized bag of candy sat near the pop can. The nameplate on the desk read "Candy Fergusson—Administrative Assistant." As she slid a chocolate orb past her corpulent lips with short, fleshy fingers, Billy Ray drew Candy's attention from the magazine she browsed, and she asked, "May I help you?" As she spoke, her gelatinous neck jounced.

"Uh, yeah. I'm supposed to get some dishes or somethin'," Billy Ray said, trying to act bored with the manufactured task. His eyes scanned the spacious interior of the office. He saw three inner-office doors across the reception area—one open. He could see Stone's friend seated in a chair in the open office, talking to someone out of view. Although unable to hear the conversation, he saw Stone's friend leaning in, explaining something and waving his arms for emphasis.

"I didn't call for a dish pick up," Candy said.

Billy Ray returned his focus to the woman. "Maybe someone else called. I could check in the offices?" he said, stepping further into the reception area toward the offices.

"I'd know if there were any dishes," Candy said. "Everything that goes on in this office goes through me ... including you." The irritation and indignity in her voice stopped him. He needed to avoid a scene. Instead of pushing it, he thought it wiser to back off and evaluate the situation. He turned toward the door and feigned meekness. "You're right. Sorry, Miss ... Fergusson," he said, glancing at the sign on her desk and smiling at her.

Candy returned his smile. She checked him out head to toe, making no attempt to mask her lecherous leering, and said, "That's okay. No harm done."

Behind a counterfeit smile he thought, *You fat, stupid cow.* He bet everything did go through her—right after she shoved it into her big mouth.

As he opened the outer office door to leave, he saw Stone's friend stand and move toward the office door. The other man came into view behind him. Billy Ray noticed his physical appearance was unremarkable, a man in the last half of his fifties of average height and weight. He had a head of short brown hair, capped by a balding pate. The expensive-looking suit he wore failed to hide his paunch.

His face, on the other hand was memorable. Deep-set mean brown eyes accentuated the man's callous face. A narrow-pinched nose over a hostile, lipless slash of a mouth emphasized an ill-tempered person used to having people kowtow to him.

Billy Ray stepped into the corridor, pulling the door part way closed, and listened. The guy in the expensive suit sounded angry.

"I don't give a damn what he said or thinks. His actions are contrary to what's best for Silver Lake, and he's in violation of his job description. I want you to handle this immediately. Is that clear—Mayor?"

To avoid becoming the unwanted focus of someone's attention, Billy Ray moved away. He would need to find out who that angry man was. The older man he'd thought was Stone's friend was the mayor. That was news. The other man sounded like he was some kind of boss over both of them.

Boss or not, if he interfered with Billy Ray's plans, he would put a stop to it—and to him. He needed Stone focused on him and refused to allow this pissant to get in the way. He needed to get some information about the man.

As Billy Ray performed his assigned duties in the main dining room, he chewed over his options. He had no idea who the man was ... but he knew who did. She'd said *everything* in the office went through her. That made the decision easy.

Chapter 35

BREAKFAST AT THE SILVER NUGGET Café was uncomfortable—too many locals pumping him for information. Stone was polite, but firm, and informed each of his interrogators that he couldn't discuss the case. That resulted in a number of curious, and a few hard, stares. At the cash register, he whispered to Molly, "I'll call so we can talk."

As he waited in his office for the others to arrive, Harry's words resonated in his exhausted mind—"Or he might want to make you suffer by taking out those closest to you first." That possibility had resulted in Stone spending the night watching Molly's house from the Marshal's Office Suburban—at least watching it between bouts of nodding off. He left at sunrise to shave, shower, and don a fresh uniform. He realized there was no way he could do surveillance on her every night.

His developing relationship with Molly was obvious to anyone paying attention. He knew the bastard was sick enough to attack her. Stone felt the added weight of knowing danger existed for the hundreds of residents and visitors in homes, hotels, motels, and campgrounds all over the area.

Will too, he realized. Will was his mentor again. He was closer to a father figure than a friend. It was possible that his continued contact with Will had put him at risk as well.

By the time Harry, Dan, and Rick arrived at the office, Stone was on his fifth mug of coffee and had made a fresh pot. With everyone seated, Stone asked the group, "Any thoughts?"

Harry was first to respond. "I think we need to put a guard dog on Molly."

"I thought the same thing," Stone said, avoiding any mention of his nocturnal activity. "But we've got more than Molly to focus on. We need help, and I think I know how to get it."

Harry, Dan, and Rick remained silent, curiosity written on their faces.

Stone took a deep breath and began, "I know the sheriff wants the murder kept quiet, but the town's rumor mill's working overtime. It won't be long until something gets out ... someone slips, or a friend of a friend says something in confidence ... so, what if we clue in the shop owners and ask each of them to keep the information confidential? It shouldn't be a hard sell, 'cause they don't want to drive tourists away either."

Rick sat a little straighter in his chair looking uncomfortable and said, "I don't know, Stone. Sheriff Davis was emphatic. He's worried a leak will open the media floodgates. The last thing we need is a bunch of reporters running amuck and causing trouble."

"We don't have to tell them everything," Stone said. "We tell them we're investigating a murder and the suspect could be in town watching us. Someone's gonna see the CBI guys or vehicle at some point and figure out more's going on than we've said. We ask them to be our eyes and ears and report anything or anyone that seems suspicious. That shuts off the rumor mill and maybe helps keep the lid on this thing a little longer."

"Good idea," Dan said, nodding. "We can't watch everything and everyone."

As they discussed the merits and possible pitfalls of the idea,

Rick called the sheriff for approval. It was a hard sell for Rick. With the sheriff on board, they discussed what information they would provide, and what they would ask the owners to watch for and report. They decided on:

- Anyone following Stone, Harry, Rick, or Dan.
- Anyone watching any of them from a fixed location.
- Anyone asking unusual questions about any of them or the police in general.
- Anyone lingering in town or visiting longer than the usual tourist stayed.

"What if he's an employee?" Dan asked.

"Shit. I didn't think of that. We'd better add that question to the list. Any new employees hired in the last month," Stone added.

"People are gonna want to know who to look for ... I mean, a physical description," Harry said.

"All we know is that he's right handed. We don't even know if he's white, black, or whatever," Stone said, frustrated.

"No point in trying to provide a physical description," Rick said. "Let 'em watch everyone instead of trying to focus on someone based on a limited description that could be wrong or change as the investigation progresses."

"I agree," Stone said as he typed the questions on his computer. He printed a stack of copies and passed them out.

"What if someone wants to know who Dan is?" Harry asked.

"I don't know—can we say he's with your department, Rick?"

"That'll work," Rick said. "He's the FNG," he added, smiling at Dan.

"FNG?" Harry asked.

"Fuckin' New Guy," Dan said, knowing Rick's comment was an attempt to lighten the mood.

"Guess out west, at the ass end of nowhere, I am," he said, smiling back at Rick.

They decided on the pairing and the division of the town and headed out on foot, Stone with Dan and Rick with Harry.

***

"The marshal and his deputy have started visiting all the shops with that sheriff's department deputy and that other man," Miss Pritchett said. "They're involved in something, sir."

"Thank you, Miss Pritchett." Hendrickson said, disconnecting. He stared at his cell phone for a moment and hit the speed dial for Will's office.

Unlocking his office door, Will heard the desk phone ringing. He rushed in and grabbed the receiver.

"Stemple Realty. Will Stemple speaking."

Without preamble, an enraged Hendrickson barked, "Do you have any idea what your marshal's doing?"

Will started to answer.

Hendrickson cut him off and snapped, "Don't bother. I'll tell you. He's continuing to conduct an unauthorized investigation into a county case. Wasn't I clear enough with you?"

Taking a momentary pause to calm his building frustration, Will said, "I've just returned to town. I haven't had a chance to speak with him, so I don't know what he's doing. If you'll give me a little time—"

"I want him gone," Hendrickson yelled into the telephone, cutting Will off midsentence. "Do it immediately!"

Annoyed at Hendrickson's outburst and rudeness, Will said, "I told you the last time you wanted him fired, it takes at least two town fathers and my vote to terminate his employment. I won't agree to terminate him, and you don't have the lone authority."

At length, Hendrickson—sounding like a lit dynamite fuse—hissed, "Fine. We'll wait for the others to return to address his employment—and yours."

In an unusual slip, in which Will allowed his anger to surface, he snapped, "I'm an elected official, not an employee."

At first, Will thought Hendrickson might have had a heart attack, because all he heard for a good fifteen seconds was the background hiss of an open line. As he was on the verge of disconnecting, Hendrickson spoke.

"I have business to attend to and will be out of town until tomorrow night. You'll instruct *Mister* Stone to arrive at my home at ten sharp, prepared to explain his actions. I don't suppose that requires two of us and *you* to approve."

"I'll tell him," Will said. He realized Hendrickson had already disconnected.

Will dialed Stone's smartphone and started telling him of the meeting with Hendrickson and the subsequent call from him.

"Hang on. I'm close to your office," Stone said.

***

Stone introduced Dan to Will, and they all sat in the tiny office. Will had locked the door and rotated the sign to closed.

"Damn it, Will. This is what I was afraid of."

"I understand, Hunter," Will said. "I did my best. Hendrickson had information that I'm certain he got from Miss Pritchett. Remember, I warned you to watch out for her."

"I remember. Look, I don't have the time or inclination to play

Hendrickson's games. What he doesn't get is that we're trying to save the town from a coming disaster. It's a matter of time until this mess bleeds across the town line."

"I understand," Will said. "But Hendrickson's out for blood."

"We're too damn busy trying to catch a killer to concern ourselves with his bruised ego," Stone said. "Meeting's a waste of time. No matter what he says, I won't stop the investigation. He'll have to fire me to stop it."

"If you ignore Hendrickson's order to meet with him, I won't be able to help you. The other town fathers are reasonable but have a low tolerance for insubordination. I believe I can convince them of the necessity of your involvement—but not if you ignore Hendrickson's demand," Will pleaded.

"Shit. Okay, I'll go. Just understand—he's not gonna be happy with the outcome."

Chapter 36

WILL CALLED STONE AND REQUESTED a private meeting to get the information he would need to make a case for Stone's involvement in the murder investigation to the other two town fathers. Harry and Dan went to dinner, and Rick went to brief the sheriff and check on CBI.

As Stone waited for Will to arrive, he thought back on Will's warning regarding Miss Pritchett and his assumption that Hendrickson had gotten his information from her. He'd seen the mysterious Miss Pritchett a few times. One day, as he arrived for work, he saw her standing at her office window, watching him. He waved to her, and she turned and walked away from the window as though he were invisible.

Because she worked for the town fathers, he had no desire to interact with her. However, if she continued to cause problems, she might leave him no choice.

Will arrived and began firing questions prior to sitting.

"How convinced are you that the person who committed the murder at the campsite is the same killer you investigated in New York? And do you and the trooper believe he's the same person who murdered those people in Ohio?"

"I'm one hundred percent convinced, and so is Dan. Hell, Will, he left me a personal note in the victim's blood at the campsite. That's the exact same M.O. he used in New York. What additional proof do you need?"

Will rubbed the back of his neck and looked out the window. "You understand what it could mean to the town if this gets out?"

"Of course I do," Stone said. I don't want to see the town suffer. What other options do we have? What if he kills again, in town this time, and we're sitting on our asses discussing what level of involvement you all think I should have? Do you understand the ramifications of taking that position?"

Will turned his head and looked at Stone. "This is your field of expertise. I'm only playing devil's advocate, so I can tell the town fathers we looked at it from every angle. You know this'll ruin a lot of businesses if it gets out of control."

Stone could see the strain on Will's face and hear it in his voice. "That's what you need to convince the town fathers of, Will. All cases are out of control in the beginning," he said. "That's the reason we need to get aggressive—to gain some control. I need to focus my total attention on stopping this killer. I don't have time to explain my every move to the town fathers. I've got to gather all the forces I can and learn how he thinks and operates. Any distraction could have devastating results, because a lot of people are in danger—and they don't know it."

Will seemed to take a few moments to digest Stone's words, lowered himself into a chair exhaling an audible sigh, and said, "I'll support you on this, Hunter, and I'll do what I can to convince the town fathers to stay out of your way. However, you know they're driven by profit, so if they begin to see a drop-in tourism—"

Stone interrupted. "Silver Lake won't have any profit if this guy turns the town into his personal killing ground. You may want to mention that to them."

An uncomfortable silence followed. Breaking the quiet, Will asked, "Have you considered calling the FBI for assistance?"

"I don't want the Fibbies storming into town—which is what they'd do." Stone envisioned a line of black SUVs snaking along Dowd Street, regurgitating a horde of buzz cut, blue-nylon-jacketed agents with large yellow letters screaming **F—B—I** on their backs. That was the last thing he needed.

"This isn't like New York," Stone said. "It's a lot harder to hide anything in Silver Lake. If we blanket the town with FBI agents, the killer will know and go to ground until things get quiet again."

"You think he'd do that?" Will asked, surprised.

"I'm certain of it. He may be uneducated, but he's street smart."

"What can *we* do? We're a small town," Will said.

Stone heard the rising fear in Will's voice. "We have more resources than you think. The fact Silver Lake's a small town is to our advantage. It'll make it hard for him to hide for long."

"If he got away with killing all those people in New York, what chance do we have of catching him?" Will asked, his words laced with doubt.

"A good chance, because I'm banking on being able to focus on the investigation and you keeping me from getting hogtied by politics," Stone said, "and—because, at some point, I believe he'll want me to know who he is."

"Wh-what?" Will said, a stunned look on his face. "What do you mean?"

"He followed me to exact revenge. For what reason, I don't know. That's the reason I think he may divulge his motive. If he does, that'll lead me to who he is. I can't be sure that'll happen, because this is new to him too. He hasn't been this close to me, or tried anything like this in a small town, so I think he's winging it as he goes. And that's good because he's apt to make mistakes—mistakes that'll lead me to him."

Stone saw the dubious look on Will's face and added, "Look, he may be a sick bastard, but he isn't superhuman. Don't believe the hype you've seen in movies or read in all those thriller novels that endow serial killers with superhuman instincts and complex agendas. The truth is that the vast majority of them aren't that bright. Most of the time, they don't even understand their own motivations. The reason they get away with multiple murders is that they're murdering strangers. If a killer has no connection to the victims, he's harder to identify. Serial killers are just murderers with a deviant pathology.

"Most murderers know their victims, or they're related, so they're easier to catch. But all killers are human, and all humans have habits and weaknesses. In other words, they make mistakes and leave clues. At some point, he'll start devolving and do the same."

Will shook his head and said, "I don't understand any of this. All I can do is pray you can stop him." Will stood and walked to the door. "Please apprise me of any action you plan to take that'll effect Silver Lake."

"I'll do that," Stone said, knowing this was the second time he'd made that promise—one he might not be able to keep.

Stone stood in the doorway and watched Will drive off. He sighed and walked back into the office, pushing the door closed.

Alone with his thoughts, he wondered if anyone understood the subtle balance he struggled to find within himself. To catch this killer meant allowing the cold, suspicious, and calculating part of himself to rear its ugly head again, even though he'd tried so hard to cast off that mantle. He needed to find a delicate equilibrium between the callous man he'd become in New York and the humanity he was so desperate to recapture. It was like dancing across a field of fragile, long-stem crystal wine glasses. One wrong step and he might slice out his soul ... lose any chance of recapturing his humanity.

***

Granted approval by Sheriff Davis, Rick arranged discreet night-time surveillance of Molly and her house. Undercover deputies would make sure she made it home from the restaurant and stayed safe through the night.

Unsure how she might react to a protection detail, Rick and Stone agreed that they would forgo telling Molly. Stone thought that after his meeting with Hendrickson he could get some needed sleep, because nervous energy and caffeine was the fading elixir keeping him upright.

***

Billy Ray finished his main dining room duties and headed for Slave Village. It was past five and the general manager's office had closed for the day. He stopped by the store to purchase a six-pack of pop and several bags of treats to ply the corpulent Miss Candy. He figured she'd have her own cabin instead of a room in one of the dormitories, because she worked in the executive office.

He found her cabin secluded back in the trees. That was good for him—maybe bad for her. Billy Ray approached, seeing lights on inside. Although dusk was a couple of hours away, it was gloomier under the forest canopy. With the inside of the cabin illuminated, he saw her lumbering about through a window.

Steeled for an unpleasant visit, Billy Ray knocked on the door, putting on the broadest, spurious smile he could muster. It could happen one of two ways, he thought. She could tell him what he wanted to know, and they would part company friends. Or she could play the hard ass.

That was okay too—because the forest *was* immense—and dense.

Chapter 37

BILLY RAY'S VISIT TO CANDY'S cabin had been beneficial. Candy had identified the angry man in the office as William Hendrickson, one of the lodge owners and a town father of Silver Lake—whatever that was. She told him Hendrickson was rich and lived in an exclusive gated community outside Aspen called Mountain Meadow Estates. Of greater interest, she'd overheard Hendrickson say he wanted Stone fired.

Based on what Hendrickson said, Billy Ray was sure that Stone knew what happened at the campground and had involved himself in the investigation. It seemed the best way to assure he stayed involved was to stop the lodge owner from interfering.

***

The last thing Billy Ray wanted to do was spend time with the elephantine Candy Fergusson. But she had the information he needed—Hendrickson's address. On his morning break, he paid a visit to the main office. Steeling himself, he opened the door, stuck his head in, and said, "Hi. Got time for a visit?"

Candy greeted him with a large, unattractive smile and said, "Sure. Come on in, Bill. I'm alone."

Following a few minutes of aimless chitchat, Candy began to interject sexual innuendos into the conversation. The smile on Billy

Ray's face veiled the queasiness he felt in his gut. When she offered to get them pop from the vending machine in the hallway, he accepted—anything to get a break from her.

With her out of the office, he would have a chance to get what he came for. Candy extricated herself from her desk chair. Instead of heading toward the office door, she moved in close and whispered in his ear, "Maybe you can come by my cabin again tonight." As if her invitation needed further clarification, she blew her hot breath in his ear. As she stepped to the office door, she gave him a lustful wink.

Billy Ray shuddered away from her lascivious actions. It took all his will power to hold his expression until Candy was out of the office. As the office door closed, his synthetic smile evaporated. He scrubbed at his ear, trying to wipe away the lecherous assault. He spun an old-fashioned Rolodex on her desk and scanned the cards behind the "H" heading until he found Hendrickson's name, address, and telephone number. He scribbled the information on a pad and returned the address caddy to its original location.

Candy returned, and Billy Ray told her he had to get back to work or face his boss's wrath. He told her he would see her tonight.

No way in hell did he intend to make good on that promise.

Escaping the office and Candy's oral obscenities, he began contemplating his options. His job at the lodge had begun to interfere with his plans. Maybe it was time to move on.

He found his supervisor in an empty dining room, haranguing one of his co-workers. "Where've you been?" Stisick scolded, wagging an offending finger. "You're late—again."

With a "kiss my ass" smile on his face, Billy Ray said, "I'm quitting, Larry. I've got enough money saved to do what I want. I'm gonna camp and see the country."

As usual, Stisick's reaction was to berate him and wag his finger in Billy Ray's face. Sick of the hand gestures, Billy Ray reached out and snatched the dining room dictator's offending digit. He twisted the finger hard enough to produce a gap-toothed wince of pain on his supervisor's face.

As he twisted the finger, he leaned close and said, "You know, someday somebody's going to snap this finger off and jam it in your ass, you pissant. You don't want to make it today, okay?" He let the finger go and Stisick scurried out of the room, rubbing his sore hand.

Billy Ray walked to his barracks and packed his belongings. He took his time and sanitized the room, removing all traces of himself, being as thorough as possible. He stripped his bedding and added it to a laundry bin in the hall.

***

Even though a knot had settled in Stone's gut since Will told him of Hendrickson's demand for a meeting, he'd chosen to keep the pending meeting to himself. Dan knew, having been privy to the conversation. Stone was thankful Dan had kept the information—and his advice to himself. The last thing he needed was for the rumor mill to get hold of it. He guessed that by morning, as if by osmosis, everyone would know anyway. He wondered if he would still have a job.

Stone, Rick, and Dan spent the day chasing reports of suspicious persons called in by the shop owners. Careful to keep the contacts friendly, and giving no hint of the real purpose behind the interactions, they stayed busy all day. None of the reports panned out. Stone wondered if his tactic was a waste of time.

Harry had volunteered to work the night shift with backup from the sheriff's department. There was nothing else to do—at least nothing until the serial killer made a move.

***

If he intended to camp, Aspen was the mecca for stores selling all manner of camping equipment. Billy Ray decided to drive by Mountain Meadow Estates first and see what challenges he might face getting to Hendrickson's house.

As he cruised along the street paralleling the perimeter of the property, the ten-foot high brick wall with columns and piers topped with capstones impressed him. The wall sat atop a landscaped slope that succeeded in blocking any view of the houses inside. It might provide a formidable obstacle to climb.

A little farther along the road, Billy Ray drove past the gated entrance. Most gated communities had security personnel who imitated real security. It surprised him to see an alert, and fit, security guard standing sentinel in the guardhouse. A black and white Mountain Meadow Estates security car parked near the guard shack looked like a police car with a blue light bar. Seated inside the car, two uniformed guards conversed.

He would have to be careful.

In Aspen, he wandered until he found a store that appeared to sell everything related to camping and mountain climbing. In addition to buying enough camping equipment to fill a large backpack, freeze-dried food, and a small, powerful flashlight, Billy Ray purchased a climbing rope, carabineer, and a cliffhanger, a device similar to a grappling hook. He added a pair of black sneakers, labeled "Approach Shoes."

How ironic, he thought.

The box claimed the soft rubber soles stuck to vertical surfaces like glue, and they were quiet as death to walk in.

On his way to the cash register, he found and rifled through a rack of topographical maps finding maps of the mountains surrounding the towns of Aspen and Silver Lake. Billy Ray decided to check out some of the other stores in town to see what they offered. It turned out to be a smart move.

In a general merchandise-type shop, he added a small battery-operated portable radio, and a battery-powered lantern to his growing collection of camping paraphernalia. He noticed a map rack on the counter with signage claiming to show movie stars homes in Mountain Meadow Estates. He saw no addresses on the maps, but they showed the street names. That might help him get closer to the lodge owner's house before scaling the wall.

Because he planned a night attack, his black clothing would make him difficult to spot. His plan was to be in and out of the house in a flash. Even if the home had an alarm, he would be a ghost in the night by the time help arrived.

The longer Billy Ray contemplated it, the happier he became with the idea of killing the lodge owner. Stone would understand the message. *This is between you and me, and no one interferes.* The thought gave him chills of anticipation. He saw no advantage to waiting either. The sooner he began making it personal, the better.

Billy Ray gassed his car on the way out of town. Satisfied he had everything he needed, he headed back toward Silver Lake. A few miles short of the turnoff to Silver Lake, he found a campground with open campsites and asked for a secluded spot. The owner pointed out an isolated site on the campground map secured under Plexiglas on the counter. The site was a good distance away from the popular slots nearer the store, showers, and restrooms. Satisfied, Billy Ray paid for a week's rental, drove to the remote section of the campground, and backed his car into the campsite. He erected his new tent and addressed the items in his car, adding the climbing gear to the smaller, black backpack he kept hidden in his trunk.

He opened and flopped into a camp chair, ate a sandwich, and downed a can of pop purchased from the campground's convenience store. Unfolding the topographical map, he searched for a fire road or some other seldom-used side road in the wooded area surrounding Mountain Meadow Estates. Satisfied with what he found, he folded the map and sat back. He was ready.

Relaxed, he smiled and tilted his face skyward, enjoying the warmth of the day as he envisioned the coming night's hunt.

Chapter 38

BILLY RAY MADE HIS WAY across the road and hunkered at the base of the wall. In his stygian clothing and hidden behind a stand of scrub oak, he was invisible to anyone passing. Security might patrol the periphery road, but he doubted it. Or a health nut might jog by at an inopportune moment. *It won't be healthy for them if they do*, he thought, smiling under his ski mask.

Once over the wall, he would move with stealth until he found cover near Hendrickson's house. People liked to landscape their property to give themselves privacy. That seclusion worked for anyone wanting to approach too.

He would watch the house for a short time before making his move. It was early, so he doubted Hendrickson was in bed. What was unknown was if Hendrickson lived alone in the house. He might have a wife and kids. Hendrickson was his target, but if anyone else were in the way, he would eliminate them too.

Satisfied the coast was clear, he stood and began to swing the rope with the cliffhanger attached in a circle by his side. He loosened his grip, and the rope slid through his gloved hands. The weight of the cliffhanger pulled the rope over the wall. The grappling hook struck the wall with a clink. He pulled on the rope until the cliffhanger grabbed the lip of the capstone.

He scanned the area again, climbed the wall, and squatted on top by a column. As advertised, the new shoes had allowed his feet to grip the wall's surface like a gecko and made the climb easy. He unhooked the cliffhanger and lowered it by the rope to the ground inside the wall. He lowered himself, gripping the capstone with his hands and dropped to the grass, quiet as an owl's flight.

Frozen behind a bush, he waited to be sure no one saw him or heard the faint noise made by the grappling hook. He secured the climbing gear in his backpack and removed his favorite knife. Comfortable he was in the clear, he moved off in the direction of Hendrickson's house.

The house was easy to find, being the lone house on the cul-de-sac with lights on. Billy Ray saw motion-activated security lights mounted under the eaves. From a distance, out of range of the sensors, he orbited the substantial structure, surveying the windows. As he circled, he spotted Hendrickson pacing in what looked like a study.

As Billy Ray watched, a butler came into view, carrying a tray. Hendrickson took a glass from the tray and waved off the manservant. Continuing to observe for a few minutes, he saw no other movement inside the house. Since he knew Hendrickson's location, he decided to make his move: take out the butler and go for Hendrickson.

This was the risky part. Billy Ray approached the front door. Large evergreens and other landscaping blocked the view of the house from the street, but his approach tripped the security lights. If someone looked out, they would see him coming in his bizarre outfit and raise the alarm.

He made it to the door unseen and tried the knob—locked.

With no other choice, he rang the doorbell and ducked to the side. He heard the distinctive click of the lock disengaging and repositioned himself in front of the door. As the door began to swing inward, he rammed his shoulder against it, knocking the unsuspecting butler to the floor. The servant grunted from the impact. Billy Ray was on him before he could regain his senses.

Silencing the manservant with a deep slice across his neck, Billy Ray turned and eased the door closed. Stealing deeper into the house, he found the door to the study. Without hesitation, he pushed the door open and scanned the room. Hendrickson stood across the study behind a desk, looking out a window into the darkness. His back was to the door.

"Is that—" Hendrickson began as he turned.

His eyes widened in surprise upon seeing the macabre intruder entering the room. Hendrickson bolted toward the desk. Billy Ray flashed across the room the knife at the ready. He was fast. So was Hendrickson. The time it took to close the distance gave Hendrickson enough time to pull a handgun from one of the desk drawers.

Billy Ray lunged across the desk as Hendrickson raised the gun. He sunk the blade deep into Hendrickson's chest. As Hendrickson staggered back into the wall and crumbled to the floor, he reflexively pulled the trigger. The firearm's explosive concussion echoed through the house. The bullet missed its mark, slamming into the ceiling.

***

Stone pulled in front of Hendrickson's house a couple of minutes before ten—fuming like a toxic dumpsite. He sat in the Suburban, trying to calm himself. It was no use. He was beyond angry. Angry was how he'd started the trip. Now he was volcanic—ready and spoiling for a fight. His outrage at Hendrickson's interference had increased exponentially as each mile had ticked by on the odometer.

He burst forth from the SUV, slamming the door. As he strode toward the front of the Suburban, a muffled gunshot from an unknown location inside the house stopped him in his tracks.

Pulling his pistol, he stared at the front door. He damn near fired as it swung open and the blood-covered butler staggered out and fell to the ground. Stone rushed to his side and felt for a pulse. The man was dead.

Stone crouched low and dashed to the edge of the door. A quick peek revealed no one waiting to take a shot at him.

"POLICE!" he shouted into the empty foyer.

He followed another quick look by rushing through the doorway into the house. Taking cover against the far wall of the foyer, he strained to hear any noise that would alert him to the perpetrator's location. The house was quiet as a tomb.

Stone dropped low to the floor and took a longer peek. Light spilled from a doorway on the left side of the hall. Other than the foyer and room light, the house was dark.

Without a sound, he moved out of the foyer and used the dark recesses of the hallway to make his way toward the open door. Outside the room, he listened again for any unnatural sound. Hearing nothing, he chanced a quick look into the room. What he saw made him freeze. A bloody message stained the far wall. It read:

NO ONE INTAFEERS.

A window near the message stood open. The house's security lights bathed the side yard with bright floodlight. Stone refocused his attention and rushed into the room at an angle assuming a firing stance. He swung his pistol in an arc, covering the room. Empty. His pistol held at the ready, he moved toward the desk.

As he neared, he saw Hendrickson seated on the floor, leaning against the wall. His head lolled on his chest, and his arms lay limp at his sides. He clutched a revolver in his right hand. The note hung above him like a gravestone epitaph.

Stone rounded the desk and removed the gun from Hendrickson's hand. He felt for a pulse. Thready, but Hendrickson was alive. His blood-soaked shirt had a tear in it near the left breast pocket. Stone could hear sucking and hissing sounds coming from the wound and saw frothy blood bubbling through the rip.

Stone had seen enough knife wounds to know what it was—a punctured lung resulting in a sucking chest wound. If he failed to seal the hole, Hendrickson would slip into a coma and die. Stone began ransacking the desk drawers. At last, he found what he needed. He ripped open Hendrickson's shirt, exposing the wound. Blood spurted out of the hole like foamy lava burping from a volcanic vent. He took the plastic bag and pressed it into and over the wound. Hendrickson was out cold but moaned as Stone worked on him.

Pressing the bag in place, he pulled his portable radio from his belt with his other hand. His hands coated in slippery blood, it was difficult to hold onto the radio. Fumbling with the knobs, he got the switch on and keyed the mike. "Silver Lake One to base. CODE ONE! I say again, CODE ONE!" That meant an officer needed immediate assistance.

"Base. Go, Silver Lake One."

Stone explained the situation and called for two ambulances and the sheriff's department to respond hot. "Notify Mountain Meadows Estates security too," he ordered. Although he felt confident the perpetrator had fled, he would feel less exposed with some backup until the sheriff's department arrived.

***

As paramedics began to move the gurney, Hendrickson regained consciousness and reached out, grasping Stone's arm. His pleading eyes fixed on Stone as his lips moved under the oxygen mask. All that came out of his mouth was a trickle of blood. Stone leaned close. The town father whispered something.

"I don't understand," Stone said.

"We've got to move," a paramedic commanded, hip bumping Stone out of the way.

Stone watched, wondering what Hendrickson had tried to say, as the ambulance sped off into the night.

Chapter 39

HOLY SHIT, **BILLY RAY THOUGHT** as he drove toward the campground. That had been close—too close. He barely had time to leave a message. His escape out the window was pure survival instinct, triggered by someone shouting police. *Someone who sounded like Stone,* he thought.

Billy Ray's quick thinking gave him time to get across the backyard, crash through the trees, and scale the wall. Outside the perimeter of the compound, a dash across the road put him into the forest, which afforded him cover. His escape successful, he wiped the perspiration from his face and neck with his gloved hand and rubbed the moisture onto his pant leg.

As his mind played back how events had unfolded, he realized how lucky he was no cops had pursued him. He had no idea how many cops had come—or how they even knew to respond to the house. He was damn lucky.

Hendrickson had surprised him too. Aggression from a victim was unusual. His victims froze—like deer caught in a car's headlights. He was aware of the fight-or-flight response, however, upon seeing a black clad apparition, his victims confused synapses misfired for the few seconds it took him to end their lives.

The unexpected move by the old man had thrown off Billy Ray's timing. If not for his quick reaction—a last second lunge across the desk—it would've been him bleeding on the floor. Even with his speed, the pissant managed to get off a shot as he fell. It missed, but was too close for comfort, and it was so loud the high-pitched whine in Billy Ray's ear felt like he had a microphone feedback squeal in his head.

Billy Ray wondered if his quarry was dead. Even under the circumstances, the stab wound hit in a good spot. He felt it would do the job.

The message he left in Hendrickson's blood served two purposes. He wanted to make it clear no one would get in his way. And he wanted to announce that the attack on Hendrickson was no coincidence.

Billy Ray eased the car along the dirt driveway to his campsite. The faint crunching of twigs and leaves under the car's tires worried him, and he scanned the area. No one was out, because it was too late to wander the campground. He could see lights on inside some of the trailers and a diffused glow radiating from a few tents.

He backed his car into his campsite, killing the lights and engine. In case some neighbor got nosy, he sat in the darkness of his car, surveying the campground. When he felt it was safe, he exited the car and stripped off his ebony clothing. The chill in the air caused him to shiver. Changing and concealing his hunting clothes and knife in his backpack, he walked to the shower room to bathe.

In the light of the room, he saw that he'd transferred blood from his gloves as he wiped the sweat from his neck and face. He stripped and showered, lucky again that no one had seen him with blood on his face.

Back inside the tent, he squirmed into his sleeping bag, allowing the warmth of the bag to relax his tense muscles. As he slipped toward sleep, he thought it might be a good idea to keep a low profile for a bit. He suspected the police would descend like a hive of killer bees, suspicious of everyone for a few days.

***

An army of cops from every jurisdiction in the area and Mountain Meadow Estates security descended on the scene. Stone sought out the senior Pitkin County Sheriff's Department deputy on scene, a Sergeant S. Nichols, according to his nametag.

Stone wasted no time briefing the sergeant, which resulted in a team of officers sweeping the area looking for the suspect and evidence. Deputies and Aspen police secured the crime scene. Sergeant Nichols had one of the deputies who'd cleared the house get a blanket to cover the butler.

Stone gave the sergeant his smartphone number and cleared from the scene. He ran his emergency lights the short distance to Aspen Valley Hospital. Within a few minutes of Stone's arrival, Sheriff Davis appeared with an entourage of brass bars and stars from the sheriff's department and Aspen Police Department.

Hendrickson was an important figure in these parts, so everyone wanted to put in an appearance. Of course, no one could do a thing except clog passage through the cop-infested halls. Aspen Valley was an excellent hospital with a superb staff. They decided that for trauma this serious, they needed to airlift Hendrickson to Denver Health Services, one of the best trauma hospitals in the entire country. The doctors worked on stabilizing him for transport. As everyone in law enforcement waited, hoping Hendrickson would regain consciousness long enough to provide some information, a helicopter landed on the hospital's helipad to airlift him to Denver.

AirLife paramedics loaded Hendrickson into the helicopter and lifted off as cops watched and the local press snapped photos. The helicopter reduced to a blinking light in the night sky, Sheriff Davis turned to Stone and said, "At least we've got CBI close by, working the campground."

Stone nodded and turned to leave.

The sheriff called out, "Stone, I'll need you to come to the department, so we can get your statement. You're a material witness to at least one murder—maybe two."

"On my way," Stone said.

***

The white-faced industrial clock on the wall of Sheriff Davis' office read one-twenty-seven. Stone's head bobbed as he fought a losing battle with exhaustion. It was all he could do to keep from nodding off, since the adrenalin surge and caffeine buzz had worn off. The emergency over and his initial report and interview done, his system began shutting down. An overload of anger, fear, and tension in the last few hours, combined with a lack of sleep, had taken its toll. With every minute that ticked by on the clock, his ability to stay focused eroded bit by bit.

Prior to writing his statement, CBI had collected a sample of the blood from his hands before allowing him to wash off the rest. In the bathroom mirror, he saw the bloodstains on his uniform shirt, and his fogged mind thought, *I won't get those stains out.* Laughing at himself, he realized what a strange and unimportant observation that was. The shirt was evidence.

He stared blankly through the slats of the vertical blinds covering the large office windows. In Stone's fatigued mind, the brown uniform-clad deputies scurrying around in the outer office looked like gerbils in a cage. The din drifted in through the closed door.

***

The office door burst open, waking Stone. He'd nodded off without realizing it. Stone lifted his head and looked at the open door as Will Stemple and Dan Deegan rushed into the office. The sheriff followed, with Rick Fowler dressed in civvies close behind.

"Are you all right?" Will asked, staring at Stone's bloodstained shirt.

Their sudden appearance snapped Stone back from his stupor. "I'm fine. What're you doing here?" Noticing Will had fixated on his shirt, Stone pointed at the bloodstains and said, "That's Mister Hendrickson's."

Will shifted his eyes and said, "Harry heard your radio transmission. I called Dan, but with the mayhem, it took us awhile to find you."

Stone noticed that Will appeared animated and agitated. "Is Harry here too?" Stone asked.

"He wanted to come," Dan said. "I suggested it might be better if he maintained a presence in town."

Stone thought a second and said, "Good call."

"I can't believe this happened," Will blurted. "If he can get to one of the town fathers, no one's safe. What're we going to do?"

Stone looked at the faces of his fellow investigators and said, "That's a good question. Any ideas?"

Chapter 40

SHERIFF DAVIS, STONE, DAN, AND Rick looked back and forth at one another. No one spoke. Will shifted his gaze from man to man, fear etched on his face.

Awake again, feeling as though he'd gained a second wind, myriad thoughts careened through Stone's mind like the steel ball in an old pinball machine. At length something clicked, and he looked at Will and said, "Wait a minute. How'd he know you met with Hendrickson?"

Everyone looked at Will in bewildered silence.

"I didn't tell anyone other than you," Will said to Stone.

"Where'd you make the call from?"

"From my office ... alone," Will said, defensiveness in his tone.

Sheriff Davis interrupted and said, "I'm going to leave you gentlemen to figure this out. I've got a mess to contend with, including a shit storm of media descending on us."

The sheriff left, and Stone refocused on Will and asked, "Where'd you meet with Hendrickson?"

"In his office at the Lake Lorraine Lodge."

"Could anyone have overheard your conversation?" Rick asked.

"Mister Hendrickson was, as is his nature, agitated and loud. I'm sure the office secretary heard him."

"Anyone else?" Rick asked.

"I didn't see anyone else."

"That means the secretary either told our suspect or he overheard her telling someone else," Stone said. He sensed the possibility of a break in the case. "We need to get to her. The killer's going to figure out she's a potential witness too," Stone said, bounding from the chair.

"The Lake Lorraine Lodge is outside our jurisdiction," Rick said. "It's in Lake County, *and* it's the middle of the night."

Stone knew what to do and his mind shot into high gear like a fine-tuned racecar. He headed for the office door. "The hell with jurisdictional boundaries or the time. This is our first solid lead. We don't have time for niceties. It'll be easier to ask for forgiveness than wait for permission."

As Stone pulled open the office door, he glanced back and asked, "Anyone coming?"

Rick and Dan looked at each other. Rick gave a "what the hell" shrug and followed Stone out the door.

***

Billy Ray snapped awake. He wondered what had pulled him from such a deep sleep. In the recesses of his mind, a prickly sensation had come to rest and scratched at the door of his *prefrontal cortex*. What was it that kept gnawing at him?

He stared into the inky tent interior trying to figure it out. At length it struck him like a thunderbolt. Stone was smart. He would wonder how the person who attacked Hendrickson had discovered his interference. That would lead to a question. Where'd Hendrickson and the mayor meet? Stone was sure to check the lodge and ask who might have overheard the conversation. And that would lead him to Candy.

Shit.

Billy Ray had shown an interest in Hendrickson—maybe he'd appeared a little too interested. He was in the office as part of the argument took place. He asked Candy about Hendrickson at her cabin. The same day he promised to see her after work, he quit his job, told his boss he intended to camp, and attacked Hendrickson.

She was the weak link. It was a mistake to let her live. With her gone, all they would know was that he was a temporary employee named Bill Hatch who left to go camping—an all too common occurrence. Temporary employees came and went all the time.

If they questioned Candy, she'd tell them he'd asked questions about Hendrickson. That could give them the link they needed to make him a suspect, and too many people had seen his face.

Billy Ray knew what he had to do.

He fumbled through his clothing piled inside the tent until he found his lantern. He clicked it on and looked at his watch. If he got moving, he could arrive before the day shift woke to begin preparations for breakfast. With the cops all focused on Hendrickson over by Aspen, he had a clear shot at Candy.

With a sense of urgency knotting his gut, he dressed in blue jeans and a pullover shirt. He lunged out of the tent and began the drive to the Lake Lorraine Lodge. On the way, he began planning how to get to her. Tucked into the trees, her isolated cabin would provide the cover he needed.

He remembered Candy was paranoid and locked her cabin tighter than her grip on her last candy bar. He would have to turn on the charm again to get her to let him in. Once inside, the rest would be easy. Except hauling her bulky carcass into the woods, he reminded himself.

***

As the two police vehicles skidded to a stop, their overhead emergency lights flashing, Stone saw the startled Lake Lorraine Lodge night doorman back into and trip over an ashtray stand outside the main doors. The four men bolted from the vehicles. The attendant had a frightened look on his face as the men rushed him. Stone demanded, "Get the manager." The doorman failed to move until Stone barked, "Move!"

The porter turned and scampered to an office located behind the check-in counter. In a high-pitched, panicked voice audible from the main entrance, he squealed, "There're cops demanding I get you. One's got blood all over him."

Stone looked at his uniform and at the other men. He shrugged and said, "Guess I should've changed first."

The manager rushed from the office, bleary eyed, with his tie loosened and his collar unbuttoned. He slipped into his suit jacket as he approached. "Wh-what's going on?" he asked, staring wide eyed at Stone's uniform.

Stone demanded, "We need to get in touch with the main office secretary right now."

"Wh-what for? The night manager stuttered. "I should notify the general manager."

"We don't have time for that," Stone said. "Get us to her—now."

"O-okay," he said, his nervous eyes darting from man to man. "Let me call Mister Ralston. I'm just the night manager."

Stone reached out and grabbed the manager by the lapels. The night manager's eyes bulged as he tried to back away. "Damn it, move!" Stone yelled into the man's face.

That seemed to provide the motivation he needed. Stone released the lapels, and the manager moved with purpose. He obtained the information and escorted the quartet to Candy's cabin, as if his life depended on it.

***

Shaken by her abrupt awakening, Candy Fergusson panicked at the banging on her door. She cringed in a corner until she realized it was the night manager yelling for her to let him in. She opened the door a crack and peeked out.

They gave her time to put on her robe and slippers, and then the entourage surrounded and rushed her to the lodge. Embarrassed by her attire and the curlers in her hair, she tried to hide her face as lights popped on in the surrounding buildings. Inquisitive employees craned their necks at the windows as they tried to see what all the commotion was, their eyes tracking the strange group as it hurried though the compound.

***

Billy Ray turned into the access road that led to Slave Village. As he approached the parking lot, he could see light glowing through the trees. He killed his headlights and cut the engine. As quietly as possible, he walked toward Candy's cabin on a dirt path that wandered through the trees. Nearing the cabin, he saw light in her window and shadowy movement behind the curtain. He ducked behind a tree as the cabin door flew open and light spilled out, illuminating the darkness.

From his hiding place, he watched Stone, the mayor, and two other men exit the cabin with Candy in tow. They headed toward the lodge. Billy Ray ran back to his car and drove with his lights off until he was out of sight of the lodge.

"Shit! Shit! Shit!" he shouted, turning on the headlights as he sped along the highway. *How in the hell had they gotten to her so fast?* He would have to disappear. The campground was no longer a safe haven for him. That meant he would have to put his plans on hold.

"Damn you, Stone."

Chapter 41

SEATED IN THE MAIN OFFICE, surrounded by three police officers and the mayor of Silver Lake, Candy Fergusson looked like a woman on the verge of a panic attack. She shivered as though someone had dumped her into the lodge's glacial lake.

"Do you remember seeing Mayor Stemple in this office the other day?" Stone asked.

"Yes. He came to see Mister Hendrickson," she answered, her nervous eyes darting from face to face.

"Did you happen to hear any of the conversation between Mayor Stemple and Mister Hendrickson?" Stone questioned.

Candy hesitated, tears welling in her eyes as she looked from Stone to the mayor and back.

"You're not in any trouble," Will explained. "Go ahead and tell him what you heard."

"Uh ... okay," she said. "I ... uh ... I heard Mister Hendrickson yelling at the mayor. He said he didn't want the marshal ... uh, you ... involved in a county investigation. And he told the mayor to fire you."

None of what Candy said was news, so Stone moved on to his most important question.

"This question is critical, Candy. You won't be in any trouble as long as you tell the truth."

Candy nodded, her eyes wide in anticipation.

Stone hesitated, then asked, "Did you tell anyone else of the conversation between Mister Hendrickson and Mayor Stemple?"

"Heavens no," Candy blurted out with conviction. "Nothing discussed in the office is ever repeated by me—to anyone."

Stone had expected Candy to say yes. Her answer threw him off and left him unprepared to ask another question. He looked to Dan and Rick for help.

Rick jumped in. "Was someone else in the office who might've overheard the conversation?"

Candy hesitated, then said, "Uh, he left as Mayor Stemple and Mister Hendrickson came out of Mister Hendrickson's office."

"Who left?" Dan asked.

"A friend of mine. He works ... uh ... worked for the lodge—until he quit. His name's Bill. He worked in food services."

The excitement in the room was electric. Stone could feel the hairs on the back of his neck prickle at the news. Each man showed a slight reaction upon hearing a name put to their elusive suspect.

"I know you said you don't discuss what's said outside the office, and I believe you," Rick said. "But did you ever have a conversation with Bill in which Mister Hendrickson's name came up ... like on a date or something?"

Candy blushed and said, "Bill did mention him in my cabin that night. He wanted to know who he was, that's all."

Stone's mind was on fire. They had confirmed Bill had gotten Hendrickson's name from Candy. If they could verify Bill got his address from her too, he would be a solid suspect. "Did Bill ever ask you for Mister Hendrickson's address?"

"No—but that reminds me. I have his address in my Rolodex. I left Bill alone in my office yesterday to get some pop. After he left, I noticed it flipped to a different name card than the last one I'd looked at. I didn't think anything of it."

"Candy, could you help a sketch artist do a drawing of Bill?" Stone asked.

Candy nodded and asked, "Is Bill in trouble? Did he do something wrong?"

"Dan, why don't you and Candy fill in the details, and you can explain what's going on to her. We'll go speak to the manager," Stone said, pointing toward Will and Rick.

As soon as Stone, Will, and Rick were out of the office Rick said, "I'll ask Sheriff Davis if we can put a couple of female deputies on her for protection. I'd better call him. He'll want to notify Sheriff Yates we're conducting an investigation in his county."

"Do you guys have someone who can do a composite sketch?" Stone asked Rick.

"One of our deputies is a pretty good sketch artist," Rick said. "I'll ask the sheriff to send him out."

"I'll have the manager pull Bill's personnel file and see what I can get," Stone said.

"What can I do?" Will asked.

"You're doing it," Stone said. "Your verifying Candy's statement as accurate was a huge help. I'm sure at some point, I'll need something else from you. Are you okay hanging in for a while longer?"

"To be honest," Will said, as he looked at Stone's shirt again and shuddered, "I'd rather be with you than alone in Silver Lake at the moment."

As night edged toward day, Stone, Rick, and Dan began interviewing different employees who knew or worked with Bill. Upon interviewing Bill's immediate supervisor, Larry Stisick, Stone discounted everything he offered because of his attitude. As he told what he knew of Bill, he spat the words with such derision, there was no mistaking his contempt. That made him an unreliable witness.

However, one thing Stisick said was of interest. He said Bill had quit to go camping.

"Will, can you compile a list of campgrounds in the area when we get back to town?" Stone asked.

"Sure. My pleasure."

"Do you think he could hide in one of the abandoned mines in the hills around town?" Stone asked.

"Doubtful," Will said. "A few years back, the county engineers blew the mines that hadn't already collapsed. As far as I know, they're all sealed."

Sheriff Yates responded to the Lake Lorraine Lodge with detectives and deputies in tow. Stone and Rick briefed the sheriff and his detectives on the events to date. The sheriff volunteered a female deputy to assist with twenty-four-hour protection of Candy and his detectives to assist with the monumental task of all the pending interviews.

By the time the sun spilled over the mountaintops, the detectives were on the last of the interviews, deputies had secured Bill's room until CBI could respond to their third scene, and the sketch artist had started working with Candy. The speed of the investigation pleased Stone. They had made excellent progress.

It surprised Stone that no one interviewed had ever seen Bill near or in a car. Although his personnel file listed a vehicle, a registration check through the sheriff's department dispatch showed the information to be false. Stone suspected the other information he'd been able to gather was phony too. Other than a name and a copy of his New York driver's license, which showed no record found upon running it, most of the required information lines were blank. Even the copy of the driver's license was so poor Bill Hatch's facial features appeared dark and obscured.

The general manager, Sam Ralston, arrived with a flourish. Stone noted he was of average height and weight, had a clean-shaven narrow face, and wore his trimmed dark hair slicked back. He wore an expensive suit that Stone bet rivaled a month of Stone's pay and glassy shined loafers with tassels. *He's a tight-assed metrosexual,* Stone thought. Only someone like that would wear shoes with tassels.

As the GM took charge of his staff and directed them to specific tasks, he seemed to think that it was within his authority to question law enforcement personnel too. He was condescending in his speech and pompous in his attitude, which pissed off Stone. It was as though all this was a great and unwarranted inconvenience; an affront directed toward him.

Stone, too tired and angry to deal with his arrogance, cornered the GM and interrogated him on the lack of information on Bill Hatch's application.

Acting offended by Stone's bluntness, the GM informed Stone they needed a temporary fill-in. They had brought him on as a busboy with no customer contact and no access to the rooms. Therefore, he saw no issue. Stone wondered if the lodge owners might take exception to the manager's blasé attitude toward screening prospective employees.

Returning the manager's sarcastic attitude, Stone said, "I guess asking if you completed a background check would be a waste of my time."

The general manager gave Stone a withering look and asked, "Anything else I can do for you, marshal?"

"No thanks. You've already been a huge help."

It looked like little else needed doing at the lodge, except CBI's check of Hatch's room. As things slowed, and they prepared to leave, Sheriff Yates approached Stone and said, "I'll make sure copies of the composite sketch get delivered to your office."

Stone thanked him for all his assistance. He apologized for the way they had bum-rushed into his county without contacting him first.

The sheriff said, "I understand. I think under the circumstances, I'd have done the same thing."

As they drove back toward Silver Lake, Stone realized he felt like a predator instead of like prey. It was time for Bill Hatch to run scared.

PART IV

PREDATOR AND PREY

Chapter 42

BILLY RAY SAT IN HIS tent, anxiety overshadowing the anger he felt. If they identified him, which they were certain to do with Candy running her fat mouth; they would check his personnel file and find the copy of his phony New York driver's license with his photograph.

A background check would follow in New York too. They would learn the license was fictitious.

He'd told his asshole supervisor he intended to go camping. They would find that out too and start checking all the campgrounds. If he were smart, he would pack his gear and get the hell out of Colorado. Let them suspect he killed the guy in the tent and Hendrickson. No real proof existed—as long as Bill Hatch disappeared.

He needed to calm himself and think things through. A change of appearance was one thing he could do. Grow a beard, dye his hair, and maybe add some fake glasses.

He needed to get rid of his phony driver's license and vehicle registration. The switch he'd made with his license plate turned out to be a better move than even he thought. A South Carolina license plate was innocuous. His New York plate would've drawn Stone to his car like a bee to honey.

He sat on his sleeping bag, contemplating his options. No way would he run. His mission was his priority. Stone had to suffer first—and then die.

Regardless, it was time to move ... but where? With his flashlight, Billy Ray rummaged through the pile of supplies in his tent and found the topographical map he'd purchased. He scrutinized the campgrounds and individual campsites.

The Aspen area was too expensive and too close. If he moved even further away, his exposure traveling would be too great. They were sure to plaster his photo all over the state. Even a change in appearance was no guarantee he would go unrecognized. No public place was safe for him. That narrowed his choices.

He noticed a number of abandoned mines, in the mountains surrounding Silver Lake, marked by X symbols on the map. An abandoned mine would give him shelter and keep him away from prying eyes—if he could find a suitable one close enough. He could strike at night and disappear right under Stone's nose.

The longer Billy Ray considered the idea, the more it appealed to him.

He had all the supplies he needed to camp. All he needed was a water supply. Several of the abandoned mines had blue lines near the X's. The map legend showed a blue line indicated a stream. He chose one that overlooked Silver Lake and provided the necessary concealment.

He packed his gear in preparation for the arduous hike that lay ahead. Policing the campsite, the sun had risen by the time he was ready to leave. He loaded his gear and eased his car out of the campground.

Paranoid, Billy Ray decided to forego parking at the trailhead. Even with the South Carolina license plate, he worried someone could've seen him near, or in, the car and might be able to provide a make and color. He drove deep into a fire road across the highway from the trailhead parking lot and tucked the car back into the trees. He hoisted the heavy backpack onto his shoulders and fastened the padded waist belt and sternum strap. Unfolding the topographical map, he traced the route with his finger. The elevation lines on the map indicated a steep climb ahead.

He followed the trail for a couple of miles until he found the cutoff that led to the mineshaft. Overgrown with grass and shrubs, he'd come close to missing it ... would've if he'd tried to find it without the map. The effort it took to climb the trail left him breathless from both the steepness and altitude. Littered with scree, the flat loose rock that skidded away as you shifted your weight from foot to foot, traction was tenuous at best.

The precipitous trail changed direction, zigzagging back and forth across the mountain. The switchbacks helped cut the steepness of the climb but lengthened the distance to reach his goal. Several times he slipped and came close to falling.

Exhausted, he reached the mine and found the entrance blocked: two chain-link gates held closed with a rusted chain and padlock blocked the entrance. An old faded sign wired to one of the gates warned, **DANGER – KEEP OUT. MINESHAFT IS SUBJECT TO CAVE-IN**. The rest of the sign was too faded and rust covered to read. He pulled on the gates to test the give, spotting a wide enough gap at the bottom. As he stood on top of the rust-streaked tailings that cascaded in a motionless waterfall over the hillside, he looked toward Silver Lake. His view of the town blocked by the thick stand of trees, the reverse would be true too.

An unforeseen benefit he discovered was an unobstructed view of part of the trail from the mine entrance. It would be difficult for anyone to approach unnoticed. He surveyed the area, spying a rusty ore cart hidden in the thick vegetation. The gurgle of a stream close by broke the silence. Billy Ray shucked off his backpack and wriggled though the narrow opening. He pulled his backpack through behind him.

Daylight penetrated a short distance into the cave-like opening. Without a flashlight, no way would he dare venture inside. Many of these old mines held unpleasant surprises—shafts descending hundreds of feet and offshoots that could spin you through a labyrinth of interconnecting tunnels until you became so disoriented you might never see daylight again.

He clicked the light on and probed the floor, walls, and ceiling with the beam. Satisfied the way was clear; he walked with care into the shaft. A short distance into the mine he saw the rusty remains of the metal rails used to guide the ore carts. Descending at a slight angle and moving a hundred feet or so into the shaft, the tunnel made a gradual right turn. He stopped and shined the flashlight beam ahead. The air temperature had dropped a few degrees and a dank, musty smell hung in the air.

"HELLO!" he shouted into the shaft.

"'Ello!" his echo answered.

Upon completing the turn, he could make out something off in the distance. As he approached, the apparition became clear. A cave-in had blocked the shaft.

"Shit."

Through debris composed of rocks, dirt, and splintered support beams he could see small openings. The cave-in looked old, but not substantial. If he could move enough of the rock without causing another cave-in, passage was possible. He dropped his backpack and propped his flashlight on it, lighting the debris pile. Tentative at first, he moved one rock at a time, listening for telltale sounds that might indicate another cave in. None of the debris shifted, and he heard no sounds other than his own grunting. With a great deal of effort, the hole grew large enough for him to walk though, bent over. His backpack and flashlight in hand, he moved through the opening, hoisted the pack back on his shoulders, and continued along the tunnel.

He continued to descend, he figured, because the temperature continued to drop. Rounding another bend, Billy Ray found himself in a large subterranean cavity. The flashlight beam showed the cavern to be a good twenty by twenty and every bit as high. Although the floor was flat and sandy, rocky protrusions jutting from the walls and ceiling and dark crevices in the walls indicated the chamber was a natural phenomenon.

His flashlight beam found a broken ax handle with the initials BD carved into it and a few old wooden boxes scattered on the floor. Across the span, two other tunnels led off into the darkness. He felt a light breeze.

The location was ideal. No one would ever look for him in an abandoned mine. With a locked gate covering the entrance, it appeared impenetrable. He would establish his base camp, fill his canteen and collapsible water bottle from the stream, and cut some brush to wipe away his boot prints at the mine entrance.

Prior to settling in, he checked the two tunnels. The left shaft extended another thirty feet and came to a dead end. The right one wound downward, twisting and turning like a snake for a short distance. Then the shaft straightened and began a steep ascent toward the surface. As he neared the surface, Billy Ray could see daylight peeking through a crush of large boulders, blocking further progress. With the cross ventilation provided by the opening, he could even have a fire without fear of asphyxiating himself. He made his way back to his new home.

As he worked, the near miss with Candy came to mind. With all the focus on finding him, it might be wise to hide out for a couple of days to let the dust settle. Let them think he'd decided to take off. They might begin to relax their guard if they thought he'd fled.

***

Billy Ray sat on his sleeping bag, rubbing his hands together over the fire he'd built as his counterfeit New York identification burned. His mind in a fog and exhausted from the lack of sleep and hike, he decided to fortify his body with food and restore his mind with sleep.

He had all the time he needed to decide how to make Stone pay.

Chapter 43

WITH THEIR PART OF THE investigation done for the time being, and exhaustion etched on everyone's face, Stone suggested they take the day to get some rest. He knew no good decisions ever came from overtired minds. Besides, the sheriff's department had the town—and Molly—covered. He asked Dan and Rick to meet him back at the marshal's office at eight o'clock the following morning.

Prior to leaving, Stone updated Harry, who'd remained at the office, awaiting their return. "If you wouldn't mind, can you hang in until the sheriff's department delivers the composite sketch? It shouldn't be long."

"You bet," Harry said. "And I'll be back this evening, so if anything happens I can handle it. Between the sheriff's department and me, I think we can keep the horse in the stall for a night."

"Okay. Don't spend the whole night working. The sheriff's department can handle it, and they'll call me if something of consequence happens. I need you rested too."

As Stone drove home, he called Molly. "Sorry I haven't called sooner," he said. "I'm sure you've heard we've been a little busy."

Molly began speaking like a buzz saw. "Are you all right? Are you hurt? We heard what happened to Mister Hendrickson and people saw you covered in blood. Tell me you're okay." Stone could hear the near panic in her voice through her rapid-fire discourse.

"Wasn't my blood," Stone explained. "I'm uninjured, and I'm

headed home to get some sleep because I've been awake since—huh—I can't remember. Can I see you tomorrow and explain everything to you?"

"As long as I know you're okay, I can wait," she said.

"I'm fine but wiped out. I wouldn't make good company or any sense if I tried to explain things as exhausted as I am."

"Okay. You promise to see me as soon as you can?" Molly pleaded.

"I promise."

Stone parked in his driveway and stumbled into his cabin. He stripped out of his uniform, reminding himself to preserve his bloody shirt as evidence. As he took a hot shower, his muddled mind wondered how much blood Hatch intended to spill in his name. He had to find some way to stop him from killing again. The simple answer was to run. Hatch followed him to Silver Lake, so it was logical he would follow again.

The logic might be sound, but Stone ran from nothing. At least not anymore. Besides, if he ran, he would have to keep running for the rest of his life, looking over his shoulder at every turn.

Done showering, he toweled off and crawled into bed. He fell into a deep dreamless sleep as his head hit the pillow.

***

Stone had slept through the day and most of the night. At four-thirty in the morning, dressed in a fresh uniform, he sat in his living room in one of the two overstuffed recliners angled in front of the moss-rock fireplace. He stared at the plastic trash bag that held his bloody shirt.

Molly's safety worried him. Maybe he could convince her to take a vacation until he could stop Hatch. He should do the same with Will. If he could get them out of harm's way, it would lower his stress level.

Stone felt the sharp edge of his past cutting into his soul. Death had followed him to Silver Lake and left him no choice except to unleash the aggressive animal locked in his brain's *amygdala*—to again become the maniacal pursuer of society's bottom feeders he'd been in New York. He'd tried so hard to rid himself of that part of his persona. Now he could feel it surging through his veins like sulfuric acid, eating away at his humanity. His quest to find peace and heal his torn soul was a pipe dream, at least until he stopped Hatch. He worried he might tip over the edge this time and lose himself for good.

No point sitting at home staring at the walls, he thought. He grabbed the plastic bag containing his bloodstained shirt and headed to the marshal's office. As he parked, he saw Harry's pick-up truck parked in front.

The office was empty. Stone grabbed the coffee pot and headed for the bathroom to fill it. Opening the door to the back room, it surprised him to see Harry asleep on the bunk in the jail cell. The noise woke Harry, and he looked at Stone as he entered the room.

"What're you doing?" Stone asked. "I thought I told you to go home."

"Figured I'd better stay close," Harry said. "You know."

Stone nodded his understanding—and appreciation. As he made coffee, Harry took a few minutes in the bathroom to make himself look presentable. Stone sat at his desk, and Harry at the deputy's table, each sipping coffee. A few minutes of quiet contemplation passed as Stone stared at the composite sketch of Bill Hatch on his desk.

Harry broke the silence. "Had some news types from Aspen, I think, come by. I didn't answer the door. I think they might be smellin' a skunk in the woodpile."

"Yeah, I'm afraid it's all gonna leak out, and we're gonna have what Sheriff Davis didn't want—a media circus," Stone said. "It started with my radio call from Hendrickson's house, followed by the cop convention at the hospital."

"You heard any news 'bout how he's doing," Harry asked, sounding curious as opposed to concerned.

"No, nothing," Stone said. "He was bad enough they air lifted him to Denver. Sucking chest wound," Stone added, pointing to the spot on his own chest.

"Huh," Harry said. "So, what do you want me to do?"

"I asked Will to make a list of all the campgrounds and campsites in the area. If he's in a local campground we could get lucky."

"I can check the ones I know," Harry said.

"No. Hold off on that. I don't want anyone looking for this guy alone. I wish they'd gotten a better copy of his driver's license. Couldn't see any damn facial features, so all we have is this composite," Stone said, waving the sketch in the air.

A Pitkin County Sheriff's Department patrol car pulled into the parking lot, and Rick walked into the office. He nodded and headed for the coffee pot. Stone said, "What're you doing here? We're supposed to meet at eight."

"I could ask you both the same question," Rick said, "and I'm guessing the answer'd be the same."

Stone and Harry nodded.

As Rick settled into a chair at the deputies' table, he sighed and said, "I'm afraid I've got some bad news. Sheriff Davis has to pull the two deputies assigned to Molly."

"That doesn't surprise me," Stone said. "I planned on talkin' to her today to see if she can leave town and lay low until this is over."

"Sorry," Rick said. "Mountain Meadow Estates is in the county and because of the attack on Hendrickson, the privileged have started screaming bloody murder for additional police presence. You know how it is—people with lots of money and political connections. Between their demands and babysitting CBI, we don't have the manpower to spare."

"I can watch her," Harry said.

"I appreciate that, Harry," Stone said. "Let's wait for Dan, so we can work on a game plan? I don't think Hatch will attack anyone in daylight. He seems to prefer the night."

Stone passed his blood-stained shirt to Rick. "Thanks. I'll add it to our thin pile of evidence."

As Stone refilled his coffee mug for the third time, Dan pulled into the parking lot. Stone looked at his watch and saw it was close to seven. He pointed toward the window and said, "Looks like no one listened to me."

Everyone seated and in possession of coffee and a copy of the composite, each man took a few moments to study the face of their nemesis.

"Before we go any further, I have a question," Stone said to the group. "Since Hatch was quiet last night, does anyone think he's decided to run?"

Everyone shook their heads no, and Rick added, "I suspect he's getting his second wind and planning his next move."

"Okay, let's get our day planned. With the composite, we can put a face to the name," Stone said. "We've got some additional information we can add to the composite too. I think we can announce that he's a white male, in his mid-twenties, six foot, average build, brown hair, and dark—maybe black—eyes. I got that from the copy of his driver's license. He'd at least need his physical description to be accurate, even if the license is phony."

"My guess is he'll change his look once he realizes we have a composite of him," Dan said.

"Even if he does alter his appearance, he may be recognizable." Stone added "WANTED" at the top of the composite with the sheriff's department number, the name Bill Hatch, and the physical description at the bottom, and then printed off a pile of copies for distribution.

"Unless someone's got another idea, I think we should flood the town and campgrounds with the composite sketch. I need to talk to Molly and Will to try to convince them to leave town until we catch him, so I need to stay in town for the time being."

Harry said, "I can see if Will has the list ready, and if someone will come with me, we can start hitting the campgrounds and campsites."

"I'll go with you," Rick said. "I'll call the sheriff to see if he can shake some deputies loose to assist with checking the campgrounds, since these are county cases. That should help speed things along."

"In that case, I'll work with you in town," Dan said to Stone.

"Okay," Stone said. "Let's meet again this evening, so we can review and plan our next move."

They all agreed to meet back at the marshal's office at six.

Each man took a portable radio and a large stack of the composites and headed out on their assigned tasks.

Chapter 44

"I WANT TO TALK TO Will before we go see Molly," Stone said as he and Dan walked the downtown area of Dowd Street. They took their time distributing the fliers to the business owners and answering what questions they could. They asked that the owners display the posters, so the tourists could see them too.

Stone had to convince Will to leave town and hoped he might have some ideas how to persuade Molly to do the same. An independent and confident woman, no one forced her to do anything.

As Stone pushed open the Stemple Realty office door, the bell at the top jingled.

Sounding morose, Will said, "Come in and have a seat. Harry came by a bit ago, and I gave him the list of campgrounds and campsites in the county."

As Stone and Dan sat, Will said, "It's starting."

Puzzled, Stone asked, "What's starting?"

"The leaks. The attack on Mister Hendrickson drew the attention of the local news people. And it didn't take them long to make the connection to the attack at the campground. They're reporting a possible connection, because of the state investigator's vehicles at both places. It won't be long until they find out it was a murder."

"Ah, shit," Stone said. "Have you heard if they've made any connection to Dan or me and the Ohio and New York killings?"

"No, but I'm afraid it's a matter of time."

Stone stared off in the mid-distance for a few moments. He drew a deep breath, sighed, and shifted his eyes to Will. "If the national media gets wind of this, they'll dig into it and make the connection. All we can do is deal with what comes as it comes. I've got other priorities that take precedence."

"Misters Langford and Feldman are back and they're a priority I can't ignore—and neither should you," Will cautioned. "I've briefed them on the events to date."

Dan looked from Will to Stone, a puzzled look on his face.

"The other two town fathers," Stone explained. "What'd they have to say?"

"Nothing to me; however, I'm certain they're discussing it."

"We'll deal with whatever comes from them as it comes too," Stone said.

Will started to protest, and Stone cut him off. "I know Will—tourism and dollars. But I told you, people's safety comes first.

Will frowned, then nodded his understanding.

"And that brings us to the reason for our visit," Stone said. "We think you may be in danger."

Will recoiled in his chair as if someone had punched him in the chest. His furrowed eyebrows knitted worry lines across his forehead.

"I'm hoping to convince you to take some time off and leave town until we get this resolved. And I need any ideas you might have on how I can convince Molly to leave too."

"Jesus, Hunter. I'm frightened enough. Are you saying you think he'll attack me or Molly?"

"I can't know for certain, Will. We think it's possible he'll target people I have personal relationships with. We have to assume he's watched me, so he'll know I spend some of my time with you and Molly. That could make you both targets."

"I don't know," Will said, looking frightened—yet resolute. "I have a responsibility to the town—and the people too. I can't run away from that."

"That's noble, Will, and maybe a little foolish."

Will stared at Stone and at length said, "As foolish as you chasing someone who followed you halfway across the country to kill you?"

"Point taken, but that's *my* job," Stone said without resolve. In truth, Will's conviction in the face of danger impressed him. At length, he nodded his acceptance and respect to Will.

Dan cleared his throat and interjected, "We know his pattern's to attack at night. That and the fact we're posting his composite all over town should make them safe during the day." Dan turned his attention to Will and asked, "Can you stay someplace else at night, away from town?"

Will focused on Dan and said, "A few years back, I bought some land with a small cabin on it between Aspen and Glenwood Springs."

"Have you gone to the cabin in the last month or so?" Stone asked.

"It's been a busy year, so no. I haven't had time."

"Okay. That'll work," Stone said. "Do you have room at the cabin for Molly?"

"It has two bedrooms," Will said. "But you know how Molly is, Hunter. She doesn't do anything she doesn't want to do."

"So how do I convince her," Stone asked.

"You don't. All you can do is tell her the truth and ask," Will said.

"Okay. I suggest you pack some clothes and personal items and plan to move in starting tonight. We'll have someone from our office or the sheriff's department tail you as you leave town to make sure no one's following. Make sure you let us know that you're headed out. And don't drive at dusk or at night without someone to follow."

Will headed home to pack some clothes, and Stone and Dan walked to the Silver Nugget Café to see Molly.

***

Stone had convinced Molly to break away from the restaurant for a short time and meet him at the marshal's office, even though it was busy. That, in itself, Stone saw as a small victory. He hoped his luck would hold.

Molly fidgeted, saying she needed to return to work. Stone asked Molly to sit at the deputy's table. The seriousness in his voice got her attention. They told her everything that had happened to date, from the New York and Ohio murders to the campground murder and the attack on the Hendrickson home as succinctly as possible.

"Please keep all this confidential," Stone said. "None of it's public knowledge."

Molly was dumbstruck. She looked from Stone to Dan with a mixture of concern and confusion on her face. Finding her voice, she said, "My God. That's why you've been too busy to see me?"

"Yeah, and before we knew he was in Silver Lake, I spent a lot of time with you and Will, and we think that may make you a target," Stone explained.

"I've spoken to Will, and he's agreed to work days and stay in a cabin he owns away from town at night. He said he had room, and you could stay with him. If you'll do that until we catch the guy, I think we can keep you out of harm's way."

Molly seemed to consider it. At length, she said with conviction, "I won't tell you I'm not scared because of what you've said, but I refuse to let him drive me out of my home. I can take care of myself." She looked at Stone and Dan, as though daring either of them to challenge her.

Stone decided to heed Will's advice and changed tactics. It was his last shot. "I know you can take care of yourself, but no one in Silver Lake's ever faced anything like this killer. If I can't convince you to leave, will you at least consider working days and staying home at night until we catch him?" Before Molly could object, Stone added, "Please, Molly. I can't focus on catching him if I'm worried because you're exposed."

Molly appeared to mull it over, and although she seemed reluctant, nodded consent.

"Thank you," Stone sighed with relief. "That's a load off my mind." Stone asked Molly to follow the same parameters Will had agreed to—no dusk or night travel without a police escort. Molly agreed to that too.

Molly stood and walked over to Stone. She leaned in, kissed him on the cheek, and whispered, "You take care of yourself too. I don't want anything to happen to you either."

Stone and Dan walked Molly back to the restaurant and resumed distributing the composite sketches to all the businesses. Many of the shop owners questioned Stone about the incident at the campground and the attack on Hendrickson. Stone deflected the questions by saying that the sheriff's department had handled the investigations. Therefore, he had the same information they did.

It was mid-afternoon by the time they finished the flier distribution. As they approached the marshal's office, Stone noticed three live-feed vans with telescoping booms topped with satellite dishes on their roofs parked in front of the office. The major Denver channel names, numbers, and logos adorned the sides of the vans.

"Shit," Stone whispered. He wanted to turn and run.

The reporters and camera operators piled out of their vehicles like rats escaping a sinking ship and approached them. Dan slowed allowing a gap to grow between Stone and himself. Stone noticed, looked back, and mouthed, "Thanks."

Dan smiled, nodded, and slowed further.

Each of the reporters attempted to speak over the other. The camera operators elbowed each other for the best filming position. *Reporters were the same, no matter if it was New York or Silver Lake,* Stone thought, watching the free for all.

Stone stopped short of the horde and held out his hands as though stopping traffic.

"Folks, I don't have anything for you," he said. "These aren't my cases. You'll have to go through the county sheriff's department for information."

The jabber started again. Stone ignored it, skirting the reporters and camera operators with his head down, and headed for the office door. Dan had beaten him inside and held the door open.

Inside and safe, Stone leaned back against the door and said, "Shit. Will was right. The media frenzy's started."

Chapter 45

AS THEY HID IN THE office, Stone's smartphone chirped. He looked at the screen and saw the caller was Harry. "How's it going with the campground checks, Harry? You need any help?"

"We got help from the sheriff's department, so we're close to done. Rick and I are at the Bar J campground out on Highway 82. We showed the composite to the owner, and he said it looked like a fella he rented a space to yesterday. We checked, and the space is empty."

"Shit," Stone said. He thought for a moment and asked, "Have you done a search for evidence?"

"No. I wanted to call you first," Harry said.

Stone mulled over his options and said, "String crime scene tape and stand by for me. Make the perimeter large. We can shrink it if we need to, but I don't want to chance losing evidence because it's outside the tape."

Stone disconnected and briefed Dan as they headed for the police Suburban. They noticed with relief the news vans had vanished.

***

"I apologize for issuing orders," Stone said to Rick. "Old habit. This is your case and jurisdiction, so it's your call. Do we search it or wait for CBI?"

"It'll be a long wait, I'm afraid. They're working the campground. And they still have Hendrickson's house and Hatch's room at the lodge waiting," Rick said. "I was kind of hoping we could put your forensic skills to work, processing this scene."

The men stood at the perimeter tape and looked at the campsite. "Looks clean," Dan said.

"Let's do a grid search first. Look for treadwear impressions, cigarette butts, or anything else within the perimeter," Stone suggested.

The search was a waste of time. The driveway and parking area near the campsite had a loose gravel surface, which prevented treadwear impressions from showing. And it appeared Hatch had policed the campsite: no scraps of paper or anything else was visible. Not even any footwear impressions in the dirt near the tent's footprint.

As the four men worked inside the barrier tape, a small knot of campers gathered to watch. Rick suggested they conduct interviews to see if they could gather any additional information. Harry and Rick headed toward the crowd.

Frustrated, Stone stood there, staring at the campsite. He remembered some classes he'd taken on criminal profiling. Hatch fit the organized type offender as described by the FBI's Behavioral Science Unit, meaning he planned and executed his crimes in an organized way.

These types of offenders were deliberate and methodical. They were self-absorbed psychopaths, lacking empathy and remorse. Most were well spoken, outgoing, and pleasant, and because of that they appeared non-threatening—at first.

Stone remembered the instructor telling the class that they brought their own weapons to the scene and took them from the scene. They were careful and took the time to remove all traces of evidence. They might even move or conceal the body.

Hatch fit the profile on most of the markers. Yet, he chose to expose and stage his victims, because he wanted the messages found. As for his spelling, either he'd misspelled words on purpose or he was uneducated. Stone sensed in is gut the misspellings were unintentional. The errors appeared to be a natural part of Hatch's syntax.

That meant Hatch should've fit a disorganized offender profile. The fact that he didn't indicated to Stone that he was an anomaly, showing both organized and disorganized traits. Stone thought that perhaps someone had taught him the skills he used.

Another piece of useless information, Stone thought.

As Stone ruminated, his eyes scanned the campground. They locked on a fifty-five-gallon drum with a bear-proof lockable lid off in the distance. Harry had wrapped the crime scene tape using the can to help form one leg of the scene perimeter. "Locard's Principle," he mumbled, pulled from his reverie.

"What?" Dan asked.

"Edmond Locard's Exchange Principle," Stone repeated. "It's the cornerstone for all forensic crime scene investigation. It means every contact leaves a trace—an exchange of evidence. Something's taken and something's left behind. You thought the campsite was clean," Stone said, beginning to walk toward the trashcan. "I agree. So, what do you do with your campsite trash?"

Stone watched as Dan sighted in on the container and realization dawned on his face. "Trashcan," he said, pointing.

They removed the lid and saw that the can was close to full. Thank God the campground owner was a little remiss in his duties. Dan guarded the can, as Stone retrieved his camera and evidence collection kit from the Suburban and carried them to the receptacle.

Stone photographed the scene and the trash container. They

donned latex gloves and began removing the trash, one piece at a time. The trash on top consisted of empty pop cans, plastic food wrappers, and receipts from the campground store.

"He camped just the one day. We start finding receipts dated prior to his arrival, we can stop collecting," Stone said.

It didn't take long to reach older trash, based on the receipts. In paper evidence bags, they had collected three plastic wrappers, two pop cans, and two receipts.

Rick and Harry had concluded their interviews and joined Stone and Dan at the trashcan. "No new information," Rick said. "No one even noticed what kind of vehicle he drove."

"Maybe our luck's changed," Stone said, showing the evidence bags.

"I'll get them over to the CBI people," Rick said.

"If that's what you want to do," Stone said. "But you said they're swamped with working the three scenes they have. I can process this stuff today at my office."

"Let's do that," Rick said. The men tore off the crime scene tape and added it to the trashcan. Excited, they raced to the Silver Lake Marshal's Office.

At the office, they pulled the chairs away from the deputies' table. Stone covered the wooden table with overlapping rows of paper towels from the bathroom. He opened his fingerprint kit, exposing a variety of dry powders and wet chemicals and assorted supplies for processing, collecting, and preserving fingerprints from surfaces. He pulled latex and nitrile gloves, a dust/mist respirator, and ventless goggles from his evidence collection kit.

As the other men crowded in to watch, Stone said, "Harry, would you please get the steam iron in the supply closet. Put some water in it and bring it to me."

Harry hurried off to complete the task, as Stone pulled a chair back to the table and sat, donning the latex gloves and a respirator mask. He removed each item of evidence from its bag, spacing them out on the tabletop.

Harry returned with the iron and plugged it in to heat. Stone photographed all the evidence laid out and each item separately, assigning the item a number by writing it on the paper towel. Stone looked up and warned the group, "Don't get too close as I use the fingerprint powder. It tends to waft into the air, and it's unhealthy to breathe."

Everyone stepped back as Stone set to work, processing the cans and bags for latent prints. He developed three partial prints on one of the cans and a full set of five on the other. He switched to magnetic fingerprint powder and recovered three partial prints from one of the plastic wrappers, but nothing except smears from the others.

After swabbing the plastic wrappers and can openings for DNA, Stone said, "I'm gonna take the receipts outside to spray them. He pulled a can labeled "Ninhydrin Spray" from his fingerprint kit. Holding the can so they could see the skull and crossbones on the label, he added, "This stuff is carcinogenic, so you don't want to inhale it or get it on your skin." Before stepping outside, he changed gloves. Nitrile gloves would prevent bleed through of the chemical, whereas latex would fail.

He covered the sprayed and dry receipts with a paper towel and allowed the huffing steam to penetrate the paper towel by holding the iron close to the surface. Upon removing the paper towel, he saw that each receipt had clear, purple-colored partial prints on the front and back.

Stone affixed a special attachment to the lens of his Polaroid

Instant Film camera that placed the camera at the precise distance needed to take one-to-one photographs of the developed latent prints on the receipts. He explained that ninhydrin developed prints faded over time, so it was vital to photograph them.

He re-photographed the evidence and transferred the prints to latent lift cards, using lifting tape, and completed the necessary information on the reverse side of the cards. Then he initialed and dated the evidence and sealed it back in its bags.

Finished, he stood and fanned the latent lift cards and instant photos.

"Let's hope we caught a break."

Chapter 46

"YOU PLAN ON STOPPING BY the sheriff's department to log my shirt in as evidence?" Stone asked Rick.

"Yeah. Want me to take the lift cards and have them entered into AFIS and IAFIS?"

Stone, like everyone else in law enforcement, knew that without acronyms, communication would be difficult ... or at least convoluted. As an example, AFIS and IAFIS stood for the Automated Fingerprint Identification System and the Integrated Automated Fingerprint Identification System. Acronyms allowed communication to be brief and provided a semi-secret means of communication.

"That would be great," Stone said, thankful for the offer. Stone figured the funding for the AFIS data entry machine had come from the same federal funds that provided them so many of their other special toys. The Fed provided a great deal of help to police departments across the country. Homeland Security provided money for specialized equipment, and the FBI operated both AFIS and IAFIS to facilitate the input and search for matching prints to identify any person's fingerprints on file.

As he handed Rick the cards, he added, "If you do get a hit on any of the prints, would you check CCIC and NCIC for criminal records and any other information available?" Secret police code again: CCIC and NCIC stood for the Colorado Crime Information Center and the National Crime Information Center, and each provided all kinds of criminal and non-criminal data.

Having done what they could, Stone suggested they call it a day. "Everyone's put in a full day, so go relax. Let's meet again in the morning at eight."

Harry and Dan began to shuffle toward the door. As Rick gathered the evidence, Stone asked, "Rick, can the sheriff have someone make sure Will gets to his cabin without a tail and maybe have a few patrols come through town tonight?"

"I called him on the way back from the campground to update him and asked him the same thing," Rick said. "He knows we've been at it pretty hard, so it's all covered—at least for tonight."

"Great. Thanks, Rick," Stone said, relieved. "I don't mean to be pushy, but how quick can we get the results on those prints?" he said, pointing at the latent lift cards and photos.

"Our latent print examiner is off duty. I could ask the sheriff to bring him back if you think it's necessary," Rick offered.

"What I think is that I'm on the verge of abusing the sheriff's good will, so let's wait until morning when your latent print guy gets in. I'd appreciate him making it a priority though."

"Consider it done," Rick said, gathering the evidence and heading toward the door.

Stone was the last to leave the office. Instead of going home, he drove to the Silver Nugget Café. He figured he could eat dinner and make sure Molly got home without incident. He had a security idea he wanted her to try too.

Molly took a few minutes to sit with Stone in his customary booth. "How goes the hunt?" she asked, a look of anticipation mixed with worry on her face.

"We may have some positive news come morning," Stone said without going into detail. "I sent everyone home for the day to get some rest."

"I hope that means you too," Molly said, looking concerned. "You look tired and stressed."

"It does. I thought I'd get something to eat and make sure you got home safe and sound," Stone said.

Molly gave him a disapproving look and said, "I'm a big girl. I don't need a chaperone to get home."

"I know—but remember our agreement: you're home by dark and stay locked in until sunrise. I want to make sure no one follows you."

"Okay, okay," Molly said, holding her hands out in surrender.

"This'll give me the opportunity to check your window and door locks too, which brings me to a question. Do you save your empty pop cans or recycle them?"

"We have a recycle bin in the back," Molly said, confusion etched on her face.

"Good. Can we wash out a bunch of cans and bring them to your house?"

"What for?" Molly asked.

"I assume you don't have a security system, so the cans are an excellent substitute. You put them on the floor inside the windows and doors. If someone does get in, he'll kick them making a hell of a racket, alerting you to his presence. Keep your gun close."

"I haven't fired at another person, Stone," Molly said, her concern evident.

"If it would make you feel better, I could stay with you."

Molly's eyebrows arched, and she gave him a quizzical look.

Stone realized that what he said came out wrong. Their relationship had intensified, but it hadn't reached the sleepover stage. "I mean I could sleep on the floor or the couch, not ..."

Molly stopped him. "Thanks for the offer, but I'll be fine."

Dinner over, Stone followed Molly home. He checked all her window and door locks and helped her set the cans in place, attaching them to each other with a string looped through the pull tabs. "Don't answer the door for anyone either. If I have a reason to send someone over, I'll call you and let you know."

As comfortable as he could be that Molly was safe, Stone drove home. He downed a strong Maker's Mark and water to help calm his nerves and prepared for bed. It was hard enough trying to catch a killer. What no one knew was that his insides were in constant turmoil. He had to hold the line and refuse to permit himself to lose all he'd gained by slipping back into the gutter of his New York life. Following a couple of hours of tossing and turning, trying to figure out where Hatch had chosen to hide, Stone drifted into a restless night's sleep.

***

Slept out, Billy Ray sat on his sleeping bag, warming his hands over the rekindled fire. It might be summer, but it got cool at night—even colder in the mine. With nothing to do, his mind replayed the events that led to his self-imposed exile—and it angered him. He knew his best move would be to lay low for a few days, but he wanted to make another statement and had no patience. He'd seen it happen in a dream.

Having eliminated the mayor's boss, it would panic Stone if he took out the mayor. Remove the hierarchy and Stone would stand alone atop the bodies of his dead bosses. The weight of that alone might destroy him. At least it would show him how powerless he was to stop the murders. With the mayor gone, Billy Ray would focus on the girlfriend. One by one, he would strip Stone of everything and everyone important in his life. After Stone had seen his life destroyed, Billy Ray would make his final act the destruction of Stone himself. By that point, he figured Stone would welcome the sweet release of death.

Billy Ray checked his watch. It was a little past one. If he got moving, he could arrive between three and four and be back on the trail or at the mine by sunrise. He grabbed his canteen and began the downhill trek to his car's hiding spot.

Turning onto Route 138 from the fire road, Billy Ray felt his nerves go raw as he headed the short distance into town. If he saw any hint of headlights coming in either direction, he would get off the road.

He drove with his headlights off. His prior surveillance had shown the mayor lived in a newer ranch-style house off the section of Lake Street on the west side of the lake, across from the main part of town.

To avoid drawing attention, he parked a couple of blocks away, in an undeveloped area. He changed into his stygian clothing and closed the distance to the house in a couple of minutes.

He saw no lights inside or out. A sliding glass door in the back provided him easy access. With no additional locks or a security bar, Billy Ray jimmied the simple handle lock. He slid the door open and stepped into the house, sliding the door closed behind him.

The stillness inside the house made Billy Ray think the house was empty. He tiptoed along the hallway to the bedrooms, his knife in hand. The bedrooms were empty. He searched the rest of the house, his frustration growing. No car in the garage either. "Shit," he whispered.

His first instinct was to back out and leave no trace of his forced entry. He could come back another night. Except his anger and exasperation had intensified like a geyser—ready to burst forth in a torrent of rage. Nothing had gone right. He'd killed the guy in the tent outside of Stone's jurisdiction. He'd just escaped from Hendrickson's. It had to have been that pissant Stone who'd interrupted him. He missed beating Stone to Candy. It still stumped him how Stone knew he intended to attack Hendrickson and how he tumbled to the Lake Lorraine Lodge and Candy so damn fast. The information they got from Candy, and who knew who else, forced him to live like a hermit in an abandoned mine now, because he had to hide his face.

Now this, his intended target missing from his home.

"Fuck it," he said, loud enough that his voice carried through the house. Overcome by his rage, he began slashing the beds and linens. Having destroyed the beds in the two bedrooms, he moved to the closets and dressers, slicing the clothing he found into strips. He strode into the living room and cut the couch cushions and two overstuffed chairs to pieces.

He wanted to smash the television and destroy dishes and glassware but knew the noise would alert the neighbors. Inside the refrigerator, he found squeeze bottles of ketchup, mustard, and mayonnaise. He used the ketchup on the living room wall and wrote **YOUR NEXT**. By the time the containers sputtered on empty, the walls, ceilings, and floors looked like a Jackson Pollock painting in red, yellow, and white condiment blobs, smears, and lines.

His rage assuaged for the moment, Billy Ray stood in the middle of the living room, admiring his handiwork. He dropped the empty containers on the floor and slipped out the sliding glass door, leaving it ajar.

Chapter 47

TEN HOURS OF UNINTERRUPTED AND dreamless sleep left Stone feeling recharged. He shaved, showered, put on a fresh uniform, and downed two cups of coffee. Revitalized and hopeful the prints submitted would provide useful information; he headed for the door, full of energy. As he reached for the knob, his smartphone chirped.

"Stone," he answered.

"It's Will. I stopped by my house on the way to the office, and it's destroyed. He left a message on the wall for me."

Stone could hear the panic in his friend's voice. "Okay, Will. Take some deep breaths and calm down. Are you at your house?"

"I'm standing in what's left of my living room," Will all but screamed into the phone.

"Don't touch anything, okay?" Stone said. "I'll stop by the office to see if anyone else is in, then head right over. It might be better if you wait outside." Stone knew victims felt the need to straighten and clean things after a crime.

Stone's composed demeanor must have had a calming effect, because the panic in Will's voice had modulated as he replied, "I'll wait out front in my truck."

Harry, Dan, and Rick were all at the marshal's office upon Stone's arrival. As he entered the office, he noticed they all held cups of fresh-brewed coffee.

Stone briefed them, and they all piled into their respective vehicles and drove to Will's house. Will sat in his truck, waiting. Stone noticed that he appeared jittery, his head on a swivel, and his eyes bulging with alarm.

"Jesus," Stone said as Will led them through his ruined home, pointing out the damage. The message on the living room wall, YOUR NEXT, was Hatch's calling card, Stone thought. This wasn't a simple vandalism perpetrated by bored kids looking to get into mischief. Hatch had come calling and took his anger out on the house upon finding it vacated. Thank God he'd convinced Will to spend his nights away from Silver Lake.

"Look at this damage," Will said to Stone in near panic as the other men wandered, took notes, and spoke to each other in hushed tones.

"It's all replaceable, Will," Stone said, sweeping his arm at the carnage. "What's important is that you're safe. Now you understand my reason for wanting you to spend your nights away from here."

"I've never in my life experienced anything like this," Will said, the fear evident in his tone.

"I'm convinced you're safe as long as you continue to do what I asked of you," Stone said, trying to reassure him.

Will nodded but seemed no more mollified as he scanned the damage to his home.

"What we don't want is the media getting wind of this. Can you call your insurance company from your office?" Stone asked. "The longer we're all parked out front, the bigger the chance someone will spot the police vehicles and get curious."

"Yeah," he said, distracted. "I need to clean all this up," Will said, lifting a dissected couch cushion from the floor.

"Insurance companies have people who specialize in cleaning

flood and fire damage and stuff like this. Head to your office, and I'll finish my investigation and lock the house as I leave."

"All right," Will said, putting the cushion on the couch and backing out of the living room.

"Try to act as normal as you can," Stone advised. "And please, other than your adjustor, keep this quiet."

Finished with the investigation at Will's home, Stone took the condiment squeeze bottles for print processing and locked the house as they exited. The men fanned out and knocked on the neighbor's doors to determine if anyone saw or heard anything. Most of the knocks went unanswered and the few people who were home provided no useful information.

Rick approached Stone as they prepared to leave and said, "My print guy just called. He got hits on several of the prints. They're assembling files for us. They'll have them finished by the time I get to my office. I'll meet you back at your office as soon as I can."

Back in the marshal's office, Stone processed the condiment containers for prints—with no luck. They waited until Rick returned and handed out the files to each man. "This guy's got a hell of a jacket," Rick said.

Everyone poured themselves fresh coffee and found a seat. Rick began the briefing. "First off, his name isn't Bill Hatch. It's Billy Ray Hatcher." Rick provided his physical description and his date of birth and added, "He's from Texas."

A booking photograph of Billy Ray Hatcher was paper clipped to the inside cover of each binder. The composite sketch they had distributed looked similar to Hatcher's photo, but nothing beats a good photograph. They would need to plaster his photo every place they could.

Rick pulled Stone from his thoughts by adding, "We sent a copy of the photo to Sheriff Yates, and he took it to the Lake Lorraine Lodge. They confirmed Hatcher's the same person they employed under the name Hatch."

Each man began to flip pages, reading Hatcher's long criminal history. "Guy's a real mudsill," Harry said.

As Stone got to the New York arrest and subsequent plea bargain, he blurted, "Damn it! I knew it."

"Knew what?" Rick asked.

"I suspected he was in the system when the New York killings stopped. Looks like they had him incarcerated for the same period. I tried to convince the powers-that-be and the homicide detective of my hypothesis. They wouldn't listen."

"I talked with the homicide detective as part of my investigation, Dan said. "He wasn't what I'd call cooperative."

"We need to see if anything in his jacket connects him to you, Stone," Rick interjected.

"I don't know the name, and I wasn't involved in his arrest," Stone said. He continued reading until he came upon Hatcher's affiliations and known associates.

"Wait a minute. I remember this name, Arnet Gantz," Stone said, pointing at the name. "So Gantz was Hatcher's half-brother, and both of them are affiliated with the White Brotherhood of Texas."

"Were," Rick corrected. "This says someone stabbed Gantz to death at the Five Points Correctional Facility in New York. And listed on the following page, under unconfirmed intel, it says the White Brotherhood threw Hatcher out following his half-brother's conviction."

"I remember the case," Stone said, slapping the folder shut on his desk. "I worked the gang unit for several years. We busted a group of White Brotherhood gang members who attacked and killed two gay men at a gay pride parade or some kind of gathering." Stone stopped speaking and looked off into the middle distance, his brow knitted in thought.

"Was Arnet Gantz one of the perps?" Dan asked.

"He was," Stone said, refocusing on the group. "We didn't have a solid case. A few worthless witnesses and no hard evidence. I interrogated Gantz, and he took a deal and rolled over on his cohorts. They convicted them all. None of the others ever confessed."

"How long ago was this?" Rick asked.

"It's got to be eleven ... no, twelve years ago," Stone said.

"So, let's do the math on this," Rick continued. "If you put Gantz away twelve years ago Hatcher would've been—what—fourteen at the time, based on his DOB. The gang bounced him out after Gantz rolled. Then someone kills Gantz, and Hatcher's criminal jacket starts growing." Rick shook his head and blew a long, low whistle. "I'd bet dollars to donut holes he started planning his revenge a long time ago."

"That's a long time to let your hate simmer," Stone said, shaking his head. He made a mental note to talk to Molly again and try to convince her to leave town or let him stay at her place.

"And if we compare that information to the messages left for you at the murder scenes in New York, you've got a pretty strong connection and motive," Dan said.

"Hatcher thinks I railroaded his half-brother."

"That—and I'd guess he holds you responsible for his half-brother's death," Rick added.

"So, we know who and why," Harry said, frustration resonating in his voice. "How's that get us closer to nailing his hide to the barn door?"

"It's one piece of the larger puzzle, Harry," Stone said. "We get enough pieces, we get him. And it adds to his profile, which helps us understand his motivation."

"What we need to focus on is his hiding place," Dan said.

"You're right, Dan," Stone agreed. We've eliminated the local campgrounds and campsites. That leaves every hotel, motel, or rented home from Silver Lake to Glenwood Springs. And all the possible places to camp in the mountains."

Chapter 48

"IT'LL TAKE WEEKS TO CHECK all the possible hiding places," Harry said.

"My guess is that he doesn't want to stray too far from Silver Lake, so I'd suggest we start by checking all the motels, hotels, and homes in town, focusing on the rentals," Stone said. "We have ready access to the information we'd need on house rentals through Will. If anyone has any other ideas, please share them."

"You're right. Start in Silver Lake and expand our search area as needed," Rick said.

"Let me see if I can get some information that might help," Dan said. He stepped into the back room to make a call as Rick, Harry, and Stone began formulating a plan.

Dan returned with his notepad in hand and a smile on his face.

"You got something?" Stone asked, seeing the rare smile.

"After our investigation at the Lake Lorraine Lodge, I contacted my partner back in Ohio about the name Bill Hatch. As part of our serious crime protocol, our troopers canvas areas surrounding crime scenes based on time of the crime and the distance a suspect can travel in that time. They contact everyone who could be a suspect, meaning they skip families, tour busses, schools—you get the idea. Because the homicides happened at a rest stop along Interstate 70, we expanded the search area and canvased all the rest stops, motels, gas stations, and restaurants within a diameter of 200 miles of the crime scene."

Harry whistled and said, "That's a lot of ground to cover."

Dan said, "It was—and all that data's been on my desk in binders, waiting for something to compare the information to. We uncovered the Hatch name, so I asked my partner to begin a search. It took some time, because he had to do it by hand. The data doesn't get entered into the computer database until a case goes cold."

"Are you going to tell us you found his name?" Stone asked.

Dan smiled again and said, "I'll do you one better. The trooper who contacted our Bill Hatch had him produce a vehicle registration and point out his car. It's identified as a 1986, four-door Ford Taurus, gray in color. We've since determined the driver's license and vehicle registration are fakes, and the New York license plate on the car at that time was a stolen tag."

"He's too smart to have left a New York plate on the car, because he knows it would draw my attention. If he thinks we don't know the make and model of car, he might continue to use it, and we'd have a chance of spotting him," Stone said.

"We might want to check the trailhead parking lots near town," Harry said. "If he decided to camp, we could get lucky and spot his car."

"Could narrow the search area," Dan said.

As the men brainstormed, Stone looked for photographs of a similar Ford Taurus on the Internet and downloaded Billy Ray Hatcher's and the vehicle's photo into the office computer.

A brief discussion ensued in which the men weighed the merits of posting the vehicle information on a wanted poster to gain hundreds of sets of eyes looking for it, verses leaving it off, which might fool their suspect into thinking his car was safe to drive. They decided to post the information.

Within twenty minutes of the decision, Stone had produced an updated wanted poster that contained the two photos and all the pertinent information. "I'm going to email Sheriffs Davis and Yates with a copy of this," Stone said, showing the completed wanted poster.

After Stone sent the posters and printed out a stack of them, they all headed out to distribute them. Stone and Dan walked the town distributing the posters, and Harry and Rick went to check the local trailheads for Hatcher's car, hang wanted posters on the trailhead information boards, and distribute posters to the campgrounds in the area.

Having done all they could for the day, Harry and Rick went home, and Dan headed to his hotel room. Stone drove to the Silver Nugget Café for dinner and—with luck, another shot at convincing Molly to leave town.

***

Stone told Molly of the attack on Will's house. It had the desired effect and frightened her. Realizing how vulnerable she was, she agreed to let him camp on her living room couch until they caught Hatcher.

Half a battle won was better than nothing.

Stone swung by his house to grab a sleeping bag and some sweats he could wear in place of his uniform. He stopped at the office too, taking the time to fax the file of information he had on Hatcher to Captain Baxter at the NYPD Crime Lab. He included a note, explaining Hatcher's motive. He saw no need to point out that his hypothesis had been correct. Baxter would see it as he read the file.

***

Angry because he'd failed—again, Billy Ray sat in the mine, contemplating what he could do. He knew one thing. He was over failures. Whatever action he decided upon, he must think it through and plan it, so it had every chance of success.

He was still fuming that Stone had beaten him to Candy. If she'd kept her big mouth shut, he wouldn't have needed to change his plans—or move into a damn mine. All of a sudden, an idea struck him like a thunderbolt. It brought a malicious grin to his face.

It was dark as he headed down the trail, crossed the road, and hiked deep into the fire road to retrieve his car. He drove straight to the Lake Lorraine Lodge and backed his car into a parking space as close to Candy's cabin as possible. It was a short walk through the woods to her cabin's location. He saw no reason to haul her carcass any further than necessary.

Cloaked in his hunting attire, Billy Ray eased his way along a path through the trees that ended in a small clearing near Candy's cabin. It was pitch black under the canopy of trees. He settled into a seated position behind a thicket of scrub oak that provided him an unobstructed view of Candy's darkened cabin.

Instead of rushing in, Billy Ray waited. He wanted to make sure everyone had plenty of time to fall into a deep sleep. Twenty minutes had passed when he saw a deputy sheriff approach Candy's cabin. He circled the cabin, shining a flashlight into the surrounding forest.

Billy Ray ducked as the flashlight beam swept in his direction. So, they had provided Candy protection. He decided to wait to see how frequent the deputy's checks were. If he could establish a pattern, he could determine the gap between checks.

Over the following two hours, Billy Ray established that the deputy came by every hour or so: plenty of time for Billy Ray to do what he needed. As he waited for another check, he planned how he would get Candy to open her door. He doubted she'd open it for him. He was sure Stone had poisoned her with lies. He decided to alter his voice and knock on her door, announcing himself as the deputy providing protection.

The deputy came and went again. Billy Ray gave him fifteen minutes to move out of earshot. He approached Candy's door and rapped on the door with three quick knocks. "Miss Fergusson," he called. "Are you awake?"

A few moments later he heard her nervous answer. "Who is it? What's going on?"

"It's Deputy Johnson, Miss Fergusson. Dispatch advised me the suspect may be in the area. They want me to get you to the safety of the office. Can you hurry, please?"

A few seconds passed, and Billy Ray heard the door lock disengage. As the door began to swing open, he shoved it as hard as he could, knocking Candy off her feet. She landed on her back, the air exploding from her lungs.

He rushed into the cabin, ramming a knee into Candy's solar plexus to keep her from regaining her breath. He reached back and closed the door, re-engaging the lock. As Candy tried to catch her breath to scream, Billy Ray raked his knife across her throat, silencing her for good.

Satisfied with how things had gone so far, he wrapped her in the blanket from her bed and waited for the deputy to make his rounds again. *Pig in a blanket*, he thought, amused. The area clear, he opened the door, dragged Candy's body outside, and closed the cabin door. He struggled to drag her to his car. Twenty sweaty minutes of work, and he had her secured in the trunk.

Headlights off, Billy Ray drove out of the parking lot and back toward Silver Lake. A safe distance from the parking lot, he turned on his headlights.

He had another task to perform before heading back to the mine.

CHAPTER 49

BY THE TIME BILLY RAY made it back to the trailhead, daybreak had begun to splash pigments of color on the monochromatic predawn landscape. Pleased with his nights work he felt fulfilled—nothing like success to make you feel good.

As he approached the trail, a wanted poster attached to the information board caught his attention and stopped him in his tracks. It showed his photograph and a photograph of a car like his.

"Shit," he said to the empty lot. They had identified him and had a description of his car too. He had no idea how they'd figured it out. He would have to abandon his car and find another one. That would be a pain in the ass. He ran back across the road and to his car, tucked into the trees along the fire road. He popped the trunk and retrieved his special backpack. With no reason to erase his fingerprints any longer, because they knew who he was, he slammed the trunk lid, jogged back to the trailhead, and began the arduous hike to the mine.

Can't one fuckin' thing go right? he wondered.

***

A busy night in the county, the deputy assigned to the area near Silver Lake had no chance to swing through town. If he had, he might have found the scene, instead of a tourist driving through town on his way to the lake for some sunrise fishing.

The chirping of Stone's smartphone pulled him from a semi-conscious sleep state. It was impossible to get comfortable on Molly's modern-design couch. The call was from a county dispatcher with some bad news. "A tourist found what?" he asked, trying to shake the fuzziness from his mind.

***

The discovery of Candy Fergusson led to evidence showing her murder had taken place inside her cabin at the Lake Lorraine Lodge and her body moved to its current location. That made the investigation a Lake County case. No matter in which jurisdiction the murder had taken place, Candy Fergusson's body was in Silver Lake—seated on the ground, her back against the memorial bolder at the end of Dowd Street—her throat cut, her housecoat blood soaked. Her hands folded in her lap, she looked as though she was contemplating her predicament. Printed on the memorial bolder in blood above her head was a message.

NO ONES SAFE STONE

The area surrounding the body buzzed with law enforcement from Lake County, Pitkin County, and the Silver Lake Marshal's Office. In addition to all the cops, Glenwood Springs and Aspen reporters had heard the radio traffic and responded, setting their cameras on tripods along the crime scene tape perimeter, as reporters shouted questions or tried to coerce anyone they could into an on-camera interview.

Stone knew the cork was out of the bottle. It was clear the information was all going to come out. The murder at the campsite, the attack on Hendrickson, and the ongoing CBI presence would lead to probing and investigating by the media. They were sure to uncover the connection to the Ohio and New York murders too. That would lead to the national news media descending on Silver Lake like a swarm of locusts. With all the people involved in the investigations, it surprised Stone it had taken this long.

Sheriff Davis' nightmare would come to fruition, and the fear that disclosure might lead to an exodus of tourists from Silver Lake looked like a self-fulfilling prophecy. Will tried his best to mollify the town fathers as news began spreading like wildfire and a number of vacationers fled town.

Stone knew that with a dead body on display, many additional visitors would pack their tents and trailers, cancel their remaining hotel and motel reservations, and depart Silver Lake as fast as they could. What began as a trickle would swell into a tsunami of fleeing tourists in short order.

Sheriff Yates approached Stone and guided him out of earshot of the press. Keeping his voice low he said, "I'm sorry, Stone. I had a deputy assigned to her, but the general manager wouldn't permit us to use a guest room at the lodge. He restricted my deputy to a chair inside the employee entrance, so he had to make periodic trips to her cabin to check the area."

The news angered Stone. He turned his back on the media, so no camera caught his angry look. Candy's death had been preventable.

"I'd ask you to arrest his ass if I could think of a charge." Stone promised to have Will talk to the lodge owners and tell them the GM's lack of cooperation led to Candy's death.

"On another subject, I understand you have a task force working," Yates said. "Do you need any help? I could assign a detective to work with you."

"Technically, this is your case, so I'll leave that decision to you.

We're doing okay, but with a staff of four, we can't handle everything we need twenty-four hours a day."

"Tell me what I can do to help," Yates said.

"We're starting a motel, hotel, camper, and house-to-house check to see if the suspect chose to hide in town, but I don't think he did. Sheriff Davis has done all he can do to help. He's under a lot of political pressure and had to reallocate his resources to provide additional patrols at Mountain Meadow Estates, so that leaves us short of help. Our problem is we need to work days to look for him, and he's active at night."

"So, you need some help with night patrols?" Yates asked.

"I'm thinking a car check for vehicles entering and leaving town, from dusk to dawn. With one road in and out of town, it shouldn't be difficult to control."

"Since we're deputized in Pitkin County as Sheriff Davis' people are in mine, I can provide a couple of deputies to run a roadblock until we nail him," Yates said.

"That would be a huge load off my mind," Stone said, relieved. "We're narrowing the number of places he can hide. I hope to have him in custody in the near future."

Sheriff Yates and Stone worked out the logistics and hours of operation for the roadblock and parted company. Stone ducked the press and headed to Will's office to do something he dreaded—update him and, as such, the town fathers.

***

Stone was right. The meeting was anything but pleasant. The town fathers were unhappy. Between the tourists leaving and a roadblock that would challenge anyone entering town, they saw nothing in that scenario that sounded like a ringing endorsement to visit Silver Lake.

As upset as they were, the body of Candy Fergusson propped against the memorial bolder with a bloody message smeared on the monument had had a sobering effect. Although reluctant, they agreed the roadblock was necessary, but railed over the potential lost revenue. They implored Stone to catch the killer as fast as possible, so the town could return to some semblance of normalcy.

Stone understood their motivation. They wanted the tourists back while summer kept its hold on Silver Lake. He doubted what he had planned would make them any happier.

***

Billy Ray sat on his sleeping bag, scrutinizing the topographical map showing Silver Lake and the surrounding mountains by the light of his lantern. With no car available, he had to either steal one or find a way to walk into town, staying off the beaten paths. Stealing a car was easy enough to do; however, the owner would report it, and they would know he'd taken it.

The map showed trails crisscrossing the mountains on the east and west sides of Silver Lake. He saw that the main trail leading away from the trailhead on his—the east side trail—showed a number of cutoffs leading to primitive campsites. That was no help. He needed to avoid hikers and campers and find a back way into town.

As he traced the main trail with his finger, he spotted a side trail that went toward Silver Lake but curved away within a short distance. It intersected with another trail that curved toward town. The secondary trail led to an area identified as the location of the town shop and water treatment plant south of town. Access into town was by a dirt road a few blocks away from the boulder where he'd left Candy Fergusson's body.

He could walk to town and sneak in, but it would add several hours of hiking. Moreover, he would have to walk wherever he needed to go and make sure he was back on the trail before sunrise. It would be a pain in the ass, but it was doable.

Billy Ray folded the map and began preparing some food. Working most of the night, he needed some sleep too. He decided it would be smart to stay at the mine for a few days. He could listen to the radio to see if he could find any news reports, rest, and plan his moves.

Chapter 50

OVER THE ENSUING TWO DAYS, the small task force checked and searched the motel and hotel rooms and every camper parked within and near the town limits. Neither the search nor roadblock produced any results, other than raising the anxiety level of the locals and encouraging the visitors to flee at an ever-increasing rate, making the search harder.

It was a monumental task, and they still needed to check every home in Silver Lake and all the primitive campsites in the hills surrounding town. On the positive side, Hatcher had been quiet. Stone figured that with the task force's activities, the exodus of tourists and all the eyes on the lookout for Hatcher and his car, it would be difficult for him to show his face.

To pour salt into Sheriff Davis' wound, all the activity had in fact drawn the attention of the big, Front Range city media outlets. They dug for news tidbits like anteaters tore into termite mounds and, in short order, had made the connection to the Ohio murders and the New York serial killer. The reporters pursued everyone at the marshal's office like paparazzi chasing movie stars. It was all they could do to duck them, so they could do their job without interference. Stone knew at some point he would have to face them.

The national news got hold of the story and gave it serious airtime every chance they got. They ran video feeds using local affiliates as their illustrious talking heads rushed cross-country landing in Silver Lake like the pilgrims landing on Plymouth Rock—except the pilgrims didn't wear fifty-five-hundred-dollar Brioni custom-made suits and twenty-three-hundred-dollar Berluti brand shoes.

Will had done a good job keeping the remaining town fathers at bay. Stone guessed his incentive was the attack on his own home. He was sure they were on Will's ass day and night since the roadblock and search had begun and the story broke open. True to his word, he ran interference like a tight end blocking an opponent for a tailback.

Something fortuitous, or unfortunate, depending on your point of view, began happening as the vacationers departed—an unusual metamorphosis. Stone recognized it for what it was. In his experience, at horrific scenes, whether fatal traffic accidents, street shootings, or jumpers, masses of people materialized from the shadows to gawk. For some reason, they were as morbidly attracted to the scene as an addict is to heroin.

It appeared Silver Lake would succumb to this macabre phenomenon too. Within the same two days, the vacationers scattered in ever-increasing numbers for parts unknown, the curious and those who pursued the thrill of being close to the action—whatever that meant—flooded into town.

The influx of media and those drawn by the television and electronic news stories began to fill the hotels, motels, and campsites in and outside of town. No empty or non-reserved hotel or motel rooms existed in town. Stone had heard reports of reservation bleed over in Aspen and at the Lake Lorraine Lodge.

The result was that Silver Lake avoided the sting of lost revenue. It remained as energetic a community as it had been, although the flavor of visitor appeared different. Regardless, they had to eat, and many craved any trinket that had the name Silver Lake embossed, printed, or embroidered on it.

The town fathers seemed satisfied with the continuing revenue stream and the free national advertising, putting Silver Lake on the map. Stone's concern was that the thrill seekers could cause additional issues by interfering with the investigation—or by becoming victims. The locals had memorized Hatcher's face and were quick to report anyone who looked even a little like him. At least two members of the task force investigated every call.

None had turned out to be Billy Ray Hatcher.

Midafternoon of the second day, as the men sat in the marshal's office, as exhausted from dodging the media as from checking hotels, motels, and campgrounds and answering calls of possible Hatcher sightings; they discussed the spectacle happening in town. The office telephone rang non-stop. Tired of the calls, Stone muted the ringer and let the calls go to voice mail. Anyone of importance knew to call him on his smartphone.

They could see the media gathering in a knot outside the office again. It had become a common occurrence. This time it wasn't a few reporters and their crews. Parked helter-skelter across the street in the fire department parking lot, and nose to ass along the edges of the streets, all manner and size of vans, trucks, and motor-home-sized news vehicles seemed to increase in number by the hour. It looked like a national media convention had convened.

They ignored the occasional knock on the office door. "They won't quit until somebody talks to them," Stone said, glancing out the window following a loud and continuous episode of knocking. "Would you like the honor, Rick, since two of these cases are your department's investigations," Stone offered.

"Thanks, but no thanks," Rick said. "They want to talk to you."

"Okay, but if I have to talk to them, I want to make it productive for us. Let's use the media to try to flush him out. The vandalism at Will's house convinced me that he's impulsive and starting to devolve. I want to use that knowledge to make statements, some true and some complete lies, that'll insult his intelligence and inflame him into acting—attacking out of anger. In other words, help him devolve faster and make the mistakes that'll result in his capture."

Stone's idea caused a flurry of responses, ranging from concern to outright disagreement. What they all agreed on was that the idea was dangerous as hell and had the potential to backfire. But no one else had any better ideas to flush Hatcher out of hiding.

"Give me a minute," Stone said. "Then we can start planning what I'm going to say."

As he opened the office door, a cacophony of clamored questions assaulted his ears and camera operators hoisted cameras to their shoulders or jumped behind tripod-mounted cameras. Newspaper photographers snapped rapid-fire photos, the shutter clicks sounding like an invasion of weird digital insects.

Holding his arms out to silence the crowd, he announced, "Folks, I know you all want a statement and have questions. Pass the word out that I'll make a statement at five o'clock. I won't respond to any questions until that time." Stone turned and walked back into the office as the shouting resumed.

For the following hour, they worked on what he would say. As they fleshed out the talking points, Stone's nervousness increased. The statement was a hell of a gamble to take. It would either work—or be the end of him.

Stone's smartphone chirped. Stone checked the caller ID and saw it was Will. "I've spoken with the town fathers," Will said, "and they're relieved the town won't suffer economically. However, they want to know what you're planning."

Stone explained the plan they had formulated.

"I don't know how they'll react to your idea," Will said, concern in his tone.

"They'll have to trust that we know what we're doing."

They disconnected, and Stone's smartphone chirped again. It was Sheriff Davis this time, sounding stressed to the point of collapse. Stone filled him in on their plan and assured him it would relieve him of a great deal of the media pressure. Stone guessed the sheriff would've balked at the idea, if not for the promise of relief.

They disconnected as Dan moved into the back room to call his boss. As they waited for his return, Stone's phone chirped again. It was Captain Baxter this time.

"I won't keep you, Stone. I know you're busy, based on the news reports," Baxter said. "I thought you'd like to know that heads rolled over your discovery that Hatcher sat in Riker's—like you hypothesized—as the homicide detective, inspector, and deputy inspector did all they could to obstruct you. The commissioner bumped both McFarland and Bussard's retirements to yesterday. The homicide division chief booted Burnside out of his unit. He's back on patrol, directing traffic on some obscure corner on Staten Island or doing some other vital task."

"Thanks for the update, Cap. I hope those who follow won't have to deal with what you and I did." Stone asked, "Any news on that other thing you're handling for me?" Stone had told no one of the paint chips he'd sent to his old captain for analysis. His enigmatic question drew curious stares from Harry and Rick.

"No, nothing's back," Baxter said. "I'll call you as soon as I have the results."

"I hope I have better news by then," Stone said. "We don't have a clue about his location."

"You'll get him," Baxter said. "Quitting's not in your DNA."

They disconnected as Dan returned from the back room. Stone placed his smartphone on his desk. He looked at his watch, stood, and looked into the faces of his three co-conspirators. He swallowed the lump in his throat and said, "It's time."

Chapter 51

BY THE TIME BILLY RAY made it back to the mine, following the killing and posing Candy's body, he was so exhausted he'd slept most of the day. He awoke starving, prepared a freeze-dried meal and what claimed to be some kind of apple compote for desert and gobbled the food with enthusiasm. His appetite satiated, he carried his portable radio to the mine entrance to catch any news broadcasts on the events in Silver Lake and the manhunt for him.

Candy's death and her link to him led many of the news broadcasts. They had aired his name and a detailed description, including his vehicle's make, model, and color. Every broadcast he listened to detailed his connection to the New York and Ohio rest-stop murders. It confused Billy Ray that with all the news flooding the airwaves, the reporters failed to broadcast any interviews with Stone or anyone else in law enforcement.

On day two of his self-imposed confinement, Billy Ray felt antsy and decided to chance going outside. He needed to refill his collapsible water container, and he might be able to find a decent country western station on the radio. He could lounge in the wooded area by the stream and remain hidden from any prying eyes—although no one had approached the mine.

He secured his canteen to his belt and grabbed a bag of trail mix for a snack. With the water container and his portable radio in hand, he strolled to the mine entrance like a man without a care in the world. He slithered through the gates and made his way to the stream. He filled the container, found a comfortable and shady spot to stretch out in the trees, and extended the radio antenna. A few seconds of fiddling with the dial resulted in finding a local station that came in clear.

***

Stone stepped out of the office a few minutes before five. The news media vans' boom armatures raised and extended, pointed into the warm afternoon sky like white skeletal fingers. Satellite dishes perched precariously on top of the booms, peering skyward in anticipation of broadcasting the live feed.

An array of streaming and non-streaming cameras glared at him. Every ilk of reporter, from print, to radio, to television—and their entourage—crowded the lot. Stone had to remind himself to breathe.

Someone had added a small metal lectern outside the office door. A large number of microphones, the stations identified by microphone flags attached to each of them, crowded the stand in front of him. Wires snaked from the microphones in a tangled mess to the mass of cameras.

Stone positioned himself behind the lectern. At five, he saw red tally lights illuminate on the cameras he faced, indicating he was on the air.

Stone cleared his throat and began, "I have a statement to read. I won't take any questions at this time, due to the sensitive nature of this investigation. Before I begin, I want to thank my investigative teammates, Deputy Marshal of Silver Lake, Harry Field, Sergeant Rick Fowler of the Pitkin County Sheriff's Department, and Trooper

Dan Deegan of the Ohio State Troopers. These men continue to work nonstop to catch the killer identified as Billy Ray Hatcher. In addition to them, the sheriffs of both Pitkin County and Lake County, the Silver Lake town fathers, and the mayor of Silver Lake continue to provide vital support."

The recognitions complete, Stone cleared his throat again, uncurled the pages of notes he gripped, smoothing them flat on the lectern, and in an authoritative voice belying his nervousness, laid out the course of events, from the murders in New York and Ohio to the murders and attempted murder in Colorado. He was careful to show the thread of criminal activity that connected all the cases.

A brief pause ensued in which Stone wondered if he'd succeeded in weaving the cases together. He took a deep breath and continued, providing detailed information related to Billy Ray Hatcher, from his physical description to his past ties to the White Brotherhood of Texas.

"Billy Ray Hatcher is the half-brother of one Arnet Gantz, who was a member of the White Brotherhood of Texas. In my capacity as a gang officer with the NYPD, I became involved in the investigation of a double homicide—a hate crime—against two gay men attending a gathering in New York approximately twelve years ago. Mister Gantz was one of the suspects, and I was the officer who interrogated him."

This was the moment Stone began weaving fiction with the truth—fictitious personal opinions with facts. "Arnet Gantz confessed and rolled over on his co-conspirators for a sentencing deal. During his incarceration, another inmate attacked and killed him. Billy Ray Hatcher seems to think I'm responsible for both his half-brother's conviction and subsequent murder. He can't accept the fact that Arnet Gantz was a snitch, a coward, and a murderer.

"As for Billy Ray Hatcher, we've determined, based on evidence and our profile, that he's an uneducated, emotionally stunted psychopath, prone to fits of childlike rage. It's possible he was an abused child and a bed wetter. He may be homosexual. We have information the White Brotherhood kicked him out too. We assume it's because he's a coward, like his half-brother, except he hides behind the notes he leaves in blood at the scenes."

Stone let that resonate for a moment and continued.

He rather enjoyed ripping Billy Ray limb from limb. "Since he killed the innocent young man tent camping, he's failed at all the other things he's tried. He failed at killing one of our town fathers, Mister Hendrickson. He failed at covering his trail at the Lake Lorraine Lodge and campground he stayed at for a day. He failed in his attempt to attack Mayor Stemple. He killed an innocent woman, Candy Ferguson, who worked at the Lake Lorraine Lodge, because of the mistakes *he* made during his temporary employment, blaming her for his sloppiness. We have overwhelming evidence against him, and he can feel the noose tightening. He knows it's a matter of time 'til we corner him. He can't show his face in the county anymore. In fact, we wouldn't be a bit surprised if he hasn't tucked tail and run."

That was it. Stone had baited the hook. They had better be ready, because if Billy Ray had access to a television, radio, or newspaper, he would go off the rails at what Stone had said.

Stone announced that he would provide updates at five o'clock every day. Finished, he turned and walked back into the office.

He leaned against the door and exhaled a huge sigh. "That ought to do it," he said to the three grim faces looking at him.

***

"In fact, we wouldn't be a bit surprised if he hasn't tucked tail and run."

"Marshal Stone announced that if the suspect, Billy Ray Hatcher, was in the vicinity, they would find and apprehend him in the near future. We will continue to follow this breaking story. Stay tuned for updates at the top of the hour. For KYNC news, I'm Brian O'Keefe."

The news ended, and a DJ announced the coming series of songs. Billy Ray tuned him out, his thoughts on the news report. He stared at the radio, myriad thoughts running through his mind.

He'd failed to realize that with his name and face made public and connected to all the murders, going home again was out of the question. The safety of hiding within the White Brotherhood was no longer an option. They might even turn him in if the police offered a reward. If the police found him, he would spend the rest of his life in prison.

Billy Ray mumbled, "You pissant."

Stone had said he would run. Run where? Stone had destroyed his life. The longer he thought, the closer his anger came boiling to the surface.

Billy Ray clicked off the radio and squeezed the plastic case between his hands until it groaned under the pressure. White flashes of light stabbed at his eyes as his mind tumbled toward the edge of insanity. His anger rising like magma, raced to the surface toward a volcanic eruption of rage.

He cocked his arm, the desire to hurl the radio against a tree overwhelming. At the last second, he stopped himself.

He placed the radio by the water container and walked to the clearing by the mine. A safe distance from his supplies, he set his rage free. Arms flailing, he kicked at loose stones, sending dirt clouds billowing into the air, and cursed at Stone.

Tiring, he tried to rein in his anger. It was like wrestling with a killer shark. He could reel it in only so far, then lose it again as the line of rage peeled out of control.

"Damn you, Stone!" Billy Ray bellowed into the surrounding trees. Out of breath, he reached out and braced himself against the mine gate. In a brief moment of clarity, he decided no one would stop him from finishing his mission.

It was time to end this.

PART V

LIFE AND DEATH

Chapter 52

BILLY RAY KNEW HE NEEDED to remain calm to avoid making irrational decisions. A stupid mistake made in a fit of rage was the last thing he needed, and what he was sure Stone hoped he would do. His focus must be on the mission. His personal animus for Stone was secondary.

He'd concluded that there was a possibility his life was forfeit. Stone would make that happen if he could. If people saw that Stone meant to kill him, they would see that what he'd said with his bloody notes had to be the truth.

Taken alive, he would spend the rest of his life in prison. However, he had no intention of letting them catch him—nor did he intend to die. His plan was to finish his mission, steal a car, and escape. He could change his appearance, buy new fake ID, and start his life over someplace new.

Billy Ray sat on his sleeping bag and added a few logs to the fire. He took several deep, calming breaths and fixated on the dancing flames. He envisioned himself going out in a blaze of glory, defending the rights of everyone denied justice at the hands of Stone. If he had to die, at least it would happen bringing vindication for Arnet.

Stone's words had cut to the bone. He'd insulted the memory of Arnet and had called Billy Ray a coward. He'd called him uneducated, and an emotionally-stunted psychopath. He'd accused him of being a homo. Stone was way off base—and Billy Ray meant to prove it.

Let Stone think he'd run away. That would make the plan percolating in his mind a surprise and catch Stone off guard.

Billy Ray settled in to plan his attack.

***

Back in the marshal's office, everyone filled their coffee mugs and took their respective seats. "That went as well as we could've hoped," Stone said.

"Except we have no way of knowing if Hatcher will hear or read what you said," Harry added.

"He's a planner," Rick said. "Odds are he'll have some means of getting the news."

"How do we work it tonight?" Dan asked, avoiding unnecessary chitchat and getting right to the point.

"I'm sorry to ask you all to work so many hours, but we need to get back to twenty-four-hour coverage, since the sheriff's department can't have someone patrolling town all night. With around the clock coverage, we can better cover the town and coordinate with the deputies at the roadblock. Because of the statements I made to the media, we need to increase our situational awareness."

Everyone nodded their understanding, and Harry asked, "What about tonight?"

"Dan and I will take off tonight. We'll take over in the morning, so you two can get some rest," Stone said nodding at Harry and Rick. "I have to give the five o'clock news update tomorrow, and I wasn't able to convince Molly to leave, so I'm sleeping on her couch every night."

Harry asked, "What're the odds he's hidin' in one of the closed houses in town?"

"I don't know, Harry," Stone answered. "I think the odds are against it with his face plastered all over. But anything's possible, so look for signs of life at any of the closed houses. If you see something, a light inside, or some other indication someone's there, don't approach it alone. You call for the rest of us, and we'll establish a perimeter and take him."

A solemnness hung in the air like a thick fog until Harry stood and broke the silence.

"I'm gonna catch a short nap in the cell 'til sunset."

***

Stone made a beeline for Molly's café to take her home after dinner. As he ate, Molly sat across from him in his favorite booth. "I'm sorry to keep bugging you, but your safety is of primary concern to me," Stone said. "I don't think I could stand it if anything happened to you."

"I feel the same way," Molly said, taking Stone's hands in hers. "I'll be careful and do everything you're asking, but I won't leave. I don't expect you to understand. Just accept that I have to do this—for me."

***

Over the following two days, the residents of Silver Lake flittered about their businesses, nervous as a preacher in a striptease joint as the influx of thrill seekers increased. Unlike the usual vacationers and tourists, those in town for the excitement of being close to the action were prone to rowdy behavior. Arguments over whose theories were right had become a common occurrence.

This resulted in calls to the Marshal's Office to handle drunken behavior and quell arguments on the verge of getting out of control. At least the reported sightings of Hatcher look-a-likes had dwindled, allowing the investigative team the time needed to handle the calls and continue to eliminate Hatcher's potential hiding places. The two-day break had allowed them to complete the house-to-house checks and begin the primitive campsite checks along the trails on the east and west sides of town.

Stone continued his vigil, sleeping on Molly's couch, although saying he *slept* on her couch was an oxymoron. He drove Molly home and to work in her car, allowing Harry and Rick the use of the Silver Lake Marshal's Office vehicles at night. He and Dan used them during the day. If Hatcher attempted to attack Molly, he would see her car in the driveway and think it was safe. It was a ruse Stone hoped would draw Hatcher into a trap.

On the second day, as the sun began its descent behind the mountain peaks and night prepared to wrap Silver Lake in its cool grip, Harry and Rick began their patrols.

As usual, Dan retreated to his hotel room. Following his press briefing, in which he was unable to provide anything new, Stone drove to Molly's restaurant for dinner and to escort her home. Silver Lake and the investigative team had settled into an uncomfortable routine. It was as if they were all holding their breath, awaiting the next attack by Hatcher.

***

Stone settled onto Molly's uncomfortable couch, prepared as he could be for the long night ahead. He pulled his forty-five-caliber pistol from its holster and laid it on the coffee table within easy reach.

With nothing to do except wait for sleep, if it would come, his thoughts turned to Billy Ray Hatcher. Stone knew that at any given time as many as thirty-five active serial killers were at large in the United States and committed a large number of murders every year. Hatcher might believe he was special and on some kind of revenge mission, but he was just another piece of crap serial killer, using Stone as his excuse.

Stone felt a mixture of anger and guilt eating away at him like sulfuric acid. Intellectually, he knew Hatcher was to blame for his actions and decision to follow Stone to Silver Lake, but emotionally, he felt a crushing guilt.

He was angry at the carnage Hatcher had caused, angry because he'd come to Silver Lake, Stone's *sanctum sanctorum.* He'd invaded the place Stone chose to rebuild his life—the place he'd come seeking his salvation.

Irrational as it was, he was angry with himself too. He should've stopped Hatcher in New York. He'd felt himself slipping, bit by bit embracing the beast inside that had been such a part of who he was in New York. The non-feeling part of him he wanted to forget, to crush so it would cease to exist.

Stone tried to clear the profusion of uncomfortable emotions and disturbing thoughts crowding his mind by concentrating on pleasant thoughts of Molly. Instead of a distraction, a migraine headache began to jackhammer his temples. Waves of nausea pulsated, forcing burning stomach acid into his throat. Involuntarily swallowing, he squinted against the pain. With his head throbbing, he stumbled to Molly's bathroom and rummaged through her old-fashioned, white-painted wooden medicine cabinet until he found a bottle of aspirin. He chewed four tablets, wincing at the sour taste as he examined his torment-ridden features in the cabinet door mirror.

He returned to the couch and lay in the dark, waiting for the aspirin to kick in and relieve the pain. With luck, he might get a little sleep tonight and escape his thoughts.

Chapter 53

APPROACHING TWO-THIRTY, EVERYTHING WAS dark and quiet. Billy Ray squatted, arms locked over his shins, behind a copse of bushes across the street from Molly's house. He would watch for a short time, and—if the coast was clear—approach and probe for any defenses.

He'd chosen this spot because it provided him an expansive view of Molly's house and the surrounding area. A sliver of moon exposed, it cast a faint glow. Enough light for him to see any movement in the trees or bushes.

One by one, he focused on each tree and bush, eliminating each as a possible hiding place. Some were evergreens that provided no good hiding places. The tall deciduous trees had better branches to perch on, although none showed the telltale signs of out of place branches or an unusual clump of leaves.

He assumed anyone on guard duty would dress similar to him. However, he doubted they would have the skill or patience to sit motionless. People had a tendency to shift their bodies if they became uncomfortable or swat at a bug buzzing near their face.

Following his inspection of the trees, he refocused his attention on the bushes. It was easier to maneuver from a ground position and bushes provided better cover. As he'd studied the trees, many of the bushes had been within his peripheral vision, and he'd detected no movement.

***

Stone's chirping phone woke him from a troubled sleep.

"Stone," he said, groggy from the lack of rest.

"It's Rick," came the urgent reply. "I'm in route to the hospital in Aspen, following an ambulance."

Stone jolted awake and asked, "What happened?"

"Bar fight," Rick explained. "Harry tried to stop it prior to my arrival, and someone hit him on the head with a beer bottle. It looks like he'll be okay. He's got a nasty cut and maybe a concussion."

"I'll be en route to the hospital in a couple of minutes," Stone said, grabbing his clothes and heading to the bathroom to dress. He was afraid of something like this, with the type of people who'd flooded into town.

The noise woke Molly. As Stone dressed, he explained the situation to her through the closed door. Exiting the bathroom, he said, "Lock the door and reset the cans. Don't open the door for anyone. I'll call you when I'm back on your doorstep."

Molly nodded and unlocked the door as Stone moved the cans.

Stone stepped across the threshold, looked back, and added, "Keep your gun close and call me if you hear any unusual noises." He rushed to her car and sped off into the darkness, as Molly watched him drive away.

***

Satisfied the area was clear of any lookouts, Billy Ray prepared to move toward Molly's house. He decided to change locations several times, keeping to cover as much as possible. As he mapped the route in his mind, preparing to make his first move, Molly's front door flew open and Stone rushed out.

As Stone drove off Billy Ray's attention shifted to the light spilling from the open front door. Molly stood in the doorway, watching Stone drive away. She looked around, moved back inside, and closed the door.

***

It had surprised Billy Ray, seeing Stone exit his girlfriend's house. Stone had set a trap and except for whatever had drawn him out, it would've succeeded in his capture or death. Luck had prevented him from making another mistake.

Billy Ray was unsure if he should leave and plan an attack another time or continue his night's mission. It was impossible to know when Stone would return, although if his rapid departure was any indication, it was something important and might keep him busy for some time. In addition, Molly was awake, so it would be impossible to sneak into her house and catch her by surprise.

Torn with indecision, he knew he should leave, but he wanted to hurt Stone for what he'd said and done. After an internal debate, he decided to err on the side of caution and leave. He would develop another plan and return some other time.

As he began his retreat, Molly's house went dark. It looked like she'd gone back to bed. Billy Ray stopped and hunkered behind the bushes again. It was such a long walk from and to the mine. If he could do the job tonight, it would save him additional planning and an arduous walk to return.

Killing Stone's girlfriend would give him immense satisfaction too.

He needed little time inside the house. The trick would be to get in and out prior to Stone's return. Billy Ray figured it would take him ten to fifteen minutes to check the house to find the best entry point. That would give Stone's girlfriend a chance to fall asleep again.

He changed from his hiking boots into his approach shoes and came at the house from the side, through a stand of trees. As he neared the house, he stopped and listened for any unnatural sounds. It was as quiet as a graveyard. He moved against the house, near a window. Curtains covered the window, blocking his view of the interior. As he circled the house, he noticed locks engaged on all the windows. None had alarm contacts on them.

He moved to the front door. The screen door creaked a warning as he eased it open. He froze, waiting to see if the noise had alerted anyone of his presence. The house remained dark and quiet. He reached out and grasped the doorknob, twisting it with caution. It was an antique knob—every bit as old as the door. The knob started to turn—and stopped. Locked. He could force it, but that would alert Stone's girlfriend of his presence.

He rounded the back of the house and approached the storm cellar doors. A large padlock secured them. She'd locked the back door too. He guessed the back door and window near it led into the kitchen. He moved to the window and examined the lock. Like the others, it was old, and he could defeat it with ease. He slid the tip of his knife between the bottom and top sections of the window and twisted. A little pressure and the lock popped.

Unlike the screen door, the window made no noise as he slid it open.

He eased the curtain aside with the tip of his knife and peered inside. A night light cast enough of a pale for him to see the entire room. It was the kitchen. He saw no dirty dishes in the sink—nothing he would have to move out of the way.

Careful and quiet, he pulled himself through the window. He eased himself off the counter and stood in the middle of the kitchen. He heard no sounds of movement. He unplugged the night light. In a few minutes, his eyes would adjust to the dark. Able to see as well as he could in the blackness of the small house, he moved to the archway leading to the living room. As he edged into the living room, his foot struck something hard and a clatter of cans shattered the silence. From an unknown part of the house, a shout cut through the darkness.

"I HAVE A GUN!"

He didn't wait to see if the woman had a gun. He spun and dashed through the kitchen toward the open window. As he clambered onto the sink, he heard someone kick the cans. His pursuer was close. Desperate, he lunged for the open window. He heard the shot and felt the bullet whiz past his head, shattering the glass as he cleared the window and collided with the ground.

As she unlocked the back door, he ran. Billy Ray knew a moving target was easier to spot, so he stopped in a stand of trees. His disguise would conceal him in the shadows.

As he froze by the trees, the back-porch light came on, illuminating him. The woman stepped out from the kitchen door and leveled a semi-automatic pistol at him. Lights came on at a neighbor's house causing her to shift her eyes for a moment. He whirled and sprinted away. He heard two gunshots and felt a searing pain rip across his right side.

"Shit!" he swore, grabbing at his side as he ran. The bitch had shot him. The bullet had only grazed him, but it still burned like hell.

***

Stone was at the Aspen hospital, and Rick had told him Harry needed several stitches to close the wound and had a slight concussion. The doctor said he would keep Harry overnight and release him in the morning. Harry's wife, Verna, had arrived and was at his bedside.

As Stone and Rick waited, they heard a dispatcher call for any available unit to respond to Molly's house on a shots-fired call. He and Rick dashed for their vehicles like madmen. In a matter of seconds, they had maneuvered onto the highway, heading for Silver Lake at breakneck speed, Rick leading with his emergency equipment flashing and screaming.

Chapter 54

THEY SKIDDED TO A STOP in front of Molly's house, the vehicles joining two others blocking the street. Stone saw a Pitkin County deputy sheriff and one of the Lake County deputy sheriffs assigned to the roadblock standing outside the house.

He slid out of Molly's car and ran toward the deputies with Rick on his heels. "Is Molly okay?" Stone asked, moving past the deputies and toward the front door without waiting for a response.

"She's fine, and the suspect's gone," the Pitkin County deputy said to Stone's receding figure. Rick joined the deputies outside the house.

Stone burst through the front door, startling Molly, seated on her living room couch. "What happened? Are you okay?"

"I'm fine," Molly said. "After you left, I went back to bed and fell asleep. Someone kicked the cans by the kitchen doorway, and it woke me."

Stone glanced at the cans on the floor, a jumbled mess of rolled aluminum containers and string. "Did he attack you?" Stone asked, shifting his attention to Molly, his eyes scrutinizing her from head to foot.

"He didn't have the chance," Molly said. She told Stone the details of the event and finished with, "My neighbors heard the shots and called 911."

"Was it the same guy on the wanted poster?" Stone asked.

"I couldn't tell. He dressed all in black and wore a black ski mask."

Stone seemed more upset than Molly. He thought her calmness might be shock related.

"That's gotta be him. I should've been here, damnit," he mumbled.

"It worked out okay," Molly said. "I told you I can take care of myself."

"You were lucky. Staying at your house isn't feasible anymore," Stone said. "You're gonna need better protection. If you did hit him and he ran off, his injury can't be bad. That means he's pissed and, because he's revenge motivated, he'll be back."

"I told you—I refuse to run away," Molly said, a hint of anger in her tone.

"We'll work out a better plan to protect you," Stone said, ignoring Molly's angry declaration.

"It'll be daylight in a couple of hours, so I need to shower and get ready for work," Molly said.

"I'll wait out front and drive you to work. I'll need a detailed written statement from you, but it can wait."

"Okay," Molly said, taking him by the arm and escorting him to the door.

Outside, Stone addressed the two deputies. "Thanks for responding. I got pulled away, because Harry got himself beaned with a beer bottle, and I was at the hospital."

"We heard," the Pitkin County deputy said, nodding toward Rick.

"Has anyone checked for the suspect or evidence?" Stone asked.

"Yeah, we cleared the area. The suspect's long gone," the Pitkin County deputy said. "We thought it better to stick close to the house until you arrived, so we haven't looked for evidence."

"I'm more relieved you decided to stay with her than you know. It'll be easier to look for evidence come sunup," Stone said. He looked at the Lake County deputy and asked, "Did you guys see any suspicious vehicles leaving town after the shooting?"

"I radioed my partner, and he hasn't seen any vehicles leaving except you, after the ambulance left with Rick following in one of your department vehicles. And no vehicles came into town since ten or so, except you two."

The information made Stone wonder if they had missed Hatcher hiding someplace in town. They would have to take a closer look at that possibility.

Stone thanked the deputies again and told them he would stand by and take Molly to work. He addressed Rick as they pulled away. "Thanks for having Harry's back. I was afraid we might have issues because of the type of people that've been comin' into town."

"Yeah, they're pretty rowdy, but I think this was an isolated event," Rick said.

"Go home and get some rest," Stone said. "We can talk tonight."

"What about Molly?" Rick asked, nodding in the direction of the house.

"We need to work out a better plan to protect her," Stone said. "Give it some thought, and we can talk it through tonight."

"We need to find that bastard," Rick added, heading for his vehicle.

Stone nodded and climbed into Molly's car to wait for her.

Racked with emotions, anger roiled inside him. If Hatcher were in front of him, he would kill him with his bare hands. At the same time, fear squeezed him in its icy grip. He was afraid of losing everything and everyone that mattered to him. If that happened, he would lose himself.

***

Mumbling and cursing all the way back to the mine, Billy Ray peeled off his shirt. The blood from his wound had dried, causing the shirt to stick to his side.

"Goddamn son of a bitch," he shouted, as the shirt tugged at the scab, intensifying the pain. With gritted teeth, he yanked the shirt free in an effort to get it over with, like ripping off an adhesive bandage stuck to hair. The effort caused the wound to begin bleeding again and set his side on fire.

"OWWW—GODDAMN IT!" He grabbed his canteen and poured cool water over the injury, flushing the blood away and cooling the burning sensation. Patting the wound dry, he waited for the bleeding to stop and the pain to subside. He dressed his side with antiseptic ointment and a bandage from a first-aid kit he'd purchased with his other backpacking equipment. He was fortunate she was such a bad shot. The bullet had grazed his right side below the ribs, passing between his side and arm. It hurt like hell, but the injury was superficial.

On the other hand, she'd damaged his ego worse than his side. When he made the decision to end someone's life, his victims were as good as dead. If not for the distraction that caused her to look away for a moment and allowed him a chance to escape—she might have killed him.

He pulled the revolver out of his backpack—the one he took from the PI he'd killed in New York and gripped it, feeling its heft. *Maybe I'll shoot you both*, he thought. The idea pleased him, even though firearms weren't his weapon of choice. Although proficient in their use, he preferred the knife—because it was personal. He'd had no opportunity to use it though. *That pissant bitch was ready—*

waiting for me, he thought. *It's because of Stone. The bastard wants me dead, and he used his whore to try it.*

What angered him most was that a damn woman had gotten the better of him. She'd made him fail in his mission—again.

As he thought through the night's events, light from the fire reflected off the polished surface of the gun. He stared into the glow dancing off the weapon's finish. The longer he thought, the more rage he felt.

This time he would let the building storm grow unchecked. Enraged, his emotions were white-hot. Explosive anger so overwhelmed him, he screamed and stabbed the gun into the darkness at the edge of the firelight. He spun and sought an imaginary adversary to shoot. As his blood pressure spiked, he pulled the trigger. The deafening report of the gunshot ricocheted off the walls of the chamber. The detonation and recoil from the revolver startled him back from the edge.

Soaked in cold sweat and his vision blurry, he sagged to his knees, unable to keep his legs under him. Head thrown back, he sucked in great masses of air, trying to clear his head and regain some control. His vision cleared, and his heart began to slow. He fell forward, catching himself with his hands. His energy spent, he crawled to his sleeping bag and slipped the gun back into the backpack. Exhausted, he slithered into the bag to rest.

A short nap, he thought. *That's what I need.* He drifted into a troubled sleep—where his nightmares waited.

Chapter 55

STONE, DAN, RICK, AND THE recent hospital patient, Harry Field, met at Molly's house to determine her fate—in spite of her protestations. As the sun dipped below the mountain peaks, Molly sulked in her bedroom, refusing to participate. The team trickled in and found seats on her living room couch and two chairs surrounding a coffee table. The modern style furniture looked good but failed to lend itself to comfort in Stone's—and his back's—opinion.

Stone had taken the day to review the recent events and the steps taken to find Billy Ray Hatcher. They were solid investigative moves. Stone tried to think in the abstract to develop additional ideas they could implement. It had been one of his strengths at the NYPD and had led him to success with a number of so-called unsolvable cases. He'd come away with some ideas and had prepared for the meeting.

Harry provided information on the events that had taken place at the bar. No arrests resulted from the attack, because Harry's attacker struck from behind. By the time Rick had arrived on scene, the culprit had fled town, according to the witnesses. Following Harry's report, he showed off his stitches. The show and tell over, the men focused on business.

"First things first," said Stone. "Any ideas we formulate must exclude Molly leaving town. She's made it clear that won't happen."

"I think we have two priorities to discuss," Dan said. "Protecting

Molly and catching Hatcher. The two subjects aren't mutually exclusive, but they need independent analysis."

"I agree," Rick said. "Hatcher has narrowed the focus of his attacks, Stone. I think he's zeroed in on his endgame—those closest to you, and you in the end. That doesn't exclude attacks on others, but it's looking personal.

Harry interjected, "His plans don't mean spit. We need to find his hidey-hole and flush him out."

Stone agreed with everything said but zeroed in on Harry's comment, because it was the third time he'd heard it said, and it irritated him like an unreachable itch. "You've all made that same point to me, so I spent the day wondering if he could've slipped past our hotel, motel, home, or campground checks. I did some additional checking today with Will and Dan's help, and I'm convinced he isn't hiding in town or at any commercial campground from Silver Lake to Glenwood Springs. I found no campgrounds going east on Highway 82, because it's too steep and rocky all the way to, and beyond, Independence Pass."

"And if he's driving in and out of town, they would've spotted him at the roadblock," Rick added.

"Where's that leave us?" Harry asked.

"Applying a principle used in forensic disciplines called Occam's razor," Stone explained. "Its basic premise is to accept the simplest and most obvious explanation consistent with all the known facts."

"So, how's that apply to catching Hatcher?" Harry asked.

"It tells us that if he isn't hiding in town, he's hiding outside of town," Rick said. "Since all the campgrounds are on the lookout for him, and we know he has camping equipment, the simplest explanation is that he's camping in a location other than a commercial campground."

"And because he can't use his car, and we've heard of no stolen car reports, he's got to be close enough to town to walk," Stone added.

"That narrows the search area," Harry said, "but still leaves a lot of area to cover."

"I don't think it's as large an area as you might assume," Stone said. "If he's walking, I'd bet he's close. He'll want to avoid exposure to day hikers and other wilderness campers."

"So, you think he's in the mountains near town?" Harry asked. "We've checked the primitive campsites on both trails."

"That's right," Stone replied, pointing at Harry. "So, if he isn't hiding in town, isn't at any commercial campground, and isn't at any of the primitive campsites near town, what's the simplest hypothesis of his hiding spot?"

"He's bushwhacking?" Harry asked.

"Bingo," Stone said. "The topography of the surrounding mountains doesn't lend itself to camping any place he wants, so we can narrow our search to areas conducive to camping."

"We got abandoned mines in the mountains too," Harry said. "Think he might try hidin' in one of 'em?

"Doubtful," Stone said, "Will told me the county engineers dynamited the ones that hadn't already collapsed a few years ago. If we can't find him camping any place else, we can check them as a last resort."

"Any idea how he's getting in and out of town?" Rick asked.

"I have an idea," Stone said, pulling a folded topographical map from his jacket pocket and spreading it out on the coffee table. Everyone leaned in or knelt by the table to see.

Using his index finger as a guide, Stone said, "I highlighted the trails in yellow, because it's hard to follow. If we trace the east side trail from the trailhead to this area south of town, even though the main trail curves away from town, several primitive and unused old trails cut off toward town. I was able to follow these intersecting trails to the city shops and water treatment plant. It's a short walk from the plant into town." Each man followed Stone's finger as he traced the route.

"From the main trail on the west side of town, I couldn't find any feeder trails leading to town," Stone pointed out, tracing the highlighted trail. "But look at this," he said, stabbing the map with his index finger. "The main trail passes close to the newer housing development west of the lake. It wouldn't be hard to bushwhack a short distance. Or, for all we know, hikers could've made newer trails shortcutting through the woods to town that aren't shown on this map."

"How feasible is that?" Rick asked.

"Off the east side trail, it'd be damn tough to navigate," Stone said. "A little easier from the west side trail. I wouldn't want to try either in the dark."

"I can't believe he can walk into town from either trail," Harry said, in a worried tenor.

"Until we figure out another way, we can't discount that possibility. So, starting in the morning, I'd like to begin hiking the trails and looking for any signs of Hatcher's camp," Stone said.

Everyone agreed it was the best option they had, so they worked out a plan to complete the search.

"The other thing I'd like to do is have someone park near the entrance of the road leading to the shops at night to see if Hatcher enters town that way. Several places in the area lend themselves to hiding a vehicle, so if he does come that way, we'll see him, but he won't know we're on to him."

"I'll do the stakeout," Harry volunteered.

"And I'll continue night patrols, if you want," Rick said.

"It'll take a little longer to check possible campsites off the two trails with just Dan and me checking, but it's a good idea to keep someone patrolling town at night," Stone said.

"Let's assume we don't know how he's getting into town," Dan said. "How do we provide better protection for Molly?"

At the mention of her name, Molly appeared from the bedroom and joined the group. "I refuse to leave," she said with finality, crossing her arms over her chest as she walked into the living room.

"I made sure to cover that," Stone said, giving Molly a reassuring look. "I called Sheriff Davis today, and I think he's got an excellent idea—and you won't have to leave town."

The group discussed the plan, and even though Molly was unhappy with it, she agreed because it met her requirement of remaining in town overnight.

***

Hatcher chose to remain hidden until his side scabbed enough to stop hurting as it rubbed against his shirt. It would give him time to plan. He could afford no further mistakes. His anger at Stone's bitch for shooting him continued to burn a hole in his gut. He'd been lucky. But luck only lasted for so long, and he'd pushed his.

With proper planning, he wouldn't need luck.

He decided to make one final hike to town and stay hidden until he could finish his mission. He could pack enough trail mix and other dry foods, and carry enough water, so if he had to wait for an opportunity, he could do it in relative comfort.

With patience, planning and a readiness to strike, he would get the opening he needed.

Chapter 56

TWO NIGHTS LATER, BILLY RAY made his move. As he approached town on the dirt road leading from the shops and water treatment plant, something in his gut told him to stop. He might be paranoid, but to avoid mistakes, he had to assume they would've increased security since his brush with Stone's whore. Walking into town as if he owned the place might be a foolish move.

Prior to reaching the intersection with South Avenue, the southernmost street in town, he cut east off the dirt road into the trees. East of his location were a number of rental cabins in a campground called Streamside Cabin Rentals. At this hour, everyone was sound asleep. He skirted along the south edge of the campground, between the cabins and a stream that fed into the lake west of town.

Past the campground, he cut north again and found South Avenue. Stone's woman lived a couple of blocks away. Billy Ray returned to the same hiding spot he'd used the last time.

This time no moonlight was visible to help him see.

He waited and watched, checking the trees and bushes as he had the last time, looking for any potential threat. Satisfied, he dodged from one clump of bushes to another until close enough to make a final dash to the house. He crept along the foundation to the back of the structure.

Standing by the kitchen window, he could see inside through a split in the curtains. The night light, lit on his last visit, was off. It was pitch black inside the kitchen. Through the new window glass, he could see the lock had been re-engaged.

This was too easy. *Was someone inviting him to break in again?*

Billy Ray backed away and made his way back to his original hiding spot. He hunkered behind the bushes to contemplate his next move.

***

Stone sat in one of Molly's living room chairs he'd moved to a corner of the living room. He sat in the dark with his Heckler and Koch, Mark 23, forty-five caliber ACP semi-automatic pistol resting on his lap. The safety was off in anticipation. Exhausted from a lack of sleep, he struggled to remain alert. At least the uncomfortable chair helped keep him awake.

With dawn an hour away, Stone slipped into a shallow and fit ful slumber. His head bobbed at first, then settled, his chin resting on his chest. Drifting deeper into a disturbed sleep, dreams of the grizzly scenes he'd investigated in his prior life at the NYPD flashed through his mind. In his nightmare, a kaleidoscope of butchered victim's faces, stained red with blood, flickered across his view like scenes out a subway train window. The screeching of train brakes morphed into the anguished screams of the victim's families, pleading for his help to solve their loved ones' murders. Red neon notes in blood flashed on and off—on and off—taunting him.

Stone awoke with a start, drenched in a veneer of cold sweat. His heart pounded—his breath coming in short, ragged bursts.

"Jesus," he said into the darkness. It was bad enough that his childhood nightmare of Benjamin Dowd's ghost, hunting those who killed him and took his fortune had returned of late, but now this? He rubbed his hands through his hair, feeling the icy dampness at the back of his neck. Remnants of the macabre nightmare lingered.

He wondered what time it was and realized the blackness of night had edged toward the dullness of pre-dawn. He interlaced his fingers behind his head and arched his sore back, causing pops in his lower vertebrae, and watched the room lighten. The floor, walls, and furniture morphed from shades of gray into Molly's choices of muted colors. To push the last of the lurid dream away, he tried to focus on what lay ahead. His heart and breathing slowed. With a sigh, he headed to the bathroom, taking his gun with him.

***

Wary he would find another waiting trap, Billy Ray climbed the steep hill along the east edge of town, working his way north along the hill on the other side of the ridge so he would remain unseen. He settled behind a large rock outcropping at the crest of the hill across the street from Stone's house.

As he settled in, he noticed a subtle change as night edged its way toward shades of gray in the predawn sky. The sky continued to brighten as daybreak crept toward sunrise. It was too late to do anything but observe.

As the sun peeked over the tops of the mountains, he saw two men dressed in black and carrying rifles with large odd-looking scopes emerge from hiding places behind a rock outcropping and a copse of bushes below him. They had been invisible in the dark. As he watched, they made their way off the hill and across the road to Stone's house.

They carried their rifles in a relaxed, ready position and approached the front door of the cabin. As the door opened, they stopped short. A man Billy Ray had seen with Stone stepped onto the front stoop and conversed with the men.

Following a brief conversation, the black clad figures trotted off until they were out of sight. Billy Ray sat back, wondering what else would happen at the cabin. A short time passed, and Stone pulled into the driveway and exited the car that Billy Ray had seen earlier, parked in Molly's driveway. This time the front door opened, and the man and Molly stepped out into the morning brightness. Molly drove off in the car Stone had arrived in, and Stone and the man left in the Silver Lake SUV parked in the driveway.

Billy Ray had all the pieces to the puzzle. Stone had tried to sucker him, hoping he'd attack the woman again. He'd tried to pull a switch by hiding her at his house. Billy Ray figured Stone had done that so he could play the hero in a one-on-one confrontation—one he would lose.

It was telltale that Stone had private security watching the woman *and* two SWAT cops across the street. That was a lot of protection for one person. That meant she was special to him. Good. In a flash, he knew what to do. Snatch the girl, and Stone would follow like a whimpering puppy.

Billy Ray crested the hill and made his way to a rock outcropping that would put him above and to the left of the SWAT cops upon their return. He removed a canteen of water and an energy bar from his backpack. He took a long drink of water and munched on his breakfast. Pleased with the results of his night's work, he repositioned himself to get some sleep. As the cops prepared for another night of surveillance, he'd watch and plan his move. They outnumbered him two to one and had the firepower—but he had the element of surprise working for him.

***

The team met at the marshal's office prior to Harry and Rick going off duty. Stone made a fresh pot of coffee and everyone filled their cups then took their respective seats.

Stone sat at his desk with his mug in his hand, took a sip, and sighed. The lack of leads worried him. They had no idea where Hatcher might be. Stone wondered if Hatcher had decided to run. *No,* he thought. Hatcher meant to finish what he started, and nothing would stop him from trying.

"Did you see anything last night, Harry?" he asked.

"Didn't catch a whiff of 'im," Harry said, frustration in his voice—the same frustration they all felt. "And I tucked myself away as deep as a tick on a dog's back. No way he could'a spotted me."

Dan added, "It was all quiet at your house too. I spoke with the SWAT deputies this morning, and they had nothing to report either."

Stone looked at Rick.

"Nothing," Rick said. "And I spoke with the guys at the roadblock, and they had nothing to report."

"Damn," Stone said, his frustration evident. It was as though Hatcher had vanished.

"I'm worried if Hatcher doesn't make an appearance soon, Sheriff Yates will pull his deputies, and your boss may want to pull SWAT too," Stone said to Rick.

"I'll find out how Sheriff Davis feels, and if he's thinking of pulling the SWAT guys, I'll do what I can to get him to change his mind," Rick said.

After Harry and Rick left, Stone asked Dan, "You get any sleep?"

"Yeah. Your couch is comfortable," Dan said, smiling. "I had the portable radio near me on the SWAT channel, so they could alert me if they saw any movement. Didn't hear a peep."

"Wish I could say the same," Stone said. "Don't tell her I said this, but trying to get a decent night's sleep on Molly's furniture is like trying to get comfortable on a medical backboard."

Dan barked a rare laugh.

"Let's get some breakfast and hit the trails again," Stone said. "I want that bastard's head on a pike."

At the café, they bumped into Will. It relieved Stone to learn the revenue flow continued to please the town fathers, as did the free advertising. They were certain once Stone caught the killer, the current negative news reports would cease, and the result would be an uptick of visitation.

"You might also want to know that they've moved Mister Hendrickson out of intensive care, and he's on the road to a full recovery," Will said.

"I'm pleased to hear it," Stone said, being polite. What he was most grateful for was that Hendrickson was out of the picture. He had enough on his plate without dealing with the man's arrogance—and pathological need to interfere.

Chapter 57

A DAY OF STRENUOUS HIKING looking for fresh campsites resulted in weary legs and further frustration for Stone and Dan. Returning to town, dejected, it seemed to Stone Silver Lake had taken on a frenetic air. The town held its collective breath, waiting for another chapter in the gruesome story to unfold. An uneasy murmur of expectation had replaced the joyful sounds of summer. The residents of Silver Lake wore the worried mask of imminent victims. Even the adrenalin-seeking tourists twittered all over town, awaiting another act of violence. If he failed to end this soon, he was afraid it might destroy Silver Lake—and him.

Finished with dinner at the Silver Nugget Café, Dan took Molly to Stone's house in the Silver Lake Marshal's Office SUV, and Stone drove Molly's car to her house.

As dusk approached, Dan prepared for another night at Stone's house with Molly. He made the couch into his bed for the night and turned on the portable radio, keeping the volume low. It gave him some relief, knowing trained professionals watched his back from across the street.

Stone resumed his vigil from Molly's living room, praying for the confrontation that would end this nightmare.

***

The sky began to darken. Bruised clouds crowding overhead foretold a coming weather change. The SWAT deputies positioned themselves in the same locations they had hidden the previous night. Dressed in the same type of clothing, they also carried the same strange-looking rifles.

Settled in, they blended with the landscape like chameleons. If Billy Ray hadn't witnessed them hide, spotting them would be near impossible. He pinpointed their positions, using landmarks to find them in the dark. One hid among a mound of boulders with shrubbery growing out of the ground in the gaps. The other, who was closer, had positioned himself behind a large copse of scrub oak bushes.

The night ticked by in slow motion. He wanted to get moving, but he knew the longer he waited the better his chance of success. With the coming storm plopping large raindrops on the ground and rocks, a downpour was sure to follow. That would hide any noise he made as he began to move.

The sky opened and a rare, but serious, deluge poured from the heavens. Thunder boomed, the sound rolling along the mountains like an echo. Billy Ray saw the movement of the deputies unfurling and hiding under camouflage rain tarps to keep their equipment and themselves as dry as possible. The weather was a welcome addition and would make the coming job easier.

As his watch dial neared four-thirty, he decided it was time to go. A planned route chosen and memorized, he began a careful decent toward the closest deputy. He crawled on hands and knees, probing the ground with his hands prior to shifting his weight to avoid snapping a twig that could signal his approach. With the ground water-soaked, the small twigs and other plant debris was too wet to make any noise.

As he neared the camouflaged figure lying prone behind the large scrub oak bush, he reached back and slid his knife out of a side pocket on his backpack. The rain continued to fall in a steady downpour and his target, covered head to foot with the tarp and focused on Stone's house, was unable to see his approach. He stopped near the deputy, a couple of feet behind the front edge of the tarp.

Frozen, he waited for the opportune moment. Thunder rumbled, and the deputy raised his head. Billy Ray attacked. The deputy lay dead before he could sound the alarm. The rain sent the blood flowing in rivulets from his deep neck wound along rain-filled gullies carved into the hillside from the storm.

Billy Ray lay prone, pressed against the deputy, examining the equipment his victim wore. The deputy's clothing would be indistinguishable from his in the quasi-light of morning, except for the tactical helmet, black ski mask, flak vest, gun belt, and boots the man wore. Billy Ray could take what he needed at the right time.

He turned his attention to the rifle. It was a Heckler and Koch MP5 equipped with a sound suppressor and night vision device with a red-dot sight system. He slid the rifle out of his victim's hands, found the safety, and disengaged it. The butt pressed against his shoulder, he pointed it in the general direction of the other deputy's hiding spot. An image of the other tarp appeared in the scope.

Billy Ray waited, hoping for a target. If he guessed at the shot placement and missed, all hell would break loose. The deputy had body armor, so the result of a shooting confrontation would mean his own death.

As the rainstorm began to slacken, Billy Ray worried that the loss of noise would cease to cover his movement. He stayed in place to avoid the possibility of drawing the other deputy's attention.

As he froze in place, waiting for the other deputy to make a move and give him an opportunity to strike, the deputy poked his head out from under the tarp. Billy Ray reacted without hesitation. He aimed the rifle, using the red dot to pinpoint a spot on the deputy's head behind his left ear, and squeezed off a shot. The deputy's head jerked to the side from the bullet's impact. Another check through the scope showed no movement. The deputy was dead. To be sure, Billy Ray fired a second time. The bullet struck a limp body that remained motionless.

The metallic clank of the bolt and a soft *pfft* of firing through a sound suppressor were the only sounds the rifle made. He doubted anyone even a few feet away could've heard the noise. To be sure, he remained stationary and scanned the house through the scope. Satisfied no one in the house had heard anything, he stripped the deputy of the needed equipment. Donning the gear, he thought his disguise would fool the guy protecting Stone's whore.

With time to kill, he resumed his watch through the rifle scope. He wanted to approach the house a few minutes earlier than the deputies had the previous morning. He knew the timing would be tight. He had to finish what he intended to do and disappear prior to Stone's arrival.

As he waited, the rain eased to a stop and the clouds broke apart, exposing the starlit sky. As the black of night edged toward the dawn, he stood and—with authority—marched toward Stone's house.

Billy Ray knew his guise had worked when the cabin door opened, and the man stepped out on the porch.

***

Dan's eyes locked on the deputy. He'd kept his ski mask on and was alone. Suspicious, Dan squinted and asked, "Where's your partner?"

When the deputy failed to respond, Dan knew. He saw the rifle, rising with the barrel pointed in his direction, and dove to the side.

Two rapid-fire shots hit their mark. The first shattered a rib and punched a hole in one of Dan's lungs, and the second ripped through Dan's heart. Dan fell to the wet ground, never feeling the impact.

***

Without a second glance, Billy Ray stepped over Dan's crumbled body and entered the house, focused on this part of his mission. He had no time to waste. A quick scan of the space showed a portable radio and a set of vehicle keys on a coffee table to his left. He pocketed the keys and clipped the radio to his belt.

With muted speed, he moved through the small house and stopped at a bedroom door that was partway open. Stone's girlfriend was asleep in the bed, tucked under the covers. The muffled noise made by the rifle had failed to wake her.

Billy Ray placed the rifle on the hallway floor. He inched his way into the bedroom and to the side of the bed. As he approached, he slipped his favorite knife from the pocket on the side of his backpack.

Before beginning, he took a moment to stand over her and watch her sleep.

Chapter 58

DRESSED IN HIS HIKING CLOTHES, and in the bathroom combing his hair, Stone heard talking on the portable radio in the living room. One of the voices sounded strained. He moved to the living room to listen. Maybe they had caught Hatcher.

Stunned by what he heard, he grabbed the radio and interrupted the exchange between Rick and the dispatcher. "Sergeant Fowler, Silver Lake One. Repeat your last."

"Silver Lake One," came the instant reply, "you need to respond to your home right now."

Stone wasted no time replying. He ran into the bathroom and grabbed his gun, securing it in his belt holster. As he headed toward the door, he clipped the portable radio to his belt opposite the gun. He jumped into Molly's car and sped to his house.

As he pulled to a stop near his house, he saw the Silver Lake Marshal's Office older SUV Harry drove, a Lake County Sheriff's Department patrol car, and a Pitkin County Sheriff's Department patrol car all parked askew in the street. The vehicles blocked his view of his house, but the yellow crime scene tape surrounding a large area on the hillside across the street was an ominous sight.

He jumped out of Molly's car and hurried toward the men congregated near his front door. He came to an abrupt stop upon seeing a bloodied Dan Deegan lying dead on the ground outside his open door.

"Molly!" he shouted and broke into an all-out sprint for the house.

Rick and Harry headed him off and stopped him. "No," Rick said. "You have to stay out. It's a crime scene."

Gripped with the fear of a man who's lost everything he values in life—everything he holds sacrosanct—Stone stopped and backed away from Rick's outstretched arms. He sank to his knees in the damp grass and with a look of anguished grief, he mumbled, "Molly and Dan dead," as though trying to grasp a foreign concept.

"No, no! Molly isn't dead—he kidnapped her," Rick said, realizing Stone had missed some of the radio traffic. "She's missing along with your Marshal's Office SUV."

"Missing?" Stone questioned. A sudden wave of relief washed over him. Molly was alive. Stone regained his footing, waved his arm in an arc from Dan to the hillside, and said, "I don't understand. How could any of this have happened?"

Stone had believed it was impossible for Hatcher to get through their defenses, but he had. Stone blamed himself for his failure to foresee that possibility. He'd failed to protect Molly and gotten Dan killed. Guilt tore at his sanity, threatening to drive him mad. Beginning to feel sorry for himself, he remembered that self-pity was an ugly suit to wear.

"Based on what little I've seen," Rick explained, "it looks like Hatcher killed our two deputies on the hill. He took the gear from one of them and must've come to the house. Dan came outside, and Hatcher shot him and took Molly and the SUV," Rick said. One of the deputy's rifles is in the hallway. I wasn't able to take a good look because Sheriff Davis is on his way with everyone he can find and ordered me to freeze everything." Rick withheld one thing he'd seen.

Harry stepped in and with his voice cracking said, "I'm sorry it all went to pieces, Stone, but you need to know somethin' else."

"Harry?" Rick cautioned.

Harry shook his head no and said, "He has a right to know."

"Know what?" Stone demanded.

"He left a message on the bedroom wall," Harry said.

Stone stared at Harry, terror embedded in his eyes. "Tell me what it says."

Harry swallowed, his Adam's apple bobbing. "It says, 'Now you pay.'"

Stone's blood ran cold. He sucked in a breath and asked the question to which he was sure he knew the answer. "Was it in blood?"

"Yeah," was all Harry could muster.

Rick jumped in and added, "It's a minimal amount of blood. Like what you'd get from a cut."

Stone's emotions morphed from fear to anger. His jaw tightened like a vice, and fire raged in his eyes. He lashed out, "Why're you waiting to mount a search for her?"

"The sheriff said ..."

"Look, I'm sorry your deputies are dead, and I'm sorry Dan is too, but there's nothing we can do for them. But Molly's alive and needs our help. The longer we wait, the more chance Hatcher will do her harm."

"I can't run off looking for Molly right this minute," Rick said, pointing at Dan and the hill across the street.

"I know," Stone said. "You understand that *I* have to go."

"I do," Rick said. "You go, and we'll follow as quick as we can. When we've got a handle on the scenes, we'll be able to provide a lot of help."

Harry said, "I'll go with you."

"No," Stone said. "We have to have someone to represent our department, since all this happened in our jurisdiction."

Harry nodded, but looked unhappy. Stone jumped in the remaining Silver Lake Marshal's Office vehicle and sped off. The truth was he wanted to find Hatcher on his own. He neither expected nor wanted any added support. It would all be over in short order, because his nightmare last night had provided him with an idea of Hatcher's location.

Molly's life depended on him using every skill and intuition he had. He owed it to her and Dan. He refused to consider the possibility she was dead—that possibility meant his life was over too.

As he sped toward the entrance to town where Dowd Street turned into Route 138, he thought back on his dream. As a child, he had nightmares because of the stories told to him of the town's founder, Benjamin Dowd, who wandered the abandoned mines in the hills surrounding town, seeking revenge for his murder and the theft of his fortune. Since Hatcher had chosen Benjamin Dowd's memorial boulder to place Candy Ferguson's body and his bloody message, the nightmares had begun to revisit Stone.

He'd failed to grasp the significance of the dreams at first. It was his nightmares that had helped him realize what was right in front of his face. Séances, palm reading, crystal balls, and all the other so-called mystical arts were a bunch of hocus-pocus as far as Stone knew. He was a man of science and put no stock in the mystical.

Using Occam's razor, a scientific principle, he'd narrowed the places Hatcher might hide, but that left a lot of ground to cover. Common sense told Stone the best place to hide was in an abandoned mine, but they were either collapsed or filled in according to Will. Yet Hatcher had to be someplace, and a mine was a good place to hide.

Stone wondered if the placing of Candy's body against Dowd's memorial might have been an unconscious slip on Hatcher's part: no mysticism involved—just thinking outside the box. The skill that helped him solve so-called unsolvable crimes in New York.

And it so happened that he knew the location of Benjamin Dowd's mine. He would know if he was on the right track if he found his Silver Lake Marshal's Office SUV in the spot he thought he might find it.

He slammed on the brakes, so involved with his thoughts he came close to missing the turnoff. He swung onto the dirt access road and sped toward the trailhead. Entering the parking lot area, he slammed on the brakes again and jammed the shifter into park. He was halfway out the door as the truck slid to a stop.

His marshal's office SUV sat gleaming in the morning sun in front of him.

Chapter 59

IT HAD ALL HAPPENED IN a blur—from sound sleep, confident in her protection, to jolted awake by tape slapped across her face and wrapped around her wrists and ankles. With no chance to resist, she'd lain helpless. Molly couldn't understand what had happened to her protection.

As she lay immobilized, she'd felt a sharp pain in her hand. She saw the masked apparition of a figure, close to invisible in the dim light, writing something on the bedroom wall as blood flowed from the wound. Then her attacker had freed her ankles and forced her to her feet.

By the time he shoved her out the front door, she'd regained her wits and prepared herself to fight and run. However, any thought of resisting had drained from her at the sight of Dan's body crumbled on the lawn. As he'd forced her onto the back-seat floor of the marshal's office SUV, she'd seen the police attire he wore.

Following a short and hurried ride, he'd poked and pushed her to keep her moving along the east side trail and onto a steep side trail. A torturous forced march on the steep trail in her socks had winded her and sliced her unprotected feet. Cut and bruised by twigs and the sharp edges of scree, the pain in Molly's feet had caused her to cry out. With her mouth duct taped, a moan was all that had escaped.

She'd made a feeble attempt at slowing the pace, met by the

stinging slap of a stick across the back of her thighs. Salty trails of sweat had rolled into her eyes, stinging and blurring her vision. Her tears helped wash some of the pain away. As she stumbled along, her kidnapper had prodded her in the back with the stick.

Halfway along the steep trail, she'd slipped and fallen to her knees. Her attacker struck her on her back, arms, and legs until she'd regained her feet. As she stumbled along, she felt sticky, warm blood trickling down her arms and legs.

At last, they had arrived at a level area Molly saw was by the gated entrance of a closed mine. She'd sagged to the ground, her energy spent. She'd chanced a glance at her tormenter. He'd removed the ski mask and guzzled from a canteen. The face she'd seen was that of the murder suspect on the wanted poster, Billy Ray Hatcher.

Done drinking, Hatcher had wiped a forearm across his mouth and stared at her. His face showed all the emotion of a person looking at a dead insect. It had made her shudder. The look in his eyes was cold, reptilian. Deciding to take a chance, she'd looked at the canteen, pleading with her eyes and mumbled through the tape. As he slipped out of his backpack, he spoke the first words he'd uttered and said, "Shut your pie hole." She'd gotten the message and stopped trying to communicate.

Hatcher had forced her to wriggle between the gates with her wrists bound behind her back. The trudge into the mine had been as dangerous as the mountain climb. Any hesitation resulted in violent shoves. One such push had ended in her colliding with the rock wall, cutting her forehead.

Entering a large chamber, Hatcher had ordered her to sit. She'd collapsed and watched him start a fire and strip off the police gear. His immediate needs taken care of, he'd ripped the tape off her mouth and given her a drink of water. A new strip of tape replaced the old, and he'd added more tape binding her ankles again.

He'd left her bleeding on the cavern floor and walked back into the tunnel, heading toward the mine entrance.

***

That had been fifteen minutes ago or so by her calculations. Frightened, exhausted, and pissed off, Molly had the presence of mind to evaluate her situation. She thought that Stone must know by now Hatcher had kidnapped her. He would move heaven and earth to find her. Her job was to stay alive until he did. To do that, she'd have to be careful. Hatcher had made it clear he had no tolerance for any disobedience and no desire to communicate.

She figured that if he'd wanted her dead, he would've killed her at Stone's house. That meant he had a reason to keep her alive—for the moment. Molly knew that at some point she might have to take saving her life into her own hands. She at least needed to prepare to help if Stone found them.

She also needed a plan in case no one found her. She knew what she had to do. She was a distance from the walls and her feet had swelled to the point she could put no pressure on them. If she could crawl to a wall, she might find a jagged rock edge sharp enough to cut her bindings.

What then? she thought. She was unable to walk, let alone run. And Hatcher had disappeared into the lone means of escape from the mine. Molly scanned the cave, desperate to find something she might use. Then she saw it. At the edge of the light cast by the small fire, she saw a large stick. If she could retrieve it, maybe she could hide it under her body and find a way to use it if the opportunity came.

Molly knew Hatcher might return any minute, but she had to

take the chance. She squirmed her way over to the stick, the pain from her swollen feet excruciating. Struggling to close the distance, she saw it was an old ax handle. She rolled onto her side and grabbed the handle in her taped hands. Under her hip, she felt the stab of a small rock. She probed for it with her hands and pushed it into her back pocket when she realized it was a piece of jagged rock.

As much as she dreaded returning to her original position, she wriggled her way back, tears of pain streaming across her face and dripping into the sand. Back in her original location, she used the ax handle to scrape a shallow gouge in the soft sand and buried it. She prayed Hatcher would miss the marks she left in the sand because of the low light.

Pulling the rock from her pocket, she held it in one hand and pressed it against the tape binding her wrists. She began to saw at the tape with the edge of the rock. Given enough time, she might be able to free her hands.

***

Stone ran to his marshal's office SUV and searched the interior. Other than a small amount of blood on the back-seat floor, nothing else caught his eye. He left the vehicle and started his trek along the trail. He looked for telltale signs that Hatcher and Molly had come this way, but the trail was hard-pack dirt from years of use. He spotted a single drop of blood on a rock protruding from the ground a quarter of a mile or so from the trailhead.

He was so focused on potential evidence on the ground, he walked right by the trail to the mine. He realized his mistake and backtracked the short distance to the cutoff. It was difficult to identify because of the overgrowth. Finding the trail, Stone noted it showed telltale signs of recent use. Unless you took a close look, you would've missed it, but bent blades of grass and weeds proved that someone had walked there.

In case Sheriff Davis sent backup to look for him, Stone realized he needed to mark the side trail, or they might miss it like he did. He stripped off his lightweight jacket and laid it on the side trail with one of the arms pointing the way. They were sure to see the sign and follow him to the mine—if they came.

Stone began to see additional signs the further along the trail he hiked. Traversing the area composed of scree, blood transfer, and a partial footwear impression in blood jumped out at him in the bright sunlight. With no pattern, he was certain the footwear impression was that of a sock.

The further he climbed, the angrier he became. Molly's forced march on the dangerous and sharp scree must have been excruciating for her. He prayed he would be in time to stop any further injury to her. At the same time, he needed to pace himself, because the climb was arduous and dangerous in spots.

He reached the tailings plateau and stopped to catch his breath. Gates blocking the mine entrance remained closed, and a chain and lock secured them, but footwear impressions in the dirt—some tinged red—convinced Stone he was at the right spot. Will hadn't mentioned a mine with a gate securing it. As he stared at the gates, it dawned on him that he was a perfect target, standing in the open. He ducked to the side of the gates.

Stone could see from his position that someone watching from the mine entrance could see a long way along the winding trail. Hatcher was a planner, so Stone had to assume he knew someone would find the vehicle and check the mine. Hatcher had most likely seen him coming.

Stone knew he should radio in and wait for backup. He had no idea what awaited him, or what trap Hatcher might have set. It was a fool's errand to go in alone.

But Molly was in there, so call him a fool. Waiting was out of the question. And he didn't intend to call it in because this was personal—as personal as it got.

PART VI

ENDINGS AND BEGINNINGS

Chapter 60

BILLY RAY PACED BACK AND forth at the mine entrance. He figured Stone would come because of his whore. It surprised him to see Stone approaching alone. Billy Ray had expected an army of angry cops. He raced back into the mine. This was perfect—a final clash of moralities. Stone represented impiety. Billy Ray believed he had righteousness on his side.

Re-entering the large cavern, he saw Molly laying in the same spot he'd left her. She was on her side, immobilized with duct tape. Hatcher hoped Stone would see her and feel compelled to run to her aid.

The fire had come close to going out in his absence. Billy Ray tossed a couple of small logs on it, so it would glow with enough light to illuminate Stone as he entered the cavern but insufficient light to expose him in the spot he'd chosen to hide. He donned his gloves and ski mask and positioned himself inside the tunnel he'd found blocked near the surface. Lying prone on the dirt floor, he stretched his arms out in front of him, holding the pistol taken from the SWAT deputy. He concentrated on slowing his breathing and waited for Stone to appear.

***

Molly saw Hatcher rush back into the cave. She was on her left side, facing the tunnel, having positioned herself in the same location and posture Hatcher had left her. He seemed to pay her little attention and threw some logs on the fire.

Molly rolled onto her back to watch him and to hide the tape on her wrists, which she'd managed to cut through part way. On her back, her body covered the ax handle's crude burial spot. She observed Hatcher disappear into a tunnel on the opposite side of the cavern.

Out of sight, Molly rolled back onto her side and resumed the methodical sawing of the tape with the small stone. Even though her back faced the tunnel Hatcher had disappeared into, she thought the dim light would cover her actions.

***

Certain no one watched from the mine entrance, Stone tested the gates, dropped to the ground, and wriggled through the opening at the bottom. He pressed his back against the mine entrance and listened for any sounds that might indicate Hatcher waited in the darkness to ambush him. The tunnel was as quiet as a tomb.

Stone pulled a mini-flashlight from his pocket and shined it into the darkness, taking a quick peek. No one waited. He pulled his pistol from its holster and followed the barrel into the tunnel. Careful to check for trip wires and other traps, he edged his way along the tunnel using the beam of his flashlight to guide him.

Nearing the end of the tunnel, he saw it opened into a large chamber illuminated by a fire, based on the flickering light filtering into the tunnel. He turned off the flashlight and slid it back into his pocket. Pressed against the tunnel wall, Stone hesitated, then took a quick peek into the cavern.

What he saw made him want to charge into the cave. Molly lay on the floor of the chamber. His emotions running close to out of control, he squeezed his eyes closed and tried to calm himself.

Reining in his emotions, he dropped into a prone position and peaked into the cavern at Molly. Obscured by the darkness, because she faced away from the fire, he was unable to see her face. He thought he saw her eyes open, looking in his direction. Or was he imagining it because he wanted her to know he'd come for her?

Stone whispered loud enough for her to hear—he hoped, "Molly."

He heard a muffled sound and saw her body shift. Her minimum movement and the muted response told him Hatcher might have bound and gagged her. "Can you speak or move?" he whispered again.

Her muffled response was unintelligible, "Umm umm."

Stone was sure he saw her shake her head no. "Okay, I'll come and get you," he whispered again.

"Umm umm!" she said louder and with emphasis, shaking her head again. She rolled part way onto her back and turned her head toward the back of the cave.

With the fire illuminating her face, Stone saw the duct tape over her mouth. He understood her message. Hatcher had hidden himself on the other side of the cave.

"Okay, okay," Stone whispered. "Stop moving."

He pulled back out of view and considered his options. He could rush in, staying low, and try to reach Molly. But Hatcher had a gun and he might shoot Molly. Maybe he could wait until the fire went out and sneak in. He wondered if Hatcher would wait that long? Stone guessed no. He would see the fire dimming and do something to Molly before it went out. Stone thought his best option was to talk to Hatcher, appeal to his survival instinct.

It would be a difficult conversation, because what Stone wanted was to rip Hatcher's heart out of his chest. Seeing Dan dead and knowing Hatcher had taken Molly, something had snapped inside. He'd buried his humanity—tucked it some place deep inside so the animal in him could take over. Hatcher was a dead man. Stone knew that no matter what happened to him, he would save Molly and kill Hatcher.

Stone stood again, his back pressed against the tunnel wall, and called out, "Hey, Billy Ray. I know you're hiding back there. Let's talk over your situation."

Stone waited, but no response came. "Come on, Billy Ray. You can't hide forever, and I won't be alone for much longer. Let's talk this out. Come to a decision we can both live with."

"Arnet's dead because of your lies!" Billy Ray shouted from the dark recesses of the cavern. "I'm gonna kill you and have fun with your whore before I cut her throat."

"I know you don't believe me, but I didn't lie," Stone said, using all his power to sound sincere. "You know Arnet came to New York to do what he did. He got caught, that's all. I don't blame him for trying to make the best deal he could for himself. If he hadn't done it, one of the others would've."

"He died because of you," Billy Ray said, the anger in his tone unmistakable.

"He died because a rival, black gang member attacked him," Stone said. "I didn't want that to happen, and I had nothing to do with it. It wasn't me who picked the prison—the court did."

"It's still your fault," Billy Ray said.

Stone thought he heard a little less conviction in Billy Ray's voice. Maybe it was time to appeal to his desire to stay alive.

***

Hearing Stone speak frightened Molly. He sounded too calm, too in control. It was as though he picked each word with great care, but his tone was flat—emotionless. This wasn't the Stone she knew. She believed Stone was in the eye of an emotional hurricane. Once that eye passed, only God knew what he would do.

Molly knew what she needed to do—hurry. If she could get her hands free, she might be able to help in some way. She increased her effort to saw through the tape binding her wrists with renewed vigor. She pulled her wrists apart, trying to tear the tape.

It held.

***

"I'm gonna guess you planned to get away," Stone said. "You still can—but that window's closing."

"I don't believe you," Billy Ray said. "You're trying to get me to lower my guard, so you can kill me like you did Arnet."

Stone heard Hatcher's veneer of anger cracking. "If that was true, all I'd have to do is wait," Stone said. "A bunch of cops headed this way want you dead. I don't happen to be one of them. So that makes me your best chance of getting away."

"How can I trust you?" Billy Ray asked.

Stone knew this was his chance. "Because neither of us has a choice. You want out of this mine, and I want Molly. If you throw your gun out so I can see it, I'll drop mine and step into the light, so you can see I don't have it. You gather your stuff and leave while I take care of Molly. That's the best I can do."

There was a long hesitation, and then Billy Ray said, "Okay. I'm throwing my gun out."

Stone watched as Billy Ray tossed the pistol out by the fire and walked out of the darkness. Stone tucked his pistol into the small of his back and moved into the cavern and light from the fire near Molly.

The thunderous report of a gunshot, amplified by the cavern, shattered the agreement.

CHAPTER 61

IT FELT LIKE SOMEONE HAD punched him in the gut. The impact knocked the wind out of him. He sagged to the floor of the cavern, unable to breathe as the pain intensified. A hole in his abdomen leaked blood that soaked his shirt in a spreading crimson stain.

Hatcher stood over him, pointing the small revolver at his face. It was the gun he'd taken from the PI he killed in New York. "You've been underestimating me since New York, you pissant."

Gritting his teeth in pain, Stone said, "Why? I thought we had a deal." As he spoke, his eyes searched the chamber.

"You know the reason," Billy Ray spat. "After what you did to Arnet, did you think I'd make a deal with you? You're a dead man, Stone! But shooting you again is the easy way out for you. I've got a better idea. I want to look into your eyes as you die."

Hatcher tucked the revolver into his waistband and pulled his favorite knife from the beltline at the small of his back. He held the knife in front of him, turning it so Stone got a good look. With a wicked smirk on his face, he said, "This is the knife I used on every one of the people I killed, and I'm gonna use it on you. But first, you're gonna watch me cut your whore's throat."

***

Molly's perseverance paid off.

As Hatcher had walked out of his hiding place, the final section of uncut tape ripped free. She rolled partway onto her back to hide her hands. She watched wide-eyed as Hatcher raised the revolver and shot Stone. On the verge of panic, she dug in the sand with her fingers until her hands locked onto the ax handle. Hatcher walked over and stood over Stone, within her reach. She watched as he pulled off his ski mask, shoved the gun in his waistband, and pulled his knife.

She tried to tune out his words and ignore the fear that made her want to curl into a ball. If she lost control, they were both dead. Hatcher spoke about the knife as if it were a holy relic and held it out, turning it for Stone to see.

With the knife held away from his body, this was her chance. She rolled over as fast as she could, swinging the ax handle from the back of her body in a violent arc with all the force she could muster. Her aim was true, and the ax handle smashed into Hatcher's wrist with a resounding crack.

Hatcher screamed in pain as his wrist fractured and the knife flew from his hand. It stuck, point first, in the sand next to Stone. Hatcher grabbed his shattered wrist with his other hand and screamed, "You bitch!" He released his wrist and bent over to retrieve his knife as he turned his head to glare at Molly.

The pure hatred in his eyes curdled her blood. The force of the impact had dislodged the ax handle from her grip. It lay useless on the floor of the cavern—out of reach.

Molly feared this was the end.

***

Hatcher meant to kill them both, unless he did something to stop him. Shot and bleeding, Stone wasn't quite finished. As Hatcher turned his head to look at Molly, Stone reached out and grabbed him by the front of his shirt, pulling him off balance. At the same time, he reached out—finding the knife—and pulled it from the sand. He rotated the blade to point toward Hatcher's moving torso. Hatcher began to fall.

With all his might, Stone plunged the knife into Hatcher's lower abdomen. With a loud grunt, Hatcher dropped to his knees, leaning over Stone. He kept himself from collapsing onto Stone by sticking out his uninjured arm, grabbing Stone by the neck.

Stone twisted the blade and ripped the knife from Hatcher's lower abdomen to his solar plexus. The knife blade cut through Hatcher's waistband, causing the revolver to come loose and fall to the cavern floor. Hatcher's grip loosened as he fell. Stone pushed him, so he landed on his side on the cavern floor.

Exhausted from the exertion and loss of blood, Stone's arms flopped to his sides. It stunned him when he saw Hatcher moving. As Stone and Molly watched, both helpless to fight any further, Hatcher managed to stagger to his feet. Without looking at either Stone or Molly, he grabbed his torso with both arms and stumbled into the exit tunnel.

In his fogged mind, Stone wondered how long a gutted fish could swim. He doubted very long. He tried to clear his head. He needed to focus on saving Molly and himself. He felt lightheaded from the loss of blood. As he wondered how long it would be until he passed out, he slipped into unconsciousness.

***

Molly saw Stone fading and cried out, "Stone! Stone! Don't leave me. Please, please—please." She heard Stone moan and, struggling against the pain, dragged herself over to him. She placed an arm across his chest and sobbed, "I'm here, Stone. It's going to be okay."

Blood flowed from his wound. She pulled at his shirt, exposing the entry wound. She ripped the remnants of the duct tape off her arms and legs, and pressed pieces of it in place over his wound. She rolled him onto his side but found no exit wound in his back. She saw his gun and pulled it from the small of his back. The movement caused him to moan again.

"It's all right, Stone," she reassured him. She was unsure what else to do. She could take his radio and crawl out of the mine to raise help, but she had no idea how long that would take. And she was afraid to abandon him. What if Hatcher waited in the darkness of the mineshaft? She had no idea how serious Hatcher's wound was.

Knowing what she had to do, she sobbed and said to Stone, "I have to go get help, Stone. I'll be right back, so you wait for me, you hear?" Molly took the radio and gun and, with great reluctance, crawled away toward the tunnel that led to the mine's entrance. She looked back at him one last time and disappeared into the darkness.

***

Harry, Rick, a bevy of deputies from Pitkin and Lake Counties, and several officers from the Aspen Police Department hiked the east side trail, looking for clues. They were unsure of Stone's whereabouts, and their radio calls went unanswered. As they hiked, they heard the faint echo of a gunshot. Harry stopped, looked at Rick, and asked, "Did you hear that?"

"Yeah," Rick said. "It sounded way off. We better pick up the pace."

As they moved faster along the trail, Harry spotted something ahead, along the side of the trail. They approached the object. It was Stone's jacket, laid out with one sleeve pointing to an obscure side trail, zigzagging up the mountainside.

"Damn smart," one of the deputies commented. They began their ascent on the side trail.

Upon reaching the mine, Harry scanned the area, dropped to the ground and crawled between the gates. A number of the deputies followed his lead.

"We'd better announce ourselves, so we don't get shot," Rick warned. As they moved into the mineshaft, they kept shouting, "Police!"

Harry was the first to come across the body. The face turned away, the body was near a collapsed section of the mineshaft, cleared of some of the rocks and other debris. Harry saw what looked like a long tail leading from the body deeper into the tunnel. A closer look showed it was a trail of intestines.

Rick rolled the body and shined his flashlight in the face of the corpse. "It's Hatcher," he said.

"Let's keep going," Harry said. A short distance further, he saw Molly struggling to crawl through the tunnel. As he approached, she started to weep tears of joy and relief.

"Harry," she said beginning to sob again, "It's—it's Stone. He's shot. He's hurt real bad, Harry."

Harry turned to the deputies, pointed at Rick and ordered, "Stay with her." To another he said, "Go back outside and call for help. Have them bring two ambulances. Bring the paramedics to give aid and additional help to carry them out." Without waiting for a reply, he turned and disappeared into the mineshaft.

Chapter 62

PACKED WITH LAW ENFORCEMENT VEHICLES from the Pitkin County Sheriff's Department, Aspen Police Department, Silver Lake Marshal's Office, two ambulances from Aspen, and enough law enforcement personnel to fill the town hall, the trailhead had gone from an empty lot to what looked like a police convention.

A lesson the press and lookie-loos who'd followed the cops and ambulances into the trailhead parking lot learned was that in law enforcement, if one of their own goes down, civilians had best stay out of the way. No cop is of the mind to take any crap from anyone, including reporters at such a time. On this day, the non-law enforcement crowd chose propriety over nosiness and headlines.

Stone was the first to come off the trail. He was alive, hanging on by a thread. Paramedics jogged alongside the stretcher, as deputies carried it to a waiting ambulance. One paramedic squeezed an IV bag, pumping fluids into Stone, and another applied pressure to his abdominal wound.

Another stretcher came off the trail, carrying Molly. Harry was on one end, helping to carry it. The paramedics loaded the stretchers into the ambulances and sped out of the lot, blaring sirens and flashing lights as they headed toward Aspen. Most of the procession followed them to the Aspen Valley Hospital. So many patrol cars escorted the ambulances, all with their emergency lights flashing and sirens screaming, that no one dared interfere with the motorcade.

***

Mayor Will Stemple arrived at the hospital, and the admitting physician advised him Stone's condition was critical. "He needs extensive surgery to stop the continued loss of blood and repair the damage the bullet caused," the doctor stated. "We came close to losing him. We have him stabilized for the moment. We're waiting for Flight for Life to arrive and airlift him to Denver Health Services Hospital."

The doctor refused to predict if Stone would even survive the flight. "The female patient isn't as severely injured," the doctor said. "But because of the nature of her injuries, and—uh, her insistence that she goes where the marshal goes, we're sending her too."

Will watched, along with two of the town fathers, Leo Feldman and Douglas Langford on one side and Harry, Rick, and Sheriff Roger Davis on the other as the staff loaded Stone and Molly into the helicopter. A mass of police officers had gathered in the parking lot behind them. The engine revved to a high-pitched whine, the whirling blades causing those close by to shield their eyes from the dust stirred by the downdraft. As Will squinted against the wind, the helicopter lifted into the clear blue sky.

"Godspeed," Will whispered.

***

Propped on several pillows, with the head of his bed raised, Stone was on his way to a full recovery.

His surgery had cost him a small piece of his colon, his appendix, and his spleen. A fraction-of-an-inch difference and the belly wound would've been fatal the doctor had told him. A week out of surgery, he felt good enough to go home.

As he stared at a mindless television show, his smartphone chirped. The caller ID showed the name Sam Baxter. "How're you doing, Cap?" Stone asked upon answering the call.

"I'm doing better than you, I hear. Your mayor's kept me updated, and I understand you'll be a few ounces lighter but will make a full recovery."

"So, the doctor informed me," Stone said. "I'm ready to get the hell out of here and go home."

"I'm sure you are. I just hope you follow the doctor's orders better than you did mine."

Both men laughed, and Stone grabbed at his stomach and said, "Don't make me laugh, or I'll rip out my stitches."

"Sorry," Baxter said. "I wanted to talk to you because I got the results of the paint chips we submitted for analysis."

Stone quit smiling, sat a little straighter in his bed and said, "What'd the tests determine?"

"It's an uncommon paint called Guards Red. It was a paint color used on the 1993 Porsche 911 RS America. Turns out they only imported 701 of them."

"That's what I needed to know," Stone said, the seriousness in his voice clear. His mind flashed back to his parents' deaths, and he knew in an instant who'd been responsible.

"It sounds like you know who had that make and model of car," Baxter prodded.

"I do. What I don't know is what I'll do with the information."

"It's way beyond the statute of limitations, so you can't file criminal charges," Baxter said. "Maybe you can use the information for a different purpose. Something that'll provide you some long overdue closure. And maybe some justice for your parents."

"I'll think about that," Stone said. They shifted the conversation to pleasant topics and said their goodbyes a half hour later. Stone sat in his bed, the thoughts in his mind swirling at the speed of light. In time, he came to a decision. He knew what he needed to do to get some justice for his parents.

Stone slept the rest of the morning until a nurse woke him for lunch. Hospital food was reason enough to get the hell out of this place. Lunch behind him, a nurse stuck her head into the room and asked him if he felt good enough for a visitor.

"Sure," he said, thinking it might be Molly. The smile slid from his face upon seeing who walked into the room.

William Hendrickson, the town father he'd saved, took a seat by the bed. "They're releasing me today, so I wanted to stop by and see you," Hendrickson said. He hesitated, cleared his throat, and continued. "I owe you a great debt, Marshal. If you hadn't come along, I don't know what the outcome might have been. My doctor said your actions saved my life."

He hadn't "come along." Hendrickson had ordered him to appear. "Just doing my job," Stone said with no emotion in his voice, but anger in his eyes.

Hendrickson saw the resentment and said, "I know we had a difficult start, but I'm willing to put that behind me. If there's anything I can do for you, please don't hesitate to ask."

Stone took a deep breath and said, "Since you offered, I would like to ask you to do something. Not for me—for Silver Lake."

Hendrickson appeared surprised and asked, What's that?"

"You can sell all your local holdings, remove yourself from the town fathers, and never set foot in Silver Lake again."

"Wha ... what did you say," Hendrickson stammered, rising from the chair. "Who do you think you are to speak to me this way?"

"Sit back in that chair, and I'll explain it to you," Stone stated, a coldness in his voice.

"The nerve," Hendrickson said, stomping toward the door.

"I wouldn't walk out that door unless you're prepared to have your reputation smeared on the national news. You know the media's dying to interview me," Stone threatened.

Hendrickson stopped and turned toward Stone. "What do you know? Nothing—that's what you know," he snarled. "You're a little nobody, a small-town peon. You can't hurt me. If you try, I'll crush you like the nothing you are."

Stone knew he had him. "If you don't sit back in that chair," Stone said, pointing, "you'll find out what I know the hard way. By the time I'm done with you, you'll be lucky to get a seat on a bus, let alone a seat on the boards of all those multi-national corporations you milk for money by lending your good name to their portfolios."

Hendrickson stood frozen, glaring at Stone. "Last chance," Stone said. "You can hear me out or watch your Dun and Bradstreet credit rating drop like the '29 stock market crash."

That had done it. Hendrickson edged his way to the chair and said, "Fine. I'll listen to you, but you're finished in Silver Lake."

"One of us is," Stone said, emotionless. Stone told Hendrickson the information he'd uncovered. "Only 701 of them sold in the United States and only one located in Colorado. You remember who owned that car, don't you? Who drove it like he owned the roads and who I arrested for DUI from that same car? I sure do, and I have proof positive that your car caused the accident that killed my parents."

Stone watched as Hendrickson slumped in the chair. Defeated, he mumbled, "What is it you want?"

"I told you," Stone said. "I'm here another week or so, but I can monitor things from here. You start detaching yourself today. Call it health concerns, I don't care. By the time I get home, you'd better be a fading nightmare in Silver Lake."

"Okay, okay," Hendrickson said. "I get it."

"Good," Stone said. "Now please get out of my room and my life."

Epilogue

"MAKE A PATH," MOLLY COMMANDED, as she propelled her wheelchair through the door. The infection in her feet treated, her doctors told her she'd walk again within a couple of days. Her other wounds, all superficial, had—for the most part—healed.

Harry, Rick, Will, and Sheriff Roger Davis had come all the way from Silver Lake and Aspen to Denver to visit and crowded into Stone's room. Flower-stuffed vases and various get well, thank you, and congratulation cards covered every surface in the room. Stone thought the place looked like a florist's shop. It surprised him that so many people seemed to care.

"You've become a media sensation and a hero in Silver Lake," Will said to Stone as Molly wheeled into the room.

"I understand you put yourself in harm's way to save Molly," Roger said.

"I'd say it was the other way around," Stone said, smiling at Molly as she wheeled her way to the bed and took his hand. Stone watched as Molly absently fingered the small scar on the side of her forehead, a reminder of her time with Hatcher. He squeezed her hand and smiled at her. As he looked into the faces of his friends and the woman he loved, he reflected on how his life had changed. He was no longer a loner or alone. The old Stone had died with Hatcher, and he'd found his soul again. Surrounded by people he cared for and who cared for him, his metamorphosis was complete.

He'd opened his heart again and found love. He squeezed Molly's hand again and broke the silence.

"Any news about Dan?"

Roger said, "I spoke with Colonel Kurt Herrmann, the superintendent of the troopers, and he said the department credited Dan with solving the murders the serial killer committed at the rest stop and awarded him their highest medal posthumously. They buried him with full honors."

"I wish I could've gone," Stone said, sadness in his voice. "He was a good man, a friend, and a dedicated police officer and investigator."

They sat in silence for a moment. Stone broke the quiet and asked, "Roger, what can you tell me about the SWAT deputies you lost?"

"Jerry Campbell was twenty-four and single, and Mike Young was twenty-seven and married with a three-year-old son. Their loss was tough on their families and the department. We're still reeling from the loss, but we all understand the dangers of the job. You walk out your door to go on duty, but don't know if you'll make it home at the end of shift."

"A sad reality of the job," Stone said with a heavy heart.

"We buried them both with honors," Roger said. "I think we had officers from every city and county in Colorado and the state patrol. We even had some departments from the surrounding states attend."

"I'm sorry I missed it," Stone said.

"I stood in for you," Harry said.

"What happened to Hatcher's remains?" Stone asked.

"No one claimed the body, so he received a pauper's burial. I don't even know the burial site," Roger said. "Don't care, either."

"I'm sorry," Stone said. "I didn't mean to cause bad memories. It's just that I've been out of the loop."

"That's okay," Roger said. "You have a right to know."

"I have some positive news," Will said.

Everyone looked at him, and Harry said, "Well, pony up, Mayor."

"It seems that Mister Hendrickson has resigned from the town fathers—for health-related reasons, I'm told. And he's selling off all his properties in Silver Lake. He's taking whatever's offered to dump them. I even purchased a couple of properties at rock-bottom prices. Seems strange to me because he's supposed to be such a tough businessman," Will said. "Has anybody heard what's going on?"

All heads turned and looked at Stone. "Hey, don't look at me," Stone said, holding out his hands and shrugging. "I'm in the hospital in Denver. How would I know anything?"

"Remember how fast news travels in a small town, Stone," Molly said, laughing. "And small towns have long arms, like the long arm of the law."

"I plead the Fifth," Stone said, and everyone laughed.

"Oops, I forgot the other change," Will added. "Without Hendrickson, the town fathers decided they had no need for Miss Pritchett any longer."

Stone grinned, licked his index finger, and made a check-mark motion in the air.

"Speaking of needs," Molly said, "Don't you need to get something, Will?"

"Oh, that's right, I do. Excuse me, I'll be right back."

As Will exited the room, Stone looked at the smiling faces and tried to hide his discomfort. He might be a changed person, but surprises still annoyed him.

Will returned with a long, gift-wrapped box and placed it in Stone's lap. "The whole town participated in getting you this small token of our gratitude," Will said.

"That wasn't necessary," Stone said, embarrassed. "It's my job."

"Oh, hush and open the box," Molly scolded.

Like a kid at Christmas, Stone tore at the wrapping and pulled the tape off the box. What he saw inside shocked and moved him.

"Take it out so we can all see it," Rick said.

Stone lifted out a polished black walnut board with beautiful scalloped edges, with an ax handle mounted to it. Engraved into the ax handle were the initials **B.D.** A small brass plaque screwed to the board read, "For those who dare to stand strong in the face of adversity." Under the inscription it read, "Presented to Marshal Hunter Stone for his unwavering dedication to the residents of Silver Lake."

As tears welled in his eyes, everyone in the room applauded.

Choking back his emotions, Stone said, "Thank you all for this. I'll cherish it, and I know right where I'm going to hang it."

"So, do you think that's the real Benjamin Dowd's ax handle?" Harry asked.

Stone smiled at Harry. "No way to be sure, Harry, but use Occam's razor. With those initials carved into it, and the handle found in Benjamin Dowd's mine, what do you think the answer is?"

"I think it would please him to know we used one of his tools to stop a killer," Molly said.

Stone nodded. "As a kid, the mines scared the hell out of me because of the ghost stories. But having been in Dowd's mine and survived, I think I'm over the fear."

"No need to fear that mine anymore. A few sticks of dynamite sealed it tight," Will said.

"How are things in town, Will?" Stone asked.

"Close to normal again. The reporters have left, and vacationers seem as eager as ever to visit. Silver Lake's returning to what it's meant to be—a quiet town and a nice place to visit."

"Speaking of Silver Lake, who's watching the store with all of you in Denver?" Stone asked.

"Pull in your reins," Harry responded. "The kind sheriff assigned some deputies to help out 'til you're back in the rodeo."

"Can't come quick enough for me," Stone complained.

Another hour of chit-chat, and the group decided to give Stone and Molly a chance to rest. They wanted to tour the big city too.

"I've got to get Verna a gift, or I'll be bunkin' in the barn," Harry said.

After they left, Molly said, "I'll go back to my room, so you can get some rest."

"Don't leave," Stone said. "I want to talk to you in private."

Molly gave him a quizzical look. "Oh, okay. What's going on?"

He cleared his throat and looked at his hands, folded in his lap. As he stared at them, he began. "You know me better than anyone and know I'm no good at expressing my feelings. But I think you know how I feel. Everything that's happened has made me realize how important you are to me." Stone stopped and chanced a glance at Molly.

She sat in the wheelchair, looking at him with one eyebrow raised and a silly grin on her face. He knew that look. She understood what he meant but had no intention of making it easy for him.

"What I mean—uh—I mean what I want to say is—you know," he said, looking at her and pleading with his eyes.

Molly looked back with that same knowing grin on her face.

"No, Stone. I'm afraid I don't know what you mean. What're you trying to say?"

Stone reached over and slid open the drawer in the stand by the bed. He withdrew a small, black-velvet covered ring box and held it in his lap.

Molly sucked in a breath when she saw it. The glib look slid from her face as she stared at the box.

"Before I ran away, I intended on giving this to you and asking you to marry me." Stone opened the box and handed it to Molly. "This was my mother's engagement ring. I've kept it all these years, because I can't imagine it being on anyone else's finger. Molly, will you marry me?"

"It's beautiful," Molly said, removing it from the box and slipping it on her ring finger.

"And?"

"And I've waited a long time to hear you ask me."

"Molly! That's not an answer."

"I have one question first," Molly said.

"Okay," Stone said. "What's the question?"

"Where do you intend on hanging the ax handle?"

www.ingramcontent.com/pod-product-compliance
Lightning Source LLC
Chambersburg PA
CBHW060601310726
48982CB00008B/1190/J
* 9 7 8 1 7 3 2 1 5 8 3 0 6 *